RESOLUTION

MASON FAMILY SERIES

BOOK FIVE

ADRIANA LOCKE

UMBRELLA
PUBLISHING INC.

To everyone doing their best.
It's enough. Keep going.
With love.

ALSO BY ADRIANA LOCKE

My Amazon Store
Purchase Signed Copies

Play Me Series
Play Me | Try Me | Show Me

Brewer Family Series
The Proposal | The Arrangement | The Invitation | The Merger | The Situation

Carmichael Family Series
Flirt | Fling | Fluke | Flaunt | Flame

Landry Family Series
Sway | Swing | Switch | Swear | Swink | Sweet

Landry Family Security Series
Pulse

Gibson Boys Series
Crank | Craft | Cross | Crave | Crazy

The Mason Family Series
Restraint | The Relationship Pact | Reputation | Reckless | Relentless | Resolution

The Peachwood Falls Series
Tempt | Truly

The Exception Series
The Exception | The Perception

Dogwood Lane Series

Tumble | Tangle | Trouble

Standalone Novels

Sacrifice | Wherever It Leads | Written in the Scars | End Game | Like You Love Me | The Sweet Spot | Nothing But It All | Between Now and Forever

For a complete reading order, visit www.adrianalocke.com.

To receive a text alert for new releases, text BOOKS to 740-206-6969. US only.

SYNOPSIS

Romance is not in Wade Mason's portfolio.

This is tragic. It's unfair that a man so maddeningly gorgeous—an architect with a deliciously squarish jaw, adorably dimpled chin, and the hottest black glasses that straddle the line between professional and provocative—rebukes all things love.

I knew this well before I walked into his office.

The man is a conundrum—a complicated, steel wall of a puzzle. On the one hand, he brushes against me in the conference room with a broodiness that sets me on fire. He demands in-person meetings about the house we're working on together. I catch him watching me out of the corner of his eye with a look that's *anything* but platonic. But any talk of hookups, love, or relationships—even in general? Completely off the table.

I'm determined to peel back his layers until I get to the bottom of the mysterious businessman. But my plan is foiled by a surprise that leaves both of us reeling. Neither of us sees it coming, but it changes everything ... forever.

Prologue

Wade

"Will you please cooperate?" Holt sighs, his face muddled with complete exasperation.

My brothers and I sit around a conference room table in their office building. The only one missing is Coy. He was smart enough not to work in the family business. My architectural firm is technically a separate entity for the sake of my sanity, but most of my projects interlace with my brothers', which is a great setup. Until it's not.

"Come on, Wade," Oliver groans.

I sigh, resting my forearms on the table. I was over this ridiculous conversation—a meeting called with the presumption of business—nineteen minutes ago. We've been in this room for a total of twenty. I'm no more inclined to indulge their request than I was the first minute because this *business meeting* is really an adult version of my brothers getting themselves into a situation and pleading for my help.

"And which project would you like me to drop to make room for this one?" I raise my eyebrows, knowing damn well they aren't about to suggest that I remove one of *their* projects from my list. "I have four Mason Limited projects *for you guys* in various stages of development, and I'm working on three homes—one that is taking up a lot of my time right now."

Holt rolls his eyes.

Oliver sighs too, frustration evident in the harshness of his exhale.

"So, which is it?" I ask as if I'm actually considering this absurd request. "Which job of yours do you want me to cancel? Actually, let's pick two, and one must be Greyshell."

Boone, however, leans forward. A smirk settles on his lips. "He's considering it. Wade is breaking. We're breaking him."

I level my gaze on my youngest brother. Before I can put him in his place and tell him that there is no way he can or ever will *break me*, Oliver steps in.

"For the love of God, Boone, don't antagonize him," Oliver says.

I arch a brow at Boone but remain otherwise unaffected—at least on the surface. The truth is, I *am* affected. *I loathe being put in this position.* My brothers rarely do this to me, but when they do, they go all in.

Oliver looks at me with resignation. "Let's just … Let's back up a little and see this for what it is."

"I've done that," I tell him. "Do you know what I was doing prior to your text summoning me here?"

Oliver doesn't move. He doesn't even blink.

"I'm sure it wasn't fun," Boone says, tossing a sunflower seed in the air and catching it in his mouth. He crunches it, then grins. "I'm right, aren't I?"

"Well, considering that this is a workday, that would be pretty evident. Don't you think?" I ask before smirking. "I apologize. Silly question. You *never* think."

Boone's jaw drops. But before he can reply, Oliver cuts in and saves him.

"Curt Bowery, the hotel magnate responsible for—"

"I know who he is, Oliver," I deadpan.

"Then you know what a score it would be to make friends with him."

"I don't care. *I don't want to be friends with anyone.*"

"Dammit, Wade," Oliver says, throwing himself back in his chair.

Holt motions for Oliver to take it easy and then takes his turn trying to convince me to participate in their scheme to befriend one of the wealthiest men in all of Georgia. *Via me.* The one who doesn't care. The one who's too busy. The one who just wants to design things that excite me and be left alone.

I'm choosy about what projects I take on and who I work with. I have a process, and it doesn't mesh with just anyone. Independence and control over my day are at the top of the list when it comes to things I value. My brothers know this, yet ... here we are.

"Listen," Holt says. "Curt just wants us to design a home for one of his granddaughters. How hard can that be?"

"Who is this *us* you speak of? Did you suddenly get a degree in architecture this morning?"

Holt looks at the ceiling.

"Curt rattled on about your work at the Landry Gala a few weeks back," Oliver says. "He keeps calling me."

"That sounds like a *you* problem."

"This could be really good for business, Wade," Holt says. "He has worldwide connections and government contacts. He can literally snap his fingers and get anything he wants."

"He can't get me."

Oliver groans. "Curt has already hinted at a possible collaboration on a project in Atlanta. He's talking about a state-of-the-art hotel, shopping—the whole bit. Just having our name associated with him would be a feather in our cap."

"Wade, *please*," Holt says, cutting in. "We *need* you to do this for the greater good of the family."

"I'd do it if I could," Boone says.

"Boone, you couldn't trace your hand with a fucking crayon." It's my turn to exhale. "Listen, I've really enjoyed this little chat, but I need to go. I—"

"Fine." Holt interrupts me, running a finger over his lips. "I have a compromise."

"You have no leverage with which to compromise," I point out. "It's *my* time. *My* skills. *My* lack of time in the fucking day to spend working with some silver-spoon princess who will have unrealistic ideas about architecture that she gleaned from a fake reality show." I narrow my gaze at my brothers. "I am not a babysitter nor am I a prostitute. *I* decide what projects I take on. You can't just hire me out to the highest bidder."

Boone tosses another sunflower seed into the air and catches it. "The granddaughter could be hot."

I don't dignify that with a reply.

"Do this for us," Holt says. "Help us get our foot in the door with Bowery Hotels. I know it will be one more thing you don't have time for. We get that. We understand you don't want to do this. But ..." He takes a deep breath. "If you agree to do this for us, I won't make you be a groomsman in my wedding."

I narrow my eyes because he's playing dirty.

Holt knows me more than I'm willing to admit. There aren't many things I want less in the world than to be paraded down an aisle in front of fifty million people in an overpriced and unnecessary ceremony like some kind of trained monkey in an expensive suit. The whole idea makes me twitchy.

"First," I say carefully, lest they get the wrong impression, "you can't *make me* do anything."

Boone chokes on a sunflower seed, earning him a warning glare from Holt.

"Second," I say after pausing to make sure Boone doesn't asphyxiate, "do you even know what Curt wants? Can I do this via email? Electronic prints? How big is this project? Are we starting from scratch? Who is the point person? Do they own the property already or is this conceptual?" I groan. "And why can't they use the architect they work with on a daily basis?"

Holt looks at Oliver. He shrugs.

"I'm not going to lie to you," Oliver says. "I don't know. I can forward you the emails he's sent, but they're basically inquiring about your availability."

"Great. It's settled. Tell him I'm not available."

"Wade, if the roles were reversed and I was refusing to cooperate," Boone says, "you'd be the first one up my ass, telling me to think beyond myself."

I sigh. "If it were you, Boone, you wouldn't have anything else going on. I have a full schedule right now. See the difference?"

They see the difference. They *all* see the difference. The problem is, they know I see it too—from both sides.

The reality is, I don't care how much pull or money Curt Bowery has. It doesn't matter to me. I have enough work to last me two years and enough money to last me a lifetime. That's part of the beauty of being a bachelor.

Unfortunately, my brothers don't think like me.

They've all started to settle down. They want marriages and children and all the domesticated life trappings that make me ill. That means that Mason Limited doesn't just have to supply them with a solid future. It also has to take care of their families—families that are my family too.

While I'm happy to walk out of here without agreeing to this Bowery Hotels nonsense, the weight of my brothers' eyes sets firmly on my shoulders. They need me to do this—not just for them but for potential future Mason generations. I know it, and they know I know it. They also know that I'm not completely heartless.

Dammit.

As if he can read my mind, Boone smirks. "I really hope my little Rosie doesn't need Curt's help someday, and I'll have to tell her that her favorite uncle Wade couldn't make time to—"

"Fine," I say, shoving my chair backward with more force than necessary. "I'll meet with whomever, but I'm not guaranteeing that I'll do it."

"Great. That's all we're asking," Oliver says hurriedly.

"And Holt—you better take me out of the groomsmen lineup," I add. "And *you* are dealing with Mom when she flips out. Not me."

"Deal," Holt says, his tone tinged with disbelief.

I'm surprised your proposal worked too.

"This is completely ridiculous," I mutter as I gather my things.

A discernible tension creeps through the room. It snakes its way across the table, pulling at my brothers and me. They're looking at each other—I know this without looking at them—but I refuse to make eye contact.

Do not look. You know they're holding something back.

The collar of my shirt is tight. My jaw sets in place. My heartbeat strums in my chest as the walls of the conference room seem to shrink.

"Oh, and um ... You have a meeting with Curt tomorrow at noon in your office," Boone says.

My hands still over my briefcase, and I look up at Oliver's cringing face. *This motherfucker.*

Oliver shrugs sheepishly. "What can I say? We had faith."

My gaze narrows. His brazenness is absurd. "No, you had a whole lot of stupid. That's what you had."

Oliver gets to his feet, relief across his face. "Thank you, Wade. You won't regret this."

I pick up my things and level my gaze at my brothers. I let it linger for a few seconds to ensure my displeasure about this entire situation is understood. Once I'm sure my point hits home, I drag my briefcase off the table.

"Famous last words," I mutter and march out the door.

Chapter One

Wade

"Eliza? Please remind me at twelve thirty that I'm needed elsewhere."

I sit back in my chair. Massaging my temple with one hand, I await my assistant's reply through the speakerphone.

"And where might that be, Mr. Mason?"

"It doesn't matter."

"*Oh.*"

I should feel guilty that I'm confusing this poor woman on her third day of work or, at the very least, regretful enough to backtrack.

I do neither. I also don't feel bad about this decision.

"Actually, make it twelve fifteen," I say, further complicating Eliza's confusion.

"Yes, sir. While I have you on the line, I believe your twelve o'clock is walking in right now."

Fabulous.

I squash back a shot of frustration and stifle an annoyed growl. *Do this and get it over with.*

That's the plan. Meet with Curt Bowery and find him and his

proposal unreasonable. Then I can tell Oliver I did my due diligence, and now I'm out.

Simple.

"Send him back," I say before the guilt that I should've felt earlier starts to wiggle its way into my conscience. "*Thank you*, Eliza."

"Yes. Of course. You're welcome, Mr. Mason."

Her voice is full of … happiness. Despite the fact that it's wholly unrepresentative of Mason Architecture, Holt insists that prospective clients prefer a cheerful person at the front desk. Such an oddity, if you ask me.

The line disconnects and I get busy tidying up my workspace. The office is the only place where controlled chaos reigns in my life. Immersing myself in designs, blueprints, clay models—it makes me feel alive.

It's what gets me up in the morning. It's why I work through lunch, and it's the reason I work late most nights. That and insomnia is a bitch.

A knock raps on the door. I run my hand down my tie and click out of the program on my computer. When I look back up, and—*what the hell?*

The human being standing in the doorway is *not* Curt Bowery.

"It *is* you," she says, a wide smile stretching across her full pink lips.

What?

I do a quick once-over of the woman stepping into my office—the woman who's most definitely *not* my twelve o'clock.

She's about my age with thick, shiny mahogany-colored hair. Her cheekbones accentuate her eyes. They're golden brown, the color of a glass of whiskey when the afternoon sun shines through it, and are framed by long, dark lashes.

She exudes a friendliness, a warm and bubbly vibe that drives home the fact I've never met this woman in my life. I'm sure of it. I don't associate with this kind of person. They're too … people-y.

The door shuts with a *click!* just before she turns around.

"I know that *Wade Mason* isn't a name you come across daily," she says, moving far too easily through my office. "But I figured that I would get here, and it wouldn't be you after all. I mean, what are the odds?"

Before I can break down those odds for her—about one in one hundred thousand, give or take—she reaches me.

And reaches for *me.*

The scent of coconuts hits me before she does. By the time I get ahold of all of these moving parts—Curt's impending arrival, this random woman in my office, and the encroachment on my personal behind-the-desk space—she wraps her arms around me and pulls me in for a hug.

Oof.

She leans back quickly. Her eyes are sparkling.

"You're a friendly one, aren't you?" I ask, taking a step back in case she has a knife. Because what kind of person hugs another unprompted? Psychopaths. That's who.

Her laughter is light and breezy. "You don't remember me."

Fuck.

I hate when women—*when people*—do this. They think they're special enough to warrant being memorable against the hundred other faces you see through the course of a week. Somehow, regardless of the number of interactions you've had within a certain timeframe, *you* are the asshole who can't remember them.

It's total bullshit.

The woman flips her hair off her narrow shoulder and allows me an even clearer view of her pretty, freckly face. She doesn't look like a psychopath.

Then again, they never do.

"Should I tell you who I am, or should we make a game out of it?" she says, moving to the other side of my desk.

I exhale, confused about so many things—w*ho she is, why Eliza let her in my office, and where the hell is Curt Bowery when you need him?*

"I'm not much for games," I deadpan, hoping she'll read between the lines and gather that I'm not a fan of ... this.

"Really?" She falls back into the brown leather chair facing my desk and laughs. Her gaze settles on me. "Games can be fun, you know."

"I suppose they have a time and place," I say, sitting back down in my chair. I grab a fresh notepad and try to avoid her eyes. "I have an appointment that should be arriving any time, so I'd appreciate it if we could get to the bottom of ... who are you? Why are you here?"

I lift my eyes to meet hers. They snap together like the last two pieces of a jigsaw puzzle. She runs a finger over her bottom lip as if she—*and I*—have all the time in the world.

"I thought for sure you'd remember me," she says.

"Isn't that a bit pretentious?"

She narrows her eyes but continues to grin. "No more than your *portentous* assumption that *I'm* not your twelve o'clock."

Confidence oozes out of her as she effectively tosses the banter-ball back over the net. Coupled with her poise at my cool demeanor—a tactic that usually softens whoever is sitting across from me—it's quite a show.

It's also respectable.

"Okay," I say. "Fair enough. But I'm still going to need your name."

She seems satisfied with my capitulation.

"I'm Dara Alden," she says finally. "We had a class together at Georgia Tech. We did a presentation together about intimacy in relationships in a communications class my freshman year."

She pauses, waiting for me to connect all the dots. And I do. Quickly.

Dara Alden was my partner for the worst class and worst project I've ever been forced to participate in. I was certain the professor matched us together just to see me suffer. He had it in for me—no thanks to a speech I presented on why communications classes weren't beneficial to all students and should be eliminated from prerequisites.

I start to respond when my speakerphone buzzes.

"Mr. Mason? You're needed on an urgent call regarding the Greyshell project," Eliza says. "It can't wait, sir."

Internally, I groan and make a mental note to remind her not to call me *sir*. "I'll call them back."

"But, sir ..."

My jaw clenches in both frustration and embarrassment. "I'll call them back, Eliza. Thank you for letting me know."

"*Okay*. Thank you. I'll ... *tell them*," she says before ending the call.

I run a hand through my hair and try to stay calm and focused. But when I glance back up, Dara is watching me with unbridled amusement.

"I'm curious," Dara says, her voice as sweet as honey. "Did your opinions on intimacy change?"

Pulling at the collar of my shirt, I grab a pen. *Have Eliza turn down the thermostat.*

"I don't recall what my opinions were a decade ago," I say, jotting down the thermostat thought in my notepad. "But it's safe to say I've always considered intimacy in relationships ..."

Why are we talking about this?

I set down my pen and level my gaze with hers. "Are you really my twelve o'clock? Or was that something you picked up on because I mentioned it, and you just ran with it?" I pause. "Did Boone put you up to this?"

She snickers. "Relax, Wade. I don't even know who Boone is."

"You're the only female in this part of Georgia who can say that with a straight face."

"Heck, maybe I *should* know him." Dara laughs. "Can you introduce us?"

I flip her a look. I don't know what I mean by it, exactly. It just radiates from me without my trying. She seems amused by it and, thankfully, also lets it go.

"All joking aside," she says, running a hand through the air. "Yes. I'm your twelve o'clock. My grandfather is Curt Bowery, and I need an architect."

Well, shit.

It feels like I've been hit on the side of the head a little bit. I'm not sure what to say in response to this news. I knew exactly how I was going to deal with Curt, but this isn't Curt. I don't know why it matters, but it does. Sort of.

"I suppose my follow-up question would be ..." I search for the right words. "You do understand what an architect does, right? I design *things* —buildings, houses, hotels. I'm not a therapist specializing in relational intimacy. As a matter of fact, I've said all that I have to say about that topic."

She laughs. It's smooth and loud and sounds foreign in my office.

"That's disappointing," she says, crossing one leg over the other and settling in. "I was hoping we could spend our afternoons discussing intimacy types and debate over whether *true* intimacy is even reachable in modern-day relationships again."

I can't help it. I smirk. "It sounds as though you've lived the past ten years reading a lot of self-help books."

Dara shrugs, teasing me. "And it sounds as though you've lived the past ten years alone and are just as cantankerous as you were back then."

I look down so she can't see my ghost of a smile. It's that gesture—the tiniest splitting of my cheeks—that kicks me out of whatever bullshit distraction was happening between us and back to reality.

There's work to be done. Commitments have been made. Those things aren't happening if I'm sitting here in a verbal tug-of-war with a millionaire's granddaughter.

"I do have another meeting in ten minutes," I say, turning toward my computer. My voice is as detached as I can get it. "Unfortunately, we don't have time to get into your project today."

Out of the corner of my eye, she flinches.

"We don't have time today?" Dara asks, surprised.

"We've used up too much of it discussing ..." *Whatever we were discussing*. I adjust my glasses. "Anyway, seeing if we are a good fit is a part of the process. I don't design many homes because it requires too much ..."

My voice trails off as I turn back to her. The way she's looking at me catches me off guard. Her brows are raised, and her head is tilted to the side. She's silently calling me out, letting me know she doesn't believe a word I'm saying.

We watch each other for a long couple of seconds. It's a standoff of sorts. Neither of us wants to be the first to look away.

It's a case of two strong personalities wanting the other to bend, each of us wanting to control the narrative. What she doesn't know is that I always win that scenario. *Always*.

I stand, adjusting my tie and attempting to clear my head.

"So, what does a person have to do to see if we're *a good fit*?" she asks.

The cheekiness in her question is not lost on me. But I ignore it.

What I don't ignore is the tension between the two of us, nor do I overlook her apparent propensity to try to push my buttons. It's a replay from ten years ago. I almost came unglued over our speech, and it was for twenty class points. This time, there will be a lot more on the line.

Too much to risk, most definitely.

"It has a lot to do with trust." My gaze burns into hers. "*You* have to relinquish control and trust that *I* understand your needs and will deliver everything you ask of me." *Where possible.*

Instead of making her blush as I intended, she grins. It's not the playful one from before or the happy smile that she tossed my way when she walked in. No, this one is darker. Seductive. Not at all what I was expecting.

I smooth my tie with my hand again, running it down my chest. Her eyes flicker to the movement for just a moment before her gaze rises back to mine.

"I think we could get there, Mr. Mason."

My chuckle is soft as I plant both hands on my desk. I lean forward and wait to see if she squirms in her chair. I'm surprised that she doesn't. She sits tall, unwavering—poised despite my efforts to break her resolve.

What the hell?

I'm starting to wonder if Curt Bowery, the hotel magnate worth millions of dollars, would've been easier to navigate than Dara Alden.

"It's not *if* we can get there," I tell her, looking her dead in her eyes. "I'm one-thousand-percent confident in my abilities *to get there*."

Dara forces a swallow but doesn't blink.

"It's about all the things that lead to that final moment," I say, my voice low and steady. "The journey, if you will."

"That's what they all say." She tucks a small purse under her arm and stands. "But you might be right. I'm not sure you're the man who should be handling ... *my project*."

Of course, she's right. It's the point I was just trying to make. But hearing her say it pisses me off.

I head to the door. "Think about it. Talk it over with your grandfather," I say, swinging the door wide open. "You can let Eliza know if you'd like to reschedule, and we'll see when I'm available."

She hums as she moseys toward me. "You seem like a very busy man."

I'm not sure if she's being facetious, so I don't respond. I think her statement was rhetorical anyway.

"Busy men always go through the motions and never have time to be creative," she says, fighting a smile. "I'm not sure that fits my needs."

I narrow my gaze.

Much to my surprise *and annoyance*, she laughs as she walks by me. Her elbow grazes my stomach in a move that I think is intentional. Before I can react, she's down the hall and standing in front of Eliza.

"That dress is stunning on you," she tells Eliza as if we weren't in a strained conversation five seconds ago. "Where did you get it?"

"Oh, for fuck's sake," I grumble as I slam my door. The framed copy of the first building I ever designed shakes against the wall.

I lean against my desk and suck in a deep lungful of air. The scent of coconuts only intensifies my frustration.

I open a window and then sit down.

"Busy men always go through the motions and never have time to be creative. I'm not sure that fits my needs."

What the hell?

Relational intimacy.

Loads of rubbish, just as it was ten years ago.

Instead of listening to spoiled, silver spoon-fed women who want their ridiculous projects handled, I have real work to do.

My heart pumps from the interaction with Dara, and I find myself replaying much of our conversation. It's not until I get to *relational intimacy* do I realize how much time I've wasted—and am still wasting.

I put my phone on Do Not Disturb and get back to the only thing I ever want to know *intimately*—my work.

CHAPTER TWO

Dara

"And that's why I'm never, *ever* having kids."

My off-the-cuff statement causes my best friend, Rusti Jameson, to laugh. Her shoulder bumps mine as we sit side by side on my couch and share a pint of ice cream.

"I mean it," I say, thinking my new kid-free stance all the way through. "They're so much work. Complicated. And gross."

"You can't rule out having children because one kid puked in your mouth."

I dig my spoon into the chocolate chip mint container and free a chunk of chocolate. "Actually, I can. You would too if you tasted sweet potatoes two weeks later at the most unsuspecting times because some little cherub baby projectile vomited practically down your throat."

Rusti gags. "*Stop it*. Stop it right now."

I laugh and shove the spoon in my mouth.

"Maybe the problem is your subjects," Rusti offers, shaking her head as if the imagery I painted is still in her brain. "Maybe you should stop taking pictures of babies and focus on ...*firefighters*." Her eyes light up as she tosses a thick black braid over her shoulder. "Think about it. Less drool, more body oil. Makes sense to me."

I toss her a weighted look. "That's great in theory. But have you ever seen a firefighter in real life—like, you've personally laid eyes on him—who's *nearly* as hot as the ones on the calendars?" I scoop my spoon in the ice cream again. "The answer is no. No, you have not."

Rusti flops back against my sequined throw pillows with her spoon hanging out of her mouth.

"They don't exist," I say. "Think about it. They *can't* exist. It would be a public hazard. There would be women all over the world setting fires just to have a big red truck show up with muscle-bound hotties and their *big hoses*."

I wiggle my brows, making my friend laugh again.

"What about men who chop wood?" she asks.

"Lumberjacks?"

She shrugs. "I think. I mean, lumberjack doesn't sound sexy, but have you seen those guys on TikTok? *Hello*."

With a giggle, I fall back next to her, squishing the pillows underneath me.

"Lumberjacks have modernized," Rusti says, running the spoon along her bottom lip. "They're not all red-and-black-plaid flannel with Paul Bunyan vibes. Could be a new niche."

"We'd have to find out where the lumberjacks hang out, and I'm not tromping around the woodlands."

"Eh. Good point. Maybe you should stick to babies and weddings."

I hum in agreement because she's right. That's where the money is. That's not where my heart is, but my heart doesn't pay the bills.

Rusti leans her head on my shoulder and yawns. "I'm never going to be able to stay awake tonight, and I don't get off work until eleven."

"If you get too sleepy, call me, and I'll come in and chill at the bar and throw ice at you."

She snorts. "That's so nice of you."

We sit quietly with the ice cream slowly melting between us. I should feel more compelled to take it to the kitchen than I do. I'll blame that on Wade Mason.

What the hell happened today?

I bite my lip and try not to smile as I think back on the time we spent together.

And his grumpiness.

And his lips.

And the way he tried to get me to crumple under his stare and wither against his words.

Damn.

It's only when Rusti jabs me in the side with her elbow do I realize that she's raised her head and is looking at me.

"What?" I ask, my cheeks flushing at having been caught thinking about the handsome architect.

"Don't *what* me, Dara."

Suddenly, the ice cream getting moved to the kitchen is of the utmost importance. I grab it and climb to my feet.

"Don't walk away from me," Rusti says, following me into the kitchen. "Now, I really want to know."

It's my fault she's so curious. I didn't play this off very well, and I always tell her everything that's going on in my life. We've been best friends for six years. That's how it works. She's seen me through some great times ... and some very hard ones too.

But I don't know how to tell her about Wade. Not that there's anything to tell, really, but this whole house-building topic in and of itself makes Rusti very opinionated. Throwing Wade into the mix will only make her more ... just *more*.

The ice cream is nearly empty, so I toss the container in the trash. And then, after taking a deep breath, I look up at Rusti.

"I had an appointment with the architect today," I say.

She climbs up onto a barstool. "Okay. I'm liking this. *I'm liking this.*"

I roll my eyes. "Well, you would've really liked it if you would've been at the meeting."

"Go on."

I walk away from her and go to the refrigerator. I take out two bottles of water and hand one to Rusti.

"The architect my grandfather chose is Wade Mason," I say.

She sets the bottle in front of her. "Who is that?"

"I had a class with him at Georgia Tech. We were partners."

She lifts a brow.

I start to grin. "He's kind of a dick. Definitely a control freak. *Mysterious*." My grin grows wider. "Tall. Dark. Ridiculously handsome."

Rusti snorts. "Got it. He's your catnip."

My laughter barrels through the room.

"You're screwed, my friend," Rusti says, laughing too. "I don't need to know anything else. Picture fully painted."

I lean against the counter and try not to melt faster than the ice cream.

"He had on these black pants that hugged his ass." I shiver. "A crisp white button-down shirt with the cuffs rolled up to his elbows."

"That's it. Now I'm screwed too." Rusti shakes her head, her blue eyes shining with humor. "If you tell me that he had a tattoo peeking out of that shirt, I'll fight you for him."

"I think he's too ..." I try to find the right word to describe what I mean but come up empty-handed. "I don't know. Maybe he's too serious to have a tattoo."

She makes a face.

"I could be wrong," I say, holding out my hands. "I didn't get a full-body shot, you know?"

"But there are plans for that, right?"

I sigh, my shoulders dipping as I pull away from the counter. I walk around Rusti and sit next to her, noting the vase of sunflowers that have seen better days.

As I get settled on the stool, I think about her question.

"Dara?"

"I don't know," I say, staring out the window on the other side of the kitchen. "We kind of left things at an impasse."

"Why? Clearly, you're into him, and there's not a guy on the face of the planet who wouldn't be into you."

I smile at her. "You are being too nice."

She rolls her eyes. "Also, he's the guy your granddaddy hired to build you the house of your dreams. I'm not seeing the problem here."

Rusti might not see the problem, but she also wasn't in that room today.

There was an intensity between us, a fire in Wade's eyes when he looked at me—one I could feel in my core but couldn't quite read.

He reminds me of the time I was driving to Atlanta for a Tennessee Arrows baseball game because my crush, Lincoln Landry, was playing. It was raining, and the semitrucks had created so much smog that it was like oil on my windshield. I could see through it, just not clearly—not enough to make out a brake light from a taillight. I had to slow down and get a hotel room until things cleared up.

"I need to get a hotel room," I say without realizing that Rusti wasn't privy to my thoughts.

She slow blinks.

I shake my head. "Let me try this again—"

"Hey, I'm not judging you. Want me to get you guys one? An all-nighter or one that takes hourly customers."

"What? No!" I laugh. "What are you—? That's not what I meant."

She laughs. "I know. Continue."

"I just mean that I'm not sure if we're even going to work together. Things were going well, and then—boom. He was like, '*I'm all out of time. You can think about this and call my secretary to see if I'm available again,*' and ... I don't know what that was all about."

"That's odd."

"You're telling me."

Rusti's phone rings, and she takes it out of her pocket. I can tell by the look on her face that it's her boss. She answers it with a look like she's being tortured.

I get up and mosey into the living room while she tries to explain where a jar of mushrooms is in the storeroom. As she gets into the specifics, my brain floats back to Mason Architecture and this whole house situation.

"Sometimes, it's a blessing, and sometimes, it's a curse," I whisper to the vacant room.

In some ways, I think it would be easier to work with someone new, an architect I absolutely don't know. This project has the potential to get emotional for me, and having some third party who doesn't know me or my grandfather from a hole in the wall might be the best answer for everyone.

But something about that setup feels like most everything else in my life—lonely. It feels like there's no potential for laughs or long conversations about where the best spot is to put the window seat that I've wanted since the third grade or which direction my bedroom should face so that I can see the sun rise from my bed.

Even though Wade *certainly* has the potential to be a pain in the ass, working with him at least seems … exciting. It gets my blood pumping—even if it's for the wrong reasons.

"Sorry," Rusti says, coming into the room. "You'd think the guy who owns the damn place would know where things are. He should pay me more."

"Yes, he should. Want me to come by tonight and tell him that?"

She grins. "No, but thank you for the offer."

"Anytime."

"I need to get down there before they just call me again looking for something else. It would totally help if the day shift stocked everything like they're supposed to."

I grin. "Want me to come tell them that?"

Rusti laughs. "So, are we working with Catnip?"

"We don't know."

"Figures. But I vote yes if for nothing else so I can meet him." She picks up her bag off the floor next to the sofa. "What are you doing this weekend? Want to go to Xavier Park and help me walk Cleo? We could grab a sandwich and people watch after."

I fake cry.

"Come on," she says. "Cleo loves you."

"Cleo peed on me the last time she saw me. She's a menace."

"*She's sweet.*" Rusti gives me a look as she makes her way to the door. "So, yes to Xavier Park on Saturday afternoon?"

I rearrange the pillows we knocked over earlier. "I have a quick photo session in the morning, but I can meet you around one. I vote without your Jack Russell terrier, but I'll be there regardless."

She pulls the door open. "Perfect. See you then unless you come by tonight."

"I'll let you know about that. I might be in bed by the time it's officially tonight."

"In bed with visions of a hot architect ...?"

Laughing, I pick up a pillow and toss it at her. It hits the back of the door as it swings shut.

While the house feels distinctly quiet without Rusti, my head is unmistakably loud.

Every clashing, thorny emotion that swirls inside me on a daily basis picks up speed. It's as if my feelings have seats on a Ferris wheel, and I have to wait and see which one will get off and take precedence this time.

Because they all exist. They all matter. They're all relevant.

"I just wish you were here to help me work through this, Mom."

I give myself a minute to miss her, to mourn the loss that blindsided me over a year ago. To grieve the loss of the only person who ever loved me for me without expecting anything in return.

And then, because I'm my mother's daughter, I pick myself up and dust myself off. I might not know what to do with so many things in my life—well, apart from my photography business—but I'll figure it out.

But will I figure it out by calling Wade Mason's office or letting him come to me?

I shrug, a smile playing on my lips, and head to my office to edit pictures.

Chapter Three

Wade

I set my fork and knife on my plate and carry them into the kitchen.

The last rays of sun pour through the window over the sink—the one that looks over the field that stretches more than two acres to the east. It's filled with grasses and trees with leaves that hint of the color eruption that's not too far away.

My doorbell buzzes. I look across the island and into the family room. A small box appears in the corner of the television screen that hangs over the fireplace. It shows my mother entering the security code and opening the door.

"Wade? Are you home?" she calls out.

"I'm in the kitchen."

Her heels patter against the hardwood floors. I take out an extra wineglass and carry it to the table.

Siggy Mason is a force to be reckoned with. She's fascinated me since I was a little boy. The way she tailored her parenting style to each of her five children yet remained neutral and fair was impressive.

"What a day, what a day," she says, plopping her oversized bag in an empty chair at the table. She nods when I hold up the bottle of wine. "I hope your day was more productive than mine."

"Actually, it was not." I hand the glass to her. "And you can blame your children for that."

She furrows her brow. "Boone?"

I snort as she sips her wine. Once she's finished, she sighs.

"I had a class with your father this morning," she says, sitting at the table. "Then a last-second meeting with a retail chain that's interested in carrying my jewelry in their stores."

"Full-time?"

"That's what it sounds like." She beams. "I never count my chickens before they hatch, but these eggs are starting to crack open."

"Interesting analogy."

Mom laughs. "Something smells good in here. Have you eaten?"

"I just threw some chicken and potatoes in the oven. There's some left. Want me to make you a plate?"

She relaxes back in the chair and swirls her wine around in her glass. Seconds tick by, and she doesn't speak. Instead, she watches me with a knowing and growing grin.

"I'm going to take that as a no," I say and sit down in my chair across from her. Since she's acting weird, I pour myself a little more wine.

"Coy called me today," she says out of nowhere. "He said the doctor told Bellamy that the baby will be here any day now."

I don't know what my face does, but Mom laughs.

"What?" I ask.

She shakes her head. "It's a boy, you know. It's not going to be another Rosie to chase you around."

"God took pity on me."

Mom sips her wine, eyeing me over the rim in a way that makes me anxious.

"Did you come here for a reason?" I ask.

"Do I need a reason to visit my son?"

"No, but you have four others to choose from. I try to make myself as unpleasant as possible, so I never get chosen."

She sets her wine down and laughs. "Wade, you are not unpleasant."

"Then something is getting lost in translation."

Though I fight it, we exchange a grin. She knows I don't mind *her* visits.

She gives me a few moments of space without peppering me with questions or tossing whatever has sparked her arrival on my lap. It's appreciated.

My mind is still busy sorting through the work I left unfinished on my desk, a design issue on the Greyshell project that's challenging me, and Dara Alden.

I shift in my seat.

That woman was so damn irritating—and I'm not sold on why.

Sure, her bubbliness was a little much. The fact that she remembered our ridiculous speech was also suspect, and her penchant for pushing my buttons—shoving back when I pressed forward—was aggravating. But it doesn't add up. None of those qualities are things that I haven't experienced before her.

To top it off, she left things unresolved. *Are we working together? Does she want to? What kind of structure does she want designed if we go through with this?*

Do I want to go through with this?

I don't fucking know. And I don't fucking know when I'll know how this is going to wind up.

"Are you okay?" Mom asks. "Your face is getting a little red."

"I'm fine."

She grins. "We'll blame it on the wine."

"Whatever makes you happy."

Her hand stretches across the back of the chair next to her. A gold bracelet catches the light and sparkles.

"So, how's Dad?" I ask, relieved to have found a new conversational topic.

"He's doing well. Addictions are a process, and my therapist told me that this is something we'll always have to contend with. But as long as he acknowledges his issues and continues his treatment and makes the right choices ..."

The levity from earlier disappears from her face. In an instant, she looks more her age. She's still beautiful and regal but weary. And that worries me.

I clear my throat. "Mom ..."

She shushes me. "I don't want to talk about me, Wade."

"Well, I do." I force a swallow down my throat. I don't know if it's the wine giving me a set of balls to challenge my mother or what, but here we are. "I appreciate your loyalty to Dad and the way you just raise your chin and get shit done, the way you take care of us all, but are you taking care of yourself?"

"Of course I am."

"Are you?"

Her lips part as if she's going to say something, but she closes them just as quickly. I don't give her any room to wiggle out of the conversation. I just watch her—pin her to her chair—because at some point, she'll finally give in.

She grips her wineglass with both hands as her shoulders fall forward. "I'm tired, Wade."

"As you should be."

"I keep telling myself that this season of my life will require more from me than some of the others. Like when you boys were small." A faint smile touches her lips. "Holt was fourteen, Oliver nearly twelve. You were ten, Coy eight, and Boone just in kindergarten. When I tell you how exhausting that was, it doesn't begin to cover it."

I grin. "Should've stopped with Coy."

As intended, this makes Mom laugh.

I sit back in my seat, my wineglass in my hand, and watch my mother. "You know," I tell her, "I can understand some of that. I don't know what it's like to have kids, obviously, but I can reflect on different parts of my life and recall that what kept me going was simply the idea of getting through it."

A chill runs down the center of my spine. I fight against the memories clawing their way to the surface.

Not here. Not now.

"That being said," I say, settling in my seat, "I don't know if that was the best way to handle those situations."

Mom cocks her head to the side. "What do you mean?"

I'm not about to discuss my life with her. This isn't about me anyway—it's about her and my father.

I've watched my mother carefully since we found out about Dad's addiction. She's remained stoic and has displayed more loyal devotion than I believed the old man might've deserved. *But what is it doing to her?*

"I mean that you've been pushing through, getting through it, for so long that maybe you need to stop," I say. "Your entire life has been about other things—your children, Dad, your business. And all of that is well and good but have you ever just paused and thought about what benefits Sigourney Mason?"

She smacks her lips together. "I'm a mother, Wade. And a wife and a businesswoman. What I do benefits me because seeing you all happy and healthy and thriving—that makes me happy."

"But does it, though?" I get up from the table and head into the kitchen. *Why is everyone so fucking philosophical this week?* "I see your point. And you're right." I look over the island at her. "But you didn't answer the question that I asked you."

"Sure, I did."

I shoot her a look as I reach into a cabinet.

"You asked if I thought about what benefits me," she says. "I gave you that answer."

"You gave an answer that would've sufficed had Boone asked it."

She sighs. "What's that supposed to mean?"

I take out a glass container and then close the cabinet. "You answered the question in the role of mother, wife, CEO. You didn't give me a first-person answer. What benefits you as a person? As an individual? As your own structure?"

She watches as I place a chicken breast into the bowl. I add some potatoes without looking up to give her space to consider what I'm saying. By the time I snap the blue lid down over the leftovers, she speaks.

"I suppose I'll have to think about that," she says quietly.

"I suppose you will."

She smiles as she gets up from the table. "Out of all of my children, you surprise me the most."

"I'm surprised every day that I'm related to the rest of them."

She walks into the kitchen and pats my cheek. "Never tell them that I said this, but you are the most special out of all of them."

"I'm fairly certain they're all aware," I deadpan.

Mom snorts and then chuckles as she walks back to her bag. I follow her with the container in my hand.

"Here," I say, handing it to her. "Midnight snack."

She takes the bowl from me. "You are a good man, Wade Edward. You'll make the greatest husband and father someday."

I make a face and recoil.

"Wade ..." She sighs. "Stop it."

"We were doing so good."

She holds the bowl with one hand and grips the back of a chair with the other. I have no idea what's coming. I just know I won't like it.

I brace myself.

"Since we officially took a turn, I can bring this up," she says. "I heard from Holt that you are no longer in the wedding party."

Oh, hell.

"I understand that an agreement was made between the two of you, and I'm going to respect that," she says. "I just want you to know that it wouldn't have hurt you to stand beside your brother on his wedding day."

"And it's not going to hurt anyone if I sit and watch him profess his undying devotion to Blaire in front of too many people—just like he does every damn day—in a venue that I've seen the price of," I say, pointing my finger at her. "It's not my money, so I don't give a shit. But it's ridiculous, and you know it."

"We aren't talking about their budget because that's none of your business."

"Fair enough. But we *are* talking about my dignity and standing up there like a monkey in a suit while my brother basically gives up his balls—"

"Wade!"

"What?"

The air moves between us as we watch each other. Finally, she starts to smile, and I see my opening.

"It's the beauty of having so many brothers. He won't miss me," I say, my voice a bit lower than before. "I will be there, sitting in a row—probably near the back, and I'll clap and bow my head. I'll welcome Blaire into the family officially because, despite my feelings about this indulgent event, I do like her, and I'm glad Holt is marrying her if he has to get married."

"I'm sure that Holt appreciates your approval."

"And people wonder where I get my dazzling personality."

She shakes her head and picks up her bag.

"Don't you have another kid to check on?" I tease. "I bet Boone is dying for you to visit."

She lifts her chin in faux defiance. "Actually, I'm on my way to see Oliver and Shaye."

"I bet they're thrilled."

Mom punches me in the arm as she walks toward the door. Her ring bites into my skin, but I don't tell her that.

"Drive carefully," I say as we approach the entryway.

"Thank you for the snack." She raises the container I gave her. "And the wine. That was a damn good bottle. What was it?"

"A Spanish red of some sort." I kiss her cheek. "I'll give you a bottle the next time you come by."

She grins. "Are you trying to get me to come visit you more often?"

"I can ship directly to your house."

Her laughter makes me chuckle.

"I love you, Wade. I appreciate your advice." She lays a hand on my chest. "There's a big heart in that chest of yours. I can't wait until you find it."

Reaching around her, I open the door. "Time for you to go."

She laughs before kissing my cheek again. "Be good."

"Always."

"Good night, my darling."

"Night, Mother."

I step onto the porch and wait until she's in her car and barreling down the driveway. Then I go back inside.

The house smells warm and spicy. Grabbing the remote, I flip on the fireplace before collecting my glass of wine. I carry it into the living room and sit down, forgetting about my dinner.

The peace that I had before my mother arrived must have left with her. The quietness of the house that I usually enjoy, that I use to recharge my energy, makes me twitchy instead of calm. Not wanting to be stuck inside my head, thinking about things that I can't control, I pull my computer onto my lap and open my email.

It's a move I instantly regret.

To: Wade Mason
From: Curt Bowery
Re: Project

Mr. Mason,

I wanted to reach out to you personally and thank you for taking on a project so dear to my heart. It's incredibly difficult to trust anyone to work closely with my family, as I'm sure you can attest. It's an honor and, quite frankly, a relief to know that Dara is in such good hands.

Should you have any questions or concerns, please call me on my personal cell phone. I will anticipate a contract in my office early next week.

Enjoy your weekend.
Best,
Curt Bowery, President and CEO

Fuck.

I pick up my glass and down the rest of the liquid.

"Dara and I didn't make any agreements," I say aloud. "What the hell is this?"

I run the possibilities in my head. Either Dara lied to him and told him that we were working together or he assumed it to be a shoo-in.

He's wrong, regardless.

My fingers strum across the armrest of the chair as I contemplate what to do. Immediately, her laughter echoes through my brain.

"I'm not sure you're the man who should be handling ... my project."

Her words fire through me. I tense immediately.

"I can handle your project, Little Miss Sunshine," I say, almost glowering at the email from her grandfather. "But I'm going to make you work for it for a change."

I poise my fingers on the keyboard and let them fly.

To: Curt Bowery
From: Wade Mason
Re: Project

Mr. Bowery,

Thank you for considering Mason Architecture. After yesterday's intake appointment with your granddaughter, it has yet to be determined if we will, in fact, be working together. Regardless, I do appreciate your faith in my work, and I look forward to potential collaborations in the future.

Regards,
Wade Mason

I hit send.

"You're welcome for that gift, Oliver," I say, pleased with myself for thinking it through and adding that little bit. That should help ease things if he completely loses his cool if I don't take this job.

Which he will.

If I do.

But will I?

I close the computer and head to the kitchen for another glass of wine.

Chapter Four

Dara

"That was the best roast beef sandwich I've ever had," I say, letting my eyes close briefly.

Rusti hums in agreement.

The afternoon is the epitome of fall perfection in Georgia. It's still fairly warm with a big, bright sun, crystal-clear sky, and a breeze that promises cooler temperatures just in time to usher in the holidays.

"How did your photo shoot go this morning?" Rusti tugs Cleo's leash to keep her from trying to run after a bird. "Was this a family or a baby?"

"Family with a baby. Fun times. My camera still smells like—"

"Don't do it! *Don't you do it.*"

I giggle as I toss my sandwich wrapper in a garbage can. "The wife wanted two time slots because she had five outfit changes for her and three for her husband and kids. It was *a lot.*"

Cleo barks at a squirrel.

"I wish I could make the same money shooting old farms and the beach," I say.

"Take pictures of dogs. They're cuter and cleaner than babies. I mean, just look at my little Cleopatra." She beams at her tiny white dog with bubble-gum pink bows beside her ears. "She could be your first new client."

Cringing, I take a step away from my friend.

"What?" Rusti laughs. "It's brilliant. You could call it … Pawtography."

"Somehow, that actually seems to be less desirable than babies."

She gasps.

"I know. I'm shocked that something can be more off-putting than a tiny human who spits up sour milk, but facts are facts."

We sidestep a butterfly on the path and come together on the other side.

"I did get an email this morning from a stock photography site that I reached out to last week," I tell her. "They're launching next month, and the submission portal will open in a few days."

"That's … good. I think?"

I grin at her. "Well, I don't know if I'd call it good quite yet, but I'm going to give it a try. I have so many pictures of random things that I might as well see if I can make some money off them."

We stop at a bench when Cleo pops a squat to pee.

"She's so immodest," I say, nodding toward the terrier.

Rusti's jaw drops as though she's offended.

"She is," I say, standing firm in my observation. "She has no couth."

"My little baby has couth! Where else is she supposed to pee?"

I shrug. "Behind a tree?"

Rusti grins. "She wasn't the one fawning all over a hot architect a couple of days ago."

"Of course she wasn't. We know what she would've done."

We look at each other and try not to laugh.

"I mean, I've never heard of a dog trying to hump a man's leg—who was it? Zack?" I point my finger at Rusti. "Yes. Zack. Cleo humped Zack's leg while he humped you."

Rusti's face turns red.

"I can only imagine what she would've done in Catnip's office," I joke.

She tugs on Cleo's leash. "You're such a little hussy." Then she looks back up at me. "But a hussy with good taste because that man was honestly ... I would've married Zack had he asked."

"He must not have been into threesomes." I wink at my friend as we start walking again. "In reality, he was overrated."

"Eh ..."

We walk a little farther down the path, stopping momentarily at a fountain for Cleo to check out her reflection in the water. Rusti and I move in silence as she undoubtedly thinks about Zack and my mind drifts to Wade.

Rusti was right when she said he's my catnip. She doesn't realize how true that is. I don't think I fully understood the truth of her words until I sat at the kitchen table at two this morning and talked it out with a brownie.

My weakness has always started with *tall, dark, and handsome*. It's the trifecta that captures my attention out of a sea of men. Add in a sharp jawline, dazzling eyes, and a smirk? I'm ready to dip my toe into the proverbial pool.

Usually, it stops there. The water will get murky. He'll have the brains of a jackass or the attention of a gnat. He'll talk out of both sides of his mouth. He'll be *too sweet*. Something typically causes me to drag myself away from him as fast as I was initially intrigued.

But of the men who manage to hold my interest? The ones who exude intelligence? The few who have wit *and* class? The men who present themselves as a bit of a challenge with an aura of mystery?

Wade checks those boxes, making them fall like dominos. I get a rush of energy, of excitement, every time I think about him.

And this can't be about him.

I don't have the space in my life for anything to be about anyone but me, and I definitely don't have time to deal with entangling myself in any way with a man who would surely do little more than disappoint me on some level.

Or break my heart.

"I don't think I'm going to work with Catnip." The words streaming from my mouth take me by surprise as much as they do Rusti.

She lifts a brow. "Really? Okay. Not what I was expecting, but ..."

"It wasn't what I was expecting either." *Especially because I didn't know that I'd made this decision until now.* "I've been thinking about it." *About him.* "And you were absolutely right when you said he was my type."

Rusti tugs at Cleo's leash to stop her from barking at a tree. "So you aren't working with anyone you find attractive now? What if you find the unicorn hot firefighter and he books a photo sesh?"

I grin and ignore her. I need to talk through this—realistically.

"This house is going to change my life—either because I have an amazing place to live in for the rest of my life or it's something that I can sell later on and be set. But getting to that point ..." I sigh. "As much as I absolutely hate crying, this might get emotional."

"I know." Rusti frowns. "You have every right to be emotional about it."

I stuff down a wave of thoughts that always float just under the surface. *Now isn't the time to get into all of that.*

"This is going to be a process," I say firmly. "The closer we get to making it happen, the more nervous I get. And I don't need to be dealing with some guy who I know, for a fact, is difficult to work with—"

"And who you're attracted to."

I roll my eyes. "Yes. That too. Because every guy who fits the bill of my catnip, as you call it, always does what?"

Her face sobers. "Breaks your heart."

"Bingo." I roll my head around my shoulders. "I'm not saying he'd even be into me. Maybe we could just forge an antiseptic working relationship. But the odds are stacked against this, Russell."

Rusti glares at me for using the nickname I created for her.

"Too many things could already go wrong here without adding in a potential issue with the architect," I say, continuing.

I hadn't thought this out. But now that it's all laid out in front of me ... it makes sense. It's logical.

It's the right answer.

I know it in my heart. I can feel it in my soul.

"My focus needs to be on me," I say.

"You've had a hell of a year. When you put it like that, I agree with you one hundred percent. You have to follow your gut, Dara, and if it's telling you that this isn't the right answer—listen to it." She digs into her pocket and retrieves her phone. "Speaking of listening to it, can you hold Cleo's leash for a minute so I can listen to work tell me that I need to come in early and they can listen to me tell them to eff off?"

I swear that Cleo looks over her shoulder and laughs at me.

"Fine. Sure. Give her to me," I say.

Rusti hands me the leash before walking off into the grass.

"I know you don't like me," I tell Cleo. "I don't like you either. So let's just keep this friendly, okay?"

She leads me down another path that heads toward a marshy area. It's one of my favorite spots in the park.

"Good choice," I tell the dog as we get farther away from Rusti.

Moss sways in the breeze, draping over the heavy branches overhead. The rhythmic movement sweeps the negative thoughts from my mind. Before I know it, I'm mentally designing holiday backdrops for a family photo session.

It's almost as though the universe teamed up with Cleo to conspire against me because just as I let my shoulders fall, the dog springs into action.

"Cleo!" I shout, my voice tinged with panic as the Jack Russell terrier jerks to my right.

I try to move the leash to my other hand, but the transfer fails. The end of the leash slips through my fingers, and Cleo makes a break for it.

"*Shit.*"

Sprinting as fast as a nearly thirty-year-old woman who hasn't run since high school, I travel across the lawn in pursuit of the dog. Her silly pink rhinestone-encrusted collar catches the sunlight, and I swear it gives her another five miles per hour.

"Cleo!" I call out, already panting. "Cleo, please stop!"

She doesn't stop.

A bead of sweat breaks out across my forehead as I chase her through the trees. *I should've worn a sports bra*, I think as I clutch a hand to my bouncing chest.

I hate this dog. I hate this dog so much.

Thankfully, like a gift from the heavens, she stops running at the edge of the marsh. She looks at me with her tongue wagging out of the side of her mouth.

I get to her as quickly as I can in my state of mid-cardiac arrest. But just before I can reach her leash, she dives into the muddy water and races through it.

"Dammit," I say, looking behind me in hopes that Rusti will be right there.

She's not.

"Cleo!"

My shout isn't as loud as before, and my steps aren't as quick—not that they were ever quick to start with. But Cleo's seem to slow too as she approaches a large oak tree.

I sense my opening. I find my Supercharger, courtesy of a Red Bull I downed just before I got here, and bolt after the dog. But as soon as I clear the trunk, my feet stumble.

As I catch myself against the rough tree and the bark scratches my palms, I watch *in horror* as the now-brown dog leaps into the air—mud flying off her fur—like a circus-trained professional, vaults onto a picnic table, and then launches herself into the arms of an unsuspecting man leaning against a bench.

"Hold her!" I scream.

His hands close gingerly around the filthy animal. Just as I reach the two of them, she puts her dirty little paws on his chest–on his crisp white T-shirt—and licks his face.

My insides shrivel as I jog the rest of the way.

"I'm sorry," I say, planting my hands onto my knees and dragging oxygen into my fire-laden lungs like my life depends on it. Because it does. "I don't know what got into her."

"I'd say it was *her* that got into *something*."

I start to reply—to apologize for her transgressions. To offer to dry-clean his shirt. To do *something* to ease the rigidity of his posture. But as I open my mouth, something stops me.

The scent of Oud Wood by Tom Ford.

The sharp jawline that I can make out despite his dipped chin.

A blast of energy that can—strangely—only be explained by the presence of one man.

I want to close my eyes and melt into the ground. I want to turn around and find Rusti. I want to hit rewind and stop this entire scenario from playing out. I want to not be panting—with one boob hanging out of my sweaty bra—and look in control of my life.

But I can't. I don't have access to a remote control.

My fears are realized as he lifts his face to mine.

Oh no.

Oh fucking no.

CHAPTER FIVE

Dara

I take a step back.

It's a purely instinctual move to put some distance between me and the man who is clearly unhappy.

Embarrassment adds to the fire in my oxygen-deprived cheeks as his gaze finds mine.

His eyes are a slideshow. Each frame offers another piece as the last few seconds connect to the one before it, snapping into place. My chest rises and falls with uncertainty, *and humiliation*, as I watch him determine—*incorrectly*—that Cleo is my dog.

"I've never seen an animal resemble their human quite like this," he mutters before glancing down at Cleo and grimacing.

His statement lights a fire inside me that dissolves my embarrassment.

My jaw falls open. "Excuse me?"

"You both have quite enthusiastic greetings." He holds Cleo out to me. "Do you mind taking her? Or him? Or ... whatever."

I make absolutely no effort to take the dog.

"Yes, I mind. I don't want to get all muddy," I say.

He blinks.

"She's not mine," I say. "I don't even like that dog."

"I assure you that you like her more than I do."

I wrinkle my nose. "I'd bet not. I wouldn't even mind if you just tuck her under your arm and take her home with you."

He sighs as Cleo squirms in his hands.

"If this isn't your dog," he says, lifting a brow, "then why were you chasing her through the park?"

Bastard.

"Why are *you* even here?" I ask, turning the tables back on him. "Aren't you *so busy*? Shouldn't you be in the office *handling projects*?"

He wasn't expecting this question. Hell, I wasn't expecting it either, but I'm not mad that I followed up with it. His response to my challenge licks the flame starting to burn in my stomach.

Wade's eyes run up and down my body. A trail of heat is left in its wake, and I'm suddenly reminded of my floppy boob.

My cheeks heat again. "Just ... *just a second*." I turn and make a point of looking for Rusti. But while I'm facing the other way, I situate myself back into my bra as discreetly as I can—which isn't very discreet. Once I'm as put together as I'm going to be, I turn to face him again. "Cleo's mom should be coming. I thought I saw her over there."

He smirks. I try not to die. Cleo squirms until she's against his chest and licking his face again.

The dog's actions give me a second to really take Wade in today. A white T-shirt hugs his lean, solid body. His shoulders look strong but not stupid. He might be able to pick me up and throw me over his shoulder, but he's definitely not picking up the back of a car.

Black athletic pants are tight enough to showcase his thighs, and running shoes are in stark contrast to his dress shoes from yesterday but are wholly acceptable. A black Atlanta Falcons hat completes the casual Wade look.

And I'm a fan. I'm a *big* fan.

"She likes you," I say as he pulls Cleo away from his face.

"She doesn't know me."

"Obviously."

He tries not to smile. "And what's that supposed to mean?"

I try not to smile either. "That means that women always like men until they get to know them."

"Are we stereotyping this afternoon?"

"I like to think of it as speaking from experience. Besides," I say, reaching for Cleo. "You're the one who implied that she wouldn't like you if she knew you."

He's not thrilled by my point. I, on the other hand, am.

I smile as I take Cleo from him. "Thank you for catching her."

"She didn't leave me much choice." He watches me set her on the ground with a bit less disdain than before. "She just leaped toward me like a little flying ..." He stops as if he's just aware of the smile kissing his lips. "Anyway, I caught her."

He clears his throat and wipes any hint of amusement off his face.

"*You like her*," I tease him. "Look at that. You smiled."

"I did not."

I hum. "I think you did."

Wade rolls his eyes and redirects his attention to his shirt. He runs a hand over the streaks of mud left by Rusti's errant pet. Through the gesture, I'm able to see the lines of his abs.

I gulp.

"I got an email from your grandfather last night," he says as he looks up at me. "He seems to be under the impression that we're working together."

My stomach flip-flops. "I haven't had a chance to talk to him yet."

"And if you had, what would you have said?"

That he has really good taste.

I search Wade's eyes to get a hint of what he's thinking. He definitely has thoughts swimming around those deep jade orbs. It's too bad he's locked them away and made them impossible to read.

He waits patiently for my answer as though he's prepared to stand in the middle of the park all day until I respond.

"I would've told him we decided we aren't a good fit," I say, even though that's not necessarily the case.

And it's not necessarily true.

He crosses his arms over his chest and leans against the bench behind him. With his legs stretched out in front of him, his body looks long and hard … and irresistible. I'm not sure which Wade is more delicious—suit-and-tie Wade or relaxed-in-sweats Wade.

Apparently, Cleo agrees and starts trying to climb him.

"Get down," I say, tugging her leash. She whines, and I really can't blame her.

"So we're not a good fit," he says, repeating what I just said. His lips press together. "Is that what you've decided?"

He screwed up. I bet he would be even twitchier if he knew the insight he just gave me without meaning to.

"It's the conclusion I drew after our meeting," I say, attempting to come across as nonplussed as possible.

"I see."

I kneel in front of him and flick the mud off Cleo's head. "I'll have to get with my grandfather about it this weekend. I know he was looking forward to working with you."

The energy between us roars as it tries to find an equilibrium. I don't dare look at him for fear of tilting the balance of power his way.

My throat goes dry as I wait for him to reply. Cleo's fur hides the subtle shake of my hand. It's not a nervous vibration pulsing through my veins, but more of a vigorous surge of adrenaline. An anticipation. The response to a curious suspense.

Where is this going? What will he say? I have no idea, but I'm dying to find out.

"Granddad mentioned before that if things didn't work out with you that he could just use Moss and Oak—his regular architects," I say, looking up at him.

"Their business isn't in home design. It's in commercial construction."

I stand and swear I see a wave of relief flash through his eyes.

"There's a new guy, Johan I think it is, who focuses on homes," I say. "Granddad said we'd work really well together."

This is news to Wade. It's also not what he wants to hear.

A dark shadow passes across his face as his arms drop to his sides. He shoves off the bench and stands tall as if he's just now giving this conversation his undivided attention.

I lick my lips. "I've heard Johan has a lot of time to *focus on my needs.*"

"I bet he does."

Wade's voice is tense. His face, though, is passive for the most part. He stares at me like he's trying to work something out, but I'm not sure if he's annoyed by my declaration or if he's bored with the conversation.

I tug on Cleo's leash. "We should be going."

"You do realize how personal it can be to design your home with someone, right?" he asks as I turn to go.

I smile before I face him again. Glancing over my shoulder, I lift a brow. "I figured."

"Your architect needs to know how you're going to use your space. What you value. The things in life you prioritize." He stands slightly taller. "They need to know your dreams."

This feels like a warning. It sounds like he's projecting that Johan can't do all of those things.

Is he implying that he can?

But as I stand in front of Wade and feel the weight of his gaze and consider being vulnerable with him—vulnerable enough to work together on this level—every cell in my body misfires.

It's overwhelming. The mere idea makes me want to run and hide. But, at the same time, a strange sense of excitement, of possibility—of completing this process with Wade Mason—feels like the best solution.

"I guess Johan and I are going to become great friends then," I say. I throw in a shrug that I hope looks apathetic because, under my clothes, I'm sweating. "Good talk. Thanks for the tips."

"You are impossible."

I smirk. "You are difficult."

Cleo barks. We both ignore her. Instead, we eye one another as though we're in a standoff in the Old West.

It's Wade's turn to lick his lips. "I can design a house a hundred times greater than anything Johan can even imagine."

So Wade has a competitive streak? This should be fun.

"Can and will are two very different words, Mr. Mason."

"They most definitely are."

"You say you can. Johan says he will. *I like do-ers.*"

The corner of his mouth flicks toward the sky in something that resembles a mixture of a grin and a smirk. It makes my knees go weak, and I struggle to stay in control.

If I'm even in control. I'm not sure anymore.

"It's a good thing I can *do* things then, isn't it?" he asks.

"It would be if it mattered." I smile. "At the moment, you're just an architect who made a very weak first impression."

His eyes narrow. "Stop lying."

"Who? Me?"

"Yes, you."

He takes a step toward me, effectively cutting the distance between us in half. The energy rippling off his body is enough to render me speechless.

My blood pours through my body, and waves of his cologne wash over my senses. I barely remember to hold tight to Cleo's leash as I lose myself in the depth of his green eyes.

"You know I didn't make a weak first impression," he says, his voice low. "You know that if I told you that I could fit you on my schedule that you'd be there on time .... *ready and willing.*"

I lift my chin. "And you know that if I said that I would relinquish control ... *you'd be all over it.*"

I actually don't know if that's true. What I do know is that I'm playing with fire.

He sucks in a deep breath, running his tongue around the inside of his cheek. I hold my breath and wait for him to volley something back.

Finally, he sighs.

"I have an opening Monday at four o'clock," he says.

"Not in your office."

"Where?"

I think quickly. "Hillary's House. Google it."

He pauses before extending his hand. I pause even longer before giving him mine.

The contact of our palms together sends a ripple of goose bumps across my flesh. It also sparks something in his eyes that makes them two shades darker.

"I'll see you Monday," he says, letting go of my hand.

"See you then."

He walks away like nothing of importance just happened.

I watch him like it did.

Chapter Six

Wade

"What is this? A daycare?" I ask as I shut the door to Boone's office.

"*Wadeeeeeeeeee*," Rosie screeches before launching herself at me. I buckle from the force. She attaches herself to my leg by sitting on my foot and wrapping her limbs around my shin.

Do I have a sign on my head asking to be jumped on today?

I lift my gaze to Boone. He has the audacity to grin.

"I love you, Wade," Rosie says, pressing her cheek against my knee. Her eyes focus on me so intently that it makes me itch. "I just love you so much."

"That's ... nice." I glare at Boone and then at Holt. "I thought you guys were running a reputable company over here?"

Holt laughs. I want to tell him that he's getting soft in his old age, but I don't bother. He'll just laugh even more, and that will extend my time here.

"Boone ... can you get your kid?" I shake my leg, but it only makes Rosie giggle. "You're going to have to let go of me at some point, you know."

She shakes her head. Each swipe to a side causes her forehead to thump against my shin. It can't feel good.

"Wade?" Rosie asks.

I look down at her. I would never admit this to anyone, but she's actually kind of cute when she's not covered in chocolate or sticky. She also has an affinity for me, and I have to give her credit for that. At barely five years old, she can tell which one of us is the one to buddy up to—me.

"What, Rosie?" I ask, sighing.

"Will you marry me someday?"

I reach down and try to pry her off my leg. She fights me, protesting both verbally and by fisting the fabric of my pants in her little hands.

"Rosie," I say through clenched teeth. "I can't marry you because I'm your uncle. That's illegal in every state. Also, you're five."

"But I'll be bigger someday!"

Finally, with more effort than I anticipated it would take to detach myself from a preschooler, I hold her up in the air and hand her to Holt.

"You are a little rascal. Do you know that?" Holt asks her.

"That's what Daddy Boonie says." She smiles wide as she looks at my little brother. "Can I go see Helena?"

Boone grabs a notepad and a pen off his desk. "It's Saturday, so Helena isn't here. But you can go out into the hallway where you can spread out and draw her pictures."

"Draw only on the paper," Rosie says seriously.

"Only on the paper." Boone nods. "Draw her something nice."

"*I'll draw pics for Wade,*" she sing-songs.

Rosie hops off Holt's lap, grabs the notepad, and heads for the door. It doesn't take two seconds until we hear everything Boone just gave her clamor against the floor.

I poke my head into the hall to ensure she's okay. She smiles broadly back up at me.

"How do you deal with her energy all day?" I ask.

"She's usually not here. That's how," Boone says with a laugh. "We had lunch with Dad today, and I needed to swing by here, so I brought her with me. Never again."

I sit next to Holt. He gives me a curious look.

"What?" I ask.

"Nothing. It's just always shocking to see you dressed in anything but a suit and tie."

I roll my eyes. "I went for a run."

"In the mud?" Holt laughs, chuckling.

"Fuck off."

"How'd the meeting go this week with Bowery?" Boone asks, tossing me an *I got you* look.

I narrow my gaze. Despite my appreciation for the segue, I'm also concerned. Boone doesn't do me favors without needing something in return.

But I don't have time to consider that. I just came by my brothers' office to grab a file that Eliza inadvertently sent to Oliver by courier yesterday.

"It went swimmingly," I deadpan.

Boone's smile falters. "You know—I've never understood that word. *Swimmingly*. What does that even mean?"

"Use context clues," Holt says.

Boone looks even more confused.

"I don't have time today to give you an English lesson." I settle in my chair and rest my elbows on my knees. "About this Bowery thing ..."

The back of my neck tightens.

"I agreed to do it today," I say.

Holt relaxes against his chair. "Thank God."

"No, thank *me*," I mutter as I roll my eyes. "It's going to be a massive pain in the ass."

Dara Alden is a massive pain in the ass.

"And I'm not sure how I'm going to swing it."

Or how I'm going to deal with her.

"But I did you guys a solid. You're welcome."

I don't look at them. I'm not confident that they won't see the hesitation in my eyes.

This morning when I left the house, I was going for a run to help me work out how to tell my brothers that I would have to pass on this job. The more I thought about Dara last night, the more it became apparent that it wasn't going to work out. It was already taking up so much mental space, and it hadn't even begun. How could I justify the hours, days—*potentially months*—that something as elaborate as I'm sure a Bowery home will require?

I can't.

But I'm going to have to.

"At the moment, you're just an architect who made a very weak first impression."

I shake my head. *She's so full of shit.*

"You still with us, Wade?" Boone asks.

I look up. "I'm still sitting here, aren't I?"

"Do you wake up already programmed to be a dick, or is it a decision you make over breakfast?" Boone asks.

"It usually falls into place once I walk in the same room as you."

He grins. *Of course he does.*

Holt chimes in about a job in Atlanta that Bowery floated Oliver's way, and I tune them out. *Let Johan work his magic on that one.*

I roll my eyes.

Fucker.

My phone buzzes in my pocket as Boone circles back to his lunch with Dad. I take a quick look at the screen.

Bowery Enterprises.

My heartbeat picks up as I consider taking the call. If I ignore it, I'll just have to call them back when I get out of here. Alternatively, if I take it now, I won't have to wonder what it's about and can get it over with.

"I'll be right back," I mutter and get to my feet. "This is Wade Mason."

I open the door and slip into the hallway. I motion for Rosie to stay put and to stay quiet. She nods, happy to make me happy. Then I pace across the foyer and slide into Shaye's vacant office.

"Wade, this is Curt Bowery," a voice booms through the line.

"How are you, Curt?"

"Fine. Thanks for asking. You?"

"I'm great," I say. *Why the hell is he calling?*

"Great. I wanted to reach out to you this afternoon and give you an opportunity to talk with me one-on-one about working with Dara. I know it's an unusual setup for companies such as yours—and even more peculiar that I'm asking it almost as a favor from you. I've been chatting with Oliver, but it occurred to me last night that I should've called you myself before this point."

"It would've been appreciated."

He seems to consider this. He also doesn't seem to know that Dara and I reached an agreement today.

In business, there's no reason to show your hand until you have to. So I don't mention it. Yet.

"Your work is admirable. Your creativity and attention to the smallest detail in your design is—"

"Curt, with all due respect, let's cut the shit." I pause, letting my words sink in. "We both know that you didn't call to tell me what a genius I am. So let's save us both the time and get to the point."

He chuckles. "I knew I liked you."

"You'd be the first."

He sucks in a long breath. "To be blunt, and I hope this stays between the two of us ..."

"Of course."

"I'm looking to part ways with Oak and Moss. There have been a variety of circumstances that have transpired to get to this point, but it goes without saying that I'm uncomfortable with them working closely with Dara."

Take that, Johan.

"You come highly recommended, and that's not me talking out of my ass," Curt says. "I've known your family for years. You are good people. Family men. I respect that."

I pace Shaye's office.

We are family men. The Masons have always put family above everything. But something about the way Curt is speaking—I'm not sure if it's his tone or the words he's choosing—but something doesn't quite sit well with me.

I brush a streak of dirt off my shirt. "That's good to hear."

"Of course, the budget is whatever Dara needs," he says. "I trust that you wouldn't run up the bill just to run it up." He laughs ruefully.

"There's more on the line here than just this project. I'm sure you realize that."

"Someone said something about a project in Atlanta."

"Well, yes. And I haven't mentioned this to Oliver," he says, "but I'm working with a few investors on a resort in Mexico. It's going to be state-of-the-art. A one-of-a-kind. I was thinking, if things go well, that it might be an opportunity for Mason Limited."

Ah, hell.

A part of me wishes that this situation never unfolded because something is amiss here. I can feel it. But another, bigger part of me is emboldened that I've already said yes. If I'm involved at the start, I can do two things.

First, I can make sure that some fool like Johan doesn't fuck Dara over. Second, I can feel Bowery Enterprises out before Oliver gets his panties in a twist and jumps all over the Mexico proposition—if it's real. Because my reservations run deep in my bones.

"Well, Curt, you'll be pleased to hear Dara and I decided to work together today," I say, withholding a sigh. "We have a meeting on Monday."

"That delights me. How wonderful."

I can hear him smile. It takes everything I have not to roll my eyes.

"Please, take care of her, Wade. And whatever you need, let me know."

"That's the plan."

I spot the file I came to the office for and tuck it under my arm.

"I'm glad to hear it. Call me if you have any issues and please don't mention anything about Mexico to your brothers. Nothing is set in stone yet. You know how it goes."

Unfortunately for you, I do. "Understood."

"Talk soon."

And just like that, Curt ends the call.

Fuck.

Somehow, this whole thing seems even *more* complicated, and I was sure that was impossible.

I wrap a hand over the back of my neck and storm through the foyer. Rosie looks up at me and smiles.

"I'm making you pictures," she says, her grin stretching from ear to ear. "See? That's your heart. It's black."

"Fitting."

"Do you love it?"

"I think you're a very perceptive little girl."

She seems satisfied with this and goes back to her scribbling. I, on the other hand, march into her dad's office.

"I have to go," I say, gripping the back of the chair I sat in before. "I have work to do."

Boone grins. "Have you told Ollie that you're doing Bowery?"

"I'm not *doing Bowery*. I'm working on the Bowery project," I correct him.

"*Ah, she's hot*," Boone says. "I knew it! You lucky fuck."

I glare at him.

"Ignore him. I'll let Oliver know," Holt says.

"You do that," I reply.

Before anyone can say anything else, all of our phones go off at the same time. We exchange a look before pulling them out.

Coy: I'm having a baby!

Bellamy: Excuse me?

Coy: WE ARE HAVING A BABY!

Bellamy: The light is green. GO or you'll have this baby in your car.

Coy: Sorry.

Mom: I'm on my way!

"I better be the godfather," Boone says, tossing his cell on the desk. "I mean, I don't know who else he'd pick, but it better be me."

"Of note, we aren't Catholic," I point out.

Boone shrugs. "So?"

"So, godparents are traditionally a Catholic thing," Holt points out.

"But I think he *is* choosing godparents for the baby, and I think they are Hollis and Larissa."

Boone gasps. "Why? Coy has four brothers, and he's picking Hollis? I call bullshit."

"It's probably not a bad idea. Larissa is Bellamy's best friend," I point out. "And Hollis ..." I release a hefty breath. "Give him a break. The guy just found out that his sister died ten years ago. Let him have this."

Holt nods in agreement, a frown on his face. "I feel so fucking awful for him."

I hang my head, fiddling with my fingers. I don't like to talk about this kind of shit. I'd rather jab my eye with one of Rosie's crayons.

"Maybe this godparent situation will make him feel like he's a part of the family," Holt says. "I think that's what Coy is going for. They've gotten really close."

Boone crosses his arms over his chest. "Fine. I agree. But one of you better have a kid then and let me be the godparent."

I turn and head for the door.

"Want to have a kid, Wade?" Boone teases. "I'll let you borrow Rosie for the night."

"Fuck off," I say over my shoulder, much to my brother's amusement. "Bye, Holt."

"Goodbye."

I hurry down the hallway and enter the elevator before Rosie can see me. I just don't have the energy to peel her off me again.

The buttons light up, and I select the parking level and then relax against the glass. A little pink sticker that's stuck about Rosie-level shines from just below the buttons. The color jolts my memory and takes me back to this morning.

And to the errant puppy.

Then to Dara Alden and her insinuation that I'm not the best architect around.

Damn her, anyway.

Chapter Seven

Dara

"This is a great shot," I say, taking a second to appreciate my handiwork.

I fiddle with the image a bit more. It's a shot with the groom and his two best friends from a wedding I worked on a few weeks ago. Their arms are over each other's shoulders, and a bottle of Corona is hanging from one of their hands. Faces lit up in smiles like someone just told a joke. The golden hour casts the perfect glow on their handsome faces.

The wedding was amazing. It was the kind of celebration that I always pictured for myself. The white tents were filled with delicious food and raucous laughter. Revelers danced until the wee hours of the morning. The music didn't stop—random explosions of confetti and sparklers didn't wane—until the closest neighbor a mile away finally complained at three o'clock in the morning.

"There. That's perfect." I stop editing the picture and pause to get a better look. "They're going to love these."

I reach for another baby carrot on my snack plate when my phone rings. I clamp a hand over the back of my neck—tense and stiff from the past four hours of edits—and answer the call.

"Hello?"

"Guess what?" Rusti squeals. "Don't guess. I'm not going to wait that long because *I can't wait that long* to tell you my news. So, guess what? *Zack called.*"

Her enthusiasm is a little much, especially for news that I already expected would happen. *Of course, Zack called.* Zack is an opportunist. There's no way he doesn't know how into him Rusti is, and Rusti is a catch by all accounts.

I recline in my chair. "He did? When?"

"Now. Just a minute ago. *He wants to see me.*"

"He wants to see you to give you back a hoodie? Or to get a little booty?"

She laughs. "Realistically? Probably the first, but I'm hoping for the second."

"Just keep that little dog of yours out of the way, or she'll clam jam you."

Rusti's laughter only grows louder. "What is that? The female equivalent of a cock block?"

"Yes, ma'am." I laugh. "Come to think of it, she might trigger something in Zack if he starts remembering all that leg humping. You should probably hide her."

"Aw, Auntie Dara. Do you want to puppy sit your little niece?"

I make a face and pick up a carrot. "Hardly."

"Hey, now," she says, teasing me. "The last time I allowed you to watch her—"

"You practically threw her at me."

"Well, you almost let her get away."

I snap off the end of the carrot. "Because she clearly hates me. You're a terrible mother for letting your child be with someone they loathe."

"She was testing you just like all kids do. You should be honored that I'd even consider letting you watch her again."

I snort and get to my feet. "That's me. *Honored.*"

Rusti's voice gets fainter.

"You know, she did you right. *She hooked you up*," Rusti says as if the phone is away from her face. "My girlie led you right to Catnip and ..."

I don't know what she says after that. My brain is already off on a tangent that leads to Wade Mason.

My body tingles as it remembers the heat of his palm. The allure of his cologne. The sexiness of his smirk.

It's impossible to figure this man out. *Does he like me? Hate me? Is he indifferent?*

I don't know.

He kicks me out of his office like I'm a time crasher. There are no follow-up calls or emails. And then he acts like he cares that Johan isn't qualified to work for me and that he's almost insulted that I would consider anyone else.

"You know I didn't make a weak first impression. You know if I told you that I could fit you in my schedule that you'd be there on time ... ready and willing."

What was that? We both know we weren't just talking about architecture. But how does one man go from not even caring if he sees me again to talking in innuendos?

I don't understand.

And I suppose that's part of the draw. It's a challenge. *He's* a challenge.

"I should do this, right?" Rusti asks, her voice loud and clear again.

"Do you want my honest opinion?"

"No," she says swiftly. "I don't because you're going to go all logic on me and point out that he broke up with me over the phone and that I still have that purple dress in my closet for the work thing he didn't end up taking me to. And you'll probably toss in that you always got weird vibes off him and *I get that, Dara*. I do. I just don't want to hear it right now."

What do you say to that?

I toss a strand of hair over my shoulder and lean against my desk.

There's no point in saying all of those things if she already knows it.

"I'm not you," she says, her voice quieter. "I can't just turn off my feelings because I know they're wrong."

My stomach knots. "I don't turn off my feelings."

"Yes, you do. And—"

"And you don't need me to tell you all of the reasons you shouldn't see Zack because you know my opinion and *I* don't need *you* to tell me all the reasons I'm *emotionally unavailable*." I suck in a breath. "Because I'm not. I have *tons of emotions*. Trust me."

As if to prove my point, a rush of feelings barrel through my brain and land on my heart with a thud.

Damn.

"I know you do," she says, a bit more carefully than before. "I actually think, if we're being honest, that you have more emotions than I do. But once you feel burned, you disconnect. Unplug. They're dead to you."

I pick up my water glass and set it on my snack plate. The remaining liquid sloshes in the glass as my hand trembles a touch.

"I'm also going to have to object to that point," I say, my tone controlled. "And I present Exhibit A in my defense—my relationship with my grandfather."

Rusti scoffs. "Okay. You win."

"You can't see me now, but I'm bowing in triumph."

She laughs. I laugh. But really—neither of us are laughing.

Curt Bowery came into my life bearing gifts of epic proportions shortly after my mother died. I was prepared, in a way, because my mother always told me that it would happen. There would come a time when he would want to meet me. *"Give him a chance because you deserve that. Don't give him a second because he doesn't."*

I never understood what Mom meant by that. Now I never will.

Rusti sighs. "I know you think I'm dumb for wanting to see Zack, but ..."

"I don't think you're dumb." I frown, my heart tender from the last few minutes. "I just don't want to see you set yourself up for another round of heartache. That's all."

"I know that. And I'm grateful you feel that way. But I miss him, Dara. And even if he comes over and we never see each other again, I feel like I need that closure." Her voice drops. "I was in Philadelphia when things went south and I haven't even seen him face-to-face since we broke up. I just ... I need to see his face. I need to watch him tell me it's over so maybe my heart can believe it."

"Then do it. As long as you know that it might not lead to anything and you're sure your heart can handle it, then do it." I grin sadly because I know this won't end well for her. "I'll leave a key in the hole in the tree in my front yard in case you need to sleep over tonight."

The line between us grows quiet. Finally, she sighs.

"You're the best, you know that?" she asks.

"It's been said. Now, you go give yourself a quick spa night before Zack gets there. Because if this is more booty, less hoodie—you need to be ready. And if it's not, then you'll just feel better about yourself afterward anyway because who doesn't like smooth skin?"

She laughs. "You're right. Thank you. I'm going to go do that and if I need to come by tonight—the tree has the key."

"Always. I'll talk to you later, friend."

"Bye."

"Good luck," I say but she's already disconnected the line.

I toss my phone on my desk.

The sky is dark outside the window. There are no stars in the sky. It seems fitting.

I rub the center of my chest, hoping to dull the ache that pulses just beneath the surface. It makes my whole body tighten. My heart hurts.

Someone once told me that you hit your stride in your thirties. They said the pieces of your life—your experiences and dreams—come together and create a life that resembles who you are. A life you want.

I don't know who that person was, but they lied.

My eyes close and I remember my mother's face. Her eyes matched mine—a hazel-like color that floats from gold to brown at a moment's notice. She had the best laugh, all light and airy like she didn't have a care in the world. But she did. Of course, she did.

At nearly thirty—a full adult by anyone's standards, I'm more alone and more confused about the direction of my life than ever. Worst of all, I'm motherless. There is absolutely no one in the world that loves me unconditionally. No one remembers the jokes and stories from my childhood. No one to root for me when I'm nervous or to pull me in for a hug when I'm scared.

Or a hug for no reason. I miss those.

I don't know if everything happens for a reason. I'm not sure I'm being led by anything but luck. But I do believe that I'm strong enough and wise enough to deal with whatever comes my way.

I try to believe that most days, anyway.

"Whatever comes my way like a new house," I say as optimistically as I can.

I grab my plate and glass and head toward the kitchen.

A sliver of vivacity spirals through my body as my thoughts are replaced by Wade. Being around him is entertaining. And despite his irritability, he's fun.

He'll definitely be more interesting to work with than Johan. Although I've never actually met Johan, but I can't fathom he's as exciting as Wade.

I sit my dishes down in the sink, my mind sorting through my last conversation with Wade.

"Your architect needs to know how you're going to use your space. What you value. The things in life you prioritize. They need to know your dreams."

"Hmm ..."

I meander through my house, flipping on each light as I go. The eat-in kitchen leads into a living room that's just off the foyer. A long hallway extends the other direction with a closet, a bathroom, two small bedrooms with a bathroom and the master suite.

I stop in the hallway and rest against the wall to think.

This house is really all I need. It's also really all that I want.

It's also my last connection to my mother since it was hers.

I'm sure I won't live here forever but, for now, it's perfect—for me and for my heart.

That's the thought that keeps popping in my brain every time I think about building something new. Something bigger. Something Bowery-worthy.

Sure, the office is a little small and the window is shaped like a porthole. It's charming. The guest room is crammed with my mother's things but I kind of like having it all close by—even if it is in boxes. I don't really need a dining room since I don't have tons of friends and people in my house makes me anxious anyway. And the butler's pantry that Rusti is convinced that I need ... I don't. I don't even know what I would do with it.

This home is cozy. It feels like a hug when I walk in at the end of the day. The sun fills the house and makes it feel less lonely.

"And there's a tree for a key," I say, laughing. I lean my head against the wall, my heart aching again. "I really love this house. I'll hate to leave it."

But leaving it feels like the only way to go forward. And the opportunity that my grandfather is presenting me with this new house—because it *is* an opportunity, even if it feels so wonky to me—is a door opening.

I just have to walk through it.

A handsome smirk flashes before my eyes.

"That gives me some time to figure out what makes Wade Mason tick," I say, shoving away from the wall. "That can't be a bad thing."

My words reverberate through my brain as I head back to the kitchen.

Famous last words.

Chapter Eight

Dara

"Where are you going looking so hot?" Lola, a server at Hillary's House that I met two years ago when I started coming to the restaurant, says as she walks across the parking lot. "You should wear blue more often. Totally cute on you."

I smooth a hand over my blouse. "Thanks. I'm trying to pull off a *business but more casual with a slice of pretty on the side*." I smile. "How'd I do with those parameters?"

She laughs. "Nailed it."

I laugh too. "Well, good, because I'm about to meet a very sinfully attractive architect and I don't want to look too serious or too nonchalant."

"I heard *sinfully attractive*. Do tell."

Lola stops in front of me, a to-go cup dangling at her side. A breeze picks up, sending her hair flying and the edge of my eggshell-colored blouse fluttering in the air.

"I don't have a lot to tell," I say. "I'm working with him on a house that my grandfather thinks will solve all of my misfortunes in life."

Lola frowns.

"Obviously, that's not going to happen but I'm not mad about working with Wade Mason for a while to prove it." I watch Lola's face transform into a knowing smirk. "What?"

"*Wade Mason*, you say?" she asks.

"Yeah. And ..."

Her shoulders sag as she pretends that her knees are wobbling. "I can confirm with every ounce of estrogen in my body that Wade Mason is, in fact, inside. He's sitting in the back right corner wearing black pants, a denim button-up with a gray Polo sweater over it. The sun is shining on his face—making that dimpled chin look bitable."

My laughter catches the attention of the older couple making their way to their car.

"I don't know him—not in a friendly or Biblical way, sadly," Lola says. "But he's at some of the events we cater. I've watched him from afar many nights as he sips his cognac or handles a cigar in a way that makes me all hot and bothered."

I giggle. "Like you are now?"

She smacks my shoulder, blushing.

"I'm not judging you," I promise. "I was close to telling Granddad that I didn't want to design a house at all. I took a chance last minute and showed up for the appointment and, *voila*—Wade Mason. So, here I am."

"Here I'd be too." She walks backward. "You better get in there and I better get home and wash off the olive juice I just practically bathed in."

"Have fun with that."

She grins. "I think you're about to have a hell of a lot more fun than me."

We wave goodbye and go our separate ways. My heart thumps wildly in my chest as I head for the building. Chimes ring when I pull the door open and step inside.

Scents of cinnamon and coffee envelop me as I stand just inside the doorway and scan the room. It takes half a second to locate Wade. He's right where Lola said he'd be.

Damn.

The first thing I notice is something Lola forgot to mention—he's wearing his uber-sexy, nearly pornographic black-rimmed glasses.

My feet falter as I take him in. *Why is that so hot?*

Wade is pouring over a stack of papers in his hands. A cup of coffee and a glass of ice water sit in front of him. Just as I approach, he looks up.

My heart skips a beat as a look of surprise flashes across his eyes. Then just as quickly, a studiousness takes its place.

"Hi," I say, sitting before he can get to his feet. This isn't a date. I don't know if he would try to pull my chair out for me or what, but it would be awkward either way. "I'm sorry to keep you waiting."

He drags his glasses to the tip of his nose and looks over the top of them. I can't tell if he's disappointed or bored.

"That's it?" he asks, catching me off guard.

I sit my purse on the chair next to me. "*That's it?* I don't know what you mean."

He takes his glasses off and sets them next to his phone. A slight, barely there smile graces his lips. "I just expected something a little … *more* when you arrived. You never come quietly."

"Interesting observation so early in our relationship."

His lips twist together. His eyes narrow. A smile or a smirk or a frown—*what's to come?* I don't know. But the anticipation that I think he's intentionally building has me shifting in my seat.

I try to play it cool by brushing a strand of hair away from my face when, in reality, a bolt of adrenaline makes it almost impossible to sit still. I lift a brow and grin.

"I'd hate to disappoint," I say, even though I know I'm potentially playing with fire. "If you'd like me to reach over and give you a big hug, I'd be more than happy to."

He fights against his smile growing wider.

It's a challenge I accept.

"But I am not, under any circumstances, jumping into your arms or humping your leg," I tease. "I have standards."

"Let's be glad for that." He clears his throat, the hint of levity in his eyes now gone. "I was about to leave. I thought you'd forgotten."

"*Wade.* I was *ten minutes late.* Relax."

He scoffs and picks up his papers again. "I'm sorry. How much time does someone wait for another person in your world?"

"Depends on who it is and what's going on." I pause to order a glass of water and to take a menu from the server. "How long does someone take in your world?"

"No more than ten. And ten warrants a call."

I wrinkle my nose and peruse the offerings. "On another note, are we eating or just designing?"

"That would depend on, I suppose, if you're hungry."

I angle the menu to my chest so I can look at him unencumbered. "I'm always hungry, Mr. Mason."

He wants to make a face. I can tell. But for reasons unbeknownst to me, he refrains.

Frustrating man.

"Do you ever just, like, I don't know—breathe?" I ask. "Go with the flow? Not run your life in ten-minute intervals?"

He stares at me for a long few seconds without blinking. Then he looks down at his menu. "No."

I roll my eyes. I'm about to make a comment when Wade's phone goes off.

Again.

And again.

And again.

I quirk a brow. "I think someone needs you."

He discards the menu with a huff and then snatches up the device. After a quick glance and an even quicker reply, he shuts off the ringer.

The aggravation on his face verges on being adorable. His displeasure should not give me so much amusement, but it does. It's too much of a juxtaposition of inherent sexiness and indignant petulance to handle.

I set my menu down too. Lacing my fingers together, I rest my chin in them. "Was that someone warning you of a ten-minute delay?"

"No," Wade says without looking up.

"That's good, I guess." I poke a little further just to get a rise out of him. "You know, if you made Eliza a little less nervous, she might remember to text everything in one long stream rather than sending you four hundred one-sentence messages."

He raises his eyes to meet mine. "First, Eliza is new. She'll settle in. And, two, that was my mother letting us know that my sister-in-law is not having her baby today." He pauses, his jaw flexing. "There. Does that make you happy?"

I sit back and hold my hands up. "I didn't ask."

"Yes, you did."

"I did not. I just made some assumptions. But," I say, leaning forward, "you're going to be an uncle. That's exciting!"

His face doesn't change. It stays mostly blank.

"Come on," I goad him. "You have to be excited."

"I can barely contain myself."

He puts his glasses back on as the server returns. We make our orders —chicken fingers for me and a chicken sandwich for Wade.

As soon as the server leaves, he gets down to business.

"I have a form I'd like to go over with you. I'm having Eliza email you a copy—provided we have your email address. You can email the office with any questions you are unsure about today or any questions you want to think about," he says, sliding a piece of paper across the table. "Here is a hard copy."

"Okay."

He clears his throat. "My first question is regarding where this house will be built. We don't have to know, but if you do or if you have a solid idea, it's helpful to take that into account."

I squirm in my seat. Despite knowing this is exactly what we would be talking about today, I'm unprepared.

All of a sudden, everything feels so *real*.

I focus on the paper Wade gave me. The words blur together as my mind chooses this moment to solidify the fact that I'm doing this. Alone. I have no one to give me guidance. Worst of all, I don't even know if I want to be doing it at all.

"Dara?"

"Sorry." I look up and sigh. "There is a place that my grandfather mentioned building it, but I'm not totally sure."

Wade's forehead mars. "I'm assuming you have a say in it."

"Of course."

Our gazes lock together moments before Wade's eyes begin to search mine. His efforts are as intense as everything else about him, and I want to look away ... but I can't.

Finally, we're interrupted by the server and our food.

"Thank you," I say as she places my platter in front of me. I tune Wade out as he converses with her briefly about his coffee.

My chest is tight as I scramble to find another talking point. Relief courses through me when Wade diverts the conversation on his own.

"Do you need anything else?" he asks, his voice noticeably softer.

I shake my head. "I'm good. What more could a girl want besides chicken strips and steak fries?"

He grins. It's slight and so fast that I would've missed it if I didn't look up at the exact right moment. But, lucky for me, I did.

I smile back at him, and it only grows when he looks away, clearly perturbed at being caught in such a ridiculous act.

"It's critical we identify how you use your space currently and how you envision yourself using the new space," he says, back to business. "Have you given this much thought?"

"Nope."

He looks up with surprise.

"Okay. I gave it a bit of thought last night," I admit. "But I don't really have any specific plans."

His fork clinks as he sets it on the side of his plate. "You do realize that I'm going to need your input in order to make this project successful, right?"

I shrug.

He sighs.

I grin.

He grimaces and picks up his fork again.

Laughing, I slice my knife through a piece of chicken. "I want to give you my input. Honestly. I just ... I don't know how I use my space. It's a weird question."

"Do you entertain a lot?" he asks.

"That would require people in my house, so no."

He seems amused by this as he takes a bite of his sandwich.

"I don't love people in my personal space," I say. "I don't hate them. I'm definitely a lover. I—"

He coughs, covering his mouth with a napkin as he regains his breath. Once his airway is cleared, he takes a quick sip of his water.

"You okay?" I ask. "I was ready to give you mouth-to-mouth."

"I'm fine." He coughs again, clearing his throat. "You were saying …"

I think back to what we were talking about. "*Oh*. Yes. I was saying that I don't entertain a lot besides my friend Rusti. Cleo's mom."

"What about family dinners? Holidays? That kind of thing?"

I lift the piece of chicken to my mouth and then chew it slowly. He watches me carefully, reading between the lines I'm trying to blur.

Once I've chewed, swallowed, and had a drink, I look at him again. The glimmer in his eye is still his trademark cool, but there's a hint of something else—something warm or concerned or maybe just curious, that eases some of the tension in my body.

"I don't really have any family," I say.

"What about your grandfather?"

Of course. I sit back in my seat and try to figure out how to handle this sticky situation.

"Well, do you really think Curt Bowery is going to be having dinner at my house when he has a however-many million-dollar home of his own on the water?" I ask, relieved that I came up with such a brilliant, honest reply.

"Fair enough," Wade says, his tone displaying a hint that he didn't totally buy what I just tried to sell him.

"What about you? Do you host family dinners and holidays?"

"This isn't about me."

"Oh, *come on*," I say, picking up a fry. "Humor me."

He flashes me a disapproving look before taking another bite of his sandwich.

"That's not going to keep me from expecting an answer," I tell him, wagging a fry in his direction. "You're the one who said this was a personal process."

He gives me a look. "I also said you need to trust me."

"How can I trust someone I don't know?"

"People do it all the time," he says, flagging down the server for a refill. "I think I need to see the site you're considering."

I nod.

"Do you know where it is?" he asks.

"You head west to the place where that log cabin sits by the side of the road with the copper-colored metal roof. Do you know where I mean?"

He slow blinks. Twice.

"Well, you turn there and go … a while, and then there's a barn with an old, faded tobacco ad on the side. And then—"

"Are you serious?"

I bite the end off a fry. "Does it look like it?"

He shakes his head. "Just …" He grabs his phone and swipes around for a minute before looking back at me. When he does, his eyes are narrowed slightly. "Can you meet me sometime tomorrow, and we can go look at it?"

My mouth goes dry. It's not necessarily because of the way he's looking at me—although that plays a part in it. But it's mostly because of the heat and intention in his tone.

I shiver. "I have a photo shoot in the afternoon."

"What about nine tomorrow morning?" he asks. "Can you be at my office then? We can drive over together, or I can follow you."

"Sure."

He holds my gaze for a moment longer and then goes back to his phone. It rings while it's in his hand.

"Hello?" he says. "Yes. Shit. Okay. I'm sorry, Eliza. Can you tell them I'll meet them there in twenty?" He runs a hand over his forehead. "Perfect. Thank you."

I bite my lip to hold back a grin.

"What?" he asks as he puts his phone in his pocket.

"Twenty minutes is ten too long," I joke. "Seems like you're going to be late."

He flashes me a look. *I'm never late.*

"Not what it sounds like."

He sighs and takes out a credit card. "We've been trying to get an inspector on a jobsite for a month now and he just showed up. This is typically none of my concern, but I might have to tweak a couple of things depending on what he says. So ... I need to go."

"I figured. It's fine. I'm going to see you in the morning anyway, right?"

He calls the server over and then hands her his card without looking away from me. His stare is intense ... *potent*, even.

I have no idea what he's thinking, but I can feel it in every cell in my body.

My chest rises and falls as I wait for him to break the silence.

He takes his card back and finally looks away. He scribbles on the receipt before handing it back to the server. His card is returned to his wallet, and his eyes, finally, are returned to me.

"Nine o'clock?" he asks.

"I'll be there."

Standing, he gathers his things. I sit quietly and watch him, both sad he's leaving and also intrigued by his movements.

How does one person embody so much confidence and give so little away?

He heaves a breath. "I'm sorry for having to cut this short, Dara."

The way he says my name—like each sound is precious and must be spoken clearly—sends a shiver down my spine.

"I'm sorry you have to leave too," I say.

"Tomorrow?"

"Tomorrow."

The corner of his lip lifts before he walks away.

And, once again, even though I have no idea how or why, I'm left breathless.

Chapter Nine

Wade

"I'm not going to be worth shit tomorrow."

My reflection stares back at me. Much to my dismay, I look as tired as I feel. My forehead is streaked with a set of deep horizontal lines that are more evident when I'm exhausted. The dark splotches that sit below my eyes are indicative of the hour.

I'm never up at one in the morning. *Ever*.

I wipe off the sink, soaking up the splashes of water on the marble from brushing my teeth, and then hang up the towel on the hook next to my robe. The light is off with a simple flick of my wrist, and I walk into my bedroom.

Sinatra croons from the surround sound, his voice pairing with the warmth of the fireplace perfectly. It should create a relaxing atmosphere to assist me in winding down from the day ... but it doesn't.

Not tonight.

I sit on the edge of my bed and run a hand through my damp hair.

My inability to relax enough to wind down did result in a wave of productivity. Instead of going to bed at ten, as I do every night, I headed to my office downstairs and caught up on a number of peripheral projects. Hopefully, it'll help take some pressure off tomorrow.

Because God knows I'll have my hands full.

A smirk touches my lips as my mind drifts to Dara. I'm not sure what to think about her. She's captivating with her quick wit and seemingly boundless energy. Her refusal to simply answer a question without spinning it into a conversation about some esoteric topic is also frustrating.

And that body? *Fuck my life.*

I should've called this whole thing off from the get-go. My gut told me to tell Oliver no, to refuse to participate in this time-consuming situation. I definitely knew it was a bad idea when she marched into my office … and hugged me.

"Dammit," I groan, tugging at the roots of my hair.

If I'm going to do this, and I'm in too far not to do it at this point, I'll have to figure out how to separate Dara from everything else. Her project will get a set time each day, just like any other project. I'm not giving it any special attention. No matter what happens, her design cannot and will not bleed into the rest of my work.

It's just another job. She's just another client.

I flip off the light and quiet Sinatra. I reach for the remote to disable the fireplace but choose to leave it on at the last second. *Maybe it'll help me sleep.*

The bed is cool, the sheets crisp, as I slide into my spot. I toss and turn a little until I finally get comfortable. The stress in my body eases as I sink into the soft mattress.

My eyes close. My mind moves away from work, and I use the moment of peace to whisper my prayers. Just as I'm starting to drift off, a buzzing sound rips through the air.

"What the hell?" I reach for my phone and flip it over. When I see Coy's name, I sit up. "Hello?"

"Hey, Wade."

Coy's voice is low, just a few decibels above a whisper.

I can count on one hand how many times Coy has called me in the middle of the night. Once was a butt dial that he never repeated. Another time he was drunk and had a math problem he'd wagered one hundred dollars on and wanted me to give him and his buddies the answer. I did not comply. The third time was for bail money after he visited a bar that I warned him not to visit.

That time, I did help him out.

But this is different. I can hear it in his voice. A ripple of something woven into his tone has my stomach tightening as I listen.

"You busy?" he asks.

I rough a hand over my face. "Well, it's after one in the morning, so take that for what you will. Why? What's up?"

There's a pause. A long one.

I climb out of bed. "Is everything okay?"

"Yeah. Everything is fine. I just ... I brought Bells back to the hospital a little bit ago."

I still. "Is she all right?"

"Yeah. Oh, yeah. She's fine. The doctor said everything looks good and that we should have a baby sometime today."

A hefty stream of air escapes my lungs as my body relaxes. "That's good news."

"For sure."

A chair squeaks in the background as Coy sighs. I walk to the window overlooking the pool below and wonder what he's thinking. But as soon as my mind triggers that thought process, my stomach twists so hard that I think I might hurl.

"Bells doesn't want me to call Mom or her dad or anyone until morning," he says softly. "She feels bad that they were here all day for nothing."

"It's not like she was wasting their time on purpose."

"I know. The doctor said it could be a long time yet, and she doesn't want people sitting around all night."

The solar lights outside light up the pool area with a soft glow. *When was the last time I spent time out there?* I have no idea. Before I can figure it out, Coy sighs again.

I scratch the top of my head. "So, did you call me just to shoot the shit? Boone is great at that, you know."

Coy chuckles, but it's not a free, easygoing sound. It's stifled. Stressed. And I read between the lines ... even if I don't want to.

This is the last thing I want to do tonight. Or, really, ever. I contemplate telling him to call Oliver or Holt—he'd be happy to moan on and on about his wedding, and they could distract each other until the sun comes up. Even though it's what I want to do, I can't.

"I'll let you go," Coy says. "Bellamy is stirring. She might need some ice or something."

"All right. Go take care of her."

"Hey, Wade?"

"Yeah," I say, my voice tense.

"Thanks for answering."

"You know it."

The line disconnects, and I head back to the bathroom.

"Thank you," I whisper and head down the corridor.

My stomach roils with the stench of artificial cleaners and soaps. I'll have to shower as soon as I get back home because the antiseptic scent of the hospital will attach itself to me somehow.

Happens every time.

I knock softly against the door to Suite 4A. Then I crack it open until I spot my brother sitting in a chair. The movement catches Coy's attention, and he looks up.

"Wade," he whispers, sitting upright. "What are you doing here?"

I step inside the room. Bellamy is fast asleep as monitors beep all around her.

My throat goes dry. "I was in the neighborhood."

Coy gets to his feet and walks across the room. Before I can change the subject, he pulls me into a hug.

"It's good to see you, man," he says as he pulls back.

I glance at Bellamy again before looking back at my brother. "You want to take a walk? Get some coffee or something in the cafeteria?"

He reaches toward the edge of the bed and rests his hand on Bellamy's foot. The trepidation in Coy's face sits right on the surface.

"She'll be okay," I tell him. "We'll tell the nurse where we're going, and we won't be gone long."

He nods, still unsure, but trusts me to lead him out of the room. After a quick stop to converse with the nurse, we're on an elevator downstairs.

I jam my hands in the pocket of my jeans and try to feel out the situation. My head is foggy from the lack of sleep. Further, I have no idea how to handle this. Despite my natural inclination to approach it from a logical standpoint, I'm aware that my brother's emotions are running high.

Why couldn't he have called Oliver?

"Mom doesn't know you're here?" I ask as the elevator doors open.

"No. I'll call her in the morning."

We start down the hallway toward the cafeteria.

"But you decided you'd call *me*," I say, putting the obvious out there.

"Funny, right?"

"It would've been more amusing around eight o'clock—morning or evening. You pick."

He grins as we make our way to the coffee bar but doesn't reply. We work quietly side by side, filling our small cups with coffee. Coy adds both sugar and cream to his while I make my way to the cashier and pay.

"I've been thinking a lot about Hollis," Coy says, his voice distant as we walk toward a table.

"How's he doing?"

"I mean, he's okay. Sad as hell. Can you imagine being separated from us, having a hell of a life, and finally getting yourself to a point when you can go back and try to locate us ... to find out we're dead?" He sits in the chair across from the one I pull out for myself. "I hate it for him. I really hoped things would be different for the guy."

I swirl my coffee around in my cup. "Guess we don't always get what we want, huh?"

Coy's head bows. "You know, I bet Hollis's parents didn't expect to lose their kids when they were born."

"Coy ..."

He looks up, his eyes wide and wild. "Wade, what if … what if I can't do this? What if I can't be a dad?"

I set my cup down and fold my hands in front of me.

"I'm sitting in this chair for hours on end while Bellamy is in a misery that I can't stop," he says hurriedly. "And in a matter of hours, there will be another human being in this world, and I will be responsible for him."

"It's a little late to be considering this angle."

He gives me a look that's half shock, half glare. "Is that your attempt at a joke?"

"It would be funny if it weren't true." I shift in my seat. "But if you're being serious and wondering if your kid is going to grow up in foster care and come looking for you someday, the answer is no. Mom won't let that happen."

He sighs and sits back in his chair.

I mirror his reaction. "I know you must be … I don't know—fearful? Anxious?"

"What if I fuck this up, Wade? What if I don't know what to do? What if—"

"What if you're great at it?"

I want to roll my eyes at my own words. They're so fucking cheesy. But I don't know how else to say it.

Despite my hope that he takes this at surface level, he doesn't. He just sits in his chair with his coffee in his hand and waits as though he expects me to expound on why he'll be a successful parent.

"Look," I say, sucking in a breath as I prepare myself for what's about to come out of my mouth. "I know you must be feeling a number of ways right now. That's what happens before the biggest events of our life. But you have to back away from all of that emotion and think back to the version of you that got you into this mess—I mean, *situation*."

Coy grins.

I shake my head, refocusing. "There was a day, a month, whatever that you were sober and of sound mind, and you made a decision to start a family with Bellamy. Although I can't fathom why she agreed." I return his smile. "And now, here you are, about to realize your dreams for a little mini-Coy, and that's exciting stuff if that's your thing. It's apparently your thing since you chose this."

"Doesn't mean I'll be good at it."

His tone lacks the conviction from earlier. It's more conversational, more *humor me*. Even though I very rarely humor anyone, especially my brothers, it's well after two in the morning, and I'm already here.

So fuck it.

"What's the most important thing in the world?" I ask him.

"Family."

"You said that without thinking. No hesitation."

He shrugs. "What's there to think about? I'd do anything for you guys. Obviously for Bellamy. For Hollis and Riss."

"And *that's* why you are going to be a great dad."

He mulls that over, sipping his coffee. If I thought I looked tired earlier, Coy looks exhausted. But there's a hint of something in his eyes as though he could flip a switch and bust out a marathon.

I do not have that.

"You aren't going to do this alone," I say, yawning. "Bellamy is entirely more intelligent than you. You have Mom. And Dad, if you're being ballsy."

We exchange a grin.

"You have Holt. Ollie. Boone and he even did something productive and had a child for you so yours has a cousin. And a babysitter in a few years." I lean back in my chair. "Look at that. Boone being helpful. Wow."

Coy smirks. "And you."

"Me? What about me?"

"And I have you."

I scoff, shoving my chair back. "I'm not the one, Coy. I assure you."

We stand, straightening our table before heading toward the recycling receptacle. We toss our cups in the bin and then head toward the elevators.

Once we get to the doors, we stop.

Coy looks at me. "Wonder why I called you tonight?"

"Well, the question did cross my mind."

"Because I knew that out of all of my brothers, you would be the one to tell me the truth."

I chuckle. "What if I would've told you that you were going to suck as a dad?"

"Then I would've called Oliver, listened to him tell me you were an idiot, and took his side."

My chuckle grows louder.

"Thanks for coming, Wade. When I called you, I didn't expect this, and it means a lot. Truly."

I take a step back. I don't want or need his gratitude. He's family, and short of taking deals that I truly don't want to touch, I'd do anything for them.

Because that's what you do.

"It's fine. No big deal," I say.

"It *is* a big deal."

"You, uh, have a wife upstairs who's probably looking for you, and I have a bed that's missing me. So, if your confidence is boosted and you're good to go, I'm going to go too."

Coy pushes the button to go up. "My ego has been restored. Thank you."

"I'd say it was my pleasure, but I'd rather not start my day off by lying." I tap him on the shoulder as I head toward the exit. "If you need me ... call Oliver."

Coy's laughter follows me through the automatic doors.

Something else follows me—a memory from long ago. It was spurred by the scent that lingers on my clothes, the same one from that night in college.

The one I try to forget.

The one I'm never fully able to forget.

I climb in my Mercedes and turn on the radio. As Ray LaMontagne begins to sing, my mind struggles to adjust. So, I make a conscious decision—just this one time—to let it fall to the one thing, the one person who I know will distract me: Dara.

In the darkness of the car, alone in the middle of the night, I let myself smile while I think of the little spitfire I'll see in just a few hours.

Chapter Ten

Dara

"Hi, Eliza," I say as I enter Mason Architecture. The door sweeps closed behind me.

The front office smells like leather. The walls are cream with a deep, almost tobacco-colored trim that matches the overhead beams. It's very masculine and clean … and drab. The only liveliness comes from a fig tree in the corner and Eliza—and even she looks too scared to breathe too loud.

She looks up at me with big blue eyes. "Hi, Miss Alden."

"Oh, please. Call me Dara." I sit in one of the chairs near the tree. "I'm early. I know. I made it a point not to be late."

Relief washes over Eliza's face. It piques my curiosity.

"So, *Eliza*," I say, getting comfortable. "How are you this morning?"

She types furiously on her computer while trying to watch me from the corner of her eye.

"Don't let me bother you," I say, feeling bad for distracting her. "I'm just chatty today."

"It's okay. It's ... nice, actually." She lets her gaze linger on the computer before facing me. "I'm normally chatty too, but ..."

Her voice drifts off.

"Wade isn't a chatty kind of guy, huh?" I ask.

She grins. "I would say that's accurate."

"I'm trying to loosen him up. He's resisting, as I'm sure you can imagine, but I don't give up too easily."

"I—"

Her response is cut short by the opening and closing of an office door. I think we both hold our breath until Wade comes into sight.

I blow out a breath mostly to hide the *fuck* that comes out on a heated whisper.

He stops in the doorway and takes in both me and Eliza. Both of us just stare back at him.

Fitted black pants are capped off with black shoes. A lightweight sweater stretches over his chest and shoulders, giving me another view of the body I saw in the T-shirt at the park.

Whether he's been running his hands through his hair this morning or if he styled it to look precisely like that—I don't know. But I love it. The contrast of the playful hair, nerdy glasses, and sophisticated attire lights me on fire.

I think it does Eliza too because a dollop of drool glistens in the corner of her mouth.

"Ladies ..." He makes a face as if to say, *"What are you looking at?"*

I spring to my feet. "Good morning, Wade. Are you ready for our adventure?"

He's not. The scowl laced with a wariness says that all too well.

I laugh. "I'll take that as a yes."

He slides his attention from me to Eliza. "I'll be gone for an hour, maybe a little more. If anything comes up that you're unsure about, call Shaye at Mason Limited, and she'll help."

"Yes, sir."

He gives her a look I can't read and ushers me toward the door.

The sun is bright despite the cool temperature. A breeze whips through the parking lot as we step onto the pavement.

"Do you want to take one car or two?" he asks blandly. "There are benefits to both, I suppose."

"I get to pick. That's fun. I expected a more here's-what-we're-doing thing from you."

He holds a paper cup in his hand and scans the lot. Then he sighs.

"What?" I ask.

"The delivery truck next door has blocked me in."

"Great," I say. "I'll drive."

"When I said *one car or two*, I meant that I'll drive or we'll drive separately." He takes a sip of his drink as he turns to me. "I'll go see if they'll move so we can go."

I scoff at him. "*I* will drive."

He's not convinced. His thick eyebrows give his eyes a darker vibe. It might scare a mere mortal. I, on the other hand, am stronger than that. *As long as he doesn't lick his lips or something.*

"Look, your car is inaccessible. Mine is free. I also carry a valid driver's license." I adjust my grin into a smirk. "And I only have, like, eight points on my license from that time that I hit and ran—"

"What?" His mouth drops open.

I laugh. "I'm kidding, Wade. Relax. *Breathe.*"

"You are insufferable."

"Back at you." I turn toward my car. "Now, let's go so we can get there. I'm sure you have another appointment today. I would hate for you to stand here arguing with me so long that it makes you ..." I gasp. "*Late.*"

He narrows his eyes. I wink and head to my car.

I appear as cool, calm, and collected as possible as I walk away from him across the parking lot. But, inside, my blood pumps through my veins so fast that I think I might stumble on a pebble and fall on my face.

I stop in front of my Mustang, then—while holding my breath—turn to see if he followed me.

Wade's steps are determined, his face unsure. Still, he marches his way through the vehicles with his coffee cup clenched in his hand.

"See? That wasn't so hard," I say, unlocking the doors.

"Can I bring my coffee? Or would you rather me discard it?"

"You haven't peeked in the windows yet, huh?"

He rolls his eyes but climbs into the passenger's seat as I make myself comfortable in the driver's side.

I didn't think this through.

His proximity in the small cab is dangerous. I say a prayer that he doesn't accidentally brush against me and that I remember how to get to the building site.

"Buckle up, buttercup," I say, stretching the belt over my body.

"Without a doubt."

I pause, giving him a look before I snap mine in place.

"Where can I set this?" he asks, glancing over his shoulder into the back seat.

"What? Your folder and notepad? You can toss them into the back."

He angles his body to face mine. His face is sober. "Should I sit them on the stuffed animal or the pizza box?"

"Oh. *Not the stuffed animal.* There's a chance that might have sweet potato puke residue."

He flinches.

"It's not likely. I said there's *a chance.* I washed it, but you never know."

"You're kidding."

"It's not *my* puke," I say. "I don't even eat sweet potatoes, and I never will, thanks to the kid who shot an orange stream of vomit all over me."

His Adam's apple bobs as he shifts in his seat.

Instead of answering the questions written all over his face, I get ready to go. I adjust my mirror and then turn the car on. Then I make sure the climate control is set at a warm seventy-three degrees.

I reach for the radio controls when he reaches toward the back seat. His shoulder brushes against mine.

Our heads whip to each other at the contact.

His breath is hot and coffee-y. Mine is probably hot and breakfast-burrito-y, but I don't think about that. I try to extract myself from the depths of his eyes.

"You in the mood for anything specific?" I ask.

It's only when his pupils go wide—only to quickly hood—do I realize what I've said.

"*I mean music-wise*," I say, heat inching up my neck and pooling in my cheeks. "Do you want to listen to anything specific?"

He tosses his folder in the back, his jaw set firmly. The folder lands on the pizza box with a thud.

"No," he says, his voice contained.

"Fine. I'll pick." I sort through the stations, giving too much thought to what he might like to listen to—only to realize that I have no damn clue. *How would I know? I wouldn't.* "How about country? Do you like that?"

He gets settled next to me. "Sure."

I focus on finding the station and setting the volume at the perfect height ... and not at the man sitting next to me.

Finally, I reach for the temperature control to lower it a degree, thanks to my flushed cheeks.

He sighs. "Are we ever going to pull out?"

My hand stills on the dial. He walked into this one—not me. And there's something wonderfully cheeky about that.

I bite my lip and look at him. "Do you pull out often?"

Being flirtatious comes with the territory of being a photographer. Word play has always come naturally to me, much to the chagrin of my mother and teachers. But when I'm around Wade, the innuendos are even easier. I can't stop myself

The car is too small for both of us.

He takes a long, deep breath, and I feel like his entire body swells to fill the cab. I lean back, my eyes glued to his, as he processes my question.

I can feel my blood pushing through the veins in my neck. My palms sweat. The temperature probably needs to be lowered to sixty-nine but I'm not about to move.

His lips twitch. "If you don't move this car onto the road, I'm going to get out and go back inside and work."

Relief at the break in tension sweeps over me like a breaking wave. I smile.

"That wasn't an answer to my question, but fine," I say, putting the car in reverse.

He sits silently as I pilot us into the street.

Traffic is light as I make my way onto the freeway and head toward the property my grandfather showed me. I hit the gas to mix into traffic when Wade stiffens next to me.

"What?" I ask.

"Nothing."

I zoom around a truck filled with lumber and then fall back into line in front of it.

"Was that necessary?" he asks. "You drive like Boone."

"Again, I don't know who Boone is. Also, yes, that was necessary. Haven't you watched those movies where the ... well, I think they were trees and not just boards but, anyway, they come through the windshield and impale people?"

"I'm happy to say I missed that cinematic experience."

"What kind of movies do you like?" I pause. "Let me take a guess. Something about math? Math or ... rocks."

"Why would you say that?"

"Let's be frank here, Mr. Mason. You aren't the most personable person on the planet."

"By design." He pauses, looking out the window. "But, to answer your question, I don't watch many movies."

"That sucks for you. I love them. Most people love them. But if you ..." I look up to see the exit quickly approaching. "*Crap.*"

After a quick check of my blind spot, I whip the car into the right lane.

"*What the hell are you doing?*" Wade asks, his voice louder than necessary.

I glance over to see him holding the *oh-shit* handle.

"That's my exit," I say. I punch the gas and hit the off-ramp with little time to spare. "Whew. We almost didn't make that one—but never fear. I got you."

The engine roars as I decelerate and come to a stop at the light. Wade's hand slowly releases the bar above the window.

"*None of that* was necessary," he says. "*Shit*, Dara."

"Don't get in my car and act like I'm not a race car driver. That's rude."

He looks at me, shocked. "You aren't a race car driver. You're a … photographer, if I'm not mistaken, and one who *clearly* has no professional driver training under their belt."

I flip on my turn signal, grinning. "Want to know what I have under this belt?"

He looks at me warily.

"A need … *for speed*," I say and tromp the gas again.

The car lurches forward. The engine roars but I let off the gas before we exceed the speed limit. Only when I'm sure everything is under control do I look at Wade.

He's eyeing me carefully, a finger stroking his bottom lip.

"This bothers you, doesn't it?" I ask, flipping my attention back to the road.

"What part?"

I shrug. *The fact that I don't have specific ideas for my own home? That I'm a little sassier than I think he's used to? That my driving skills are on point—even if he disagrees?*

"I don't know. *All of it*?" I offer.

His gaze lingers on me for a long moment. Its weight is heavy on the side of my face. Finally, he settles back in his seat and picks up his coffee.

"You have no idea," he mutters. "No idea at all."

Chapter Eleven

Dara

I kill the engine.

A stillness settles over the car—over me and Wade—as we look across the property. Stately, oversized trees surround us, the morning sunlight filtering through the branches. A path was made at some point long ago, leading deeper into the forest. It's magical.

"Wow," Wade says, sweeping his gaze over the expanse. "This is incredible."

"I know."

"Can we get out? Walk around?"

"Sure."

We climb out of the car and shut our doors behind us.

Birds chirp overhead, singing songs and alerting each other of our presence. The blue sky peeks through the leaves and it feels like we are truly tucked inside our own little cocoon.

"How much land is here?" Wade asks as he walks to the front of my car.

I shrug. "I don't know. A lot. If you follow this path, it leads to a lake. It's pretty special."

His brows raise and he points in that direction. "Could we walk that way?"

"Yeah. Definitely."

Our shoes pad along the trail cut through the trees. Wade walks beside me with his hands in his pockets.

"Is this where your home will go?" he asks. "Or is this just an option?"

My heart tugs in my chest. "I believe it's an option. Grandpa brought me here a while back and said how he always thought this would be a great spot, but his new wife, Tyra, hated being so far away from the city. He thought maybe I'd like it."

"So do you?"

Wade's question sounds simple enough. But there's something heavy laced in his tone. When I look at him, I can see a skepticism in his eyes that I feel deep in my soul.

"Yes," I say, forcing a swallow. "Of course, I like it. What's not to like?"

"I was getting the feeling that you weren't sold on it."

"Eh."

He narrows his eyes as if he's deciding whether to poke at me about this or not.

My brain wars over how honest to be with him, how transparent. Yes, he said we'd need to work closely together, but he'll also be working with my grandfather on this project. That means that Wade isn't my friend. He's not automatically on my side.

"My grandfather and I ..." I sigh, reaching for the words. "I just met him almost a year ago."

Wade lifts a brow. It's clear he didn't expect this bit of information.

"My biological father was his only son," I say. "I never knew him."

"I'm sorry. That must've been difficult."

"It's not difficult when it's all you know."

Our pace slows and turns more into a meander. The rhythm settles my nerves with its consistency and ease.

"I hate to make judgments about my father," I say, choosing my words slowly. "I've hated him, loved him, idolized a version of him that I completely made up in my head. My mom said that he came around a few times when I was a baby but never for long."

Wade swallows hard. "I don't mean to pry and you can absolutely tell me to fuck off and I won't be offended. But your father was a Bowery. He had money. He had ... *the world* at his fingertips."

The thought feels unfinished and, when I look at Wade, it confirms my suspicions. He's watching me with a hesitation that I've never been able to escape about my past.

"I guess he did." I kick at a rock on the ground as we walk. "I know the story my mom told me and I believe it. I believe her. But I'm sure that if he were around, he'd have another version or at the very least his side of the story. So, as far as I know—what I've always been told, is that he wanted no part of having a child. And my mother, coming from a lesser socioeconomic background, would've humiliated him and his father. My granddad."

Wade's brows pull together into a furrowed line. His jaw sets.

"Mom got pregnant—he left. He didn't want children, least of all by a woman with debt up to her eyeballs and no obvious way out," I say sadly. "He thought she was digging her claws in for his money."

We stop next to a pile of sticks. They're on top of one another in a triangular shape. Wade inspects them as if his life depends on it.

"But it's fine," I say, my voice rising over the lump in my throat. "I'm fine. I had a great childhood without the Bowerys and I wouldn't change any of that for the world."

He walks to the other side of the pile and looks up at me. I can't read the look in his eyes but whatever it is has me holding my breath.

The space between us feels vacant and uncomfortable. Something happened as I told him this story—one he was a partner to just a few seconds before. I wipe my hands down my jeans and take a step back, unsure how to navigate this awkwardness.

"What happened to your father?" he asks, his gaze both intensifying and softening at the same time.

"He died a few years ago. I got a notice in the mail. There was a clause in his Will that said he acknowledged a claim of fatherhood—which was weird because my mother never made any claims against him or put him on the birth certificate or tried to get money from him. Anyway, it said he acknowledged my existence, basically, and left me nothing."

My voice is steady, my words even-keeled. It's just facts. I'm sure it would hurt a lot more that I was acknowledged in a legal document had I ever known the man. But it doesn't. What hurts is that he never wanted to know me.

"Shit," Wade rumbles.

Yeah. That about sums it up.

Wade picks up a stick off the top of the pile and twirls it around his fingers. Finally, he tosses it aside.

"I'm sorry you've gone through all of that," he says.

"Yeah. Me too."

He nods as if that somehow tidies up the conversation. "Can we walk down to the water? I'd like to see it in case you choose to build there."

"Sure. Yeah. Follow me."

We start down the path again. The ground turns a bit sandier as we make our way to the water. With each step we take, the heaviness of our conversation seems to slip away.

I've never told that story to anyone in full. Rusti knows bits and pieces—more of it than anyone else ... until Wade today. I'm not sure why I opened up to him, but it's done. And there's a bit of peace settling over my soul.

Wade rubs his hands together in thought.

"So," he says once we've been walking a minute or so. "What is your daily routine?"

"Is this like an easier option than stalking me?" I joke. "Wade Mason —architect and lazy stalker."

He shakes his head. "I'm trying to get a feel as to how you use the space you're in. Where do you have your coffee?"

"Who says I drink coffee?"

"See?" He motions with his hands. "Do you work at home? What time do you go to bed? What time do you get up? Do you like to watch the sun set with a glass of wine in the evenings? Are you a light sleeper? Things like that are important to me."

I clutch my chest. "How sweet."

He rolls his eyes, making me laugh.

"I get up around eight," I say, gasping at the offended look on his face. "What?"

"Eight in the morning?"

"Yeah. So?"

"So that's ... I have half a day of work in by that point."

"Good for you. I bet I'm still enjoying my night when you go to bed."

He grins. It's slight and doesn't last long, but I see it and it sends a blast of heat up my spine.

"Continue," he says, shaking his head.

I clear my throat and try to rid myself of the image of his smile.

"*Up at eight,*" I say, looking at him over my shoulder. "I do like a coffee in the morning. I sit at the kitchen table because the sun comes in the windows and I like the feel of it while I wake up."

"Good. Keep going."

"Then I get a shower, grab something to eat, and then I go to my desk. My day then is either editing pictures, scoping out new locations, putting together marketing packets, scheduling appointments, meeting clients, taking photos—things like that. It depends on the day." I shrug. "I'll get lunch somewhere in there and usually wrap it up by six or seven. Dinner is in the living room with Netflix or with Rusti at a restaurant somewhere. I'm in bed by midnight or one o'clock."

He nods. "Do you like a lot of sunlight in your house?"

I consider his question as we approach the end of the forested area. In front of us is a deep blue lake with tall grass wrapping around the edge.

It's like the water comes out of nowhere—like it's another cocoon attached to the forest. It's magical in its own right.

A breeze ripples across the water, bringing the humid, salty air of Savannah swirling around us. With the rays of sunlight sparkling across the lake, everything that I was just describing about my normal day feels eons away.

My fingers twitch to grab my camera and capture some of the magic sparkling around us. I mentally frame the bird scooping into the water, droplets falling off his feathers. I can see the frame of a boat in the distance through the lens of my camera. The tree that's laying on the water's edge would be amazing if photographed right at dusk.

I close my eyes and breathe in the air, filling my lungs with oxygen. The warmth on my face, the movement of the air takes my worries and, for the time being, tosses them away.

"This is where it needs to be." Wade's voice is quiet, bordering on soft. "This is it."

My eyes pop open. "This is what?"

"This is where you need to be. The way you ..." He steps back and takes me in again. "You came alive when you saw the water. It's like when my mother sees someone wearing a piece from her jewelry line or Rosie sees Fluffy."

I laugh. "I have questions."

"My niece and her dog. Not the point." He yawns. "I was just making a comparison."

"Hey, speaking of nieces and puppies—did your brother have his baby?"

He shakes his head and yawns again. "I think that's happening today."

"I think you need another cup of coffee."

"I think you're right."

"Have you seen enough?" I ask, grinning. "We could swing by the donut shop on the way back to your office and get a coffee and a treat."

"A treat?" He looks mildly amused. "That sounds interesting."

I grin. "It sounds *delightful* and I can promise you that it won't entail sweet potatoes."

He laughs. The sound stops me in my tracks. I think it stops him, too, because his eyes widen and the sound I was reveling in stops.

"Yes. I think I've seen enough," he says, running a hand down his jaw and looking out across the water—pointedly *not* at me. "This gives me a lot to think about."

We head back toward the tree line, walking side by side. But even though we're close to one another, it might as well be a mile.

He doesn't say another word until we're at my car. It's not that I expected him to suddenly become Mr. McChatty, as that is not who Wade Mason is. That much I know for a fact. But he's so hard to read.

Although he's shown me several facets of his personality—and I bet that was unintentional—who is this man?

Aloof, moody, a perfectionist, hard, punctual ... but there's a man who can look at me, study me, and envision my home. *Is that what he's focused on now? My future home? Or—*

"Donuts, huh?" he says as we round the hood.

I laugh. "Is that what you were thinking about this whole time?"

He opens the door but doesn't climb in. Instead, he grips the top of the car and looks at me with the automobile between us.

Fitting.

"Would you believe me if I said that it was?" he asks.

"Probably not."

His lip twitches. "Would you believe me if I said it wasn't?"

That *is* what I thought—that he wasn't thinking about pastries. But the look on his face has me reconsidering that assumption.

"Probably not," I say again.

"Then what's it matter?" He wiggles his brows as if he's just won some kind of game and climbs in the car.

I laugh. *Color me surprised by that.*

I look around, taking in the scenic beauty and releasing my worries into the breeze, before climbing in beside Wade.

"This is where you need to be."

Is that true?

I bite my lip and watch a squirrel race across the forest floor.

I do love it here. The water has always soothed my soul, and if I had to pick one place to relocate to, this would be it.

But how did Wade know that? How did he look at me and read me that well after spending so little time with him?

The thought is alarming. And, if I'm being honest, a little exhilarating.

Let's just hope he doesn't read all of my thoughts.

I laugh as I climb in the car.

Chapter Twelve

Dara

My favorite donut shop in all of Savannah sits like the legend it is in front of us. Wade climbs out of the car, a heavy splash of suspicion on his face, and meets me on the sidewalk.

"Judy's?" he asks, giving a nod to the bubble-gum pink lettering spelling out the name.

"Are you judging the establishment based on the sign?"

"No. I'm judging it off the pink door."

I roll my eyes. "I'll have you know that this is the best-kept secret in the whole city."

"Is that so?"

"It is."

Wade looks down the street toward the hotels and more popular restaurants like Paddy's. The juxtaposition of the polished, dapper man who looks like he should be having a fancy brunch somewhere standing in front of a window with pink-and-white checkered curtains is fun.

I run back to my car and snag my camera from the back seat. Luckily, Wade isn't concerned with my doings. His attention is still pegged elsewhere.

Then as if the heavens open and shine down, he slips one hand into his pocket.

My inner photographer springs into action. I lift the camera and shoot.

Close-up. Farther away.

He takes his hand out and lifts his chin.

Snap! Snap! Snap!

Wade gives me a solid minute of unbridled action. But then that action halts.

He looks at me, his brows raising, and holds out a hand. "What the hell are you doing?"

"This is a camera," I say, holding it out to him. "It takes things called photographs."

"Don't be dense, Dara."

My shoulders slump. "*Come on*. Let's at least look at them."

"I have no interest."

"*Wade*."

He stares at me as if the intensity will make me relent. I hold his gaze just as sharply. Our standoff lasts until a man on a scooter barrels down the sidewalk and forces Wade to move.

I try another angle.

"Why did you want to be an architect?" I ask.

He glances at the camera and then to me with a curious, if not suspicious, expression.

"I designed a log cabin in the fourth grade for a history project," he says. "Holt helped me build it out of sticks and hot glue."

"Your mother let you use hot glue in the fourth grade?"

"Well, there are five of us boys. Holt was a little older, and I think we did it when she wasn't home." His suspicion melts into amusement. "Coy ended up gluing his finger to Boone's, so your concern is well placed."

I laugh. "I can't imagine living in a house with that many brothers."

"It will make you or break you in many ways."

I step onto the sidewalk but keep a few paces away from him, lest he decide to grab my camera and delete the photos I just took.

"What did it do to you? Make you or break you?" I ask.

He doesn't answer for a long second. "Probably both. Now, about those pictures …"

"Okay, but let's circle back to the architect thing. I was going somewhere."

He shakes his head.

"Architecture is your art, right?"

"I suppose."

"How do you feel when you design something?" I grin. "I mean, if your cold heart feels anything."

He makes a face.

"I'm serious. How do you feel when you show someone a design you've created?"

"We're here to eat donuts, not to discuss feelings."

I hold up two fingers. "This will take two minutes."

He squares his body to mine. "Two minutes we don't have."

"Says who?"

"Says me."

"Well, *I* say this—I have the keys to the car, and I'm not taking you back to the office until you answer me."

He almost grins. "I'll call an Uber."

I sigh dramatically. "Just answer the question, Wade."

He rolls his neck, his eyes glued to mine. I'm not sure what his reaction is going to be but, dammit, I think I might win this round.

We step to the side to let a woman out of Judy's. She's carrying a box. She nods politely at me but stutter steps when she sees Wade.

"*Oh!*" she says, her face breaking out into a full smile. "Excuse me."

I roll my eyes at Wade's total obliviousness to her attempted come-on.

When the woman is down the sidewalk, Wade turns to me.

I have to catch my breath.

His face is lit up. The lines around his mouth are invisible. His brow isn't furrowed in agitation. He almost looks like a different man—still gorgeous and striking. Just … different.

"When I show someone a design I've created for them, I'm energized," he says, his voice low. "It's a hit of dopamine. I ... I feel a connection to them." He shifts his weight. "I've hopefully transferred their dreams and wishes into a tangible item, and that's ... there's nothing better than that."

A softness settles in his words. It washes over my heart. I don't move, don't speak as he nibbles on his bottom lip.

I'm not sure that he's ever verbalized this to someone. I'm not positive that he's ever thought it through to himself. But as the realization hits him that he's just said this out loud, *to me*, he clears his throat, and —*poof!*—the vulnerability is gone.

I spring into action before the moment is lost.

"That is how I feel when I look at someone through my camera," I say. "I crave that hit of dopamine. To think that someone trusts me enough to capture their emotions—to see them without any distractions ..." I suck in a breath. "I get to peek into someone's soul and that's such a beautiful thing."

I don't move, don't breathe, don't even dare to blink while Wade contemplates what I said.

His body stills and then, ever-so-slowly, his shoulders relax.

"Will you at least look at them?" I ask, extending my camera toward him. "Just see you like I just saw you?"

He starts to speak but stops.

"Fine," I say, resolved. "If you really want me to delete them—"

"I'll make a deal with you."

Really? "Okay."

He shifts his weight again. "I'll let you keep the pictures if you let me take a photograph of you."

What?

He reaches for the camera. I'm not certain what's going on, but I hand it to him.

"Do you want me to pose?" I joke, trying to lighten him up. "Like this?" I lay my palm up on my forehead like a dramatic pin-up girl.

He tries *so hard* not to be entertained.

"Stand in the middle of the sidewalk," he says. "With your back to Paddy's."

I walk around him in order to stand where indicated. As I do, his hand brushes my side.

My body registers the contact before my brain has time to prepare. I exhale an inaudible moan at the circus that takes up shop in my stomach.

I ignore the chaos rippling along my skin and get into position.

One foot slightly in front of the other. Stand tall. Create distance between my body and my arm.

I lean slightly forward and look toward the street.

"Look at me," Wade says.

"Oh, you're going for a portrait?"

His face stays blank.

"Fine, fine." I adjust my position and look into the camera.

A car blasts its horn on the street. The scents of food from Paddy's grows, swirling through the air like a kite. A group of people laughs as they walk down the other side of the street, but all of that fades away.

I haven't been on this side of the camera much. Being the subject when Wade Mason is the photographer is different than the handful of times I've allowed someone this much access to me.

Because that's how it feels—*like he has access to me.*

I can feel him watching me. The heat of his gaze blazes across my body. My chest rises and falls at a quick, anxious pace, and I know he can see it if he looks.

Not knowing what he's looking at, what he's thinking, *what he's capturing* amplifies my anxiety, and I'm the one who breaks.

I stick my tongue out at him and walk his way.

He lowers the camera and smiles. *I wish I would've captured that on film.*

"Get what you were after?" I ask, taking the camera back from him.

"Did you?"

His question feels loaded but I'm not in a place to start trying to piece through it. So, I ignore it. Wade is too ... complicated. Insightful. And he's seen enough—taken enough—from me today.

Time to move things along, Dara.

"Are you ready for the best donut that you've ever eaten?" I ask instead.

"It won't be hard to accomplish that, considering I've eaten maybe five in my life."

I gasp. "You're joking?"

"You act like that's a crime of some sort."

"Basically, it is." I narrow my eyes playfully. "It's definitely a red flag."

He shakes his head and leads me to the door.

Judy's is empty except for the smell of cinnamon and yeast. I take a deep breath and sigh.

"That's the best smell ever," I say.

"It reminds me of my mother's house during the holidays."

My heart squeezes because it does the same for me.

"Hello, there." Judy, a round little woman with silver hair, comes to the front of the store. She wipes her hands on a white apron. "May I help you?"

"We're here for donuts," I say.

She laughs. "Of course, you are. I haven't seen you around here for a while, Dara. How are you, sweetie?"

Judy pulls me into a quick, warm hug. It feels good to have physical contact with someone.

"I've been good," I tell her. "How about you?"

"Well, I'm still kickin', so I'll take it." She laughs and turns her attention to Wade. "I've seen you before. You're a Mason, aren't you?"

Wade nods and tosses her a restrained grin. "Wade Mason, ma'am. You're Hollis's grandmother."

Her laughter gets louder. "I love that boy. Yes, I'm his honorary grandmother. I'm glad you remembered me. I was at your mother's house for Blaire's bridal shower. Larissa brought me."

He nods. "I hope you enjoyed your time with them."

"I did. Very much. Your mother is a lovely woman. All of the women in your family, actually." She glances at me and grins. "And those men—*whoo we!* But you obviously know that, having snagged one yourself."

I laugh, but my face heats to a nuclear level. "Ah, no. That's not ... what this is."

Wade's stare from beside me doesn't help.

"So, do you have any cinnamon sugar cake donuts left?" I ask, pleading with her silently to move the conversation along.

She nods. "Get your butts in a seat, and I'll bring them over."

Wade and I walk to a corner booth beneath a flamingo picture and sit. Neither one of us speaks. I don't even look at him. If I would've known that he knew Judy, I wouldn't have brought him here. Judy has no filter and is a major flirt at seventy-five years old. I could've predicted this type of situation unfolding.

"Small world," Wade says just loud enough for me to hear.

I place my camera next to me and then inhale deeply before looking up at him. "That it is."

He sits back in his seat. "Do you make friends everywhere you go?"

"Why?"

He shrugs.

"Well, I don't know about friends, but, yeah, I usually walk out of a place and know someone's name ... or life history." I laugh. "It's a much nicer way to live than the alternative."

"Which is?"

I lean forward. "Stuck in your head. Alone. Not living your best life."

"What does that mean to you?" He quirks a brow. "What does *living your best life* mean to you?"

I shrug. "Happiness, I guess. Having people around me to share experiences with. Feeling fulfilled and that my life has a purpose."

Judy sets two oversized donuts and two cups of coffee down but is pulled away to another customer before she has the chance to potentially embarrass me again—*thank God*.

"What does it mean to you?" I ask.

He picks up his coffee and holds it in his hands. "I'm not sure."

My eyes go wide.

"What?" he asks.

"I'm surprised you gave me an honest answer."

"Do you think I lie to you?"

I pinch a piece of donut off the one closest to me. "No, but you don't really share a lot with me either."

"I have nothing to share."

"*Okay*," I say, calling him out without saying it outright.

He exhales. "What would you like me to share?"

"Simple. What makes you happy?" I pop a piece of the donut in my mouth. "What does *living your best life* mean?" I grin. "Why do you shy away from intimacy in relationships?"

"Not that again," he gruffs.

"I'm using it to prove a point. I doubt you ever share anything meaningful." *At least not with me.*

"We talk about house designs. You're my client. What's meaningful to our relationship is me knowing where you like to sleep at night."

My hand stills in the air with a piece of donut in it.

He sets his coffee down slowly, his gaze piercing mine.

"Do you really want to know that?" I ask.

The air between us is heavy. The tension is thick. Wade presses his lips together as his eyelids hood.

I'm afraid to press any further because I'm not sure if he's going to tell me he does want to know via the innuendo that I don't think he meant to imply or if he's going to get up and walk out and take an Uber as he threatened earlier.

"I shy away from intimacy in relationships ..." He blows out a breath. The action seems to change his line of thinking because he relaxes, and a smirk graces his lips. "Because people start asking nosy questions about things they don't really want to know the answers to."

He takes a napkin from the container on the table, picks up his donut, and grabs his coffee. "Now let's go, or I'm going to be late for my next meeting."

"Are you eating that in my car?" I ask, finding my equilibrium again.

He gives me a look. "I'll use the pizza box as a table. Get your stuff. I'll go pay."

I watch him walk with authority toward the cash register. Judy is all too happy to meet him there. I grab my camera and start to get up but pause.

After a quick glance to make sure Wade's busy, I swipe through the pictures I took of him.

They're as good as I expected, and the contrast between him and the playful backdrop is perfection.

But as I sort through them, there's one picture—the second from the last—that catches my attention. It's just before he catches me snapping away.

He's mid-turn and appears to be just about to say something. There's a free, easy, happy look on his face.

I'd give anything to know what he was thinking in that photo.

"Thanks for coming in," Judy says, pulling me back to the present. "Come see me again, Dara."

I look up to see Wade waiting for me by the door.

"I will," I say, getting to my feet. "Thanks, Judy."

The nerves that I expect to feel as I walk toward Wade aren't there. Instead, there's a peace, a contentment that settles through my body.

Despite what I insinuated, there might be more openness in Wade Mason than I expected.

But does it matter if I'm a client? Does it matter at all?

"Are you ready?" he asks as he opens the door.

I stop and look at him. He's so mercurial. And delicious. I smile.

And, for some reason unbeknownst to me, he smiles back.

Chapter Thirteen

Wade

I can't take it much longer.

The sitting room in Bellamy's hospital suite is filled with an over-whelming exuberance. Everyone is happy. Their cheerfulness is bubbling over, and it's wearing on my nerves.

I rest my elbows on my knees and hold the sides of my head. Exhaustion settles in my bones.

"Bellamy promised she'd make it to the wedding," Blaire tells Jaxi with a laugh from across the room. "I told her not to worry about it. I can't imagine feeling like attending a wedding a week after I had a baby."

Jaxi nods in agreement. "I can barely imagine having a baby at all, let alone getting dressed up right after."

Blah, blah, blah.

I hold my head tighter.

The door to the room where Coy, Bellamy, her dad, and our parents are located swings open. Mom beams from the other side.

"He's so sweet," she says, her smile stretching from ear to ear. "Are you guys ready to meet baby Kelvin Joseph Mason?"

Boone heads toward Mom. "They named him Kelvin? I thought I had him talked into McCoy."

Mom swats Boone's shoulder as he and Jaxi walk past her. Holt and Blaire follow close behind them.

"Are you coming in?" Mom asks.

"I think I'll wait until it clears out a little."

She grins. "Want me to sit with you?"

"I do not."

Her grin turns into a laugh. "Come in if you get lonely. There's always enough room for you."

"That's not my concern." I sit upright. "My concern is that ... my head will explode."

"It's a happy occasion. Your head won't explode."

I quirk a brow.

"Fine," she says, coming over and kissing me on the top of the head like a child. "Wait until everyone leaves and then come in. Or just pop in and tell Coy that you'll be back later. He'll understand."

After last night? "He fucking better," I mumble.

"What was that? I didn't hear you."

I sigh. "Nothing. I might do that. I'll just hang out here for a while and see what happens."

"Okay, honey." She starts toward the room but stops at the doorway. "Are you feeling okay? You look tired."

Astute observation, Mother.

"I didn't get a lot of sleep," I admit.

She watches me closely, in a way only a mother can. "Make sure you take care of yourself, Wade Edward."

I nod. This seems to suffice because, with a final smile, she disappears back into the room of joy.

My head rests on the wall behind me, and I stretch my legs out in front of me. Thoughts swirl in my head like they always do ... just at double speed.

Notes for projects I'm working on, calls I need to make, and looming deadlines all bounce around my brain. But the largest part of my thoughts is held hostage by a very particular woman.

I run a hand down my face as a smile threatens to break on my lips as if the gesture will wipe them away.

Damn her.

I groan, stretching my body again before sitting upright with an *oof*.

On the one hand, I think she's doing all of this on purpose. I think she's fucking with me, needling me, pushing my buttons just to drive me crazy. But, on the other ... I'm not so sure. If that's the case—*what does that mean?*

My temples throb as the conversation Dara and I had earlier rolls through my memories.

So many things about what she had to say bother me. How could her father walk away? What was it like growing up with a single mother who, by all accounts, struggled? How can she be so kind about the situation because, if it were me, I'd be fucking pissed to get a note that my dad said a proverbial *fuck you* specifically to me when he died.

I'm curious why she has a relationship with her paternal grandfather. Why is he building her a house now?

I have so many questions ... and I'm pissed that I have them.

A groan slips through my lips. *This is why I don't get involved with people.*

But I'm not involved with her. I'm not involved with her any more than I'm involved with any of the men and women who I work with on a daily basis.

So why does this sit differently in my gut?

Why am I still thinking about her?

And why in the hell did I tell her anything about my life? I don't do that. I know better.

My stomach tightens because I know why. I know all the reasons, but I'm not ready to deal with that.

Dad walks out of the suite, bringing me out of my thoughts.

"I didn't know you were out here," he says.

"Been out here for a long time."

"Have you seen Kel yet?"

"Kel?" I laugh. "He has a nickname already?"

"I didn't want Coy's middle name to be Kelvin. Your mother was adamant thanks to some character on a soap opera or something." Dad shrugs and stands straight again. "So, Kel. Works for me."

"Makes sense."

"He's a cute kid. Looks just like Coy but with Bellamy's eyes."

I nod. I don't know what to say to that.

Dad shifts his weight from one foot to the other as he mulls something over.

"You all right?" I ask him.

He clears his throat. "Wade, I wanted to talk to you."

Fuck. "Okay. What's going on?"

"Nothing, exactly. I just ... We haven't connected in a while, and I wanted to check in, make sure things were good."

"Yeah." I sigh. "Things are good. Things good with you?"

It pains me to ask that. Whomever decided that asking how someone is doing as a pleasantry was a fool. Why use an emotional prompt as a societal norm when no one usually cares?

Not that I don't mean it with my dad. I do. I hope he's good. I want him to be good. I just don't want to get into it right now if he's not.

I can't take much more peopling today.

"Things are getting better every day," Dad says. "And you are the only one of my boys I haven't apologized to."

"You don't have to apologize to me, Dad."

"No, I do. I put you all through a lot of bullshit that none of you should've had to go through. And, for that, I'm sorry."

I wave a hand through the air. "It's fine."

"It's *not* fine." He blows out a breath. "I know you don't want to hear that you're a lot like your old man, but you are."

My gaze snaps to his.

"You're strong and smart, and you do your own thing—to hell with what anyone says," Dad points out. "And that's all great ... until it's not. Just remember that, okay?"

"Fine."

"I mean it." He looks over his shoulder at the closed door before turning back to me again. His face is ruddy. "It's okay to ask for help when you need it. It's better than digging yourself a deeper hole because you think you can climb out yourself."

Why is he doing this right now?

"I'll remember that," I say.

He pats me on the shoulder and then disappears down the hallway.

I glance at my watch. Tension pulls across the back of my neck. *I wish he hadn't brought it up here. At least he did apologize, even though I didn't feel like I needed one.*

My stomach screams for food since I skipped lunch. I look at the suite door and contemplate going in, but the idea of dealing with everyone nixes that idea quickly.

Just as I start to stand, Larissa and Hollis walk in. Riss pulls me into a big hug and kisses my cheek.

"Have you seen the baby?" she asks.

"No. I'm just about to leave," I say.

Hollis nods a greeting.

"How are you, Hollis?" I ask.

"Good, man. Good. How about you?"

Larissa pushes the suite door open tentatively and bounds through once her gaze settles on the baby. Hollis stays behind, shaking his head.

"Grab a seat," I say, motioning toward one of the many available chairs lining the room.

He sits with a huff. "Been a long day."

Why do these people think I want to talk?

But out of all the people in the universe to talk to, Hollis is the least irritating right now.

I fall back in my chair. "I feel that."

He runs a hand through his floppy hair. "Sometimes I feel like my life is changing so fast that I can't keep up with it."

"Riss?"

He shrugs. "She goes a hundred miles an hour whichever direction she's going. I have to sprint to catch up."

This reminds me of earlier today and speeding down the exit ramp. I try not to smile.

"And then this whole family of yours ..." He blows out a breath. "It's a little intense going from no family to all of you."

I chuckle. "Yeah, well, it's a little intense being born into this family too."

He grins. "I heard I'm going to be a godfather."

"Really? That's awesome."

"It is. I think." He scratches his jaw. "I know Coy, and I have gotten close with our music stuff, but I never dreamed that he'd ask me to be the godparent to his kid."

"He likes you," I say. "You're a good man. I'm sure he feels honored that you accepted."

Hollis's hand falls slowly to his lap. "Thanks, Wade. That means a lot."

"Sure."

We sit with a clumsiness between us. I don't know how to make it less awkward. Typically, I'd just excuse myself and leave, but I don't want to do that to Hollis. *Because apparently I fucking care.*

I need sleep.

"I thought Coy would pick you," he says, a laugh in his voice.

"Me?"

"Yeah. Didn't you?"

"I thought I was the last person Coy would choose."

I shift in my seat, wondering how well Hollis actually knows us after all. Coy is the wild one, the party boy—or he was. I've always been the studious, intellectual of the Mason men. No way in the world would Coy have picked me, and that's fine by me. Just a problem I don't have to deal with.

"Really?" Hollis looks surprised. "Coy talks about you like you're some kind of genius saint who can fix and do anything. Why would he not pick you?"

Wow.

"I am a genius, and I can fix and do just about anything," I deadpan. "But I suspected it would be Boone—no offense."

"Of course not."

The air around us grows heavy, and I can't ignore the topic that I'd like nothing more than to avoid. I don't know what to say to Hollis about Harlee. How do you succinctly share with someone that you're sorry they just got the worst news of their life? Hell, Hollis might not even want to have it brought up.

But when I look up and see him sitting there with his head down, I know what I have to do. *Shit.*

"I, um, just wanted to say that I heard about your sister. I'm sorry, Hollis."

His head lifts. "Me too. I know it's not my fault—"

"Of course, it isn't. How could it be?"

He lifts his head and frowns. "You'd be surprised at what you can talk yourself into if you're not careful."

"I'm sure she wouldn't want you to blame yourself."

"Sadly, I didn't know Harlee long enough in her life to know what she'd want, and that fucking sucks."

My stomach clenches. I can't believe I'm doing this—again. *Today.* But here I sit, and I don't know what else to do.

"If Harlee was anything like you, she would be pressing on and figuring shit out," I tell him. "You've done that your whole life, and look at you now."

A slow smile slips across his face.

"She'd be happy you're doing so well," I say. "And I know this because I have brothers and I can imagine what I'd think if, say, Boone went missing as a child."

Hollis chuckles. "Do I hear a little *missed opportunity* there?"

I shrug, making his chuckle turn into a laugh.

Spotting an opening, I get to my feet and yawn. "I'm going to head out. I had a long night and an even longer day."

Hollis stands, extending a hand. "Thanks, Wade."

We shake, his grip firm.

"Don't thank me," I say. "Just don't knock out Boone when he gives you shit about the godfather thing when you walk in there." I start to walk away but say over my shoulder, "But, if you do hit him, knock him out cold. You're in a hospital. They can resuscitate him."

Hollis's laughter follows me out the door.

I make my way to the elevator and push the button to go down. I shove my hand in my pocket while I wait.

Something in the bottom of my pocket is crunchy, and I pull it out. And laugh.

In my hand is a wrapper from Dara's car. I found it stuck in my folder as I was walking to my office. I took it out and shoved it in my pocket until I could find a trash can. I must've forgotten about it.

I start to throw it into a trash receptacle by the elevators but stop before I let it go. The small piece of plastic is blue and has a white design on it. It reminds me of the water and the sky and the color of Dara's Mustang.

I stick it back in my pocket, shake my head, and step into the elevator to go home.

Chapter Fourteen

Dara

"All right. One more," I say, adjusting the lens. "Don't look at me. Don't even smile intentionally. Just look at each other and … *be*."

Bronwyn and Eric turn toward each other. Within seconds, it's photo magic.

She looks at him like they share a secret. *Snap!*

He reaches down and brushes a strand of hair off her face. *Snap!*

She tilts her chin, her eyes shining, and … *Snap! Snap! Snap!*

"That was awesome, you guys," I say, taking a quick glance at the raw images on the back of my camera. "These are going to be great."

"This was so much fun," Bronwyn says. "I was so nervous."

"There's nothing to be nervous about. We're just capturing your love. Nothing to do except let me into your lives for a few minutes."

She looks up at Eric and beams.

"You'll email us when the images are ready?" Eric asks.

I nod. "Give me a few weeks. I'll work as fast as I can, but I'm a little behind on edits."

"That's fine. We're so glad we got to work with you," Bronwyn says.

We walk back to our cars, chatting about their engagement story and the weather. By the time my gear is packed up and loaded, and my clients have driven off, I'm ready for a bath and then bed.

I climb into my car and make quick work of getting onto the road. As I hit the off-ramp, a noise from my cup holder captures my attention. I smile without even looking down.

Wade's cup.

I noticed it as soon as I got home this morning after dropping him off, and I should've taken it inside and thrown it away. My hand was wrapped around the lid to do just that ... but I didn't pick it up.

It's juvenile to leave the cup sit in my car for the simple reason that I like it there. Every time I look at it, a little burst of humor fires through me. Having him in my car, toying with his control-freak tendencies was so much fun. His cologne scenting my vehicle is a win. And then being allowed to talk about my family and not feeling judged was something I think my soul needed.

I've only been able to talk to Rusti about my parents and grandparents. Our familial relationships and the way we grew up are all so different, and I'm not sure she can understand my point of view. She takes my side blindly and, while I appreciate that and love it about her, sometimes I'd like to just talk and not get her input. Sometimes I'd prefer her to come back at me with a question challenging my opinions instead of simply raising her pitchfork.

My phone rings as I get into the flow of traffic. I answer it via Bluetooth.

"Hello?" I say.

"Hi, you. How was your day?" Rusti asks.

"I was just thinking about you."

"That's ... curious. Why?"

I check my blind spot and then change lanes. "No reason. What's up?"

"*Well*, I slept with Zack last night."

My spirits sink, but I put on a happy face for her. "And that's a good thing, right?"

"It was a very, *very* good thing." She giggles. "I know you hate him—"

"I don't *hate him*. I just ... I'm not sure he's the perfect guy for you. That's all."

"And I hear that and value your opinion. It's taken under consideration."

Snorting, I roll my eyes. "Sure."

She laughs again. "But I'm also taking into consideration how much Zack misses me and needs me in his life."

"Oh, I'm sure he does."

"Dara!"

"I mean it," I say as convincingly as I can. "I'm sure he misses ... certain things about you. But I'm really hoping that you remember that he had the audacity to break up with you over the phone like the man he is not."

She sighs. "And you say you don't hate him."

"I don't like him enough to hate him, Russell."

"I'm pretending like this whole conversation hasn't happened yet, and I'm starting over. I fucked Zack last night!" She pauses. "Now's the part where you get excited for me."

"You are so eloquent."

"Hey! Are you going to play along, or do I need to look for a new best friend?"

"Good luck replacing me," I joke as I take an exit toward my house. "So, how was Zack?"

I roll my eyes again as she chirps on about how sweet Zack was, how he took her out to dinner and then stayed the night—something he didn't love to do when they were together. I listen to her gush because that's what she needs to do, peppering in an appropriate *ooh* and *aah* as necessary.

"Okay," Rusti says just as I'm pulling into my driveway. "I'm done."

"Finally."

She laughs. "What did *you* do today?"

"Well ..." A rush of warmth flows through my veins as I glance back down at the coffee cup. "I picked up Wade, and we drove out to the property by the lake."

"*You did not.*"

I grin. "I most certainly did."

"*So,*" she says, reading more into it than there is, "you're seeing him a lot lately. What's up with that?"

"We're just working together."

"Uh-huh."

I struggle against a shiver shimmying through my body. "We have fun together. I'm not sure he'd agree," I say, laughing, "but he's funny in a not-funny way."

"Okay. *Keep going.*"

With a lingering glance at his cup, I climb out of my car and into the early evening air.

"I don't have a lot to keep going about," I admit. "Our time together is mostly me poking at him and him trying to ignore my provocations. And some time talking about the house design and whatever. It's fun."

I can hear Rusti's wheels turning. The fact that they *are* moving—that she's thinking something is going on between Wade and me by what I said—springs my anxiety into action.

"There's nothing there," I tell her. "Not like you're thinking right now."

"You sure about that?"

"Yes. I am. Completely."

"The last man you talked about ... Well, it was so long ago that I'm not even sure who it was. The teacher, maybe? The dude who worked at the sawmill. Maybe him."

Looking at the sky, I remember both those men who I dated briefly months ago. They were both nice men, just lackluster in almost every way that mattered to me. They weren't motivated. Neither of them valued anything that mattered. Worst of all, neither of them was particularly creative.

"We don't need to talk about this," I say as I walk up the sidewalk leading to my porch.

"Maybe we do."

"No, we can talk about you and Zack, but I have a working relationship with Wade Mason. That's it. That's all."

She inhales slowly as if she's considering that.

I consider that too.

As amused as I am when it comes to Wade and as alive as he makes me feel, it's a little crush at most. I can't deny he's gorgeous, and there's little point in trying to convince myself that I don't look forward to seeing him. But I'm not stupid enough to think there could ever be anything between us or that I should ever even consider it should the opportunity arise.

Between working through this house—an event that everyone and everything says is one of the most stressful things in a person's life, my budding relationship with my grandfather, healing my heart after my mom's death, and growing my business—how would I have time to even consider a relationship?

And how, and why, could I risk my heart when I'm just feeling strong again?

"I'm way too smart to get involved with him." I unlock my door and step inside my house. "Guys like that break my heart. Catnip, remember? Because *I* remember, and I won't forget it."

My words are true. They still sting.

"Yeah, yeah, yeah," Rusti says. "I hear you. I just wish you didn't feel that way. I'd love to see you in love. I'm not sure I've ever seen you like that before."

"I just haven't met The One ... unlike you, maybe," I say, twisting the conversation away from me. "Are you seeing Zack again?"

"Tonight. He's bringing over dinner so we don't have to go out."

"Sounds fun."

"It better be. I got someone to cover my shift tonight in hopes it will be *a lot* of fun."

We chat about her job and how she's ready to do something different before she cuts our talk short to grab a shower.

I set my phone on the table and fix myself a glass of sweet tea.

My spirits are muted.

What I said to Rusti was true—all of it. But saying those things out loud, even though I already know them to be true, hits differently.

It's so easy to forget all of my problems when I'm with Wade. I find myself flirting with him, mainly laughing at him but with him too. I don't think about all the reasons I need to keep my guard up. There isn't a moment when I consider if what he's saying to me is for my benefit or his, and I don't find myself feeling lessened or put into a box and sat on a proverbial shelf.

I'm sure all of that is apparent to Rusti. But it doesn't mean anything.

It can't.

My phone rings, and I pick it up, answering it without looking at the screen.

"Hello?"

"Well, hello, darling," Grandfather says. "How are you?"

My heart pounds in my chest. I lick my lips. "Hi, Grandad. I'm good, thank you for asking. How are you?"

"Oh, I'm good. I haven't heard from you in a good bit, and I thought I would check in and see how things were going."

"I called you a couple of days ago. Did your secretary not give you the message?"

He chuckles. "She might have. What prompted your call?"

I pace my kitchen and hope he can't hear the panic that rides up my throat.

"Oh, I just wanted to let you know that I'm working with the architect you suggested," I say, wiping a hand down my jeans. "We've been discussing concepts, and we looked at the lake property today."

"And how did that go? Did he think it was a good location?"

Something in his tone—a curiosity—makes the hair on the back of my neck stand on end.

"I ... yes," I say, choosing my words carefully. "He said if it worked for me, he could work with it." I pause. "Why do you ask?"

"Just curious. It's always interesting to hear what other people think of an idea."

"Oh."

"Tyra and I would like you to come to dinner," he says out of nowhere. "Maybe next weekend? How does that sound? I need to check with Tyra and my assistant, but I'd like to have you over soon."

What? "I'm sure I could make something work."

"Splendid. I'll get with you in the next few days, and we'll iron out the details. Sound good?"

"Sure."

"Great." He sighs. "I need to go. I golf early in the morning and have a few calls to make before I can retire for the evening." He pauses. "Take care, Dara."

"I will, Grandfather. You, too. And thank you for calling."

"Be safe, dear girl. Good night."

"Good night."

The call ends abruptly. I'm not sure if he even hears my farewell.

I hold the phone to my chest and close my eyes.

The hole in my heart that gaped open the day my mother died rips a little wider. It always feels like this after I talk to Granddad. It reminds me vividly how I don't have my mom.

Or my dad.

I acknowledge that I have a biological child, Dara Alden. I choose with a sound mind and in front of the witnesses named below to exempt her from this document.

Tears fill my eyes.

And that hurts.

So much.

Chapter Fifteen

Dara

"I should've held out."

The statement is a mixture of a whisper and a grumble as I make my way toward Wade's office. Poor Eliza was extra sweet as I inundated her with my nervous, random-ass questions and comments.

That's what not hearing from your architect for a week will do to you.

I knock, holding my breath in preparation to hear his voice. I've played our conversation from last week until I've either committed it to memory or just made up what I wanted it to say. I'm not sure which is the truth at this point ... and that is a huge part of the reason my heart is thundering in my chest.

That and he sent me a text that simply read: *Can you be here in an hour?*

There was no follow-up. No explanation. No reply to my over-enthusiastic *Okay!*

It's impossible to know why he hasn't called before now. I know he has other clients, and I'm probably the least important out of them all.

He designs shopping malls, hotels, and mega-mansions for the uber-wealthy.

I know. I looked at his website while contemplating the lack of communication over a bottle of red wine and a box of Teddy Grahams three nights ago.

Wade also just might not have anything to say. I've never worked with an architect before, so I don't know the process. But I thought we had our version of fun together last week, and I thought maybe I'd hear from him.

I didn't. And now I don't know what to expect. *Will things be serious again? Is he upset with me for pushing him to open up a little?*

Was he appalled at the back seat of my car and decided I needed to be handled with care?

I grin. *He'd be right.*

"Come in," he says, both before I'm ready and after I've already worked myself into a tizzy.

I take a long, deep, shaky breath and open the door.

He's reclining in his chair, one ankle crossed over the other knee. His pants are black just like his shirt, and I wonder if he's trying to exude alpha male vibes or if it's a happy coincidence.

"Hi," I say, closing the door behind me.

He runs a finger over his bottom lip and doesn't say a word.

I think I can hear my nerve endings fry as his gaze singes them.

"We aren't doing this today," I say, taking a seat across from him.

"May I ask what in the world you're talking about?"

He doesn't smile—God forbid he grace me with that overt gesture—but I do pick up on something. I may be hearing what I want to hear, but I think I can distinguish a smile in his voice.

"You may," I tell him, getting settled in my chair. "But I'm not explaining the obvious."

I blow out a breath, my body still, and look at him as intensely as he looks at me. It's a standoff for a long few seconds. My temperature peaks so high that I think my cheeks are going to burst into flames. But I achieve my goal: I outlast the handsome bastard.

He bends forward, dipping his chin, and sits with his arms resting on his desktop.

Relief comes off me in waves. I hope he can't tell.

"I never quite know what greeting I'm going to get from you," he says, his lips twitching. "It could be a hug. It might be a dog attack. Admonishments are apparently on the table."

"Which do you prefer?" I grin, relief coursing through me. "I like to please."

He shakes his head and looks away, fiddling through a stack of papers.

Good try, Mason.

"I like Eliza," I tell him.

The statement catches him off guard. His attention whips back to me.

"That's random," he says.

"I know. But ..." I sigh. "Look, I know none of this is any of my business, but I can't help myself."

"Here we go."

"But she's *so sweet*, Wade, and she sits out there like someone is going to say *boo!* and she's going to pee her pants."

He takes his glasses off and sets them on his desk. "And what would you like me to do about that?"

"I do have potential solutions. I never come unprepared."

I'm pretty sure he wants to tell me to fuck off, but he seems resolved to the inevitable.

I appreciate that about him.

"So," I say, crossing a leg over the other and really getting comfortable. "My first suggestion is that you relax a little. I think she's jumpy because you're a little ... overbearing."

"I've never heard that before."

"Sure, you haven't." I roll my eyes. "And maybe ... compliment her occasionally. Do you do that?" I pause, taking in his unmoving reaction. "Didn't think so."

"You want me to *compliment* my assistant? My employee? That's asking for legal trouble, Dara."

"*Not like that.* Just tell her she's doing a good job. Appreciate her attention to detail. *Oh!* I know—this should be easy for you—tell her you notice that she's always on time."

I might as well have told him to ask her to marry him. He just looks at me blankly like we are living on different planets.

"I'm going to point out something—one more thing that's none of my business—"

He sighs and falls back into his chair.

"—that your refusal to make your employee feel seen is a reflection of your apparent disregard for intimacy in relationships."

As the last words fall out of my mouth, Wade's office door swings open without warning. In walks a taller, slightly older, and much friendlier version of Wade. His steps come to a screeching halt when he sees me.

"I ..." He swallows and looks at Wade and then back down to me again. "I didn't mean to interrupt."

"You're not interrupting." I extend a hand. "I'm Dara Alden. It's nice to meet you."

A smile breaks out across the man's face. His attention flips to Wade in a moment of incredulity before he takes my hand.

"I'm Holt Mason. It's a pleasure to meet you, Ms. Alden."

Wade says something under his breath that I can't quite make out.

Holt sits next to me. "So, I heard something about intimacy in relationships?" He stares down his brother with an amusement that he doesn't even try to hide.

Wade scowls at him, also without trying to hide it.

"Well, since your brother is tongue-tied," I say, twisting my body to face Holt. "We were talking about Wade's refusal ... failure?" I glance quickly at Wade and then back to his brother. "Let's go with refusal. His *refusal* to introduce intimacy into his relationships on any level."

Holt quirks a brow. "Oh, really?"

"That's enough," Wade says, shaking his head.

I pivot in my seat until I'm facing Wade again. "That's *not* enough. You won't even listen to what I'm saying, and I'm right. I know that pains you to hear and even more to admit, but you need to—"

"Dara," he says, his voice rising over mine. "*Let it go.*"

"Fine. It's your life."

Holt clears his throat. "So ... Are the two of you ..." He motions between Wade and me.

"*She* is Bowery's granddaughter," Wade says with a tinge of disdain.

I don't have time to really process that before Holt hums in understanding.

"I haven't seen your grandfather in quite a while," Holt says. "How is he?"

How the hell do I know?

Knowing I can't say that—I can't tarnish the family reputation—I grin.

"Granddad is great. I just spoke with him the other night. We're having dinner soon," I say. The words sound like they're coming from someone else's mouth. I'm completely disconnected from them.

"Give him my regards, please." Holt nods, capping off the respect in his tone.

"Of course."

The space between the three of us is unwieldy. I don't know what to say, but I can't take the thickness of the air and the tension in the room.

"So, Holt, are you the brother who just had a baby?" I ask.

Wade's chair creaks as if he's moved, but I don't dare look at him.

Holt grins. "No. That's Coy. He and his wife had their baby boy last week."

"Can I ask what they named it? I love baby names. I'm a photographer, and I have a fascination with what people name their kids."

"Kelvin Joseph Mason. Kelvin is after Coy, and Joseph is Bellamy's father. That's Coy's wife."

Wade groans.

"Kelvin is unique," I say.

Holt's chuckle is loud and smooth. "It's a terrible name. Let's be honest."

I shrug, my cheeks heating as I laugh too.

"So you're a photographer?" Holt asks.

He looks briefly at his brother. I don't. I can feel Wade's vibes of displeasure smashing against me, and I'm not sure what my reaction will be if I see his moody face.

"I am," I say, carrying the conversation along. "I do family portraits and weddings, mostly. I'm trying to move into architectural and landscape photography, but it's a whole different world."

"My fiancée found our wedding location from a picture," Holt admits. "She saw it in a magazine somewhere. She's not from Savannah, so she doesn't know all the niche places. You know what I mean?"

"Of course."

"Anyway, she saw a picture of the Bartholomew Gardens and fell in love." He shrugs, unable to hide his love for his soon-to-be wife. "So, that's where we're getting married."

"I know that place," I say. "I've never been closer than the road in front of it because it's so tightly controlled. It's never open, and when it is, I think it costs a fortune. No offense," I add quickly.

Holt laughs again. "Hey, speaking of my wedding ..." He looks at his brother, his face lighting up and a smile spreading across his cheeks. "Between me, my mother, and Blaire—my fiancée—we've invited so many people that we've lost count."

I sense Wade's movement. My heart starts to race.

"Why don't you come to the wedding?" Holt asks. "It's on Saturday, so last minute, I know. But you'd get to see the gardens and have some excellent food and drinks because Siggy Mason does *nothing* halfway." He laughs happily. "Maybe you'll even meet some people who can help you expand your business. Can't hurt, right?"

My racing heart levels up to a full-blown sprint.

Is he serious?

I look at Wade. As expected, he's staring at me.

I can't make out what he's thinking—both because reading him is like reading tea leaves and because I'm so excited at the possibility that just landed fortuitously in my lap. Not only that, but it would be such a fun thing to get all dressed up and do something different.

"Are you serious?" I ask Holt.

He nods. "We'd love for you to come."

I fidget in my seat. "I wouldn't know anyone, so that might be weird."

"Wade doesn't have a date and isn't in the wedding ..." Holt says, letting his voice drift off.

My gaze snaps back to Wade's.

"You aren't in the wedding?" I ask.

He clenches his jaw and shifts his eyes to Holt.

"*Wade*," I say, my voice rising. "*That's perfect*. We can go together."

"I'd be happy to add you as his plus-one," Holt offers.

I turn back to Holt. "You would? I mean, I don't want to intrude, but it would be an awesome opportunity, and since Wade doesn't have a date anyway—it's kismet."

"That's what I was thinking," Holt says.

"Perfect then. Saturday, you say?" I ask.

Holt smiles. "Yes. The ceremony starts at six. Prepare to dance all night. This is going to be one big party."

I squeal and get to my feet. "Thank you for the invitation. I would be *thrilled* to come. And thank you for considering a fabulous networking opportunity too. I'm just ... *wow.*"

"Not a problem."

I look at Wade. He's not smiling, but when is he ever?

"You," I say, pointing at him, "can pick me up at four. I'm going to go find a dress and leave you two alone to ... whatever it is that you came here for," I say, waving goodbye. "Thanks again, Holt."

He puffs out his chest. "Not a problem at all."

I stop at the door and turn around. "Wade?"

He's sitting at his desk with his head in his hands. He looks up at me like a sad puppy.

"Don't worry. We're going to have *fun*," I say, tossing him a wink.

He nods ever so slightly.

That's good enough.

I let myself out the door, unsure what Wade even wanted, and nearly skip down the hall.

Chapter Sixteen

Wade

"What. *The fuck*. Was that?" I narrow my gaze at my brother. "Please, explain."

Holt sits back with a smug grin. "What?"

His cheekiness is fuel on a fire that's erupting into an all-out blaze in my chest. I clench my hands at my sides to keep from smashing them on my desk.

Be calm, Wade.

I uncoil my fingers. Blood rushes to my fingertips.

The past few minutes replay through my mind so quickly that I can't keep up. *And I always keep up.*

"Can you please explain to me what the hell you were thinking by inviting Dara to your fucking wedding?" I ask, my voice wavering with the anger I'm trying desperately to hold back.

Holt's unaffected. He crosses a leg over the other and stretches an arm over the back of the chair that Dara just vacated.

"Well, I was thinking that it could be a good opportunity for her," he says breezily. "She said she wanted to get into landscape photography and the Bartholomew Gardens—"

"Holt? Shut the hell up."

He chuckles. "You just asked me to explain what I was thinking."

I get to my feet. The suddenness of the movement sends my chair rolling backward until it hits the wall.

This is my fault. I held out from seeing her for a whole week. Why did I call her today? Why?

I knew having her come by was bullshit, but I did it anyway. I didn't need to see Dara this morning. Nothing about her project was pressing or demanded that I summon her to my office. And when I sent her the text to come by, I was already conjuring up an excuse that she … and I … would buy.

This is why I don't let my guard down. It's never worth it.

This situation—one I can't even start figuring out how to negate— is a product of *my* failure. Had I just focused on the multitude of projects on my desk and not on the sparky little brunette, then Holt wouldn't have met her, and she wouldn't be going to his wedding.

With me.

Fuck!

"Did you have a date?" He raises a brow. "I'm sorry. I didn't know you had already acquired someone to—"

"You know I didn't have a fucking date. Stop patronizing me."

My words don't affect him, but he pretends they do. He leans back and presses his lips into a thin line.

"Do you not think she's hot?" he asks. "Because she's gorgeous, Wade."

"No fucking shit." I groan in frustration. "She's my client. I can't take *a client* to your wedding. When did we start mixing business and pleasure?"

He grins cheekily. "I'd correlate her with *pleasure* too."

I turn away from him before I blow up.

Holt knows my reaction has nothing to do with Dara being a client. Hell, Boone has mixed business and pleasure every day since he was old enough to come to the office and pretend he was working. And Oliver? He married his executive assistant, for heaven's sake.

Clearly, that's not the issue.

The real issue is something that Holt doesn't understand.

I tug at the collar of my shirt. I feel trapped—in my clothes, in the office, and in this fucking situation.

"Hey, if I overstepped ..." Holt says.

When I glance at him over my shoulder, my gaze locks with his. His eyes are wary, full of concern, and a streak of sympathy rips through me.

There's no way he could know.

I pull my chair in front of me and grip the headrest as if my life depends on it. My brain scrambles to unearth an excuse that will make sense.

"She told you that she is Bowery's granddaughter," I state.

Holt shrugs. "Yes. So?"

"So what's going to happen if I take her to this family event, she reads too much into it, and then the project falls through? What happens then? What happens to your relationship with Bowery?"

He sighs and wanders around my office. I'd tell him to stop touching everything if I wasn't afraid it would distract him from our conversation.

"She's an adult, Wade. You didn't invite her. *I did*." He blows out a breath and stops next to a fig tree in the corner. "Look, by all accounts, I just did her a favor. She wanted an in to the gardens, and I just handed that to her. And she expressed feeling awkward, and I pointed out you would be there. She won't be in a sea of people she doesn't know."

Dammit.

"Unless something is going on between the two of you that would give her some impression that there's something more there, I think she'll understand that this was a professional opportunity. And," he continues, "if you think about it like that, this will probably help our situation with Bowery, if anything."

Not what I wanted to hear. I wanted him to panic and help me find a way out of this.

"I think it's a terrible idea," I say through gritted teeth. "And if this does get ugly, *you* are handling shit with Oliver and Bowery. I'm not."

"Fine."

"*Fine*," I say back.

My brother stands tall. "I came by to ask you if you'd be up for giving a speech at the reception. I didn't choose a best man, but I need someone to do the honors before dinner. I thought maybe you would help me with that."

I release the air out of my lungs.

The hope in Holt's eyes shines, and I hate that I see it—especially now. And I hate even more that this is happening on the heels of the Dara debacle because it feels like he gets one over on me. Twice.

"Do you think I want to give a speech?" I ask.

He grins. "No."

"But you asked anyway?"

"Yes, Wade. I asked anyway."

I hum.

"Just tell me that you'll do it so I can get back to the office," he says. "I'm sure you have shit to do too."

This visit has been nothing but manipulation in its purest form.

"You opted out of being in the wedding," Holt says. "Surely, you can find it in your cold, black heart to give a speech and pretend you've enjoyed being my brother for the past few decades."

I sit at my desk. "You know, Blaire is making you soft. You used to drive a hard bargain. Now you just get sappy and expect everyone to capitulate to your wishes."

"Is that a yes?"

My head falls back to the headrest, and I close my eyes. "Yes. Fine. But it's going to be short. I don't have a lot to say."

"I would expect nothing less."

"Good." I lift my head. "Now get the hell out of here so I can figure out what just happened."

"Will do."

He turns toward the door.

"And Holt?"

"Yeah?"

"Next time—knock."

He grins before escaping.

As soon as he's gone, the room feels smaller. Eerily quiet. The energy is definitely stained with the events of the last hour.

I growl, getting to my feet as if I have somewhere to go. But I don't.

Every cell in my body wants to move, to do—to fix some of the mess I've found myself in.

But I don't know how to fix it.

Dara Alden is a slippery slope. I knew that the day she walked in here spouting off about relational intimacy and giving hugs like they're free.

Still, I saw her again.

She drove home the potential hurricane my life would become with her in it the day I saw her at the park.

Still, I saw her again.

It was crystal clear at Hillary's House and even more apparent at the property with the lake.

Still, I saw her again.

I saw her again because she's embedded herself in the back of my brain like some kind of parasite that I can't shake. I'm not sure what it is about her that makes me think of her on and off all day.

She's beautiful. Her smile is infectious. She's smart and clever and creative.

Everything about her frustrates me. *She* frustrates me. *And now she's my date to Holt's wedding.*

I run my hands through my hair and tug on the roots.

"I'll be with her for hours," I say out loud, trying to work through the situation. "There will be pictures. Dancing." I tense as the thought of having her in my arms on a dance floor barrels through my brain. "*Fuck.*"

I'm stopped in my tracks by the sound of the phone buzzing.

"Mr. Mason? Sir?"

"Yes, Eliza," I say, my tone tense.

"Mr. Correra is on the line for you, sir."

My body stills as I hear Eliza—maybe for the first time. I hear the caution in her voice, the heavy hesitation. She doesn't ramble on like her predecessor and doesn't fumble around for the information she failed to prepare.

Dara is right. Eliza isn't comfortable, and while I don't particularly want her *that comfortable*—comfortable people don't do their job to the best of their abilities—I also have no interest in her being anxious.

"Eliza?"

"Yes, sir."

"First of all, please, for the last time, do not call me *sir*."

"I'm sorry."

I sigh and squeeze my temples. "Also ..." I grimace. "Thank you for being so efficient."

The words come out in a rush as if I'm spitting them out to get it over with. Maybe I am. But the fact is that I said them, I meant them, and now she knows.

Even if it was cheesy and ridiculous that I have to be so ... whatever that was.

"Wow. Um, thank you, si—Mr. Mason."

I roll my eyes again. "Can you send the call to my voicemail, please?"

"Absolutely. And, Mr. Mason?"

"Yes, Eliza?"

She pauses, the line crackling. "Thank you for saying that. It really means a lot."

A brief shot of warmth shoots through my veins, and I try to shake it off. But as I war with the feeling, another one sparks through me too.

Dara is the one who pointed out Eliza's discomfort.

"Maybe ... compliment her occasionally."

This second sensation is a chill that puts out the heat of the first.

"Your refusal to make your employee feel seen is a reflection of your apparent disregard for intimacy in relationships."

Whether she was reaching or speaking from a place of understanding, Dara was right. I do have a disregard for intimacy in relationships. The main point being—I don't want it.

Never again.

But what did Dara mean by that? Was her focus on Eliza as an employee or Eliza as a potential recipient of a relationship with me that would include intimacy?

"Surely not ..."

I pace around my office, going back and forth in front of the windows. No matter how I look at it, I can't conclude anything that I feel good about.

But what if Dara thinks I'm interested in Eliza? What if she thinks I keep Eliza at arm's length because I'm attracted to her?

The more I think about it, the more it makes sense. And the more it makes sense, the less suffocated I feel about accompanying Dara to Holt's wedding.

I collapse in my chair. Relief comes in small waves. If Dara thinks I'm into Eliza, then maybe this won't be as bad as I fear.

I need to think about it more, but this is a start.

My cell phone rings, and I look down to see Boone's name flashing on the screen.

"What?" I ask in lieu of a formal greeting.

"We *are* brothers, after all."

I sigh, the sound filled with exasperation. "What are you talking about?"

"I'm proud of you, Wade. I really am."

"Boone, I don't have time for your bullshit today."

"Imagine my surprise when I heard from a little birdie that you have a smokin' hot date to Holt's wedding. I almost couldn't believe it. But, do you know something? I've always suspected that you were a pimp beneath those dorky glasses—"

I hang up the phone.

Then I look at the ceiling and wish for the day to end too.

Chapter Seventeen

Dara

"If you don't buy that dress, you're out of your mind." Rusti shrugs, slurping her iced coffee. "It's absolute *perfection*."

I spin in a slow circle, watching my reflection in the changing room mirrors to get the full effect.

The dress fits me like a glove. The champagne color offers a rosy hue to my skin. I can move and breathe easily in the cotton and polyester blend fabric. Somehow the band at the waist gives me a deep curve while holding everything in place.

It's basically magic.

And it makes me feel magical.

"You can pull the sleeves up for the wedding and cover your shoulders," Rusti says. "And then you can do a little off-the-shoulder, sexier vibe for the reception. It's really two looks in one."

"What shoes do I wear with this?" I turn side to side, wondering if the slit is too high. "Heels, of course, but what color?"

"Something nude. *Oh*! What about that pair you wore when we went to that comedy show in Atlanta last year? I think there's a strap at the ankle and one over the toe? Maybe?"

The longer I wear the dress, the more excitement begins to spread through my body.

"Those would work," I say.

"No. Those would be perfect."

I smile. "Okay. I think this one is it."

"That is *definitely* it. You're going to be Catnip's *catnip* Saturday night."

I bite my lip and try to keep a level head.

Holt's invitation was a gift that I didn't know I needed. Weddings, parties, holiday dinners—I used to do all of that. I used to love having a big weekend celebrating someone or something because my natural inclination is to stay home and work. Getting dressed up and letting my proverbial hair down was something I would look forward to.

But that hasn't been the case lately with the grief and fear of the last year and I'd forgotten that.

So, the fact that I'm genuinely excited for the weekend makes sense. But making sense of the buzz in my body over spending an afternoon with Wade is a little more difficult ... and something I didn't really expect.

I mull over the situation and try to justify it while Rusti slurps the rest of her coffee.

It's been a long time since I was excited to see a man, really. I can't quite put my finger on what it is about Wade that makes me forget the myriad of things in my life that usually takes up most of my brain space. But it's a fact that when we're together, I feel lighter. Funnier. More confident.

And I like that. I like that me.

"Get dressed so we can get some lunch," Rusti says. "This iced coffee is all I've had today."

"Okay." I return to my fitting room and lock myself in. After a final glance at my reflection, I slip off the dress. "Thank you for coming to help me pick something out."

The toe of Rusti's Doc Marten boot pokes under the door.

"You couldn't have stopped me if you wanted to," she says. "You have that thread of self-sabotage that probably would've had you picking the black dress with the lace overlay."

I did like that dress.

"I do not self-sabotage," I say, laughing at how well Rusti knows me.

"Not always. Just sometimes." Her boot moves back and forth. "Want to get foot-long hot dogs from the cart guy outside the shoe store?"

"Of course."

I get myself sorted and the dress back on the hanger. Rusti is waiting for me when I open the door.

"What?" I ask, raising a brow.

Her head is cocked to the side. She nibbles the end of her straw as she watches me with a curious yet contented look.

Rusti is a romantic if she's anything, and I know that glimmer in her eye.

"Stop doing that," I say as I walk by her.

"Stop doing what?" She spins around and follows me. "I'm not doing anything."

Ignoring her question that should be rhetorical, I deliver the dress to the cashier.

"This will be it," I tell the pretty blonde, pointedly ignoring both Rusti looming behind me and the rush of nervous energy spiraling through my veins.

"Did you find everything okay?" the cashier asks.

"Yes. Thank you."

I pay for the dress, wait for the saleswoman to place it in a bag, and then carry it right past Rusti and to the exit.

I squint as my eyes adjust to the sunlight.

"So, you bit, huh?" Rusti asks.

"I don't know what that's supposed to mean."

She laughs. "You actually like the guy."

I stop in the middle of the sidewalk, nearly causing an old man to run into my back. I offer him an apology, but he just steers a wide berth around Rusti and me and keeps trucking.

The anxiety that began to trickle through me in the store surges.

I don't know how to answer Rusti's question. *Do I like him? How do I not?* He's handsome, successful—a gentleman. But none of that matters because of one simple, tiny little fact: it doesn't matter.

From the moment I walked into his office and saw him sitting behind that stately desk, I knew it wouldn't make a difference if I liked him or not. I crushed on him in college. It got me more huffs and eye rolls than I could count.

Wade Mason doesn't do love or relationships or, hell, I don't even know if he does one-night stands. He's married to his job, and he has every right to be. Random people don't achieve the things he has by screwing around on the weekends.

I respect that.

But the only way to keep our ... *friendship? working relationship? whatever it is* manageable is not to think about it—not to think about the possibilities or if there was any chance whatsoever that Wade might be into me.

"Rusti, stop." I open my car and hang the dress up in the back. "Let's get a hot dog and talk about ... anything. When are you seeing Zack again?"

I close the door.

She leans against the side of my car. "Like you're interested in Zack."

"I'm not," I say, looking her in the eye. "But you are. So, let's talk about him. Are you guys a thing now or what?"

She shoves off the car and follows me across the parking lot.

"I'm seeing him tonight. I don't know if we're back together," she says. "We're hanging out. We're fucking, obviously. But we haven't had a conversation about tomorrow or the next day or next week or next month."

I slow my steps, relieved that she's shifted topics. My breathing returns to a normal pace, and I look at Rusti without trying to build in a silent message.

She looks down and toes a rock as we walk.

"I'm sorry," I say, putting my arm around her shoulders. She rests her head against mine. "I know you want something more with him. It must be hard to be in limbo and unsure about the future."

She raises her head and sighs. "Yeah. It sucks."

"But you're young. You have time to find a man and settle down if that's what you want."

"I'm *three years* younger than you."

I giggle. "Yes. Barely old enough to drink."

She laughs. "I do want to get married. I *want* to be a young mom. My mom was twenty-two when she had me, and she had all the energy in the world while I was growing up. And she was still cool, you know? Liked the music I liked, liked to shop." She smiles sadly. "I want that kind of a relationship with my daughter someday, but it's never going to happen at this rate. I'll be a new bride at seventy."

"Dramatic much?"

A half-grin tickles her lips. "What about you?"

We round the corner and spot the hot dog stand. The lunch line is a solid twenty people long.

"What about me?" I say.

"Do you want to get married? Be a mom?" She rolls her eyes. "I know you've shunned men in the past, and the puker made you swear off kids, but do you want that kind of life, Dara? No judgment either way."

We take our place in line behind a man wearing a fedora with a feather stuck in the side.

I consider Rusti's question as she answers a text. *Do I want to be a wife and mom?*

The question feels wobbly in my heart.

I've never been a woman who's prioritized having a family. I suppose I've always assumed that I would get married someday. I've never been in a relationship where I considered such a thing, so I haven't really given it much thought. And kids haven't been on my radar either. My life has been enough to keep me emotionally and financially strapped; there hasn't been a lot of excess energy to dream about adding another human to my responsibilities.

But over the past few months, something has changed.

Since I buried my mother and the well-wishers went home and stopped calling—went about their normal life as though mine wasn't just completely thrashed—a deep sense of loneliness has embedded in my bones.

It's not just spatial loneliness. It's not having anyone to call at the end of the day, and no one to call in early December and demand a list of options for Christmas dinner.

There is no one to call who will love me and console me whether I'm right or wrong. I'm not building memories with anyone, and no one in the world shares my past experiences.

This kind of emotional loneliness is different. And it's fucking hard.

"I don't know if I want kids," I say when Rusti slips her phone back in her pocket.

"Well, that's a change from your usual stance."

I shrug as I ponder the thoughts rolling through my brain.

"When I say this," I say, "I don't mean you."

"This is starting off well."

I laugh. "You know I love you, and I know you're there for me, and we're family and all of that—yada, yada, yada."

"I love when you *yada, yada, yada* me."

I smile, but my laughter drifts away. "I ... I miss having a family."

A lump pops in my throat, causing the word *family* to get stuck. I bat my lashes and hope the tears that burn like fire don't spill over.

Stop being a baby.

Rusti watches me warily for a long few seconds. Then she reaches out and flicks the tip of my nose.

"Ouch!" I say, smacking at her hand.

"That's so you don't cry." She winks at me. "Get mad instead. You'll thank me later."

I rub the tip of my nose. "You're a jerk."

"No, I'm your best friend, and best friends don't let best friends cry in public."

I laugh and nod. I know she doesn't mean that. There's nothing wrong with crying in public. But she knows that if I start down the rabbit hole of missing my mother and wondering why my grandfather— the only relative I have in the world—doesn't want much to do with me, I'll be digging my way out for a week.

And that will be what pisses me off.

We move forward a few spaces toward the hot dog guy.

"Just for the record," I say. "My grandfather hasn't called to schedule dinner with me like he said he would."

"And, *just for the record*, you should be busy if he does call." She shrugs in her Rusti way. "I don't care how much money the man has, Dara. If he doesn't make you a priority, especially knowing that he's your only grandfather, then don't prioritize him."

"I know."

"He's not *family* by default. He's a genetic similarity."

She bumps my shoulder. When I look over at her, she's flashing me a devilish grin.

"Rusti ..." I warn without even knowing what she's about to say.

Her laugh is loud. It's bright. And it picks me up and lifts me out of the headspace I was falling into.

"Speaking of genes," she says before biting her lip. "I know a dark-headed stud that probably has some good genes that you—*Ow!*" She laughs. "What are you shoving me for?"

The man in the fedora looks over his shoulder. The feather in his cap flutters in the breeze. He quirks a brow, shakes his head, and then faces front again.

"Will you quit it and behave?" I ask.

She laces her arm through mine.

We wait a few more minutes before we get to the cart. We place our orders, and then Rusti pays for our lunch. As we walk away, I thank her.

"You can pay me back," she says, taking a bite of her hot dog.

"I'm happy to, but really, it was two dollars."

She grins. "Not financially."

"I'm not taking boudoir photos for Zack. He has to earn those."

"Not that. Although ..." She quickly considers, then dismisses the idea. "I was going to say that you could pay me back by having a good time at the wedding tomorrow night."

I give her a look. "I plan on it."

"I mean it." She takes another bite and chews thoughtfully. "I'm happy—*surprised*—but happy that you agreed to go. You never do anything spontaneous or fun."

"I do too," I say automatically, even though I really don't.

Rusti ignores my protest. "This is a good sign, a solid step in the right direction."

"And what direction is that?" I ask before biting off the end of my hot dog.

"Toward ... happiness. Forward progress. Resolution to all the pieces of your life that have been dangling for the past year."

We walk quietly back toward our cars, eating our meals and lost in thought.

I'm not sure that this wedding will be a step in any direction, nor do I believe it has the power to offer resolution to anything in my life. It's not even *my* wedding. But I do hope, maybe even pray, that something good comes out of it.

I might meet a new client. Maybe I'll book a job for landscape photography or be introduced to someone who has contacts in that world. And maybe all I'll get out of it is a good time with Wade Mason.

I'd be happy with any of that.

I finish my hot dog and toss the paper in the trash.

Chapter Eighteen

Wade

The amber-colored liquid burns as it slides down my throat.

I eye my phone and twirl the remainder of the liquid in the glass.

I've sat at my kitchen table for far too long—long enough for the leftover potatoes in front of me to grow ice cold. Much to my dismay, time hasn't delivered an answer to my problem.

Do I reach out to Dara or not?

If I do, does it send the wrong message? It would be communication that's not related to the house design. Would she get the wrong idea?

But if I don't, is that rude? Moreover, will it make the task of picking her up tomorrow even more cumbersome?

I growl into the air.

My entire day was spent with half of my brain where it was supposed to be—on work. The other half was mulling over what to do about Dara and this stupid fucking wedding that I don't want to go to anyway.

It shouldn't—there's not a reason in the world for it to—but this feels like a date.

I look at the chandelier and flex my jaw.

The stress of the day—the pressure of the impending ... *doom*, and the fact that I have no resolution and may not until I pick her up eats at me.

I can't take it anymore.

Before I can overthink it, I reach for my phone. My fingers fly across the screen. When the send button has been pressed, I drop the phone like it's hot.

> Me: I'll pick you up at four.

Dara responds almost immediately.

> Dara: Sounds good.

I stare at the words. That's it? *Sounds good?*

I chew on my bottom lip and wonder if she's even in possession of her phone. She doesn't sound like that.

> Me: Do you have any questions?

I grimace after I've hit the button to send the message to her. It was a stupid question to send, but it was the first thing that came to my mind.

Almost immediately, her response appears on my screen.

> Dara: I've been to weddings before, Wade. I
> think I understand how it works.

It's her.

A grin slides across my mouth thanks to the whiskey. I get up and head for the shower, needing a little relief from the day ... and in preparation for seeing her tomorrow.

Dara in a dress?

Lord, help me.

Chapter Nineteen

Dara

"*I'm not going to overthink this,*" I singsong for the thousandth time in the last hour.

A flutter of impatience flies through my stomach as I fasten a gold hoop in my right earlobe. It's the final touch.

I run my hands down my sides and take in my reflection.

My dress fits like a glove.

Curls gently spiral over my shoulders, the ends of them brushing against the middle of my back. Somehow, I located the nude heels Rusti suggested from the dredges of my closet and accessorized my look with gold bangles and hoops in a way that I can never manage alone.

I twist side to side.

"Not bad," I say, wishing Rusti was here to bolster my confidence. While things may have come together in a slightly easier-than-normal way, I could still use my best friend for moral support.

As I turn away, the flutter in my belly turns into an all-out wave of not just impatience—but of apprehension.

What if this is totally underdressed? I cringe. *What if they all wear dark colors, or what if there's some dress code to the gardens that Holt assumed I'd know because everyone knows ... except me?*

"I have no business going to this wedding," I say. "None at all."

The doorbell rings before I can talk myself into the flu. My entire body jumps, air hiccupping from my body as though I wasn't expecting anyone.

My palms sweat. I have to pee. I rethink taking a shawl in case it gets chilly because of course I forgot to ask if this is an indoor event or outdoor.

Ding dong!

"You can do this," I say, breathing in a haggard breath. "It's just a wedding. You've been to a hundred of them."

Have other guests ever been this unsure and nervous? Have I ever captured that behind the lens?

I adjust my posture, pick up my clutch from the bench in the hallway, and head toward the door.

My heels tap against the hardwood as I make my way through the house.

"Breathe, Dara." I take my advice and inhale. Then I blow it out. "Breathe."

I twist the knob and tug the door toward me.

Oh!

My heart skips a beat, then two, as my eyes settle on Wade Mason.

He's standing on the edge of my porch and is turned toward the street. I catch his side profile—the sharpness of his jaw, the heaviness of his browbone—and the glimmer of his Rolex before I see his face.

It's like an appetizer before the main course. Because when he faces me with his hand running through his hair, it's a whole damn feast.

My knees wobble, making me rethink my shoe selection.

He runs a hand down his jaw. His lips—those full, kissable lips—part. Those gorgeous eyes widen, and for the first time since I've known him, he doesn't immediately catch himself.

"Hi," I say, my voice breathier than I'd like.

His hand falls to the side, and he clears his throat.

"Hello, Dara."

The huskiness of his voice is too much. I grip the side of the door.

He takes me in, his chest shuddering in the slightest way beneath his vaguely silver shirt. Everything else in black—his jacket, long tie, and even his pocket square—and it paints one hell of a picture.

"You look very nice," I say, my voice getting stronger.

His eyes sparkle, but in typical Wade fashion, he doesn't smile.

"You look lovely," he says.

Lovely? My brain scrambles to put the word lovely in a box.

You say *lovely* to your grandmother or a child. You don't say *lovely* to a woman who's picked a dress with the care of a heart surgeon to impress you even if she won't admit it.

"Thank you," I say instead.

Our eyes perform a dance, searching one another over the threshold. I would look away—I probably *should* look away—if I wasn't so determined not to wither in front of him.

I'll do that in the restroom on my own time, thank you very much.

"If you're ready, let's be on our way," he says.

"Absolutely."

I step into the late afternoon. The air is warm, the breeze minimal, and the sun hangs lazily in the clear sky.

Wade waits patiently as I shut and lock the door.

I deposit the keys into my clutch. With my heart racing, I pivot to face him.

"All set," I say.

He holds his hand out to me as he descends one of the four steps to the sidewalk. I know I stare at it a moment too long, unable to prepare myself for the feeling of his skin against mine because he clears his throat. When I flip my gaze to his eyes, a shot of amusement fires through his features.

"Thank you," I say, pretending that all didn't just happen.

I place my palm in his and, just as expected, a zip of fire burns through my body. He wraps his fingers around my hand. I take the first step and then the second, letting him support me as I move. I catch a breath of his cologne—the same peppery amber scent that I've come to associate with him—and laugh to myself.

Here he is, trying to keep me from falling while his cologne threatens to knock me on my ass with my legs wide open.

"You okay?" he asks as I get to the bottom of the steps.

"Yes. Why?"

He makes a face, removing his hand from mine. I miss it immediately.

"No reason," he says.

We start toward the street. I look up, and my eyes nearly pop out of my head.

"You have a Mercedes GLS?" I ask.

"Well, I didn't steal it on the way over, if that's what you're asking."

"Oh, I see," I say, grinning. "It's going to be like that today, is it?"

His lips twitch as he opens the passenger's side door.

"This just happens to be my dream car," I say, taking his hand again and sliding into my seat. "I've never been in one, though."

He rests one hand above the door and lets his attention rest on me. "I guess it's your lucky day then."

My body floods with the heat of his gaze. I hold my breath, certain that I'm going to be blessed with one of his rare smiles ... but I'm not.

He shoves away, grips the door, and swings it shut.

I watch him walk around the front of the deep blue vehicle. He moves in such a confident, almost arrogant way with his chin up, shoulders back, and purposeful strides. If I didn't know better, I'd expect him to get in, turn on some music, and talk my ear off.

I do, however, know better. And I wonder if I'll ever get to know what makes this mystery man tick.

Probably not.

He climbs in, buckles up, and pulls into the street.

No smile. No music. No, "Hey, how's the family?"

"So, how's the family?" I say, grinning at the line I just plucked from my thoughts.

He furrows his brow. "The family?"

I laugh. "You know—the brother with the baby? The brother getting married? The ... other brothers? I can't remember how many, but there were a lot."

He taps his finger against the steering wheel. I'm not sure he's going to take the bait and converse with me, much less tell me about his family. But if he's expecting me to throw him a lifeline and change the subject—he's wrong.

I'll wait him out all night.

Finally, he sighs. "I suppose I should tell you a little about them since, in all likelihood, you're going to meet them tonight."

"I think it's fair to say that's a possibility."

He glances at me briefly out of the corner of his eye. Then with a hesitant resolution, he speaks. "I have four brothers. Holt, the brother getting married, is the oldest."

"That makes sense."

"Why?"

"Okay, I guess that was silly of me. You don't have to get married in the order you were conceived."

He looks at me, puzzled.

"It was a joke."

"Right," he deadpans.

I sigh. "Anyway ..."

"Oliver is ..." He makes a face. "I don't know if my brothers are engaged or dating or what."

I shift in my seat, turning my body to get a better look at him. "How do you not know if your brothers are engaged? Like, isn't there a ring or a party or something?"

"My mom designs jewelry. There are always rings."

"*Ooh,*" I say. "Fancy."

He scoffs. "As far as parties go, my family is large, and they get together often. It always feels like a party for something. I tune out the reasons and show up. I generally know when to bring a gift. It works out."

The tick of the turn signal is the only sound reverberating through the car. Since Wade seems lost in his own thoughts, I take the opportunity to do a little investigation.

The lines around his temple are relaxed. His mouth isn't pressed into a firm line. No lines are marring his forehead.

It doesn't add up. *He* doesn't add up.

Despite Wade's hard exterior and grumbliness, it doesn't match how he talks about his family. It doesn't match how he looks right now after talking about them, and it doesn't match the glimpses that I've gotten, albeit briefly, of the man behind the glower.

He tries so, so hard to be a broody bastard. You can't be that grumpy without serious effort. But I have a sneaking suspicion that it's an act, a carefully constructed shield he's built around himself. Because as growly as he is, as detached and as irritated as he makes himself out to be, his body gives him away.

Why does he do this? I have no idea.

Yet.

Wade pilots the car around a corner and then proceeds down an oak tree-lined street.

"Oliver is with Shaye," he says, snapping me back to the present. "And Coy is with Bellamy, although Bellamy is likely going to miss the wedding."

"Coy and Bellamy had the baby."

He looks at me and gives me the softest, briefest smile. "Yes."

"Baby Kelvin." I wrinkle my nose. "Holt was right. That's a pretty terrible name."

Wade's lips twitch. "And then there's Boone."

"Ah. *The* Boone? The race car driver like me?"

He rolls his eyes. "That would be the one."

"Why did I never realize he was your brother?"

"Probably because I don't tell people that willingly." He smirks. "Boone is the baby of the family, through and through."

"I like him already."

Wade turns his head to mine. His expression is unreadable. He turns away before giving me too much time to figure it out.

"Boone is with Jaxi, and they have a little girl, Rosie." He chuckles to himself. "She's a pistol."

"That's an adorable name. Rosie is so cute."

"She's a cute kid." He pauses, as if he's considering that, and then just shakes his head. "But that's it. Those are my siblings. They'll all be there tonight."

There's a note of pride in his voice that I can't miss. It's adorable.

"Where do you fit in?" I ask.

"In what? The lineup? I can't remember."

"I'm third—between Oliver and Coy."

I scoot around in my seat and face forward. "Well, if that doesn't just make all the sense in the world ..."

"What's that supposed to mean?"

"You're the proverbial middle child," I say.

He scoffs, regripping the steering wheel.

"*You are*," I insist. "You're independent."

"How would you know?"

"*Oh, please.*"

He looks at me, confused. "Please, what? Do tell. I'm riveted here."

"You're an asshole—which is also a middle-child trait, I think."

"I'm an asshole because I have a woman in my car who thinks she's figured out who I am based on my birth order." He shakes his head, chuckling. "That's rich, Dara."

I sit up straight. "It's *the truth*. Are you not strong-willed? Even-tempered? Competitive?"

He withdraws one hand from the steering wheel and places it on the middle console. His arm brushes against mine. The contact is brief, but it's enough to send a flurry of goose bumps across my skin.

I withdraw my arm so he doesn't see the way my body reacts to him.

"You're also starved for attention," I say, knowing I'm walking a thin line but going for it anyway. "That's why you act out."

"Act out? What are you talking about?"

My stomach tightens, and I swallow a lump of anxiety down my throat. I should walk away, backtrack, point out the line of cars ahead of us going into the venue—but I don't. I foray into the minefield I've just marched into.

"You didn't just put your arm here on purpose?" I ask. "Because it felt pretty intentional, Mr. Mason."

The man is a vault. He doesn't flinch, doesn't recoil, and heaven knows he doesn't smile. He just watches the road in front of us like I told him I liked pecan pie.

"I don't know what you're talking about, Dara."

"Bullshit, *Wade*." I settle back in the leather seat. "Do you want to know what I think?"

"If I did, I would ask."

He looks at me as he presses the button for his window to roll down. A smirk graces his lips before he pulls his attention to a suited man with a headpiece who jogs up to the door.

"Hey, Wade," the man says. "You can cut around this way, and then Dominic will let you in at the gate."

"Thanks, Silas."

What the hell?

Silas steps back, and Wade pulls the Mercedes into the left lane. He hits the gas, and we fly by a train of cars to the gate. Then just as promised, a gap in the traffic leading into the Bartholomew Gardens is made, and we cut in front of a Lexus waiting patiently.

"How did you ...?" I make a face. "Are we friends with Silas?"

"He works for Landry Security. We use them for all of our events."

All of our events.

"Oh. Okay," I say, my world starting to spin.

We roll along the asphalt until we're directed to park next to an Audi. Wade pulls the car into the spot marked *Reserved* and then cuts the engine.

Car doors open and close around us. People talk, shout, and laugh. But, somehow, it feels like they're background characters in the story of Wade and me in the car.

He fixes his sleeves and repositions his watch. I pull my clutch onto my lap.

I have no idea what I'm supposed to say or do. We aren't in his office where I'm a client courtesy of the powerful Curt Bowery. We aren't in a restaurant or the middle of a forest—both of which are neutral grounds.

We are in a sea of expensive cars, tailored suits, and women carrying bags worth more than I'll make this year. I might be blind from the diamond's sparkling on the woman passing in front of the Mercedes.

This isn't my world. This is one hundred percent Wade's universe, and I'm aware that I'm not well-versed in navigating it.

Finally, he sits back and looks straightforward for a long moment. Then he turns to me.

His face is sober. It's not irritated like usual, just serious.

I still, my gaze searching his for something to go on. He's trying to tell me something, but I don't know what it is.

"Wade?"

"There will be a lot of people here tonight," he says, his voice softer than I've ever heard it. "Don't drink anything that isn't given to you by my brothers or me. The security team has solid guys. If you need something and can't find me, you can go to them. Tell them to find me."

What?

"Is this unsafe?" I ask, my heart racing for all the wrong reasons.

"I wouldn't have brought you here if it were unsafe, Dara."

Okay ...

I force a swallow. "So, what's with the whole security team spiel? Because you're kind of freaking me out right now. Not gonna lie."

His eyes flutter close for a second. "Any time you're going to be with a mass of people who are unfamiliar to you, it behooves you to understand the situation and to know what to do in case something goes wrong."

That makes sense. My mother always told me various forms of that over the years, and it is common sense. I've watched enough movies and the news to know just how badly things can go wrong if you're oblivious.

"Have fun," he says. "Just be cognizant of what's going on around you. *Promise me.*"

My mouth opens to say something silly—to downplay his seriousness or make a joke to add some levity back into the conversation—but as I start to let whatever I'm about to say roll, I stop.

Something is different. Something has changed. He still has a shield up around him, but it's ... cracked, maybe. There's a warmth, a slight vulnerability in his beautiful green eyes that softens my heart. It also settles a bit of the butterflies in my stomach.

"I promise," I say.

He nods and rewards me with a half of a grin. *I'll take it.*

"Are you ready then?" he asks.

"Yes."

He starts to get out of the car when I stop him.

"Wade?"

He looks at me over his shoulder. "Yeah?"

I grin. "Don't think our conversation is over."

His forehead mars until he realizes what I'm talking about.

My breathing halts. My heart pounds. My stomach clenches so hard I think I might yelp out in pain.

But when he casts me an *oh-so-slow, kill-me-now* smirk, I forget about everything except committing that view to memory and not disintegrating into the seat.

"We'll see about that," he says and climbs out of the car.

Yes, Mr. Mason. Yes, we will.

Chapter Twenty

Dara

Oh, wow.

Whatever I thought the Bartholomew Gardens was like, I was wrong.

So incredibly wrong.

I walk beside Wade through a set of stone pillars that look hundreds of years old. Moss is buried between the rocks like a natural concrete holding the stacks together. We pass beds of flowers, shallow pools with colorful fish, and fountains that trickle in the calmest way.

An old, stately brick building with a plaque reading *Hardwig* sets to the side. Each window holds an electric candle that flickers warmly. People filter in and out of the front with flowers, garment bags, and, most of all, wide smiles.

We pass through another set of pillars into an area tucked into the back of the property. The far wall of the enclave consists of thick, deep green vegetation. A white carpet leads to an arch filled with white and soft pink flowers. On either side of the carpet are rows of white chairs capped off on the end with oversized gold vessels overflowing with roses.

"This is ... *unbelievable*," I whisper to myself.

To the left of the setup is a giant glass greenhouse. The doors are held open by the same flower-filled vessels found beside the chairs. Lights glow from inside by what appears to be giant chandeliers and lights strung from one side of the venue to the other.

People move about—all dressed in their finest, chatting easily with one another. Couple that with the violinists playing to the right of the arch and the ambiance is absolute perfection.

I wish I had my camera.

"What do you think?" Wade asks.

I look up at his handsome face. "I'm ... I'm in awe. It's *so beautiful*."

Before he can respond, an older man wearing a suit and a newsboy hat ambles up to us.

"Wade, I still hate that you aren't standing up for your brother," the man says.

He grabs Wade's elbow to steady himself. It's only when he catches his breath does he notice me.

"Well, hello, darlin'. Who might you be?" he asks.

Wade clamps a hand on top of the man's knuckles as if to give him more support.

"Gramps, this is Dara Alden," Wade says. "Dara, this is my grandfather. He doesn't have a name. Just Gramps."

For a reason unbeknownst to me, this tickles Gramps. He laughs. The sound is full of joy, and it makes me laugh too.

"It's nice to meet you, Gramps," I say.

Gramps puts his hand against the side of his mouth between him and Wade.

"I'm hoping that he introduced me that way because that means he's finally come around and will get married before I kick the bucket," he pretends to whisper.

I giggle as Wade's jaw sets. Still, he doesn't look *as annoyed* as usual. Just more uncomfortable.

"I'm here as a guest of Holt," I say.

Gramps's eyes go wide. "*Oh.*"

"*Not like that*," Wade says.

Gramps chuckles. "With these boys, you never know."

"Well, that bodes well for them," I say, eyeing Wade's reaction.

He refuses to look at me.

"Not this one." Gramps sticks a bony elbow into Wade's stomach. "This one is as straight as an arrow. The best one of the bunch when it comes to matters like that."

Wade struggles so hard not to smile that it must pain him.

"Wade, excuse me," a woman says, coming up to us. She's wearing a pretty blush-colored dress with her hair in a fancy updo. "I don't mean to interrupt, but Holt would like to see you before the ceremony starts. I stopped by to check on Walker and got lassoed into finding you."

"Where is Holt?" Wade asks.

"On the third floor of the Hardwig building with the groomsmen," she says.

"Tell him that I'll be right there, Sienna."

She smiles at Wade, then at me, before disappearing into the crowd.

Wade blows out a breath. "That was Sienna Landry. Her ... husband? Boyfriend? Is Blaire's brother. Blaire, the bride ..."

"Didn't you say the security company was also Landry?" I ask.

"That's her family's business. It's a small world."

"Must be."

Gramps sighs. "Well, help me get settled in a seat before you take off. I can't stand around here all night."

"Are there seating assignments?" Wade asks. "Or do we sit wherever we want?"

"Oh, who cares?" Gramps scoffs. "I'm eighty-five years old. What are they gonna do? Tell me I can't sit where the hell I want?"

I laugh. Gramps's eyes light up at my amusement.

"Second thought," Gramps says, reaching for me. "Dara can help me while you go find Holt. Tell him I said not to cry. Crying is for girls."

Wade helps transfer his grandfather to my arm.

"Are you okay with this?" Wade mouths over Gramps's head.

I nod.

"All right," Gramps says, huffing and puffing. "Let's get a seat before I pop a squat right here and make the bride walk around me."

I clutch Gramps's hand the same way I saw Wade do. We start toward the chairs in what might be the slowest walk I've ever done.

"You're here as a guest of Holt," Gramps says as we approach the seating area. "But are you here with Wade?"

My cheeks flush because I don't know how to answer.

We reach the chairs in the nick of time, and Gramps chooses a seat in the back row on the far end. He collapses with a hearty exhale. Then he pats the seat next to him.

I sit hesitantly.

"You know," he says, catching his breath, "I've never seen Wade with a woman."

"Really?"

"Oh, I'm sure he gets a little something somewhere, if you know what I mean." He winks at me. "But he's never brought anyone around. Not with me, anyway. Maybe to his parents, but I've never witnessed it."

This information rolls around my brain. I didn't expect it. Sure, he's standoffish, but I never imagined him to be that much of a loner.

The idea makes me sad for him. It's possible he's with someone in his own private time like Gramps said, but how much of that time even exists with how much he works?

"I used to spend a lot of time with Holt," Gramps says. "When he was little, he used to visit me in the office—Ollie too. I'd set them up with fake jobs to do, and they'd eat it up." Gramps chuckles to himself. "Coy and Boone come by and watch golf with me sometimes. Boone used to do it to hide from Holt. But he's straightening up now thanks to Jaxi and that little pipsqueak of theirs. That little girl is as cute as can be. Have you met her?"

I shake my head.

He hums. "I'm sure you will." He digs around in his jacket pocket and pulls out two spearmint Life Savers. He hands me one. "How long have you known Wade?"

"Not long," I say, figuring that was a better answer than a few weeks.

He pops his candy in his mouth. I follow suit. It tastes like men's cologne and a hint of tobacco.

"He's a tough cookie. But I'm sure you know that," he says, rolling the candy around his mouth.

I suck on the Lifesaver, too polite to spit it out, and contemplate my situation. Is it ethical to pump information out of an eighty-five-year-old man?

I'm not sure until I look at Gramps. He's grinning a toothy grin with a twinkle in his eye.

Game on.

"I'll bite," I say, making him laugh. "Why is your grandson such a tough cookie?"

He keeps chuckling. "That I don't have the answer to, darlin'. But I do know this—I've never gotten anything worth a damn without working for it, if you know what I mean."

Gramps reaches over and pats my hand. Movement catches my attention out of the corner of my eye, and I turn around.

Wade sits beside me, watching his grandfather with a heavy dose of skepticism. "You didn't fill her with a bunch of garbage, did you?"

Gramps chuckles. "Just a Lifesaver." He looks at me and winks. "How's your brother, Wade?"

"He's ... happy."

I laugh. "That's a good thing. Don't say it like he just drank poison."

Wade makes a face and adjusts his tie.

"Want a Life Saver, Wade?" Gramps asks.

"No, but thank you." Wade leans back out of Gramps's sight and makes a face in disgust.

I giggle.

The violins begin to play louder as people file in and take their seats. Gramps gets into a discussion with a gentleman on his other side, leaving Wade and me to ourselves.

I take in the beauty of the gardens. There are so many moments I could capture, and I wish I'd have brought my camera.

"What are you thinking?" Wade says loud enough only for me to hear.

I turn to face him, not realizing how close he is to me. My breath sucks in past my lips.

Whether it's the reflection of the lights strung overhead, or it's his eyes themselves, there's a twinkle there that takes my breath away.

"I was thinking about ..." *You*. "About all the pictures I could take here," I say.

His brows pull together. "Like what?"

"Well ..." I glance around. "Imagine if you stood at the pillars at the entry and got the Hardwig house in the background at the perfect angle to capture the glow from the setting sun." I close my eyes and imagine the feeling of contentment that picture would bring to anyone viewing it. "Or if you stood in one of the windows of the Hardwig and captured a view of the gardens from that vantage point. Or ... who knows what's all in this estate? This is just a little piece."

I open my eyes to see him watching me. "Those sound intriguing."

He means it. I can tell by the tone he used and the inflections in his voice. He listened to me as a professional, as someone with a passion for what I do.

"Thank you," I say, my cheeks aching.

He rolls his eyes but grins too.

The crowd grows quiet. I have no idea where they get their cues from, but the violins fade. As their notes soften, a piano begins to play.

The music flows so beautifully that it fills the entire garden with joy. I search the area until I find a white piano on a small platform covered in flowers.

"That is my cousin Larissa's boyfriend, Hollis," Wade whispers, pointing at the pianist.

I can feel the heat on my skin from his breath. Instinctively, I want to lean into him, but I don't. I'm not sure what he would do if I did.

"You used *boyfriend* pretty certainly," I joke.

"Trust me. If Riss got engaged, we'd all know it."

I look at him over my shoulder and smile. "Do I sense a little protective big cousin?"

He shrugs and looks away ... and I was wrong when I thought he couldn't get any sexier than when he was standing on my doorstep in a suit.

Ushers walk various people up the aisle and get them seated at the front. And then the music changes again. The violins join back in this time, and the wedding party makes their way to the arch.

"Those dresses are gorgeous," I say softly, admiring the pale pink fashions of the bridesmaids.

Wade leans in. "Those are Blaire's brothers' wives, I'm pretty sure, and Larissa since she's like our sister. I think some of Holt's groomsmen are Blaire's brothers. I'm not sure."

"You sure know a lot about them for a guy who didn't want to be involved."

He gives me a look. "I had dinner with them all last night after their rehearsal. I tried to learn as little as possible so I don't feel obligated to talk to anyone tonight."

"You are *such* an asshole," I tease.

He shrugs and redirects his attention back to the parade of bodies coming down the white carpet.

Finally, the telltale notes of the "Bridal Chorus" ring through the garden, and the guests all stand. I assist Gramps, holding on to his elbow.

The bride is stunning with her long, dark hair in contrast to the slim-fitting white dress with a train to die for. She joins her groom under the arch, and we all sit again.

Gramps slides me another Life Saver, and I take it. Luckily, he doesn't pay attention, and I slide it into Wade's palm. He tries to push it back into my fist, holding it in place with his other hand, but I jerk it away. He gives me a stare that makes me smile ... and swoon.

We settle into our seats as the mechanics of the wedding take place. I appreciate the gardens and the perfection of the setting sun ... and of the man sitting next to me ... until I hear the vows.

As the groom clears his throat and then the words he wrote on a piece of paper begin to be read aloud, tears dot the corner of my eyes.

His love for Blaire is evident. It's palpable. It's the kind of love that a woman wishes for if they wish for that kind of thing at all.

It's the kind of love that touches my heart just from witnessing it.

My gaze trickles over the men standing next to him. Some are near carbon copies of Wade and others are bigger, stronger, bulkier but also extremely handsome. They watch Holt give his vows with the utmost seriousness. It's clear they, too, love Blaire.

Gramps hands me a handkerchief, a red silk piece of fabric with orange diamonds embedded into the cloth.

"Thank you," I whisper.

He pats my leg with a shaky hand.

I dab my eyes and watch the action in front of me.

Wade leans his head to the side. "You all right?"

I grin but don't look at him. "Yeah."

"Why are you crying?"

My chest shakes as I try not to laugh. I turn toward him so as not to disturb anyone else and lean in close to his ear.

"Aren't weddings supposed to be emotional?" I ask.

"No."

I smack his leg softly. "Do you get emotional about anything?"

I'm not sure what I said, or if he's irritated by the contact I initiated without thinking, but his eyes narrow, and he leans back. "No." He nods toward the ceremony as if he wants to watch it without me disturbing him.

So I keep a distance and pretend not to notice that he's staring at me when he thinks I'm not paying attention.

I'm not a fool to think that this seemingly emotionless man will change because of me—that he'll ever want an emotional connection with me. But I can't help feeling stirred to want to know why and how he is the way he is. Why does someone who has so much to give avoid connecting with people ... *intentionally*. Like it's his damn job.

Maybe it's the emotion of the evening, or maybe it's Gramps's words, "*I've never gotten anything worth a damn without working for it,*" but I'm resolved about one thing: come hell or high water, I will get to the bottom of Wade Mason.

Even if it kills me ... or my heart.

Chapter Twenty-One

Wade

"Would you like a drink?" I ask Dara, touching her lightly on the small of her back.

She turns away from her conversation with Oliver's girlfriend, Shaye. Her eyes sparkle.

"I'm sorry, Wade. What did you say? I didn't hear you."

I force a swallow down my throat and ignore the amused glance from Shaye. I'm sure I look like a fool. I feel like one. But it's impossible to look at Dara without being rendered speechless.

She shines tonight. I don't know if it's her fucking dress that's driving me out of my mind or the relaxed, carefree way she greets my family that keeps stealing my breath, but it takes everything in my power not to stare at her.

"Would you like a drink?" I ask again.

"No, thank you."

I look at Shaye and ignore the grin on her face.

"Can I get you something, Shaye?"

She shakes her head.

"I'll be right back," I say and head to the bar. It's only when I'm a solid ten yards away from Dara that I can breathe normally again.

I order a whiskey on the rocks and avoid conversation with the bartenders. Luckily, they're busy and hand my drink over without too many pleasantries required.

There is a spot next to the gigantic cake, which Holt should really be ashamed of, and I tuck myself between it and the wall. I can keep an eye on Dara from here and gather myself.

I can't relax with her here. I can't think. Not that I was going to enjoy myself tonight anyway, but it's impossible now.

Dara Alden possesses a quality that perturbs me. I've only known one other woman in my life who got under my skin, and that taught me a lesson. *Don't let people in.*

It's one I'll never forget. And if I'm as smart as I think I am, it'll behoove me to shut this shit down before it gets out of control.

The whiskey goes down smooth. I down the rest of it and start toward Dara when Rosie intercepts me.

"Wade!" Her little voice squeals through the greenhouse, and she bolts in my direction. "Hi, Wade!"

I brace myself for the impact that's undoubtedly coming.

Rosie launches her body toward me and attaches herself to my leg. I look around for Jaxi or Boone, but they're nowhere to be found.

"Hi," I say, looking down at her.

"Hi." She grins so wide that I think her face might split into two. "I'm so happy that you're here. Did you see me sprinkle the flowers? They made my fingers a little red. See?"

She holds up her chunky little hand. Sure enough, her fingers are stained pink. *As are my pant legs, I suspect.*

"You did an excellent job," I say, trying to extract myself from her grip. "Where are your parents?"

She shrugs. "I don't know."

"Let's ... separate ourselves." I pry her right off from my leg. "And find Boone."

"But I found you."

"Yes, you certainly did."

I glance up and spot Boone by the bar. He has watched this entire exchange and failed to save me.

Fucker.

"Who is this?" Dara stands next to me. "You were the flower girl, right?"

Rosie watches Dara with the skepticism most people save for politicians. She nods her head slowly.

"Rosie," I say, "can you say hello to Dara?"

"You're the famous Rosie." Dara squats down to Rosie's level. "I've heard so much about you."

"Who are you?" Rosie asks, clutching my leg with both arms again.

"My name is Dara. I'm a friend of Wade's."

Rosie's head tilts to mine. "I'm a friend of Wade's too. I'm his *best friend*. Right, Wade?"

Dara giggles and stands again. "He mentioned that. He said, 'Rosie is my best friend, but you can be my second friend, Dara.' Didn't you, Wade?"

"Funny," I say. "I don't remember that."

Dara winks at me.

Before I can reply, the violins stop playing and a voice takes its place over the speakers hanging discreetly above.

"If everyone will take their seats, dinner service will begin shortly."

I peel Rosie off my leg and hold her hand, keeping her far enough away from me so she doesn't reattach herself like a fucking octopus.

"Rosie, we need to find Boone," I say, looking through the crowd of people making their way toward the tables.

"Why?"

"It's almost time to eat."

"But I want to eat with you."

Dara laughs, moving closer to my side to allow an older couple to pass. Her breast runs along my arm as she moves.

Fire bolts through my veins and congregates in my cock. My entire body flexes under my suit as I try to stay composed.

"There's Boone," I say through clenched teeth.

"No!" Rosie shouts. "I want to eat with you."

Boone walks toward us as Rosie stomps her foot.

I bend down so we're at eye level. "Hey."

She crosses her arms over her chest and pouts. "What?"

"Why are you acting like this?" I ask her.

"Like what?"

"Like a little girl who forgot her manners."

"I didn't forget them. I'm just not using them because you are going to eat with *her*." She pauses to glare at Dara. "And not me."

Well, she boiled that down and communicated it effectively.

"That's because your Iggy," I say, using the word that Rosie uses for my mother, "wants you to sit beside her tonight. There's even a little sign at her table with your name on it."

Her arms fall back to her sides. "Really?"

I nod. "But maybe, if you remember your manners and choose to use them, we can share a piece of cake later."

"Cake?"

"That cake." I turn her around and point at the mega-cake in the corner. "I bet we could snag a piece and share it after dinner if you make good choices."

She turns around and faces me. "Like sitting with Iggy?"

"Yes."

She huffs. "Fine."

"Good girl."

Boone's laughter gets to us before he does. "What's going on over here? Are you behaving, little girl?"

"Yup," I say, standing tall. "We were talking about the cake."

"It's beautiful," Dara says. "I wish for the thousandth time tonight that I would've brought my camera. Or a phone. I'd be happy with phone pictures."

Boone grins at her. "Why didn't you?"

She shrugs. "I didn't want to be rude."

"Well, stick around," Boone says, his grin growing wider. "I'm sure someone's birthday is coming up, and you can take all the pictures that you want."

What are you doing, Boone?

My insides cringe as I glance nervously at Dara. If she picked up on anything—on my brother's suggestion that she might accompany me to other family events—she doesn't show it.

"Are you ready to find our seats?" I ask Dara.

She nods.

I slide my arm behind her—more to guide her than to touch her, but she moves in such a way that my arm is wrapped around her.

My fingers tap against her side as we move through the greenhouse and find our table. Various people stop me to say hello, and to both my surprise and frustration, Dara doesn't move away from me.

It would be easier if she did. Instead, she says hello to everyone like she's been to a hundred of these parties with me. Like it's what she does.

Like she's with me in a way that she's not.

I pass a swallow down my throat and pull out her chair. She sits with the grace of royalty. I take my seat beside her.

Gramps chats away with an older couple I've never seen before. They look up as we get situated.

"Hello," I say, nodding a greeting at them all.

"Wade, Dara," Gramps says, "this is Blaire's grandmother, Greta, and her significant other, Dave. Greta, Dave—this is my grandson Wade and his girlfriend, Dara."

Gramps looks at me, grinning cheekily, while my insides coil up and threaten to explode.

My girlfriend? That's not what I said when I introduced him to Dara tonight.

And the cheeky bastard knows that.

I look over my shoulder at Dara as she lays her hand gently on my thigh. The contact disarms the bomb inside me; her smile and all its sweetness pacifies the growing need to set everyone straight.

My shoulders relax as we exchange a look.

"It's nice to meet you, Greta and Dave," she says, flipping her attention to them. "Did you travel far?"

Whatever they say—I don't have a clue. I know there's a conversation because I see Dara's mouth moving, and I watch her patiently pause between replies. But I have no idea, and no interest, in the conversation.

My head spins, and I try not to panic. Panicking never helps.

This situation with Dara has been complicated tonight in ways that never should've happened. It's spun out of control—out of *my* control—and I don't know how to get it back.

It was a setup for failure. I knew it from the moment Holt suggested that Dara attend.

How am I supposed to keep my distance from her when she's here with me?

Dara should be here with someone else, someone who's easy to be with. A man who wants to chat and dance and tell her how stunning she looks tonight.

I'd want to kill him, but she deserves it anyway.

She's the walking embodiment of what men want in a woman. She's fun, smart, sweet. Dara is spirited and strong.

I know all of that. I recognize it. I'm not blind.

But I'm also not stupid.

Dara's fingers tap against my leg. My eyes whip to hers.

"Are you ready?" she whispers.

I furrow my brows. "What for?"

"Your speech." She smiles. "They just said that was happening next."

Shit.

My palms start to sweat as I imagine all of these people looking at me, which is exactly why I didn't want to be in the wedding party in the first place.

I should've told Holt no.

But as a microphone is passed my way and I get to my feet, I take a look at my brother sitting at a raised table with his bride.

He's happy. *He's so fucking happy.*

I clear my throat. The sound echoes through the greenhouse.

"On behalf of the Mason family, I'd like to thank you all for coming tonight to celebrate the marriage of Holt and Blaire," I say.

The crowd claps. I use the opportunity to inhale and exhale as deeply as I can to settle my nerves.

"My brother asked me to say a few words because I opted out of the wedding party." I scan the long tables extending from the bride and groom. "I didn't think anyone would miss me with that many people involved."

Everyone laughs, much to my surprise.

I clear my throat again. My mind is working overtime, trying to figure out what to say.

"I tried to write a few things down before I got here," I say, keeping my gaze focused on a basket of hanging greenery just above the violinists. "But nothing felt quite right."

"That's why I should've given the speech!" Boone yells from his seat next to Oliver.

Laughter bursts around the room.

I use the moment to watch Holt and Blaire.

When Holt first fell in love with her, I thought it was silly and irresponsible. We were in the middle of a giant contract, and Blaire was the ultimate distraction. But now, as I watch her lean her head on his shoulder and him kiss the top of her head, something about the two of them together is ... right.

I glance down at Dara. When she smiles up at me, my insides tremble.

"Holt has always been someone I can count on," I say into the microphone, trying my best to focus on the task at hand—and not the woman sitting right beside me. "He's superbly intelligent, decidedly rational, and an incredible businessman. He values logic and wisdom, and if there was a problem with anything, Holt could find the solution."

I take another breath and glance at Holt. He's a damn good man.

I know what has to be said next.

"I have admired this about him throughout my life," I say. "But when he told us that he was going to hop on a jet and fly to Chicago to convince Blaire to marry him, I thought he was out of his mind."

A chuckle ripples around the greenhouse.

"But now, as I watch him with Blaire, I realize something," I say.

My eyes lock with Holt's, and an understanding passes between us —something of respect and loyalty—that only we understand.

"I realize that he was right," I say. "He was right to go to Blaire because she fulfills something in his life that only she can."

Dara's hand flexes against the back of my thigh, and whatever I was going to say next is gone.

"With that," I say, finding a way to wrap up the speech, "I would like to welcome Blaire into the family."

I hand the microphone back to the woman who brought it to me and sit back in my chair. Holt and Blaire's family and friends clap, cheering on the newlyweds.

On cue, dishes are placed in front of us. Glasses are filled. Silverware clinks against the sides of china as the reception dinner kicks off.

I gather myself, grateful no one is staring at me after that show, and can breathe again.

Dara leans in, filling my senses with her presence.

"Hey," she says, her hair swishing against my suit. "That was a great speech."

"Yeah."

"It was." She giggles. "I think you should be a professional speech giver."

I look at her warily. "Do you now?"

She grins.

I stretch my arm across the back of her chair. Sitting this way, she appears nestled in the crook of my arm, and even though I try not to dwell on it, I can't stop.

She looks beautiful cozied up to me and completely natural in the midst of the Masons and our friends. *If only I wasn't me …*

"Wade?" she asks, her voice quiet.

"Yes?"

Her grin turns from sweet to sinful. It heats my blood as I pull my arm away, needing distance again.

"Are you going to dance with me tonight?" she asks.

Damn this woman.

I face the table. "How about you drink your wine and stop talking?"

Her laughter mixes with the weight of her hand on my forearm.

Maybe it's the festivities.
Maybe it's the whiskey.
Maybe it's her.
But something tells me that tonight is going to get out of control.
Fast.

Chapter Twenty-Two

Dara

I still can't believe this is real.

Dinner has been whisked away. The cake has been cut. Wade commented on the extravagance of the dessert, making it clear he wasn't a fan. I, on the other hand, argued that it was beautiful and a once-in-a-lifetime thing. It should be extravagant.

We agreed to disagree.

The sun has set, and golden-hued lights glow from strands strung overhead. Brilliant chandeliers adorn the center of the venue, casting a radiant sparkle on the glass walls. The ambiance creates a sophisticated, beautiful vibe. It makes *me* feel beautiful by association.

Wade catches my eye as he stands with a group of men, all of whom hold a glass of liquor. He nods in the slightest way as if acknowledging and answering the question rolling around in my head—*has he been watching me this whole time?*

I swear that I can feel his gaze following me around the room with every move I make. If we're together and conversing with someone, he stands close to me. They might be talking about the stock market or acquiring real estate—things I know nothing about. But when I speak, Wade listens as though I'm the resident expert. He has treated me with a marked preciousness that I didn't expect. *That I'm not complaining about.* But despite all of the attention and respect he's shown me, he's made an infuriating effort to keep *just enough* of a distance.

My core burns as his gaze sears into mine from across the room. The heat that's built up in my body from the moment I saw him standing on my front porch might make me melt. I can't understand Wade Mason. I can't fathom why he holds himself back when I know—*I'm almost positive*—that the energy he's giving is anything but platonic.

And that was fine for a while. Platonic totally worked for me in a past-tense sort of way because right now, seeing him in that bespoke-fit suit and looking at me *like that*—I'm over platonic.

Fuck. That.

I narrow my gaze at him. The corner of his lip quirks. To hide it, he lifts his glass to his mouth and takes a sip of his drink.

Good-looking bastard.

"What are they doing?" Larissa stands beside me, amusement etched in her voice. "Tell me they're not."

I pull my gaze away from Wade and look at his cousin who introduced herself just before Wade's rant about the cake.

"Who is they and tell you they are not what?" I ask, switching my brain back to the present.

"*Them.*"

She points at the dance floor just as I hear the first few notes of Ginuwine's "Pony" being blasted through the otherwise prim and proper event.

Everyone turns toward the commotion on the dance floor. A crowd has gathered around the edge, making space for the three men in custom-fit tuxedos to ... dance.

Larissa turns to me. "Aunt Siggy is going to kill them," she says, laughing. "I can't believe Boone had the guts to pull this off."

I look at Holt. Amusement meets mortification is written on his face. He shakes his head and holds up a glass toward the dance floor.

"Who is that with Boone?" I ask, taking in the other two.

"Lincoln Landry and Peck Ward. Lincoln is a family friend, and Peck is Blaire's cousin, I think."

I gasp. "Lincoln Landry as in the Lincoln Landry? *The* baseball player?"

She nods, confused.

"Of course, he's here," I mumble, my mind blown.

Lincoln is tall, dark, and lean—definitely an athlete's body. The third man, the one who must be Peck, has lighter-colored hair and is not quite as tall with a trim and strong *I do physical labor* physique.

Both are *absolutely gorgeous*.

The blond one undoes his tie as he gyrates toward the crowd. He takes a woman's hand and pulls her into the circle with them, much to her embarrassment. A circle of people near them start shouting, "*Peck! Peck!*" This only encourages him.

Lincoln turns toward us, making eyes at a woman near me. An older, polished lady shakes her finger at him. "Lincoln Landry—*behave yourself!*" She then turns to the woman he was making faces at. "Your husband is out of control. I didn't raise him to act like this." And then, after a long pause, they both laugh.

Not to be outdone, Boone hops onto a chair.

The entire wedding party begins to shout at him—some encouraging his antics and the others slinging various friendly insults and jabs. He begins to unbutton his shirt when Holt comes from out of nowhere. He easily tosses Boone over his shoulder to the delight of everyone watching and spins him in a circle before carrying him away from the dance floor.

"Does this kind of thing always happen at Mason weddings?" I ask with a giggle. "Because, if so, I'm going to need to score more invitations. This is the most fun I've had in a long time."

Larissa laughs. "I'm going to blame this on the open bar. But, speaking of more invitations to family events ..." She winks. "What's happening with you and Wade? Are you guys dating or just friends?"

Heat colors my cheeks, and it doesn't go unnoticed by Larissa. She smiles at me.

"I'm sorry if I put you on the spot," she says.

"No." I hold out a hand and shake my head emphatically. "You didn't. Not at all. We're just friends."

I don't think about it. I just look up to see Wade looking at me. It's as if he knows what I've just said, and he's curious about my answer. *Can he read lips?* I turn my back to him and exhale.

"That's great," Larissa says. "But weird."

"Why?"

"He doesn't have a lot of friends."

My heart tightens, and I look at her with a frown. "Really? Why?"

She shrugs. "He's just not very social. He never has been. If he goes out for a beer or has girlfriends—no offense ..."

"None taken."

"If he does those things, then no one knows about it."

I wonder if he's lonely at night or if he has someone to vent to after a hard day. *Who eats dinner with him? Who takes care of him when he's sick?*

"That's ... *really sad*," I say, my spirits sinking.

Larissa nods. "I know. I agree. I love Wade. He has the best dry humor ever. And he's always so sure of himself. I've never been that way and always thought that he was so cool because he knew who he was, what he wanted, and how to get it. No amount of ribbing by his brothers ever fazed him."

That makes sense. It matches everything I've witnessed in my interactions with him.

She excuses herself, giving me grace for my distractedness, and makes her way through the crowd. I stand, clutching my champagne, and let loose of the reins that have kept my mind from spinning.

The alcohol warms my stomach. My head is light, affected by the bubbly. I move through the well-wishers, needing the movement to work through the thoughts in my brain.

The idea of Wade being such a loner staggers me. I hate it. A ripple of worry trickles through my veins. *Why would a man like him be alone?*

Then again, *I'm* alone much of the time.

I take a sip of the champagne and ponder the situation.

I'm alone because it's been a very shitty year. I had to pick up the pieces of my shattered heart, and that's something you can't do with an audience. It's ugly and dark and snot-filled, and the biggest work is done in the quiet dredges of the night.

But I've made it to the other side. All I have left to navigate, to solidify in many ways, is my relationship with my grandfather. I don't know how or when that will happen or what it will look like, but it's manageable.

"Excuse me." A man holding a large round tray smiles at me. "Would you like a fresh champagne?"

"Sure."

We exchange my empty glass for a filled one before he moves on.

Adele's voice sweeps through the sound system, filling the room with a special touch. I close my eyes. My body sways to the vocals as a peacefulness descends over me.

A sudden touch at the small of my back makes me jump. My eyes fly open, and I start to spin around but stop.

I know who it is without looking.

Wade takes over my senses with his proximity. His cologne ripples through the air in a subdued yet bold way. The light pressure of his fingers just above my behind sends a flicker of excitement through my body. His voice is controlled as he speaks next to my ear.

"Where did you get your drink?"

The heat of his breath makes me shiver. I turn to the side to see him.

"A server," I say. "Why?"

He plucks it from my hand. "Did you drink it?"

"No. Not yet." I furrow my brow. "Why? And how did you know I had a new one, anyway?"

We look at each other, neither of us flinching.

"I thought I told you in the car not to accept drinks from anyone but me?" he asks.

"Well, technically, you said you or your brothers, so ..."

He's not amused. His lips form a tight, thin line as he looks at me with enough intensity to make me wither into the floor.

That is, if I wasn't me.

I square my shoulders to his. "I got it from someone *your family* paid to walk around passing out free champagne. I'm not really following your whole daddy vibe."

My choice of words register with both of us at the exact same time. *Oh, shit.*

His brows shoot to the ceiling along with mine. My brain screams to fix it before he can react.

"Bad choice of words," I say, backtracking.

He grabs his tie and works his neck back and forth, his eyes never leaving mine.

"That is," I tease, "unless you like being called daddy."

He clears his throat. "Dara, *please*, let's not—"

"*Wade!*"

Rosie runs across the dance floor and stops between us. She turns her back to me and faces Wade.

My heart thunders in my chest and I'm a bit happy for the little clam jam. *I need a second.*

"Do you like my dress?" Rosie asks Wade.

"It's very nice."

"Oh." She chews on her fingernail, directing a side-eye on me. "Want to watch a show with me?"

"What are you talking about?" Wade asks her, fidgeting with his tie and trying to keep his exasperation in check.

"Iggy brought an iPad for me in case I got bored because this is a grown-up thing. You can watch it with me if you want."

Wade places my stolen glass of champagne on a table behind him, casting me a pointed look before settling his gaze on Rosie again.

"Who is supposed to be watching you right now?" he asks her.

"I am." A regal woman stands next to Wade and grabs Rosie's hand. "You, little lady, just got yourself no iPad this weekend."

"Iggy!"

"Don't *Iggy* me." She gives her a stern look before affixing her gaze on me. "Pardon me for the poor introduction. I'm Sigourney Mason. You must be Dara."

"Yes. It's so nice to meet you," I say, my heart kicking it up a notch again. "I was honored to score an invitation."

She beams. "We are *thrilled* to have you join us tonight."

Wade shifts his weight. I can feel his uneasiness, and I clamor to help diminish it.

"When Holt asked me to come, I couldn't believe it," I say, much to her confusion.

She looks back and forth between us curiously.

"I basically invited myself as Wade's date." I laugh. "He was kind enough to let me tag along."

"*Oh.*" Sigourney's features soften as she looks at her son. "I'm sure he's enjoyed himself too."

Wade tucks his chin and watches me. I grin, knowing it makes him want to say something, but he can't with his mother and Rosie close by.

"I think he has," I say sweetly. "He's about to dance with me, so I'm sure he'll enjoy that as well."

Sigourney nearly explodes with joy. "Well, I'll leave you to it then. It was such a pleasure to meet you, Dara."

"You, too, Mrs. Mason."

"Please," she says, waving a hand through the air. "Call me Siggy."

Wade exhales, making me giggle.

"It was a pleasure to meet you, *Siggy.*"

She laughs. "Perfect. Now come along, Rosie. Let's go have a chat about you running off."

As soon as they're out of earshot, I look at Wade.

"Seems like your mother loves me," I joke.

"She loves everyone."

"Really?" I make a face. "I'm not sure about that."

He crosses his arms over his chest. "And how would you know? You've just met her."

"It's a feeling. Women's intuition."

Soft, jazzy notes whisper through the air. Norah Jones's purposeful yet breathy voice breezes between us. I unknowingly hold my breath as I watch something filter through Wade's eyes.

"Do you want to get a drink?" he asks.

It's a deflection, a mode to fill the space between us with a method of *his* choosing.

"No," I say.

"No?"

I reach out with more confidence than I actually embody and take his hand in mine. To my surprise, he lets me without a fight.

"We, Mr. Mason, are going to dance."

His Adam's apple bobs in his throat. "Now?"

"Now." I grin at him. "You *do* know how to dance, don't you?"

He rolls his eyes.

I hold his gaze and ignore the warmth and steadiness of his hand in mine.

"Prove it," I whisper and pull him toward the dance floor.

Chapter Twenty-Three

Dara

The commotion of the room disappears around us.

I pull Wade toward an open spot on the dance floor between couples swaying to Norah's sexy croon. I lead him near the edge and look at him over my shoulder.

My heart lodges in my throat.

His eyes are deep—hooded even, and sparkle with something akin to *trust*. Wade doesn't do things like this. He doesn't dance with women at family weddings. I didn't expect him to dance with me either and figured that he'd make an excuse or pull away.

But he didn't.

He follows me without a word. There's a slight hesitancy in the way he moves, a slight vacillation, but I can work with it. His fingers flex. His eyes are glued to mine as though if he blinks, I might disappear.

Silently, we pick a spot, and I turn to face him.

He slips his hand from mine, trailing his thumb over my palm. A spike of adrenaline fires through me, and my gaze flips to his.

A smile ghosts his lips as if to say, *"You asked for this."*

Yes, I did.

I can barely breathe as he presses his hand against the small of my back. I shudder as his other hand wraps around me, boxing me in. His fingers lace together just above my behind, and he drags me closer to him.

I blow out a shaky breath, wishing for the confidence Larissa said that Wade always has, and move my arms over his shoulders. The motion is smooth and easy and without evidence of the chaos that's taken up shop inside me.

There are too many details to categorize and file away for later.

His chest against mine is more solid and muscular than I imagined. The ridge in his shoulder feels like a tease. The skin on his neck is hot to the touch, and his hair is silkier and softer than it was in my filthy dreams last night.

"See?" I ask, needing to break the ice. "That wasn't so hard, was it?"

"You make everything hard, Dara."

He grins, turning me in a half-circle so that I'm facing the open doors to the garden.

"Is that so?" I ask, my shoulders releasing the anxiety that had built up in them.

"I don't know what you mean."

I give him a look. "I make everything *hard*? Come on, Wade. You could've used another word. Difficult, maybe?"

His chest rumbles with his chuckle. Each movement causes his torso to brush against mine.

"Well, you're that too," he says, looking down at me. "You're just brimming with moxie."

"My mother used to say I'm full of piss and vinegar, but moxie sounds nicer."

He chuckles again. It's my new favorite thing.

"What about you, Mr. Mason?"

"What about me?"

I block out the way his arm feels around me and stay focused on his face.

"Why are you so difficult?" I ask.

His forehead pulls together. "I didn't know that I was."

"Oh, *come on*."

"I'm not difficult. I'm just ..."

"Cantankerous?" I offer.

"No."

"Crotchety?"

He chuckles for a third time. "No. Did I leave you alone with Gramps too long? You're starting to sound like him with all of these random words you're throwing around."

I grin as we sway.

"I like old-fashioned words. They're so much more fun than *irritable* or *grouchy*," I say.

"None of those words define me."

"No, but they *describe* you."

He rolls his eyes but pulls me closer. A piece of paper couldn't fit between us at this point. Every breath I take has my chest pressing against his, and I wonder if he can feel it as acutely as I can.

I relax in his arms. It isn't deliberate or calculated, but I'm well aware of the tranquility at this moment. My cheek wants to press against his jacket, and my eyes want to fall closed. I want to sway with this man and listen to this music and feel the softness of the evening for as long as I can.

But I don't.

Instead, I gaze up at him.

"What?" he asks, almost as if he doesn't want to ask at all.

"Here I was thinking that you couldn't dance."

He hums. "Well, I think it's safe to say you don't know a lot of things about me."

"Want to share them?"

"No."

He narrows his eyes, making me laugh.

The song changes to a Ray LaMontagne tune about being born to love. It's a bit livelier than the one played before it. The choice seems to agree with Wade.

He repositions his hands, splaying his palms against me with his fingers unlocked. His hands touch my body from his wrist to his fingertips, and the contact is intoxicating.

"Do you know what I think?" I prod, gauging his reaction.

He groans.

"I think," I say, tapping the back of his neck, "that you aren't as testy as you make out."

"It's dangerous to underestimate people."

He guides me in a circle, but I refuse to be distracted. Again.

"Do you want to know what I think?" he asks.

"Sure."

He tries not to chuckle. "I think that *you* spend your time trying to figure out other people because it's easier than trying to figure out yourself."

I gasp. "That's rude."

He can't hold it back any longer. He full-on laughs.

I thought his smile was wonderful, but his laughter is glorious.

"I've figured myself out, thank you very much," I say in protest. But, despite the words, a quiver of uncertainty quakes in my soul. "I admit all the good *and* all the bad."

His laughter slips away. He looks at me with a soberness that makes me shiver.

"There's bad?" he asks.

I think, *I hope*, the question is rhetorical because I can't answer it. Of course, there are bad things about me. But the fact he pretends there's not ... makes me feel good.

Grinning, I toy with the back of his hair.

"Well, there's not a lot of bad," I tease. "Can I ask you something?"

He groans, lifting his chin to the ceiling. "Did you get me to dance just so you could ask me a million questions?"

"That and so you'd have to touch me."

Our bodies slow as our eyes crash into one another.

I can't believe I said that.

The longer we stand, *touching*, trying to sort out my admission, the more I realize ... *I don't care.*

I said it. *I meant it.* I did want him to touch me. And I wanted it so badly that I didn't care, *don't care*, that I got it under the guise of a dance.

"I wouldn't have had to trick you into it if you weren't so *difficult*," I say, hoping he latches on to the playful part of that and not the other.

Wade flinches. He leans back far enough that my hands can't touch behind his head anymore.

My breathing stalls. A ball of acid swirls in my stomach as I try desperately to read his reaction.

"I'm sorry—"

"You think I *don't* want to touch you?" he asks.

"Well ... yes."

He snorts, looking over my head at something in the distance.

"I shouldn't have admitted that." I run my hands over his shoulders and onto his chest. I press gently. "I just made things very awkward and—"

"*Dara.*"

My eyes flip to his. His gaze catches them like an award-winning baseball player and holds them hostage.

"Never apologize for saying what you feel," he says, his voice quiet yet firm.

"I obviously don't take direction well, you know. Like, the drink thing ..."

He closes his eyes briefly and exhales.

A wave of frustration mixed with panic seeps into my soul. Truth be told, it's probably mixed with champagne too, and that's not helping things. But we're already waist-deep in this conversation. If I don't say all the things I want to say, there won't be another opening.

I know that for a fact.

He will make sure of it.

"I shouldn't be doing this," I say. "I shouldn't be standing here with your arms around my waist while I admit to you how much I wanted this very thing."

A shadow filters across his features.

"But ..." I bite back a lump in my throat. "But tonight, I feel more like myself than I've felt in a long time. I feel ... happy. Interesting. Wanted. Not wanted by you in a way you don't mean, but I feel like my presence is wanted here."

Tears form in the corners of my eyes, and I blink them back. I will them not to fall.

The sudden eruption of emotion is unexpected, and I curse myself for not managing it better. But here I am, and here all of the feelings are, and—as is common in my life—there's not a whole lot that I can do about it.

"Your gramps was so sweet. Your mom is so kind. Larissa was a doll. The only person who hasn't been nice to me is Rosie because she thinks I'm trying to steal her man."

Wade grins.

I take a deep breath. "Little does she know that's out of the question."

"You think you know things that you know nothing about."

I rip my gaze from him and study the buttons on his shirt instead. I'm flushed, both from the champagne and from this conversation.

"I know that I shouldn't be talking about this with you," I say. "Because tomorrow morning when I wake up and remember tonight, I'll kick myself for embarrassing myself like this."

"Dara—"

"And I *also* know that I'm not emotionally ready for conversations like this. My life is still messy. I'm too vulnerable. If I'm going to put forth the effort to figure out any man, it should be my grandfather." I laugh, more from humiliation than levity. "Strangely, he's not too interested in me either."

Wade stops moving. "Dara."

I look up. "What?"

He licks his lips.

His palms press heavily into the fabric of my dress as he studies me so intently that I try to look away. But I can't.

"I just wanted to get to know you," I whisper. "I'm sorry for pushing you."

"I…"

He releases one hand and runs it through his hair. Frustration is evident in his face as he sweeps the room, looking for an out. Probably. I don't really know what he's thinking, or else I wouldn't be in this situation to start with.

"Are you about ready to go?" he asks.

The question throws me off. I step away from him and wish I could fall into a black hole.

"I'm ready whenever you are," I say.

He nods. "I'll ... I'll be right back."

"Sure."

He walks a few paces to a man standing next to the door. They have a quick conversation before Wade steps outside.

I dart off the dance floor. Partly because I'm ready to cry and partly out of defiance, I take a glass of champagne from a server and down most of it in one gulp.

The alcohol goes down smooth and sweet. The bubbles in my stomach dilute the ball of tension that has twisted itself into an unforgiving knot over the past few minutes.

"Hello," a man says, coming up next to me. Beside him is a woman wearing one of the blush-colored bridesmaid dresses. "I'm Oliver Mason, Wade's brother. This is Shaye."

"We met earlier," I say, hoping my voice sounds normal. "It's nice to meet you, Oliver."

"I'd say that I've heard a lot about you, but you obviously know Wade, so you know that's a lie," Oliver jokes.

I try to laugh. "He doesn't give much away, does he?"

"He wants to kill us half the time," Oliver says. "But there's a reason Holt chose him to give a speech tonight."

Shaye nods. "I was surprised that he agreed."

Me too.

The longer I stand with members of Wade's family, the more of an imposter I feel like I am. I'm not here with him—not like they think. Hell, he didn't even invite me.

It doesn't matter that I feel alive when I'm with him. It matters even less that I think he feels the same way. Because he won't admit it. Not now, not ever.

"It was nice meeting you, Oliver," I say, setting my glass on a passing tray. "But Wade mentioned being ready to leave, and I don't know where he went."

Shaye points at a door. "I saw him heading that way a few minutes ago."

I smile at her. "I'll look there. Thank you. And, again, it was a pleasure to meet you both this evening."

I don't wait around for their niceties. I just need to get away before my heart pounds out of my chest.

My steps are quick and measured as I head for the exit. Cool air blows in from the outdoors as I reach the open door.

I step onto the stone walkway. The breeze is crisp, and I cross my arms over my chest to keep warm. As I scan the area, there are a lot of revelers chatting, drinking, smoking cigars—but no Wade.

Lights glow faintly around the corner. My heels sink into the soft soil as I make my way to the side of the greenhouse. It doesn't take long for me to spot him.

Wade is sitting on a bench with Rosie curled up in his lap. Her head lays on his chest, her body formed into a little ball.

The sight makes my heart clench. He tries so desperately to keep himself walled off from everyone. Yet at every turn, people clamor to get in.

Doesn't he see that? Doesn't he care?

He looks up at me. "She just hopped up here and fell asleep."

"She looks pretty out of it."

He nods. "I have no idea what to do with her. I think my mother was going to leave and take her home early. I think I heard that, anyway."

"You could take her home with you since we're leaving now," I say.

He bites his bottom lip before looking at me. His eyes search mine for a long time.

I want to fight him, to prevent him from seeing the vulnerability in my eyes. I want to make a joke or blow everything off like I'm so good at doing.

But the fact that I *am* good at doing that hits me like a ton of bricks.

Maybe he was right. Maybe I don't want to figure myself out. Not all the way.

"Dara?"

"Yes?"

He looks up at me through his thick lashes. "I made you feel a certain way tonight, and I—"

"Please. *Don't.*" My cheeks flush. "It's fine."

He stands, the child still in his arms.

There is no confusion or trepidation in his features, no hesitation. He licks his lips and straightens his shoulders.

"I want to have a conversation with you," he says, "but I don't want to do it here."

"We can do it in the car on the way home—no innuendo intended this time. Just, you know, to be clear."

He fights a smile. "Fine. How do you feel about coming to my house tonight?"

"We can do this another time, Wade—"

"No." The words are sharp. "I want to do this tonight."

I'm not sure what *do this tonight* means, but I'm sure it doesn't mean what I hoped it might when he picked me up. I'm also certain this is unnecessary. But at least if we're at his house and not surrounded by the entire Mason family and half of Savannah, I can get my phone out of Wade's car and call an Uber. I'll just sit outside until I get picked up.

This is where I am in life. Taking the smallest wins.

"Okay," I say, giving in.

His shoulders sag either from my capitulation or Rosie's weight.

"Let's find her parents and get out of here," he says.

CHAPTER TWENTY-FOUR

Dara

Wade holds the door open for me.

We enter a mudroom that I'd bet has never seen a speck of mud in its existence. Then I follow him into the kitchen. A light glows beneath the cabinetry along the back wall. Moonlight streams in from a large rectangular window that hangs over the sink. Our movements are slow, deliberate, and aside from the occasional nod or exchange of routine conversation—we don't speak.

It's been like this the entire ride from the Gardens. Every minute that passes without any kind of inclination as to what he wanted *to do tonight* makes me think I'm going to lose my mind.

"Would you like a drink?" he asks.

"No. I'm fine."

He nods and then disappears through an oversized archway that leads into the living room. Flames begin to dance in a stone fireplace. The shadows filter through the room, lending a romantic ambiance to the space.

I wonder if this was Wade's intention or a coincidence?

I place my clutch on the white stone counter and glance around.

The kitchen is three times the size of mine. A matte black Viking range sits like the showpiece it's meant to be, the brass trim shining in the low light. The range sits beneath a husky black hood with the same shiny trim.

Hardwood floors run from the mudroom as far as I can see. The same wood appears as thick beams overhead. The deep color contrasts beautifully with the white cabinets.

Soft footsteps catch my attention, and I look over my shoulder just as Wade walks back in. He shrugs off his jacket and places it on the back of a chair.

He blows out a breath. The tension between us and the stress of the evening are visible in the way he holds himself.

"Wade, I can go," I say as a host of anxiety rears its head. "This isn't necessary."

His eyes snap to mine. "No. Stay. Please."

Why?

I walk toward the window and pretend to be engrossed in his yard. In reality, I just don't want to be engrossed in *him.*

"Dara?"

The sound of his voice so close to me makes me jump. I clutch my heart and spin around, nearly bumping into him.

He's closer than I realized—only a couple of steps behind me. The look on his face is unreadable.

"Thank you for joining me tonight at the wedding," he says, his voice softer than I've ever heard it. But embedded in his tone is something else that I've never heard in it—uncertainty.

"I don't think I really gave you much choice."

His weight shifts. "I always have a choice, as do you."

What's he saying?

He runs a hand through his hair.

"I'm sorry that I made this weird between us," I say. "Can I blame the champagne?"

He searches my eyes like his life depends on finding something hidden in their depths. I can almost feel his gaze percolating all the way to the bottom of my soul, sifting through the debris caused by the events of my life.

Finally, he leans back. Resolution is awash on his face.

"I hope that you wouldn't *blame* anything." He forces a swallow. "I hope that you'd say you meant the things you said and that you would stand by them like the woman you are."

My lips part as I lug oxygen as ladylike as I can into my body. My heart pounds in my chest. I look at Wade as he looks at me and try desperately not to react.

He stands tall in front of me and doesn't move. He leaves himself open for me to inspect, to peruse—*for me to understand.*

I want to reach out and touch the side of his face, to get more of the contact that we had tonight. But I'm afraid to, despite the slight opening he might have just given me. *Might have.* Because I'm still unsure.

"Honestly," I say, "the champagne probably is the reason that I was so ... forward. But did I mean what I said in my moment of glory?" I breathe deeply. "Yes. I did."

I lift my chin and leave myself open for *his* inspection. If he wants to try to understand me, I'll give him the chance.

He shifts his weight from one foot to the other, biting his bottom lip. He's deciding how to proceed with this conversation, and that's fine with me. I have no interest in leading this discussion.

I've said enough.

He releases his lip before licking it. "I had a really nice time tonight, and I'm glad that you came. I was pretty pissed at Holt when he invited you, but it worked out."

"It worked out?" I raise a brow. "*I'm glad.*"

Sarcasm is written all over my words to hide my embarrassment.

"I'm attempting to share my feelings with you," he says. "Can we not pick my words apart?"

"*Okay,*" I say, contemplating his point. "I'll give you that. But I also know you're a wizard—I heard someone say that tonight—so my expectations of your linguistics are a bit higher than normal."

He sighs. "The thought of you next to me for an entire evening was initially disturbing, but it was the highlight of my night." He raises both brows. "Better?"

"Slightly."

Wade rolls his eyes.

"So did you bring me here to tell me you were wrong?" I ask, holding his gaze. "I'm not mad about it, if that's what this is. Just checking. And there are much, much simpler ways of doing that than ... whatever you're doing."

"You really are insufferable."

I shrug. "You've managed to tolerate me pretty well so far."

"I've only had you in small doses."

The sentence is small, compact, and it says very little on the surface. But when I couple it with the way he looks at me, it says a hell of a lot more.

"Whose fault is that?" I ask, gently poking to see if I'm reading too much into the moment or ... if I'm right.

I steady myself.

He moseys toward me, erasing most of what little space was left between us.

I am right.

In this setting—in his home that's clearly *his space*—in the low light at the late hour ... Wade Mason is amplified to the *nth* degree.

He's larger, sexier, more mysterious. I'm not sure what that means for me, but I think I'm about to find out.

Breathe, Dara.

"You said you wanted me to touch you tonight," he says.

It's more of a question than a statement, and it sends a spark to my core. My stomach clenches as I watch a transformation occur in his green eyes. As the color deepens, so do the depths of desire. The hesitation in his face is now gone. In its place is a man who is tired of playing games.

Right on.

"I shouldn't touch you, Dara. I shouldn't even take you home. I should call you a car and call off the entire house project."

His eyes narrow. I narrow mine right back.

He's right—I always have a choice. And even though I don't know if it's the right one, I know the one I want to take. Because despite all of the reasons I gave Rusti and myself that I wasn't going to get involved with Wade, I forgot one thing: me.

I can handle this, regardless of what happens. And if I have to barter a little to keep feeling this way—I will. At least for now. And if the day comes that it doesn't suit me, I'll make a different choice.

"Do it then," I say, straightening my shoulders. "Call me a car and I'll wait outside."

"You'll do no such thing."

I shrug. "You're the one throwing out options, Mr. Mason. Not me."

It takes him a long couple of seconds for his brain to catch up with his body. But, when it does, a deep, undeniable smirk settles across his lips.

"Do you live to drive me crazy?" he asks.

"Don't give yourself that much credit." I try not to smile but fail miserably. "I live for pizza."

He rolls his neck. I think it's meant to be a distraction so I don't see him react. God forbid I see him smile.

Unfortunately for Wade, I'm not distractible tonight.

"So ..." I say as nonchalantly as possible. "What, exactly, did you need *to do tonight* that couldn't wait?"

The longer I wait for a response, the more confused I become. I'd thought that maybe he wanted to talk. There was always the prospect that he just wanted to have sex and, if that turned out to be the case, I already decided that I would likely leave.

I'm not against sleeping with him, but not without being comfortable with it first. *He doesn't have to be transparent, but I do need him to give me something to go on.*

But now? I'm not sure.

"Follow me," he says.

A large black sofa faces the fireplace in the living room with a floor-to-ceiling river rock chimney. It's grand and glorious, and I can imagine sitting here with a book on a chilly evening.

I ensure there's enough space between us for air circulation as we sit on the sofa. I need the room to think.

Wade stretches out his legs, running his hands down his thighs. He clears his throat. He runs his hands down his thighs again.

"I ..." He exhales. Then he clears his throat. "I made you cry tonight ..."

Oh. So that's what this is.

I slip off my heels and tuck my feet up under me.

"I didn't cry," I say. "No wetness fell down my cheeks so that means there were no actual tears." I smile. "See that? We're both off the hook—you for being a total dick and me for being a baby. It's a win-win."

He's not amused.

"Let it go, Wade."

"No." He furrows his brow. "Trust me when I tell you that I don't want to talk about this, but logically speaking, this will be worse if we don't address it now."

I roll my eyes.

"I ..." He takes a quick breath. "I'm sorry for"—he gulps—"hurting your feelings. And I apologize for not reacting properly to your admission."

"That I wanted to be in your arms on the dance floor?"

His eyes darken as he nods.

"Well, in retrospect, I probably didn't give you a whole lot of time to process that," I say. "But that's not what made me cry—or ... non-cry, I guess. I was just embarrassed, and that's not on you."

He moves around in his seat until he's finally facing me. The fireplace snaps and crackles to the right of us. Shadows dance across his face. He's so unbearably handsome. And in his handsomeness, I also see ... a gentleness. *Empathy.* And empathy is a ... *nice trait.*

Tall, dark, and handsome is my type. Mysterious is my jam. Nice guys are too boring for me to stay interested in for long. So what does it mean that when Wade gets nicer, I want him *more*?

"Having you in my arms tonight—having you *with me* tonight ... I think I crossed a line," he says.

I flinch. "Okay then."

He tries to read my reaction. "I don't think you understand, Dara."

"So make me understand."

He hesitates. Whatever he's about to say, he almost doesn't. He fights with himself over the words, and I hold my breath because I don't know what that means for me.

Finally, he blows out a breath. "I don't think I can go back to not knowing what you feel like against me."

My eyes go wide before I can stop them. This is not what I was expecting. I want to press him, ask him what that means—but I don't dare say a word. If I ruin the moment, I'm sure I'll never get it back again.

"But I have to warn you," he says, his voice wobbling in the slightest way. "I don't know what that means. I'm aware it might be unfair to you. You're a question-asker, and I'm not in a place to answer them all. And, honestly, I don't know if I ever will be. That's a bullshit thing to do to someone—to ask them to spend time with you yet be unable to be honest and open. I know that."

There's the smallest blush of vulnerability on his cheeks and the tiniest blip of hesitation in his eyes.

I sit back, my world thrown off-kilter by his honesty. He knows I might not want to hear that—that he may never be emotionally available to me.

But earlier, he reminded me that I always have a choice. And he's right. I have a choice right now.

And I was right too. I have to consider myself.

I know what I want—*I want him*. Not just physically, although if he touches me in the right way, I might combust. But I want the Wade Mason I'm slowly getting to know. The man who makes me laugh. The one who eats donuts on a random weekday afternoon even though I know he doesn't want to. The guy who let me snap his picture on a sidewalk ... and then snapped mine.

No one ever wants to snap mine.

I'm cognizant of the fact that he might have intimacy issues, and I respect the hell out of him for admitting that to me now—*before we sleep together.*

This situation works for me right now. *If the day comes when it doesn't suit me, I'll make a different choice.*

"You know," I say, narrowing my eyes, "I like you better when you don't talk a lot anyway."

"That's bullshit, and you know it."

I can't help but laugh. "You know what's *not* bullshit?"

He hums.

"You just asked me to spend time with you," I say.

"Did I?" He twists his lips. "I don't know what's gotten into me tonight."

"Well, I know what's *not* gotten into me."

His eyes darken. All levity from the past few minutes washes away from his features. His shoulders shove back, and his chin lifts.

"Patience, Dara, is a virtue."

I shiver against the timbre of his voice.

He can't be serious. He can't wind me up like this—make weighty insinuations, promises, even—and then pull out a patience card? *To hell with patience.*

But as I look at him and see the shadows shift over his face, I realize what's happening. He's backtracking.

This is his way of trying to stay in control.

My lips twitch.

Nice try, Mr. Mason.

Chapter Twenty-Five

Wade

Dara smirks. "Excuse me?"

"Patience, Dara, is a virtue."

Even if my own patience is wearing thin.

I almost growl the words out as I'm about to snap. This beautiful, sexy woman in my home, in my space, is more intoxicating than I even imagined.

"You'll be fine." That's what I told myself. Apparently, I'm a liar now too because I am not *fine*. I'm two seconds from losing control, and as crazy as it is, I really don't give a shit.

Dara is here. With me. After everything I've said, the vibes I've delivered—*making her think that I don't want to touch her, for the love of fuck,* she's still here. Trusting me. Wanting me.

I close my eyes to recenter myself.

I want her. Pretending that I don't is a lost cause, and I have no idea how I'll smooth this situation over.

My eyes open, and I see the little smirk on her lips.

"Well, I know what's not gotten into me."
I know what's about to be, you frustratingly beautiful woman.

Chapter Twenty-Six

Dara

I reach across the sofa and lift the edge of his tie. My knuckles drag against the wall of his chest.

"Patience is *not* a virtue," I say, running my fingers up the silk to the loose knot at his throat. "That's just an old proverb."

"Actually, it is." His throat moves as my hands brush lightly against it. "It's a complexity consisting of many fundamental virtues like humility, generosity, and self-control."

Leave it to Wade to give me a philosophy lesson while I'm trying to seduce him.

I keep my outward attention focused on his tie. "I think it's safe to say that you get an *A* in self-control."

My chest shakes. Each breath is a struggle to stay even-keeled and not a full-on pant like my adrenaline level demands.

The knot frees with little effort. I pull one end. The fabric slides across the back of his neck and then down the other side of his torso.

"You don't do too bad when it comes to self-control either," he says, the words strained.

The playing field has been leveled—at least a little. I'm getting to him as much as he's getting to me. I'm certain, without a reasonable doubt, that if I made an effort to kiss him that he would kiss me back.

But that would be too easy.

I look at him, winding his tie around my hand. His eyes darken as one of my sleeves falls off my shoulder and lands midway down my arm. I'm aware of it; cool air kisses the once-covered piece of skin, but I give it no attention. I just wrap the silk around my knuckle and otherwise sit still.

There is a cushion between us—just enough space for me to get a full view of him. In the low, amber-colored light, all of the traits I love about Wade are amplified. He's sharper, taller, darker. *Sexier*. And with the heat dissipating off the fireplace in front of us, my need to find relief from my overstimulation is nearly too much.

He reaches across the cushion with a deliberation that makes my insides quiver. He takes the tail end of his tie and gives it a tug. The other end is nestled in my palm with the rest of the fabric wrapped around my hand. I don't let go. I can't—not without letting the silk unwind first.

His lips form a sinful smirk as he guides me toward him. Once I'm closer, he drops the material and grips my hips instead.

His eyes lock with mine.

I bunch my dress at my hips, and then, as he lifts me, I move across his lap and straddle him.

I sink against him *slowly*.

His lips part. I raise a suspecting brow. Together, we grin.

Every cell in my body buzzes as I try to process the beauty of his unguarded smile, the feel of his hands cupping my ass—how hard his cock is, and how close it is to my opening.

I shift my hips, earning a slight hiss from Wade, and begin to work on his shirt buttons.

"Keep that up, and my self-control will be out the door," he warns.

"Isn't that the point?"

He chuckles, the sound scuffing against my already raw libido.

I can't resist. "You know," I say, smirking, "this is adding a level of intimacy in our relationship."

He doesn't answer me. He just hums in an acknowledgment that I spoke ... and as a deflection.

I scoot back, ensuring that I rock against him as roughly as possible, and finish unbuttoning his shirt. He works his shoulders around, helping me rid him of it. Then he leans back against the sofa as if he's not sitting there looking like a Greek god.

Damn.

I stare at his chest. I know I do. But the lines on this man's body are insane.

Who knew the architect looked this ... hot? Because it *is* hot. It exceeds handsome and good-looking and even gorgeous.

He. Is. Divine.

A heavy line runs from his neck out to the balls of his shoulders. A hollow spot just above his clavicle is a perfect spot for a kiss. His pecs are defined, his stomach is rock hard, and his sides go from wide to narrow at his hips in a way that makes me crazy.

"I don't know how I like you better," I say. "In a suit with glasses or like this."

"I would imagine most women would prefer this, yes?"

"Some, maybe."

I place my hands tentatively on his stomach and lean forward. His breath is hot against my lips. His eyes burn into mine. I hold them and smile.

"Despite all of the dirty things I hope you do to me with this body tonight," I say as he tightens his grip on my waist, "I think I like your brain the best."

His fingers relax a bit. "*What?*"

"Any guy can go to the gym and get a six-pack."

"That's an eight-pack, but thanks for noticing," he teases. "I've worked really hard on that."

I trail my fingers across the dips of his muscles and look him in the eye. "Good work. I approve."

He shakes his head.

"But how many men *can do* what you do?" I ask, my voice sincerely curious. "How many can design homes and hotels? I mean, geez."

A grin ghosts his lips.

"Most men can't admit they're wrong, and you kind of did that tonight."

The almost-grin is gone, and a warning look is planted on his face. I laugh at it.

"*And*," I say, ignoring the silent plea from Wade to stop talking, "not many men can walk into a room full of people—their families, even—and have everyone give them their full respect."

He forces a swallow.

This wasn't what he was expecting. But sometimes, the truth hurts, even when it shouldn't.

"I don't know if that's true, necessarily," he says.

"*It is*. I watched them." I smile at him. "Every man in that room tonight wanted to be you and every woman wanted to be with you. Except maybe Blaire. She looked pretty in love. And the ones you're related to because, you know ..."

He chuckles, moving his hands back to my ass.

"*If* that is true, it's because I walked in *with you*," he says.

"Wade Mason," I say, my cheeks flushing. I smack him gently on the chest. "Are you being sweet?"

"I know. I apologize."

I laugh. The sound breaks the moment, and I'm suddenly acutely aware once again of where I'm sitting.

On top of Wade Mason.

I roll my hips, pressing down on his lap. He raises *his* hips to accentuate the motion.

He growls. "You are *really* testing my self-restraint." His fingers slide beneath the hem of my dress. And as soon as his skin touches the lace of my panties, I shudder.

My movement slows, and I still on top of him. Heat rushes from my pussy, and I wonder briefly if he can feel it.

As if he knows my thoughts, he smirks.

"Let me ask you a question," I say, forming an eight with my hips in one long, deliberate movement.

"No."

"No?" I grin. "What do you mean, *no*?"

"I mean I'm done answering your questions."

I narrow my eyes and create another eight. "For how long?"

"Patience, Miss Alden. Patience."

I lick my lips and press my thumb against his partially open mouth. He nips the pad of my thumb with his teeth, grazing the skin with a sharpness that somehow radiates through me.

"I assure you, *Mr. Mason*, that my patience bandwidth isn't going to grow with your mouth—*oh*!"

In one swift move, Wade sits up, wraps his arm around my waist, and flips me onto my back. He hovers over me like a predator eyeing prey.

Shit.

My chest rises and falls quickly. Blood pounds through my veins. Anticipation thickens around us, and I wonder, for the slightest second, if it's possible to pass out from a look.

His hand cups the base of my neck and tilts my chin. "Are you sure?"

I force a swallow. "Am I sure of what?"

"Are you sure about *this*?"

He looks so deeply into my eyes that I'm pretty sure he can see the answer.

"Last chance." His words are intentional, each syllable clear. "If we go forward, we can't go back. Everything will be different."

I nod, but that doesn't suffice.

He narrows his gaze. "I'm not going to be able to feel the way I felt before I knew what it was like being inside you."

Oh. My. Fuck.

My body temperature spikes. My core clenches and my body hums, demanding him to follow through on that promise.

"Come on, Miss Alden," he goads. "You want to talk so damn bad. Where's your cocky little mouth now?"

It takes a moment longer than I'd like to gather my wits. It takes a full minute too long to remember how to speak. But when I do, it's with all the confidence I can muster.

"Are you done?" I ask.

He grins devilishly. "What? You don't want to talk anymore?"

I give him his grin right back. "I was hoping you were finished giving me the terms and conditions of getting fucked so we could get on with it." Although he still has a hold of the back of my head, I lean up as far as I can. "*So you can get inside me.*"

He crashes his mouth to mine, his fingers wound roughly in my hair. It's wildly reckless yet dizzingly controlled at the same time.

Everything is heightened from the weight of his body on mine to the smooth strokes of his tongue past my lips. I wrap my arms around him and pull him tighter against me, needing as much of him in every way as I can get.

We kiss as if we're teenagers with an impending curfew—lips moving, hands roaming, *wills bending.*

The overwhelming tension between us melts away as we give in to the moment.

He lifts himself and slides a hand down my body. His palm rolls over my breast, presses against my stomach, and moves between my legs. One knee falls to the side as I try to fiddle with the buckle of his belt.

Kisses are planted across my jaw, down the side of my throat, and onto my collarbone.

His fingers dip beneath the lace of my panties, and with a distinct tug, the fabric gives way at my hips.

"Wade—*shit!*"

My cry interrupts my attempted suggestion that he disrobe, thanks to his thumb pressing hard against my clit.

"Shit?" He lifts a brow, pressing small circles against my sensitive bud. "Where are all the words now, Dara?"

"I still have them," I say, squeezing my eyes shut before they pop out of my head. "Damn, that feels good."

"Does it?" He slips one finger deep inside my pussy. It's quickly followed by another. "I wouldn't have known."

"Don't be a dick."

I rock against his fingers as he strokes them in and out of me. I lift my hips and hold still, giving him more access ... and easier access.

"Do you want to come first on my hand or on my cock?" he asks. "I'll let you pick."

"So sweet of you," I moan as his fingers find the spot inside me that drives me wild. "That's two sweet things in one day."

A wicked grin sweeps over his lips. And his fingers stop.

"That's my mistake," he says, getting to his feet.

My jaw drops as I scramble to sit up. "*Wait*. What are you doing?" I watch him walk across the room toward a set of stairs. "Wade!"

He takes the steps two at a time and disappears on the landing.

I stand, my heart pounding, and pull my dress down.

The room is quiet except for the roar of the fireplace. I glance around, wondering what the hell just happened, and try to remember where I set my purse. I don't even have my cell phone.

Dammit.

Before I can descend into an all-out panic, the lights overhead brighten just a touch. It offers me just enough light to see Wade coming down the steps.

His belt is gone. So are his shoes and socks. He still has his pants on, but they're unbuttoned.

He doesn't look at me until he takes the last stair and turns toward the couch. But when he does meet my eyes, my knees wobble.

The look in his eye is pure power.

He's unhurried but still determined as he moseys my way. Once he's in front of me, he tosses a condom on the coffee table.

He doesn't say a word as he turns to me, grabs the hem of my dress, and pulls it over my head.

I don't object for obvious reasons.

Goose bumps break out across my skin as the cool air envelops me. Wade reaches behind me and unclasps my bra. He tosses it somewhere into the night.

He takes a step back. His gaze rakes over my body from my toes to the top of my head. Then it meets mine.

I stand completely naked in front of the hottest man I've ever seen in the flesh. I'm normally not self-conscious but something about this situation—the care and detail in which he looks at me—makes me tremble.

He flexes his jaw. "Dammit, Dara."

"What?"

My voice isn't as strong as I'd like it to be, but I'm working with what I have. Right now, I have nothing but a wet pussy and a need to be satisfied.

He clears his throat. Still, when he speaks, he's hoarse.

"You are ..." He grins seductively. "*Fucking gorgeous.*"

My body sags in what might be relief and what almost might just be another heap of desire.

I saunter toward him, my confidence boosted by his compliment, and make quick work of his zipper. He steps out of his pants and boxer briefs. They get discarded to the side.

Even in the low light of the living room, the length of his cock is surreal. It stands at full attention with a bead of pre-cum glistening on the tip.

I run my finger over the head and swipe up the drop onto my fingertip.

"Dara ..." He groans as he reaches for his condom.

I lift a brow, and then, with more boldness than I've ever had in my life, I plop my finger into my mouth.

"Damn you," he says, his voice thick with want.

"No, *damn you*. You're the one who preached patience for twenty minutes."

He ignores me, making quick work of the condom. Then he takes my hand and leads me to an oversized, armless chaise next to the fireplace.

The heat singes my skin as he lies back on the chair. He then guides me on top of him.

His cock lies between the folds of my sex as I straddle him with a knee on either side of his delicious body.

He reaches up and tucks an errant strand of hair behind my ear.

"I want to see you," he says softly. "I want to feel as much of you as I can while I bury myself inside you."

"You're killing me."

"Likewise."

His lips twitch before he cups my face in his hands and pulls it toward his.

We kiss—softer this time. Each motion of his tongue is more deliberate than before. It's less frenzied and more like he's committing this one to memory.

I run my hands over his shoulders, feeling the warmth of his skin beneath my palms. My core pulses, my clit screams for action, while his length teases my opening.

Finally, I can't take it anymore. I reach between us, lift myself, and slide painfully slow down his erection.

He hisses as each inch of him becomes enveloped by me. I moan as I'm filled with as much of Wade's cock as I can take.

I lean forward, planting my hands on his shoulders, and let my body get used to the sensation. It's been quite a while since I've felt this.

He presses a kiss on my shoulder. Of all things, *this* makes me blush.

Wade leans back and grins. It's a soft smile, and if I were feeling ballsy, I'd remark at how this might be a step toward intimacy.

But ballsy, I am not. Not right now.

He palms my breasts as I start to move, his fingers playing with my pebbled nipples. My hair swishes against my back as I rock back, forth, and around.

"This was so worth it." I groan, lifting my hips up and down. I stroke his cock with my pussy and watch him struggle not to come apart.

"So worth what?"

I grin, my eyes fluttering closed. "Dealing with your bullshit."

The vibrations in his chest rumble against my palms. He slides his hands down my sides and squeezes my ass cheeks.

I move up and down faster, grinding harder at the bottom. Each plunge on his length brings me closer to the climax I've been so desperately chasing.

"I think you're the one dealing bullshit." His words are difficult to decipher through his gritted teeth. "But, fuck, it might be worth it."

"It might be?" I flash him a look and move my knees until I'm squatting. "Really?"

He shrugs. "I'll let you know when we're—*holy shit*!"

I giggle as I drop my weight *quickly*, plunging him into me without warning. He grips my hips, his eyes going wide before a slow, sinful smirk graces his lips.

"Hell, woman," he says, surprised.

I swirl my hips. "Do you like that?"

"Yes, please."

I raise myself until he's nearly all the way out of me and then drop back onto him in one swift glide.

He calls out, his fingers burning into my skin.

I adjust my feet and steady myself and pump him in and out of me.

The contact is out of this world. His reactions are even better. It takes a couple of minutes before I'm clawing at his shoulders, begging myself not to come.

"Wade ..." I pant as a five-alarm fire spreads through my body. It starts in my core and roars through me with an intensity I've never felt before. My stomach coils and then recoils as I get close to the edge. "I can't do this much longer."

"Good. Because I can't either."

I open my eyes long enough to see him watching me. And that's it—the straw that breaks my orgasm.

"Wade!" I shout, trying with everything that I have to keep moving. A flurry of glitter infiltrates my eyes as my body begins to shake. "I can't—*oh my gosh!*"

I can barely register his hands urging me up and down. The bite of his fingernails. The pain of his grip.

When I can't move again, he flexes his hips into me as he stiffens and finds his own release.

A bead of sweat dots his forehead as his head tilts back against the chair. His cock pulses inside my body as he groans in pleasure.

I pant as he opens his eyes and releases my hips. He, too, struggles to catch his breath.

"Damn, Dara," he says, his disbelief ending in a chuckle.

"Damn you too."

I start to climb off him, but he stops me. He stares at me for a long second before pressing a lingering kiss to my shoulder and then helping me up.

Something in my chest blossoms. Even though I pay it no attention, I know it'll be there for me to worry about later. But it'll only get in the way for now, so I push it to the back of my mind.

Wade slips off his condom.

"What now?" I ask, looking for my dress in case this gets awkward.

To my surprise, he shrugs. "Shower sex?"

As my lips form a smile, his do too. *Beautiful man.*

"I like shower sex," I say.

He picks me up and throws me over his shoulder.

I yelp. "Hey!"

He smacks my bare bottom. "Don't act like you don't like it."

All I can do is laugh.

Because *of course I like it.* I think I might like everything with him.

CHAPTER TWENTY-SEVEN

Wade

Well, fuck.

Dara sighs. A sweet little breath of air blows across my chest.

Her arm dangles over my stomach, and her ankle crosses mine beneath the blankets. I'm acutely aware of her breasts as they press against my side because they move each time she breathes.

I try to reconcile having her here. In my home. *In my bed.*

I'm not an idiot, just a fool.

The events that led to this moment are fuzzy. I asked her to come home with me. I remember that. I also recall this ... *need* ... to bridge the ravine between us—never mind that I'm the one who dug it. And I'd be lying if I said that her body in that dress wasn't eating at my resolve to do the right thing and stay away from her.

I glance down at her still, peaceful face. My chest constricts.

What are you doing, Wade?

I rough the hand that's not curled around her over my chin. Then I run it over my forehead. And then rub it against my temple.

This is wrong, *so very fucking wrong.*

That's what logic says, and logic is king.

I groan as the reality of the situation hits me like a ton of bricks. This isn't some broken rule or a way to protect myself. My avoidance of her in any meaningful way is for *her* own good.

So why am I allowing this to happen?

Dara stirs, pulling the edge of the sheet toward her chin. Her eyes are sleepy as she looks up at me.

I know the moment she realizes that she's here. Her body stiffens, and her eyes go wide, but then she smiles and relaxes against me again.

Sweet fuck.

I close my eyes and pray for guidance.

"You aren't asleep?" she asks in a yawn. Her arm takes its spot across me again. "I thought you were out before me."

"Insomnia and I are old friends."

She grins against my side. "What keeps you up at night?"

"Oh, the usual." I glance down at her. "Just every wrong decision that I've made in the last thirty-some-odd years."

She laughs. The sound whispers across my skin, easing some of my tension.

I stroke the middle of her back while I tell myself I'm not going to. *So much for self-restraint.*

"Wanna see something?" I ask her.

"*Wade.*" She rolls onto her back and nearly glares at me. "While I have thoroughly enjoyed myself tonight, I cannot possibly go another round with you and still have legs to walk out of here tomorrow." She glances at the clock. "Or in a few hours since it's already tomorrow."

I chuckle. "I like your line of thinking, but I was actually wanting to show you something in my office."

This gets her interest. She scoots up in the bed. The linen drops from her clutches and pools at her waist.

In the soft moonlight streaming in the windows, she's the epitome of beauty. Her skin is soft and glowing. Her breasts are full and heavy, hanging in a perfect teardrop. And the way she looks at me? *Fuck.*

I stop myself from reaching over and touching her because I know she doesn't want that. She told me. And there's no way in hell that I'm about to make her think that she's here just to touch.

She's so much more than that.

Get up, Wade.

I climb out of bed and head to the closet. I slip on a pair of sleep pants, and despite being perfectly content with her walking around my house nude, I find a long Alexander Industries T-shirt that I got from my old friend Cane a while back. I never wear it.

I definitely won't now.

"Here," I say, tossing the shirt onto the bed. "If you'd like to refuse it, I'm perfectly fine with that."

She grins, slipping the material over her shoulders. "Not that you haven't seen everything that I have to offer, but I'd appreciate it if we could pretend that I have some modesty left to protect."

I offer her a hand. "You do."

I help her off the mattress and onto the floor. My intentions are to lead her into the hallway. But once I see her doe eyes looking up at me—her flushed cheeks and lips swollen from me ravaging them—all intentions are out the door.

Pulling her against my chest, I grin. "There's one spot that I haven't explored yet." I grab both of her ass cheeks in my hands and give them a rough squeeze.

She yelps, her eyes going wide. "No. *No, no, no, no, no.* No."

I snicker.

"Not funny, Wade." Her laugh is strained as she swats me away. "Just the thought of ... that." She gulps. "It makes me all ..."

She fans her cherry-red face and exhales.

"You know, I was just kidding, but now that I see your reaction—I'm into it," I say.

"Be into whatever you want, but you are *not* going to be into this ass."

She strolls out of my bedroom like she knows exactly where she's going. I follow her, appreciating that ass.

If only things could be different.

"Down the stairs," I say as we pad into the hall.

Light pours into the house thanks to all of the glass I had installed when I rehabbed the place ten years ago. Dara takes the steps carefully, her unfamiliarity with them obvious, and then steps onto the hardwood below.

She looks at me. "Now where?"

"To the left."

She pivots and starts through the formal sitting room that I never use and should really revamp. Then she comes to another hallway.

"The only door on the left," I tell her.

We make our way past pictures of structures that I've designed, a sketch my father helped me with in college, and a photograph of Gramps's old homeplace where he was born.

She flips on the light in my office.

I walk around her to my desk. She stands beside me while I pull out a sketch pad. I hope she doesn't notice the slight tremble of my hand as I lift the cover.

And there it sits. The reason I haven't been getting much sleep.

Or one of them.

"What's this?" she asks quietly.

She peers over my shoulder at the drawings I etched out over the past two nights.

"It's ... insomnia." I shrug.

"Funny. It looks strangely like a house."

I look up to see her grinning.

"Scoot," she says.

I roll my chair away from my desk so she can get a better look. Her hair drapes down her back in messy waves.

She looks at me over her shoulder. "This is ... *my house,*" she says softly, her eyes shining. "Isn't it?"

I nod.

She looks back at the sketch and drags her fingers over the edge. "I mean, it's not done, I don't think. But this is ... This is exactly what I was thinking."

My chest burns with relief and a bit of pride.

Those words are the ones that I always yearn to hear. To know that I've read the client well and can anticipate their needs before they know them for themselves.

And the fact that I nailed it with her? Fuck.

I roll closer. I shift her to the side so that I can see the paper.

My face is next to her hip, and as much as I love architecture, I can barely concentrate.

All I can feel is the soft curve of her body. I breathe in coconut and her natural musk. I hear her little breaths in the quiet of my house, and I struggle to detach myself from Dara and focus on ... anything else.

Anxiety fills the hole in my heart as an overwhelming dread begins to build inside me.

Stop this, Wade. Stop this now while you can.

"This is where you would have your coffee in the morning. *At eight o'clock*," I say, teasing her.

She points at a part of my sketch. "Is that an atrium?"

"It is," I say, my voice low. "You have to think about the way the sun moves through the sky. So having a sunny room for your coffee in the mornings would make sense here."

I don't have to look at her to know she smiles. I can feel it somehow. *Can she feel the way her smiles make me want to smile too?* I don't know.

I'm better off not knowing.

"Your office could work over here," I say, pointing at the paper. "Or we could move things around and put it here, next to the master bedroom."

"My office?"

"Yeah."

She leans away, a grin growing on her face. "Like an actual *office-office*?"

"Are you not the CEO of your business?"

"Yeah," she says quietly. "I guess I am."

I shrug. "Then let's give you CEO space to work and grow your business."

She looks at me with a glimmer of disbelief. "I ... I don't know what to say to that."

"Did I say something wrong?"

"No. It's just ... it's been a long time since someone believed in me like that."

Her voice starts to crack, and her eyes start to blur. I have no idea what to do with that, although I'm fairly certain that it's not my fault this time.

Thank God.

She looks so beautiful, yet so … alone.

How can she seem so lonely when I'm sitting right here?

"Come here," I say without a hint of the reservation that my brain screams at me to heed.

She moves toward me and I turn her around. Gently, I arrange her on my lap.

My heart pounds so hard that I'm sure she can feel it. I war internally with a mixture of instincts—both to move away and to pull her closer.

One wins.

I sit back in the chair, scooting her with me, and wrap my arms around her.

My mouth is hot, my swallows nearly painful. It's so fucking strange to feel so at peace yet so conflicted.

I shouldn't be doing this. I also can't do anything else.

"Can I tell you something?" she asks.

"Sure."

She pulls her knees up into the chair too. "I'm not sure about this house."

I flinch. "*Okay.*" I gather myself. "What are you thinking? I can do anything, Dara. I told you. I'm the best."

"No. Not like that. Not what you designed. I love that." She grins sadly. "There are moments when … I'm not sure I should accept it."

"From your grandfather?"

She nods.

"May I ask why?" I ask.

She lays her head on my shoulder. I splay my hand against her hair and hold her tight to me. I choose to ignore the red flags popping off like a bull fight and just … be.

I can gather the red flags later and burn them.

"Like *you* of all people want to hear about it," she says, snorting.

"What's *that* supposed to mean?"

I know what it means. She's right too. Still, I'm a bit offended.

"Let me put it like this—anything that has to do with my grandfather includes a lot of emotions, and I know how you are with intimacy in relationships."

That motherfucker again.

"I hear your judgment," I say, my voice wary.

"And I feel yours." She looks up at me. "You exude this aura of inaccessibility that I know is intentional."

"Like that's ever stopped you."

"True. But this isn't some random question. This matters." Her lips dip. "So when you blow me off ... I'd rather not do that on this one."

She nestles against me again, effectively giving up the fight.

We sit quietly for a long time. I wonder what she's thinking— mostly because it's easier than dissecting my own thoughts. *Which is what I accused her of before.* The entire situation will be more easily handled if I stay out of my own damn head.

But the longer we sit, the more I feel the tension in her body. And the longer I have to ponder what's rolling around in her head, the sorrowful tone of her words settle deeper into my heart.

"I'm not sure about this house ... I'm not sure I should accept it."

I have no right to ask her to open up to me because I won't do the same. I realize that. But Dara is here, in my arms, and I'm logical enough to know that it won't kill me to listen to her. She also needs to be heard. And, deep inside the pits of my internal hell, I want her to talk to me.

Why? I don't know.

"Hey," I say, jostling her gently on my lap. "Talk to me."

Her shoulders fall forward. "You don't want me to do that."

"Yes. I do."

She looks at me with a hopeful hesitation that I can't deny.

"Just, you know, don't turn this into a Q and A," I say with a wink.

She laughs. "Really?"

"I'm not asking you again."

Finally, she shifts in my lap and blows out a breath. It's the sound of resignation.

I brace myself.

"I've tried to be really optimistic about this whole house thing," she says, each word guarded. "I was a bit overwhelmed by it at first. Heck, I still am. Building someone their dream house—especially after knowing them for only a few months? That's kind of ... Well, it's a lot of things."

"He has the money."

"Exactly."

I furrow my brow. "I'm not following along."

"It's just what you said, Wade. *He has the money.*" She pauses. "I want to believe that he's doing this for me in some *'Hey, my son kind of fucked you and your mom over, so let me do something for you since you've lived your whole life on the razor's edge.'* Or, even better, maybe he realizes he's the only blood relative I have left, and he wants to make me feel like a part of the family in some kooky, rich-person way."

That tracks.

"But ..."

The word floats through the air and hits me right in the heart. I drag her even closer to me. I let her know I'm here. *Because I don't know how to say that.*

"But I know that's not true," she says, her voice breaking. "If he wanted to make anything up to me, if he wanted me to be in his family, he would invite me to dinner. Not build me a house."

The splinters of her voice dig at my soul.

"Maybe they aren't the family dinner type?" I offer, hoping it can give her something to grasp on to.

"Sure, except they do everything with their other granddaughter." She sits up and looks at me with a pained, sorrowful look that sours my stomach. "I'm Curt Bowery's only granddaughter by blood. I guess his wife, Tyra, has a daughter Curt has raised, and she has a daughter, Kimberly, who's the apple of Curt's eye."

That motherfucker.

"I know I'm grasping at straws," she says, tucking a strand of hair behind her ear. "I know I just ... I want a connection with him so badly that I overlook so many things. I ignore so much so I don't ... so I don't see it, I guess. And that's not me. I don't do that. But ... *I am.*"

I brush my thumb across her cheek and wish I could tell her what I'm thinking. That I, too, am doing things I don't do.

But like Dara, I don't know how to handle it. It'll just have to be a fight for another day.

"Come on," I say, urging her up. "Let's go back to bed."

As she gets to her feet, her spirits rise.

Mine don't. I didn't love Curt Bowery before. I hate him now.

"Are you going to cuddle with me?" she teases.

"No."

"Oh, *come on*," she says, taking my hand. "Just a little cuddle."

I look at her and try not to let her pouty lips soften my resolve.

"I already answered you," I say, heading up the steps with her at my heels.

"That doesn't mean I won't ask you again."

"Don't I know that," I mumble.

She laughs.

I follow her into my bedroom and ignore the ache in my chest. Nothing can be done about it tonight.

We slip between the sheets, and just as I knew—and hoped—she would, she curls up against me.

"Good night, Wade. Sweet dreams."

"Night, Dara."

We lie still, and it's not long until her breathing evens out. Then I kiss the top of her head and go to sleep too.

Chapter Twenty-Eight

Wade

"What the ...?"

I squint into the bright light streaming through my window. I cover my face with the back of my hand and wonder why in the hell the sun is out so early in the morning.

Reaching out to my bedside table, I rough my hand around until I find my phone.

9:30 AM

"What?"

I sit upright, jolted awake by the time. And sun. And ... *Dara*.

The side of the bed that I don't sleep on is made—but not the way I do it. Even if I could justify that somehow in my mind, my body doesn't lie.

Coconuts still scent the air. A strand of her hair shines against my white pillowcase. There's a distinct red mark running down my forearm from her fingernail.

I rub my hand over my face and exhale sharply. It takes me a little longer than necessary to piece together the events of last night and to figure out what day it is.

Sunday.

I stumble out of bed, thrown by the late time, and step into the hall-way. The house is eerily quiet. I'm not sure whether to call her name or just creep around like a nutjob looking for her.

I choose the latter.

The doors lining the hallway are all shut, so I go downstairs. There are still no sounds, no scents of breakfast, or any other indication as to where she might be.

I head to the kitchen, my hand clamped around the back of my neck, and stop short of the refrigerator.

A note is propped up against a box of donuts next to my coffee pot.

"What the hell?" I walk over and pick up a piece of Mason Architec-ture stationery from my office.

Good morning!

I had a ton of work to do today, and you were sleeping so peacefully that I didn't want to wake you. (Don't be mad. You can't be "late" on a Sunday. Besides, you're the boss.) I had my friend pick me up—but not before she grabbed some donuts for you. (And me. And she ate two on the way over so there's that. Sorry. I'm friends with scoundrels. A scoundrel. One. I have one friend.)

Anyway, I had a very nice time with you yesterday. Thank you for stepping out of your comfort zone and showing me a (really) good time. Feel free to invite me to all of your family events from this point forward. Ha!

I folded your suit and my shirt from last night and set them on the sofa.

Also—you snore.

Xx,

Dara

I lift the lid of the donut box. Three donuts—one with a bite taken out of it—await me.

"*Dara, Dara, Dara.*"

The words echo through the kitchen. Somehow, it feels emptier than usual.

My feet smack against the hardwood as I wander into the living room. Just like she said, our clothes are neatly folded and placed on the end of the sofa.

I stand in the middle of the room. The space feels different. Maybe it's that I'm seeing it midmorning—something I never do. I've never realized that until now.

I'm either in the office at this time of day or in my office here. Rarely, I'm with one of my brothers or having brunch with my mom, but I'm never here.

Is that weird?

Or maybe it's because *she* was here.

My breath stalls in my chest as last night replays vividly through my mind.

Her mouth on mine.

The way she took what she wanted.

The way she let me take everything that I asked for.

"Damn you," I say, collapsing onto a leather chair.

My head starts to throb as reality rears its ugly fucking head and settles in for the kill.

"What have I done?"

A zip of fear hits me so hard that I shift in my seat. The power of the memory leaves me reeling.

I don't think about it often. *I can't.*

The peace I woke up to is suddenly thrashed to the side with as much impact as the events of that night so long ago.

I squeeze my eyes shut and pull my mind back to the center. I focus on my breaths—in and out. *In. Out.*

"This isn't that," I whisper before inhaling again and then deflating my lungs slowly. "This is different."

But it's not.

I can look at other people and lie. I doubt that I'd be good at lying about things that matter, but I'm an expert in the field of lying to save someone trouble. And I can lie about my feelings—and make people believe it—with the best of them.

The problem is that I can't lie to myself.

I'd forgotten what it was like to be with a woman. Not one as a means to an end, but someone you laugh with. Tease. Look forward to seeing again.

Someone you could imagine yourself potentially seeing every day for a long time.

And now? Now I remember. And I'm not sure I'm going to be able to forget.

My eyes open, and I glance around my living room. It's everything it was meant to be. It's stately and grand and, to the world, it was a sign that I'd made it. *How could you possibly live here and not have your shit together?*

It's simple. You move in ... and on.

But as I take in the pile of clothes, the spot on the couch where I kissed her last and then the chaise, I'm reminded of something else that I wanted at one point in my life. And I remember why.

For the first time in over a decade, I give myself a second—the briefest second in the history of mankind—to contemplate that kind of life again.

It makes me smile.

But I'm still too scared to hope.

~

Dara

"So did you sit on his face?" Rusti asks before stuffing the end of a donut in her mouth.

I gasp. "Russell!"

She rolls her eyes and carries her napkin to the trash can. Cleo trots behind her like the princess she thinks she is.

"What? I'd give you the sordid details of *my* sex life if you asked," she says, leaning against the counter in my kitchen.

I turn my attention back to my computer and work on an image of a family of four.

"I don't want that imagery of you or Zack," I say.

"So did you?"

I look up long enough to give her a look.

"You're an awful best friend," she says.

"Why would you even want to know that?" I ask. "Like, fine—yes. At one point in the night, his face was between my legs."

She squeals. Cleo yelps in response.

"And it was an absolute *masterpiece*." My heart flutters as I giggle, ignoring the now-howling dog. "But I'm not sure why we need to discuss that."

"Because I need to know how serious this is getting. Also, because I'm nosy."

My gaze snaps right back to my computer.

What bothers me most about her innocuous question is that *it bothers me*. Plain and simple.

I've never been a person who gets weird about the status of relationships. Actually, I prefer there not to be a status more times than not as of late. Sticking labels on things you know from *hello* isn't going to last seems ... unproductive. Trippy. Dumb.

But this thing, whatever it is, with Wade, is anything but normal.

Rusti props her feet up on a chair and sighs. "So it's that serious, huh?"

"No. It's not serious at all."

"Liar."

I slam my computer lid with more disrespect than its price demands.

"Look," I say, using my best stern voice, "I don't know what it is. Okay? That's why I called you this morning and left before he woke up."

She narrows her eyes as if she's deciding whether to believe me.

"What do you want it to be?" she asks.

"*I don't know.*" Exasperation oozes from my words. "He's not ... He's complicated."

"They always are."

I sigh. "I mean it, Rusti." I try to come up with a way to explain it. "Wade is ... *Wade.* He's calm and controlled, right? But there's a really sweet side of him too. Like, *for example*, he has this little niece who's just a doll, and she's obsessed with him. So I go looking for him last night, and where was he? Holding her while she slept."

Rusti clutches her chest. "*Aw.*"

"I know," I say. "And then last night, he took me down to his office and showed me some drawings he'd been working on. For me, by the way. But then we started talking about my grandfather and that whole mess, and he ... *he was sweet.*"

"So do you think he likes you like that? Like could this be something between you?"

I laugh quietly—more to myself and out of disbelief than anything —and avoid Rusti's gaze.

Do I think it could be something between us? I don't know.

"You had all of these reasons why you weren't doing this," she says. "I'm just reminding you of that."

"And you had all of these reasons you weren't going back to Zack again too." I lift a brow. "When is he coming over again?"

"He's asleep at my house right now, but that's not the point."

I laugh.

"So this guy is worth you forgoing your whole spiel about how you needed to stay focused on yourself and tend to your healing heart?" She shrugs. "If you say yes, I'm in. But if you stutter around, I'm keeping him on as the DH."

I furrow a brow. "A DH? What's that?"

"Designated hitter. Zack loves baseball and has been teaching me stuff."

"*Okay.*"

I get up from the table with nowhere to go. I meander around the table, around the kitchen island, and back to my chair again. It gives my brain a chance to think without Rusti staring at me.

Is Wade worth it?

He's my catnip, for crying out loud. He's all of the things I like in a man. But that also means it won't end well because those men don't settle down—at least not with me.

But there's a little blossom of something, hope maybe, in my belly that makes me want to say yes—that he is worth it. I think he could be someone who treats me with respect and kindness and fun. And I think I could be a partner for him who thinks what he does for a living is cool, could support him, and remind him to ease up on himself a little bit.

And I wouldn't mind riding his face regularly, either.

"What are you thinking about over there?" Rusti asks. "You're blushing."

I wave her off, and I certainly don't tell her. Not that she doesn't put two and two together, but I'm not saying it out loud. Because as soon as I do that, this *thing* with Wade will be over. I'm almost sure of it.

"Your phone is ringing," she says, pointing at my vibrating device on the table. I pace over and pick it up. "Hello?"

"Hello, Dara."

Wade's voice is warm and smooth ... and also sleepy. It fills me with the warmth of being in his bed with his arm around me.

"Good morning," I say, feeling him out. "Did you sleep well?"

"Until nine thirty."

I gasp like I'm shocked.

"Very funny," he says. I know he's smirking. "Thanks for the donuts and the note."

I turn away from Rusti and grin. "Are you being facetious?"

"Me? Never."

I laugh. "I'm sorry I snuck out. I didn't want to wake you, and I had a ton of edits to do this morning and then a photo shoot tonight. It's a retirement party or something, which is really odd to include a photographer, but whatever. They paid a deposit."

The line goes silent.

"Wade?"

"Do you go to those things alone?" he asks, his voice hollow.

"Yeah. Usually." I pause. "Why?"

He clears his throat. "I'm just curious. Is that safe?"

"I've done this for a decade, and it's been fine. I don't book things that feel off."

I think he says *okay*, but I'm not certain.

"What are you doing today?" I ask, redirecting the conversation.

"Working."

"You're kidding! I'm so surprised."

He chuckles. "Smart-ass."

"Better than having a smart ass." I run a hand along the curve of my butt. "Speaking of—my behind is a little sore from you smacking it."

He doesn't say anything. And as the moments pass, I start to flush.

Did I say the wrong thing?

Oh, hell. I just said that in front of Rusti, and she's not going to let that go.

"Rusti is here," I say. "I probably need to go and make sure your pal Cleo isn't in my trash or something."

"Sure. Yes. Of course. I just wanted to make sure that you made it home all right."

My cheeks break out into a full-blown smile. "I did. Thanks for checking."

"Have a good day, Dara."

"You too, Wade."

"Goodbye."

"Bye."

I end the call and turn around. Rusti is staring at me.

"Stop," I say, shaking my head. "It's just a ... *thing*."

She hums. "I'm sure."

Me too.

I think.

Chapter Twenty-Nine

Wade

"You've got to be kidding me."

I search my briefcase again. Then my pockets. Then the middle console of my SUV for my office keys.

No luck.

"What the fuck?"

I always, without fail, toss them into my briefcase at the end of the day. I really only need them to get into the side door. Otherwise, I have to walk in the front and parade through the lobby on my way to my office.

People are very chatty in the mornings.

Since I have no clue where they might be and really no other choice, I gather my things and head for the main entrance.

The lights are already on, thanks to the cleaning crew that arrives as early as I do on specific days. It saves me from going back home and getting my spare set of keys.

I yank on the door handle and step inside. And then stop.

Eliza is sitting at her desk looking as bewildered to see me as I am too.

My brows shoot to the ceiling as the door swings shut with a *pop* behind me.

"*Oh!* Good morning, Mr. Mason." She withdraws her hands from her keyboard and stiffens. "I didn't expect to see you so early."

"I'm here every day at this hour. But why are you here?"

A vacuum roars to life somewhere in the building.

"This is going to sound ... a little obnoxious," she says, glancing briefly at her computer screen. "But the files Stephanie left for me were a mess. And I can't work efficiently when I have to spend five minutes finding a phone number or a project number or where to buy your Keurig pods. It's really ridiculous."

I regrip my briefcase and look at her with surprise—a gesture she must misinterpret.

"Don't worry," she says in a rush. "I didn't clock in. I won't clock in until six thirty like I'm supposed to. After yesterday, I knew I had to find time to get things in order, and I couldn't do that during normal business hours. I ... I hope you understand."

Wow.

"I appreciate your effort," I say. "It's nice to see someone take such responsibility for their work."

She smiles.

"Make sure you clock in. Now. You're working. You should be compensated," I tell her.

"Are you sure?"

There's a hint of *friendly conversation* in her tone, as if this exchange somehow demonstrates a desire on my part to now discuss the weather when I arrive.

I start to walk away but then Dara's voice trickles through my mind. *Compliment her.* I can almost see Dara give me the look that says— *Don't ignore me.*

So I stop. But I'm not happy about it.

"Eliza?"

"Yes?"

I clear my throat. "I love what you've done with your ..." I glance quickly around the room.

Do I say something nice about her hair? Her outfit? The red jacket hanging on the back of her chair?

Eliza watches me expectantly.

"With your desk," I say, giving her a quick nod and tight smile before retreating to the safety of my office.

I plop my briefcase on my desk and tug at my collar. *Damn this day already.* I glance at the calendar and see it's already Wednesday. *Damn this entire week.*

I have rested on my discipline for my entire life. While everyone around me hopped, skipped, and jumped with emotional reactions, I did not.

Logic has always been king, and I've always worn the crown. Calm, cool, and collected. I act with prudence.

And it's almost killed me for days.

I sink into my chair and don't even bother with the computer. The aroma of coffee drifts through the air from the Keurig in the break room, but even that isn't enough to lure me out of my reverie.

It's been a couple of days since I saw Dara. Long, frustrating, *hard* days—hard in so many ways. I keep thinking the need to see her will subside. It's what I always told my brothers when they acted like this. *Give it time. You'll get over it.* But I'm not getting over it.

I pick up my phone and pull up her number, just like I have a hundred times this week.

Should I reach out to her? No. She would likely assume I'm interested in her—interested in something more—if I call to say hello every day or send her a text to say good night or ask her to come by the office so I can see her smile.

I scroll down the one break in my restraint on Sunday night.

Me: How did your photo shoot go?

Dara: Great! They weren't weirdos after all.

Me: That's great.

Dara: Wade Mason—were you worried about me? 😵

Me: I was concerned for your safety.

Dara: Well, thanks. I guess.

Me: I found an earring in the bathroom.

Dara: I've been looking everywhere. It must've fallen out when my face was pressed against the counter. 😌 🔥

Me: Should I apologize?

Dara: Only apologize for never doing it again.

Me: I need to get back to work.

Dara: Same. Night, Wade.

Me: Night, Dara. Sleep well.

My cock gets hard just thinking about her bent over my bathroom vanity. And my heart softens just thinking about her asleep in my bed.

I growl into the room. "I can't do this. I can't get all fucked up like this."

But what if I already am?

My insides twist so tight that I grimace. I close my eyes.

I drift back to that day over ten years ago. I know it's coming, but I can't stop it. Since I met Dara, I've thought about it so much more.

Her face was distorted from crying so much. Tears stained her cheeks, and I wondered if there would be permanent rivers in her skin when she stopped crying. If she stopped crying.

Bile rises in my throat, catching just before it spills into my mouth.

My helplessness. The cold sweat running down my back. The deep canyon of loneliness among faces that judged me in that brisk, acrid room.

I grip the edges of my chair.

Her heart bled on the hospital floor. But it wasn't just her heart. It was her body, her spirit—our life together—that was battered and bruised, and she sat in the middle of it all.

Because of me.

My mouth goes dry as I snap out of my memories. Each breath is quick but not deep enough.

I get to my feet and bow my head, willing myself to calm down. I try to remember that was ten years ago. She's not broken anymore. *She's better without you.* She healed as much as a person could.

Maybe I've healed as much as I can too.

And maybe that's why Dara has me all fucked up. Because I am. And it's just getting worse.

The sun is still an hour from rising, but I don't wait. *I can't.* I reach for my phone.

> Me: I have some ideas to run by you if you're available today.

I set the phone down. *There's no way she's up at this hour.* But almost immediately, my phone dings with an incoming text.

> Dara: Hey, you. Yeah, I can come by whenever. I have something to run by you too.

Relief rushes through me. I sigh.

> Me: How does nine this morning sound?

> Dara: Well, I'm up now, so how about eight?

> Me: Perfect.

> Dara: See you soon. I have to get out of bed now.

There's an opening to continue the conversation, but I don't take it.
That's how it's done. That's what I know how to do.
Do not ask questions that you don't need or want answered.
Now, all I need is to brainstorm the *something* to run by her.

CHAPTER THIRTY

Dara

Knock! Knock!

I don't hear the voices on the other side of Wade's office door until it's too late. As I step inside the room, the two men look at me.

Wade is sitting at his desk looking more relaxed than usual. A man I think is Coy, but wouldn't swear to it, sits in the chair opposite him.

"Good morning," I say, carrying a cup of coffee and my camera with me.

"Well, hey, there. I'm Coy. I know there were a lot of people to keep straight this weekend." He smiles warmly at me. "Here. Take a seat. I'm just getting ready to leave."

"Oh, stay. It's fine. I can even come back."

Wade feathers a finger over his bottom lip. His gaze is soft but curious.

I think he needs a hug.

"Sit," Wade says, nodding to the chair.

Outwardly, I give them a show that I'm only capitulating to his demands because I choose to. Inwardly? I wish he was asking me to sit elsewhere.

I take the empty seat next to Coy.

"That is a fancy camera bag," Coy says.

"I'm a photographer. I took some pictures last week and wanted to show them to Wade."

Coy smirks. "Sounds kinky."

Wade narrows his eyes. "I know you just told me that you have somewhere to be."

"Yeah. Bellamy sent me out to get some formula." Coy makes a face of helplessness. "The baby lost a little too much weight, and the doctor wants to supplement her breast milk to try to counter that."

"Does she have a lactation consultant?" I ask.

He shrugs. "I think. I will ask her, though. Why? Do you have kids? Do you know anything about this because I'm all ears."

I laugh. "No. I just hear a lot of things with new moms, and I know lactation consultants are very much a thing."

"I'll relay that information." He grins cheekily. "And if she already knows it, I look like a genius, caring father, and husband. So thanks."

I laugh as he gets to his feet.

"See ya at Mom's this weekend, right?" Coy asks Wade.

Wade nods. Then, slowly, he glances at me before switching his attention back to his brother.

"Hey, Coy," Wade says, shifting in his seat. "Dara takes baby pictures."

Coy looks at me. "Seriously?"

There's not enough oxygen in the room with *both* Mason brothers looking at me at the same time.

Forget firefighter calendars. I wonder if their family would be willing to pose?

"I do," I say carefully. "Families. Babies. Weddings. Apparently, retirement parties." I shrug. "I don't do dogs, though. I have limits."

Coy laughs. "Well ..."

He glances at Wade and seems to see what he needs to see. What that is? I have no clue.

"How would you feel about taking some shots of Kel? Bells has been stressing because the pictures she had taken in the hospital didn't turn out very good, and she thinks the baby will grow up and hate her because there are only ten million phone pictures of him in the first month of life."

I laugh.

"You can send me home with lactation consultants and a baby photographer session already booked." Coy wiggles his eyebrows. "You'll definitely help me get laid … like six fucking weeks from now."

I look at Wade. He grins at me, and I take that as approval.

"I'd be honored," I say.

"You're the best. I'll have her get with you and make sure we can all hook up at the same time. I'll get your number from Wade."

Coy pats me on the top of my head like you would a younger sibling. It makes me smile. *Wide*.

"I owe you," Coy says.

"You're paying her," Wade warns.

Coy turns at the door. "Yes. I know. I'm not an idiot."

"That's debatable," Wade mumbles.

Coy looks at me. "Good luck with him. He's extra grouchy today."

"Thanks for the warning," I say.

With a cheeky grin, Coy leaves and shuts the door behind him.

The energy in the room shifts as I twist in my seat to face Wade. He's watching me in much the same position he's been in since I arrived.

"Hi," I say.

He drops his hand from his face. "Hi."

We feel each other out, our lips forming slow smiles that are anything but professional.

"I didn't think you were ever going to text me," I say.

"I texted you Sunday night."

"Yes. And today is Wednesday."

"Were you not working?" he asks.

I sigh. "Yes."

I wait for him to continue, to make his point. It doesn't come.

"You know that it's possible to work and text at the same time, right?" I ask. "Or is that why you texted me at five thirty today?"

He fights a grin. "You said you have something to discuss with me?"

"More like … show you." Opening my bag, I pull out a folder and hand it to him. "Look at these."

He takes the folder, sets it on his desktop, and opens it.

I hold my breath as he picks up the first picture of himself looking down the street in front of Judy's. It's my favorite. It's not my favorite just because his jawline is showcased and his lips are parted in the way that I now know they are just before he orgasms. I love the softness around his eyes and the curiosity in his gaze. The way he looks as if he's about to say something that will make me laugh.

Wade sorts through the images one by one. He studies each photo with the same attention, the same eye for design that puts me on edge.

He's creative too. What if he hates my art?

"It was a risk to show you these," I say quietly. "But I wanted you to see them. I think they turned out great."

He holds the last image—the one where I just finished posing ridiculously and am laughing as I walk toward the camera. My hair is tousled from the wind. A flush paints my cheeks from being in front of the camera for once. I look … happy.

"This one." He turns the photograph around. "This is my favorite."

I blush. "Maybe you picked the wrong business because your camera skills are amazing."

He chuckles and sets the picture down. Then he tidies up the stack and closes the folder.

"You really do have quite an eye," he says. "I'm very impressed."

"I had an excellent subject."

"I don't know about that."

"I do." I smile at him. "What did you want to talk to me about?"

For a moment, he seems confused. Then he sits up so quickly that I jump.

He marches over to his drafting table and motions for me to join him. So, I do.

"What's this?" I ask.

"This is a house I designed for a man in Portland a couple of years ago. It's not exactly what you're after, I don't think, but it's similar." He drags a hand down what I think is the front of the home. "What I showed you the other night was just a sketch, but this is a bigger layout. I thought you might get a better idea of what the flow would look like if we continued with the concept we discussed."

This is bullshit. I can tell. He's talking too fast.

But am I about to complain? Hardly.

I've fantasized about being in Wade's presence again. I've wished I could touch his body and watch his eyes darken. I've imagined him buried deep inside me a thousand times over. *No complaints here.*

"I love the open concept from the kitchen to the family area," I say. "It reminds me of your house, actually. But without the fireplace."

Wade pivots, squaring his shoulders to mine. "Did you like my fireplace?"

There's an edge to his voice that's an innuendo all its own.

I grin. "I will always remember the heat of that fireplace very, *very well.*"

He hums.

"I'm not averse to having one of my own," I say, quirking a brow. "Maybe I can create lots of memories in front of my own fireplace someday."

He cuts the distance between us in half. Towering over me, he looks down with hooded eyes.

"Do you remember what I said to you Saturday night?" he asks.

I know what he's getting at, and so does my vagina, but I'm not giving in that easily.

"Not to take drinks from anyone but you?" I ask coyly.

"Don't fuck with me, Dara."

"But I like it when I *fuck* with you, Wade."

His Adam's apple bobs. "I told you, *explicitly,* that if you chose to let me inside you, things would change."

"Yes."

He holds my gaze. "And you acquiesced."

"No, I asked you to fuck me, but thanks for making it sound so proper."

He widens his stance, almost boxing me into the drafting table.

"I would really appreciate it if you wouldn't suggest that you might be fucking another man in front of the fireplace that I design for you or elsewhere." His eyes grow darker. "Understood?"

My lips part as I haul precious oxygen into my lungs. *Holy shit.*

"I meant that maybe you'd bend me over whatever piece of furniture that I place there and would drill me from behind," I say, fighting fire with fire. "But if you want to think about another man in your place—"

My words are captured by his mouth slamming against mine.

His hands cup my cheeks and hold me still.

I don't think I could stop him if I wanted to.

Wade kisses me like he means it. Like he wants it. Like he needs it. And I return the touch with as much fervor as he gives.

Every swipe of his touch, dip of his fingers, pulse of his breath drives me wilder.

I yank his shirt out of his waistband and let my fingers roam his back.

He walks me backward until my back is against his drafting table, the edge biting into my skin. He presses kisses from my mouth to just behind my ear. Each motion is deliberate; each kiss is pointed.

"Wade," I moan, giving him access to my neck.

A buzzing sound rings through the room.

"Mr. Mason? Your brother Oliver is on the phone."

He stiffens and places one final kiss on the hollow of my throat.

He's panting when he pulls back. "*Shit.*" His eyes are wild as he looks at me. "Tell him I'll call him right back, Eliza."

"Will do."

We watch each other with ragged breaths, trying to regain our equilibrium.

Despite the number of times we ravaged each other just a few short nights ago, the fact that this got out of hand so quickly surprises us both.

"Well, then," I say, straightening my shirt.

He tucks his back into his pants. "Dammit, Dara."

"What? Don't *Dammit, Dara* me. This is your fault."

"My fault?"

I stick my finger in his chest. "You texted me to come here."

"And you showed up wearing ... *that*."

His gaze roaming my body is like a match to a dry forest floor.

"You mean leggings and a sweatshirt?" I laugh. "This is hardly seduction material, Mr. Mason."

He stills and grins. "You could wear a ski suit, and I'd still want to manhandle you."

"I hope you'll never hold yourself back." I wink before turning back to my chair.

It's clear that a couple of days apart did him some good. He missed me. And it was good for me too because I had some time to think.

Wade is worth taking a chance on. Me, the person who trusts no one, trusts him. I don't really know what to do with that, but pretending it's not true would be a lie.

The question is—will he take a chance on me?

I don't know. But if I give him all the access he wants, he won't.

Besides, I have work to do, and I'm not about to let my life get sidetracked over a man who might decide I'm expendable.

Like so many people in my life have chosen.

"I need to go," I say, picking up my bag. "And you need to call Oliver."

"Yes, I do. It's about this Greyshell project that's the biggest blunder in our company's history thus far."

I grin. "If anyone can fix it, it's you."

He dips his chin, but I spy his smile. "It's not all in my hands, but I'll do my best."

"I have faith." I head for the door with as much detached confidence as I can gather. "Call me sometime. But not before the sun is up."

"Dara," he says before I walk out.

I turn on my heel and take in how handsome he is.

"Yeah?"

"Do you have a lot of bookings this week in the evenings?" he asks.

"I have one, I think. Tomorrow."

I don't ask why. I think I know, and the last thing I want to do is put him on the spot.

His phone buzzes again, and I give him a wave. He nods before flashing a smile that's the brightest one I've seen yet and then picks up the phone.

I walk out.

Chapter Thirty-One

Dara

I sink into the tub.

Thanks to a bath bomb that Rusti got me for my birthday, the water is lavender. The scent should match, but it's more like grapes to me, which is weird.

My toes press against the tub floor to keep me in place. I've always wondered what it's like for tall people who can stretch from one end to the other.

I close my eyes and let the piping hot water that will probably make me look like a wrinkly prune when I'm sixty massage my muscles. The photo shoot today required a million steps up and down a sharp incline and a ladder that nearly took my life. The pictures were totally worth it, but now I need a little R&R.

Imagining sandy beaches and one particular hot architect, I'm dozing off when my phone buzzes on the stool beside the tub.

"Oh, crap," I say, grabbing the towel behind my head.

I dry my hands and peek at the screen.

My stomach spirals into a well of joy.

I grab the device and unlock it to read the message.

Wade: Are you busy tomorrow evening?

I have no idea. I forgot to check.

Me: No. Are you?

Wade: Would you like to join me for dinner? I
could pick you up at six.

I can't type fast enough. But once the words are printed on the screen, I wait a few seconds before hitting send. I don't want to look thirsty.

Me: Six is perfect. May I ask where we are
going?'

Wade: You may ask, but I will not tell you.

Me: How do I know what to wear?

Wade: It doesn't matter.

Me: Give me something. Jeans or a dress.

Wade: It doesn't matter.

Fucker.

Me: I suddenly became unavailable.

Wade: I will be at your place at six. I will pick you up and put you in your dream car, and you will accompany me to the place of my choice.

Me: You seem pretty certain.

Wade: No. I am absolutely certain.

Me: I do like a confident man.

Wade: Tomorrow at six.

Me: We'll see. 😉

Wade: Good night, Dara.

Me: Sweet dreams, Wade.

And then, because he went out of his way to drive me crazy, I do the only thing I can do. I take a picture of the water and cut the photo off just before it shows anything important.

Wade: Ms. Alden …

Me: Phone is dying. Good night, Mr. Mason.

I power off my phone and toss it to the floor. Then my fingers slip under the water, and I go back to my architect fantasy.

Chapter Thirty-Two

Dara

"What are we doing *here*?" I ask.

The parking area of the Bartholomew Gardens is empty. Lights shine here and there on the other side of the aging stone wall that's held together by moss and prayers. The estate is stoic and graceful—the type of place where fairy tales are created.

Wade shuts off the ignition.

"Did you leave something here at the wedding?" I ask. "Not that I mind as long as you take me with you if you go inside the gates."

He gives me a sideways grin. "This is our destination."

"For our date?"

He nods.

I try to temper the surge of excitement building inside me.

"Wade, you can't just come to the Gardens for a date," I tell him. But he must know this. "I think it's privately owned. Access is limited to the public and—not that a date must include dinner, but there's no restaurant here. It's a couple of old meeting halls, a house, and acres of beauty."

"Are you done talking yet?"

I shrug, unsure if I am or not. This still doesn't make sense.

"It turns out that Philip Bartholomew is pretty tight with Gramps," he says.

"Your gramps? Golf cap-wearing Gramps? Yucky Life Saver-wielding Gramps?"

Wade chuckles. "That's the only Gramps I have. Now come on. We're wasting time."

I take quick stock of my outfit as I climb out of the SUV. I didn't do bad, considering I had no idea where we were going.

Black skinny pants with a silky black tank topped with a garnet-red blazer-style jacket. I accessorized with black heels and gold jewelry. It just so happens to match Wade's black jeans and black sweater perfectly.

He holds a hand out for me as I round the front of the Mercedes. I take it without a second thought.

"I really do wish you'd allow me to open the door for you," he says.

"Why? It would just waste more time."

He grins and leads me to the gate that was open when we arrived here the last time.

We're ushered in by a sweet woman named Marjorie.

"It's such a pleasure to meet you both," she says. "We don't get to entertain here as often as we used to. The staff misses the excitement of putting together a scene."

We walk farther into the grounds.

"You know," she says. "We used to have a full-service eatery here."

"I had no idea," I say.

"We did. It was really something. It was on the back corner of the property, and you could access it from Mayweather Drive. The owners used the revenue to fund improvements, maintain the plants and animals, and pay the staff. But Mr. Bartholomew decided to streamline things. I suppose we all have to understand. Things change." She looks at Wade and smiles. "But that's not always a bad thing."

Once we reach the greenhouse from Holt's wedding, she stops. She extends her arms to each side and smiles proudly.

"The grounds are yours for the evening. Please use the phone just inside the door to call when you'd like dinner," she says, clasping her hands together in front of her.

"Thank you, Marjorie," Wade says. "We appreciate your hospitality."

"The pleasure is all mine."

With a wink, she plods silently toward the Hardwig house.

I turn, curiosity getting the best of me, and look at Wade. He's grinning.

"What did she mean by the grounds are ours for the evening?" I ask.

"That would mean that you are free to roam to your heart's desire."

I want to thank him. *I need to tell him that.* But I'm stunned.

In his office the day Holt invited me to his wedding, I mentioned that I'd never been able to see the Gardens because it was always closed and so expensive. And now, here we are.

"You did this for me," I say, working through my thoughts aloud.

"Of course. But it's not as though spending some time in nature will kill me either."

There's more. I can see it in his eyes.

"What's going on?" I ask as we stroll through the hedges and note a particularly perfect wall of green vegetation. *Graduation photos would be perfect there.* "Tell me."

He roughs his free hand down his jaw. "Well, I had a cup of coffee with Phillip Bartholomew today. He's an interesting fellow."

"I bet," I say warily.

I want to tell him to get on with it, but I don't. *Push Wade, and he might push back.*

"It turns out that the Gardens need a bit of ... a facelift," he says, nodding as if he approves his word choice. "Right there—you can vaguely see a walkway beneath those magnolia trees."

"I see it," I say, coming to a stop. "It's so overgrown."

"It is. It's one of the problems they're facing right now with an aging staff and a lack of community interest."

"That's so sad."

He shrugs. "For now. They're about to undergo an overhaul in preparation for a new marketing effort."

Makes sense.

"And I told Philip that I know a woman who would probably be more than happy to take some marketing photos in exchange for access to the grounds," he says.

I stop in my tracks and smack his chest. "You did not."

"I did."

Oh. My. Gosh.

My heart leaps with a blast of joy unlike anything I've felt in a while.

I drop his hand and bring mine to my mouth. "Why would you do that?"

His brow crinkles. "If you don't want to—"

"Shut your mouth! Of course, I want to! I just ..." The shock starts to wane, and my heartbeat begins to settle. "I ... I don't understand."

"It's pretty fucking easy." His lips twitch as his eyes search mine. "I referred your work to a colleague. What's so complicated about that?"

I hold my breath and study this man.

Does he remember our conversation at Holt's wedding? I told him that this type of photography was my dream.

My heart swells so big that I think it might burst.

Why ... Why would he do this?

"You didn't have to do that," I tell him.

"No. I didn't. But I did. I respect your hustle. And I can see how passionate you are about photography. It reminds me of how much architecture is a part of who I am. It motivates me. It drives me. It's ... It's how I communicate in a lot of ways."

His eyes sparkle under the setting sun.

My mind wonders what he'll want in return but, for the moment, I put that thought away and just revel in his kindness.

I slide up against his body and wrap my arms around his neck. It takes him aback for a moment before he locks his hands on my backside.

"Thank you," I whisper.

He rolls his eyes. "It was just a referral, Dara."

"Not for that. Well, for that but not *just that.*"

We begin to sway easily with the breeze—just Wade and me beneath the magnolias.

"Thank you for believing in me," I tell him. "I really appreciate that."

He runs his hands over the globes of my ass. "I appreciate *this*."

Even though his redirection takes away from my gratitude, and I'm not sure he understands just how grateful I am for the opportunity he just gave me, I let it go.

I glance around the Gardens and spot a little bench hidden under the trees. The limbs are overgrown and drape around it like a private canopy.

Perfect.

I run a finger over his lips. "I'll make you a deal."

"No."

"Wade!"

He chuckles. "Why would I make any kind of deal with you? I hold all the cards."

"You just think you do."

He grins, shaking my ass cheeks with his hands. "I actually do."

I giggle. "Well, as riveted as I am about walking the entire expanse of the Gardens, I'd really like to do one thing first."

"What's that?"

"*You.*"

His eyes darken. "I could get behind that."

I grin. "I'm hoping you can get under me, actually."

"Fuck yes." He straddles my feet with his and presses me against his body.

Oh, shit. He's already hard.

I missed that. I missed him.

"There's a bench to your right," I tell him.

"Say no more."

He takes my hand and leads me quickly through the grass. We dip beneath the branches and find the small area I spotted a few minutes ago.

"Sit," I tell him. "And take your cock out."

He grins. "Okay. I'll play."

"Tell me you have a condom. Please tell me you have one."

He looks at me like I'm silly. "Do you really think that I'm going to see you and not be prepared to fuck you? Come on, Dara. I'm more of a professional than that."

"Thank God."

I unfasten my pants. He sits on the bench, knees far apart, and rolls a condom down his already erect length.

Shit.

My breathing is ragged as I bend over and press a wet, aggressive kiss to his lips. He tries to grab my head and keep me there, but I pull back.

Then, before he can give me orders, I tug my pants down and back up to his lap. I grip the base of his cock and slide my body down on top of his.

He hisses as he penetrates me. I moan as I'm filled with his length.

The air is thick and heavy as I arch my back and lift off him.

"The view from here is the best view in the place," he says, smacking my ass.

"I'm pretty partial to this seat."

He chuckles until I fill myself with him again. I rock my hips slowly, deliciously—his cock touching every wild nerve ending in my pussy.

He pushes deeper. I roll my body in a circle. His fingers dig so roughly into my hips that I call out in sweet agony.

He leans up, holding me still with an arm around my middle, and bites my ear.

"*Shhh,*" he warns. "You'll give poor Marjorie a heart attack."

I giggle as he presses a kiss behind my ear and then sits back. He flexes his hips as I start to pump him in and out of myself.

The sound of our bodies hitting each other carries through the trees. Wade sits up, pushing a hand between my legs, and presses a finger to my clit.

My body trembles. Colors burst through my closed eyes. I can't stop the moan from slipping past my lips.

"Fuck!" I almost scream.

He pulls my head back by the end of my hair and captures my voice with his mouth. He runs his tongue roughly, expertly, through my lips and takes command—maybe even ownership—of my mouth.

His voice rumbles against my tongue. The vibrations carry down my throat and radiate through my body.

I can feel his reaction in my toes.

He stiffens, his throat bobbing against the side of my face as he pulses inside me.

We collapse at the same time. I sink against him as he falls back onto the bench.

His chest rises and falls in the same frenzied tempo as mine.

"That was good," I say, panting.

"If that was just good, I want a second try."

I slide off, wincing as I get to my feet.

"You have to feed me first," I say, tugging my pants back up. "And I could use a bathroom if at all possible."

He grins as he slips off the condom. "You were wet as fuck."

"It happens."

"What do you mean, it happens?" He situates himself but keeps an eye on me. "Please. Elaborate."

I'm just messing with him, but I can't back off now.

I grin. "That's what I've heard—that I get wet as fuck."

He moves in front of me before I can protest. His hand winds through my hair as he pulls my face to his.

He kisses me the same way I kissed him earlier—hard and intentional.

"No more of that," he whispers against my mouth, his eyes glued to mine.

The look in his eye—the point he's trying to make—is hot as hell. And although I'm not sure what it means, exactly, or why my knees wobble at the sound of it, I relent.

"No more of that," I say.

He pulls back and then looks at the condom in his hand. "Let's find a place for this and a bathroom for you."

"Then what?"

We dip from beneath the trees and head toward the greenhouse. I grin when he takes my hand and laces our fingers together.

"Then we have dinner here," he says. "If you want."

Anything with you.

"Okay," I say instead.

Because although my heart may be smitten with Wade Mason, my brain is still leery.

Feelings aren't always reciprocated. I know that from experience. The men I go for always break my heart. Wade is different, I think. Maybe I even hope. But I'm not letting my guard down.

For now, anyway.

CHAPTER THIRTY-THREE

Dara

I yawn. "I should probably get going."

Still, I don't move. Not a muscle.

Wade's bed has quickly become my favorite place. It's ridiculously soft, has the best pillows, and has a view at eight in the morning you can't get at the finest hotels in the world.

I bet. I haven't been to the finest hotels in the world, but I don't know how they could get any better.

Wade doesn't reply to my statement. He just stays still with his arm under my head and one over my waist.

It surprises me that he doesn't want to get up and get to work. Saturday is a workday for Wade Mason. But he doesn't seem determined to move, and I don't have the discipline to get up either.

Not now while he's still here.

"I've been thinking," I say, my voice the only sound in the room.

He hums sleepily.

"I want to make an adjustment to my house," I say.

"To what?"

I trail my fingers down his back and look out the massive window.

The grass is green, as are the evergreen treetops that extend as far as I can see. Although I love to watch the sun rise from my kitchen table, I've learned over the past few weeks that waking up to the sun low in the sky is pretty special.

Not as special as waking up with Wade, but special enough.

"I want my bedroom to face the direction of yours," I say. "Not that I plan on waking up to the sun rising many days, but I even like it midmorning. It starts the day off with some Vitamin D."

He rolls his hips against me. "I have your Vitamin D right here."

I laugh and hug him tighter.

Things between us have been so … easy.

Over the past couple of weeks, we've seen each other nearly every day. I've stayed here more and more, and instead of going home when he left for work, he's left me sleeping the past couple of days, and I went home when I got up. He's trusting me more and more as the days go on.

There are still moments where I catch him watching me as if he's trying to figure me out. He stares out the window sometimes instead of watching the movie with me. He's still slow to smile on occasion as if he's trying to remember that smiling for me, *and with me*, is okay now.

I don't know what this means. I'm afraid to consider it too much. Living for the day is working for now, and until he's ready to talk about more, I'm good with this.

I'm better with him.

He groans and rolls over onto his back. I watch the beauty of his body unfold as he stretches.

"You make me feel like a piece of meat," he jokes.

"How many men in their mid-thirties would complain about that?"

"Excellent point."

He curls up on his side and looks at me. "So, the house."

"*The house.*"

Conceptually, I'm more at peace with the idea of building a home than I used to be. I can't live in my mother's house forever. I know that. It's probably not even healthy at some level. But I'm no more certain about my grandfather's role in the whole thing than I ever have been.

"My grandfather still hasn't called."

I cringe but try to keep Wade from seeing it. It's humiliating to tell a man who's so family-oriented that my own flesh and blood has seemingly forgotten about me.

And his promise about building me a house.

"I just wish he'd admit it if he's changed his mind," I tell him. "I've lived this long without him. I don't need him now."

Wade strokes my arm. "You don't need anyone."

"I know."

My feelings swell up inside me, and I try to hide that from Wade, too.

I know I don't need anyone. I can make it on my own. I can live my life and be a success by all of society's measurements for such a subjective thing. And I largely have my mom to thank for that assurance, that self-confidence.

She was a single mom. A stern disciplinarian. Gracious. She ensured I was independent and capable.

I miss her so much.

But as much as I thrive living alone and not have to people every day, I don't want to live like that forever.

I don't want to always have to have a stiff upper lip. I want to be able to protect myself and watch my back. Where is the fun in finding all of these successes in life and not having anyone to tell? To share in it? To experience it with?

I've thought about it even more than usual lately.

Maybe I'm just a baby.

"Stay with me today."

Wade's request catches me off guard.

"What?" I ask.

"Stay with me. Stay here. Let's do something."

I snuggle down in the blankets and face him. A bubble of happiness erupts in my belly.

"Are you sure?" I ask. "Don't you have work to do?"

"Yes. I do. I have a shit ton of it, and I'll have to answer to Oliver on Monday as to why I don't have the revisions done on part of the Greyshell project."

I slow blink. "So, do it. We can hang out later."

"But I want to *hang out* today."

I narrow my eyes and search his, trying to figure him out. But the longer I watch him, the more confused I become.

The shield that I generally see over his eyes when anything remotely serious comes up between us isn't really there. *Wow.* His shoulders are relaxed. A small smile graces his lips.

"Did you just say *hang out*?" I tease.

"Isn't that what the cool kids are saying?"

"So you're trying to be a cool kid now? Interesting. I think you're going to have to put your cardigans up."

He feigns offense.

"They're super sexy when *you* wear them," I say, lifting his chin with my knuckle. "But they're probably not considered cool."

"I'm bringing cardigans back."

He rolls over and hops out of bed. There's entirely too much energy in that movement for me this early.

"Let's get breakfast," he says. "Let's order it in. And then we can watch a movie."

I struggle to sit up. *Watch a movie?*

"*Okay.*" I rub my eyes with the back of my hand. "A movie it is."

His phone buzzes on the nightstand. He picks it up.

"It's Oliver," he says. "Will you run down to my office and get my glasses? I'm going to see what he wants, and then we can DoorDash something. Good?"

"Great."

I climb not so gracefully out of bed.

"Hey, Ollie," he says. He stops me as I walk by and presses a kiss to my lips. "Tomorrow? Yeah. I think that's fine. I'll check."

I pad into the hallway and down the steps. The calm vibe of the house sinks into my soul. I don't know if it's because it's Wade's space or the way he decorated or simply because my life stressors aren't present here, but I'm relaxed here more than anywhere.

I make my way down the hallway and into Wade's office. His glasses are on his desk right next to his keyboard. I walk around to grab them but stop.

"What the hell?"

In a frame, tucked just to the side of his desktop computer—visible only if you're sitting at his desk—is a picture of *me*.

My breath catches in my throat. I reach for the gold frame but stop before I touch it. There's something precious about knowing that Wade took the picture from the folder that I left here, framed it, and placed it here where only he could see it.

It's from the day at Judy's. I'm bent over and laughing. I think I'm about to walk toward Wade and stop the impromptu photo session.

Little did I know that day what he would grow to mean to me. I'm not even sure how to define that now. I just know, more with each passing day, that my life is different with him in it.

It's fuller. More fun. Better.

So much better.

"Dara? Where are you?" he yells from somewhere in the house.

"I'm coming!"

I grab his glasses and start back down the hallway.

"You will be when you get your ass in here," he shouts back.

My laughter trails me as I race up the steps ... *to my man*.

Chapter Thirty-Four

Dara

"You are having lunch with me tomorrow," I say through the phone. "I'm not taking no for an answer."

Rusti sighs. "I want to. I just need to check on Zack—"

"No!" I flip on my turn signal and pilot my car down into a cozy neighborhood filled with ridiculous houses. "*Come on*, Russell. I haven't even seen you for a week."

"*I know.*"

Her voice sounds defeated … which is exactly why she's having lunch with me tomorrow whether she likes it or not.

"Zack will survive without you for a couple of hours," I say. "It'll be good for him. Absence makes the heart grow fonder, you know."

The line quiets as she either gets distracted or mulls over my words.

"I need to see my best friend," I say. "Just because we both have … well, I don't know if what Wade and I have is a relationship or not—"

"Clearly, it is."

A wave of gooeyness washes through my body.

Is it clear?

To me, it's not.

I hope for that kind of situation in a very muted, extremely hesitant kind of hope there is. He's wonderful, and our lives keep entwining in the most natural of ways. Our steps have fallen in sync with talk of work, sharing meals—he even laughs at the silly GIFs I send him now.

Most of the time.

Slowly, I'm overriding my natural instinct to keep a buffer between us. But a habit of almost three decades, something you learned by osmosis as a child, is hard to battle. I'm fighting it, though, because Wade deserves a chance to stand on his own.

And I know deep down that I deserve a chance to be loved by someone too.

Not that Wade loves me. This is a process for him too. But he's trying to work through it. He's opening up slowly. There's still some resistance there—a bit of pulling back and needing his space. I need that too, so it works.

It's ... us right now. *Who knows what we'll look like in a year? Or five?*

A shiver runs down my spine at the thought of potentially still being with Wade five years from now.

"I don't know if we're clearly in a relationship," I say, grinning, "but you wouldn't know because you're never around. And I'm putting my best friend foot down to that bullshit right now."

"Okay. You're right."

I gasp. "Are you saying you're wrong?"

"No. I'm saying *you're right*." She laughs. "I do miss you, Dara."

"And I miss you and ... hell, I even miss Cleo."

Her laughter grows, and the sound of it warms my heart. *Damn, I've missed her.*

"All right. Cleo and I will be over tomorrow for ... Let's get bagel sandwiches on Court Street and then watch *Yellowstone*."

"Haven't seen it. Sounds fun."

"Perfect. See you then. And ... thanks, Dara. I needed this call."

"I know. I needed it too." I cringe as I pull into a car-filled driveway. "Hey, Russ?"

"Yeah."

"You don't *have* to bring Cleo."

"*Oh, no*. She's coming. She heard the invitation, and she'll be heart-broken if Auntie Dara cancels on her now."

I roll my eyes and park behind a Lexus. "Fine."

"Are you there?" she asks as I put my car in park.

"Yup."

"Okay. Go have fun with the Mason family. I'm going to pick up some dry-cleaning for Zack and then figure out dinner."

I pop my lips together in a loud kissing sound. "Bye, Rusti."

"Bye."

Wow.

I should've expected something this extraordinary after the wedding festivities, but somehow it escaped me how wealthy these people are.

Four garage bays are facing me. Cars worth six digits are parked in front of every one. The driveway extends along the far side and through an open gate. Cars seem to be parked back there too.

"And I thought this was just a baby photo shoot," I say, trying to quell the pounding of my heart.

The front door opens, and Wade steps onto the porch. His eyes find mine immediately. They're kissed with a softness like he has a secret I'm not privy to ... and I love it. I love that this is where we are in things.

He lifts a glass to his lips and takes a long, leisurely swig. Dressed in a pair of dark denim and a deep gray sweater, he looks relaxed and comfortable.

I'll never get tired of seeing him like this.

I'll never get tired of seeing him at all.

And that scares the shit out of me.

Chapter Thirty-Five

Wade

"Are they still taking pictures?" Mom laughs. "Bellamy might have Dara in there all afternoon if we don't have them come in to eat."

"I would too if that baby were mine," Jaxi says, handing Mom a stack of plates. "Kel is so beautiful."

Mom beams. "He is. He's such a good little boy. Coy and Bells are so lucky."

I try not to make a face as I lift my glass of sweet tea to my lips.

"I wonder who will have a baby next out of you all?" Mom asks, arranging meats and cheeses onto two huge boards.

"Me, if Boone has his way." Jaxi laughs. "I keep asking him to wait until the first of the year. I'll have a new manager at the apartments and can step back a little then. But this whole thing with Kelvin has made Boone want babies now."

Mom grins. "I wouldn't be disappointed." Then she looks at me. "How are things with you and Dara, Wade?"

She didn't just do that.

I narrow my eyes, silently asking my mother why she chose violence today. She grins like the matriarch that she is, knowing that there's really nothing I can say back to her to express my displeasure.

Or so she thinks.

I set my glass on the counter with a thud. "Do you remember Gran's tea? Remember how sweet it was?"

Mom lifts a brow. Her lips form a thin line. "*I do.*"

"I really wish we had that recipe in the family."

I look Mom in the eye and smile. She places a little jar of fig jam onto the board with a touch more force than necessary.

"You're bringing out the big guns today, huh?" she asks, trying not to laugh.

I roll my tongue around my cheek. "I have no idea what you mean."

"So, I'm taking it we aren't Gran fans?" Jaxi asks, looking back and forth between us.

Mom presses a hand to her hip and looks at Jaxi.

"My mother-in-law was insufferable. No matter what you made, baked, bought—it was never, *ever* as good as hers. All we heard was how everyone just died over her pudding. Her meatloaf won a ribbon at the County Fair back in the thirties—I don't know." She sighs. "I'm sorry she's gone, and may God rest her soul. But ..." She looks at me with a warning glance. "*My* sweet tea is the best."

Jaxi grins cheekily. "I'm also taking it Wade isn't going to tell us about him and Dara?"

I flip my eyes to her. "I like you, Jaxi. Let's keep it that way."

Her grin breaks into an ear-to-ear smile. "Come on, Wade. Give us something. What's going on with you two?"

"She's here," Mom says. "On a weekend. For dinner. With the family."

"And taking pictures of Kelvin," Jaxi offers, watching me carefully. "I think it's great. *I adore her.* She's *exactly* what you need."

"And what do I need?" I ask her. "I think you've been spending too much time with Boone if you think you know what I need all of a sudden."

Jaxi laughs. "You need someone who makes you do *this.*"

She crosses her arms over her chest and looks at me like she just made her point.

Bullshit.

Kind of.

I blow out a breath and carry my glass to the fridge. I take my time refilling my glass.

This was to be expected. I can't bring a woman here after explicitly *not* bringing anyone here before and not anticipate a little ribbing from my family. But she'd met them before, albeit quickly. And the opportunity for her to get to know Coy and Bellamy was perfect. *Who knows? If things go well, maybe Dara could take some pictures for Bellamy's real estate company?*

"*I like her,*" I say.

The words tumble out of my mouth like a juvenile admitting his first crush and not with the confidence that a man like me should have.

My cheeks heat as my admission saturates the room. I don't turn around. I don't want to see Jaxi or my mother's face.

"We know you do," Mom says, her words gentler than before. "That's okay, you know."

"Yeah."

I clutch my glass like it might run away if I don't hold on tight. Or maybe *I* might run away if I don't because escaping this situation sounds like a damn good idea.

Of course, I know it's okay that I like her. I know it's reasonable for a man to admit this to his family as well. But I haven't worked this all out. I haven't deciphered what this might mean in the grand scheme of things.

I have no idea what it even means or if it matters.

The Wade Mason that she knows is a carefully constructed version of myself that I've allowed her to see. That I've chosen to share with her. But God knows she doesn't know it all. And if she knew my failures, she wouldn't want to be with me anyway. Just because I like Dara—because I breathe easier when she's around, my designs are stronger, and my days go by faster—doesn't mean that I have the right to assume she would be okay with things.

Because she wouldn't. *She couldn't.*

Not if she's the intelligent woman I know she is.

"All done," Bellamy says.

I turn around to see Bellamy and Coy walking in the kitchen. They are on top of the world.

"She. Is. *Amazing*," Bellamy says. "I had no intentions of getting my picture taken today, but she convinced me, and ... I'm so glad I did it."

Coy kisses Bellamy's hand.

"She's wonderful, Wade," Bellamy coos.

I take a drink as a response.

"Jaxi, let's get everything to the table," Mom says. "Coy, grab those charcuterie boards, please."

Everyone files out except for Jaxi and me.

"Where is Dara?" I ask.

"In the bathroom, I think." Bellamy takes a pickle spear off a plate and chomps on the end. "You got a good one, Wade."

"Thanks."

She moseys out of the room, nearly running into Oliver on his way in.

"I just got the call of a fucking lifetime," Oliver says, smacking me on the shoulder. "Bowery just called about a job in Mexico."

I look up as Dara enters the room. Her smile wobbles as she hears the word Mexico, and I wonder if her grandfather mentioned the project to her like he did me.

"This is going to change everything for us, Wade. *Everything*." Oliver looks over his shoulder. "Dara, your grandfather is my favorite person today."

Dara tries to look happy, but I see the truth in her eyes. It's a glimmer of fear, of concern. Of uncertainty.

"Come here," I say, motioning for her to move closer.

She stands next to me. I put my arm around her back and hold her close.

"Grandfather is something else, all right." She looks into my eyes. "He wants me to come over tonight for dinner. His assistant just called."

Her attempt to slide in that last piece of information isn't missed by me. I study her face and see the hesitation brimming at the surface.

And the pain.

His fucking assistant invited her to dinner? What the fuck? What a fucking asshole.

But I don't say that. I don't want to make it worse for her. She won't like going, but as she's said before, she wants to know her grandfather. I can't blame her for wanting to get to know her blood family, even if the thought of them sits like a rock in my gut. She can do that easier alone. I get it. I hate it, but it's logical.

"I'll go with you," I say without thinking it over first.

The fuck? Why the hell did I offer that?

"You don't have to do that," she says.

I look up to where Oliver was standing, only to realize he's gone.

My hands ball into fists as I try to work my way through this conundrum. How do I justify my presence when it's not wanted, and I'll probably be a hindrance to the point of it all.

Shit.

"You don't have to go alone," I say. "You shouldn't. Not when … not when you look like that when you're talking about him."

"It's fine."

It's not.

I brush a strand of hair out of her pretty face. "Let me run interference. If something goes wrong, I can say I had a call, and we can go. I'll be your out."

She holds her breath and studies me. It takes longer than I would like, but eventually, the confident woman who has my heart—whether I like it or not—comes back.

She lifts her chin. "I appreciate that more than I can tell you, but I need to do this alone. I need a relationship with him that's solely mine. I don't even know this man, really."

I want to argue. I want to tell her that's even more reason for me to go with her. But I can see this is important to her and … *fuck.*

Dara raises on her tiptoes and presses a kiss to my lips. It's chaste and simple. Meanwhile, she slips her hand into my pocket.

"I'm going alone," she says, pulling away. "But I'll come see you after, if you want."

She gives me a wink and disappears from the kitchen without another word.

What the fuck?

I put my hand in my pocket as I head toward the chaos in the dining room.

Then I pull out my hand and stop.

A pair of black lace panties are in my hand.

My cock hardens immediately as I look at the doorway.

That little vixen.

I grin, sliding them back where I got them and take off to find her.

Chapter Thirty-Six

Dara

This isn't awkward at all.

I turn away from *my family* and look out the window. I don't want them to see my eyes roll at the fact that even my internal sarcasm is dripping with sarcasm.

The view outside my grandfather's dining room window is fabulous. I've never been to Europe, and I definitely haven't personally seen the gardens surrounding the royal castles there, but in my mind, this is pretty freaking close.

Hedges in tidy rows separate perfect squares of green. Even the trees look hundreds of years old and like they were planted exactly where they needed to be to play a role in the landscape.

It's head and shoulders above the view from Wade's house in a fancy kind of way. Yet the longer I look out the glass, the more my heart wishes I was with Wade.

There's no warmth here, no touches of anything I can identify with. It's not lost on me that this is the third time I've been to my grandfather's house, yet I felt more comfortable at Siggy's for the first time today.

I frown.

I miss Wade.

A burst of laughter from Grandfather and Tyra billows from the living room behind me. Kimberly's voice rises above them all, engaging them with tales of an African safari it seems they sent her on recently.

I wish Wade was here.

If only I hadn't walked into Siggy's kitchen when I did and heard Oliver's announcement. If my grandfather is going to work with the Masons on an international level, I can't afford to mix my personal life with Wade's professional one—especially when I don't know what kind of personal life I have with either of them.

That would be unfair—to me, to Wade, to Oliver and the rest of the Mason family. I imagine it would be unfair to my grandfather, too, but something tells me he'd find a way to come out smelling like a rose.

I frown again.

"Dara, darling, please join us," Grandfather says as if just remembering that I arrived nearly an hour ago.

I paste on a smile and walk toward them.

"Dinner smells delightful," I say, perching on the edge of a chair across from Grandfather and Tyra. Kimberly takes a seat on a sofa to my left.

Kimmy, as they call her, is twenty-five with long blond hair and the brightest blue eyes I've ever seen. They would be the focal point of her face if she weren't iced out in so many diamonds that my head spins.

"Mildred is such a wonderful chef," Tyra says. "I don't know what we'd do if she ever retires."

"Mildred has been a part of the family since I was born, I think." Kimberly laughs, keeping a side-eye on me. "I can't remember a part of my life without her."

"Because there hasn't been one." Grandfather winks at her. "That's the way it should be. Staff should be family. Remember that, sweetheart."

"Of course." Kimberly smiles like a princess back at him.

What an odd interaction.

I clear my throat.

Tyra raises a brow as if I've somehow offended her.

"I'm sorry," I say, holding my neck as if it's paining me. "It's allergies."

"Right." Tyra looks at her husband.

"Kimmy was just telling us about her time in Kenya," Grandfather says. "We'd love to hear stories about what you've been up to."

My heart leaps in my chest as my lips part to tell them about my life —about the beautiful Bartholomew Gardens and photographing a music star Kelvin McCoy's baby today. And the movie that Wade and I watched last night and how I made a Barefoot Contessa chicken recipe and it tasted almost like my mother's.

But as I take in their faces—cold and aloof, I realize that the offer was rhetorical. They don't really want to hear what I've been up to. They want to move the conversation along.

Besides, how can roasted chicken compete with Kenya?

I lift my chin and steady my breath, hoping I can talk past the lump in my throat.

"Where did you go in Kenya?" I ask Kimberly.

Her grin is smug. "The Massai Mara National Reserve. It was beyond wonderful. It's not quite as amazing as Mykonos, but definitely in my top five."

My top five includes New Orleans, Sedona, and Nashville. We are not the same.

"I've heard Mykonos is beautiful," I say politely.

The room falls silent. The stillness scratches at me, clawing at my soul, and I need to fill it with something. Anything. *Anything* is better than thinking that they are watching and judging me.

Tyra and Kimberly look at Grandfather expectantly. It's a pointed move that says loud and clear that something is about to happen.

Something I'm afraid I won't like.

The room grows bigger. The three of them sit on one side like a pride of lions before me. I slide down into my seat and prepare for whatever is about to hit me.

I ignore the burn across the bridge of my nose and stiffen my shoulders.

My instincts say to run, to catch flight, because I know that this situation is about to be for my survival, and fighting for my life isn't going to work out well.

Thoughts fly through my mind, shuffling across like snowfall in a blackout.

My mom's face. The smell of her mother's meatloaf. Rusti's laugh and Cleo's annoying little bark that I would give my left arm to be hearing instead of this right now.

And Wade. The smell of his Tom Ford cologne. The feel of his hand caressing me while I sleep. His smile while I dance to Post Malone while we cook dinner, and the safety of his arms when I'm feeling a particular way and he somehow understands it.

When I'm feeling like this.

Alone. *So, incredibly alone.*

"So, Dara, darling," Grandfather says, each word paced. "I wanted to bring you here tonight to discuss with you some big family news that will be announced in the coming days."

"Okay."

He sits up in his chair. "I have decided to make a bid for president."

President. President of what?

Oh.

President of the United States.

Although we're sitting at the same height, Tyra still looks down at me as if I'm a plebian. And maybe I am. Maybe I'm the scum on the bottom of her red-bottomed heels. I certainly don't have a string of pearls around my neck or a diamond bracelet that has to be hard to lug around all day.

But I am not beneath her. *No.* Fuck that.

I turn my attention solely on my grandfather.

"That's exciting," I say, measuring my response.

"It is. It is indeed. We were hoping that you would attend the press conference with us in Atlanta next week. On Thursday, I believe."

What?

I'm still trying to figure out what any of this has to do with me when Kimberly speaks.

"Yes," she says, smiling ruefully. "We would hate for the media to harass you if you aren't there."

"And why would they harass *me*?"

"Because ..." Kimberly bats her lashes. "How would it look for the family if news breaks that Curt Bowery has a granddaughter that's a bastard?"

"*Kimmy*." Grandfather admonishes her with a scowl. "That's not what we mean."

But it *is* what he means. I can see it on his face.

I acknowledge that I have a biological child, Dara Alden. I choose with a sound mind and in front of the witnesses named below to exempt her from this document.

My breaths can't quite get enough oxygen to my brain. Every thought takes a few seconds too long to process. My mouth goes dry.

Grandfather scoots to the edge of his chair and rests his elbows on his knees.

"The media are vultures, darling," he says. "They are going to pick through my life with a fine-tooth comb and expose any unsavory pieces that they can find."

Tears dot my eyes. "And that's me, right? I'm the unsavory piece."

Kimberly's shoulders shrug, but I don't acknowledge it.

I can't.

Oh, my God.

I'm too in shock to process the entirety of this conversation. I'm too blindsided to react.

He doesn't want me here. He doesn't want me in his life.

"That's not what I mean, Dara," he says, his words firm. "You are a delightful young lady who we are just getting to know. And I think it behooves everyone involved if you join us from the beginning so that we may show a united front. It leaves little for anyone to investigate."

My body is eerily still.

"You mean that you want to show a united front so that people don't realize that you have a granddaughter that you've never bothered to get to know," I say.

My words are as firm as his. I lock eyes with Curt and wait for him to react. I learned this from Wade—how to be strong and not bend to someone's will.

Wade. Why didn't I just let you come?

Curt sighs. "We are getting to know each other now. I'm building you a house, for heaven's sake."

No, you're buying me off.

I stand. They all flinch, surprised by my sudden movement. I stand above them.

"Bless your hearts," I say.

Tyra rolls her eyes. It makes me chuckle angrily.

"You've made a lot of money over the years, so you're clearly not an idiot," I say, looking at Curt. "But let me explain something to you."

His jaw sets.

"If you wanted to get to know me, you would've called. Texted. Invited me to dinner—and did it yourself. Not through your assistant," I say. "Building me a house is not getting to know me. It's manipulation. You're trying to put me in a situation where I can't say anything bad about you to the press."

"Dara—" he booms.

"Dara *Alden. That's* my name. *Not Bowery.* I have never been a Bowery, and it's clear I never will be."

Curt stands. "While I appreciate your backbone, I do think it might be best for you to sleep on this before you make decisions that you can't take back."

"Your son already did that."

He narrows his eyes. I narrow mine right back.

"I'm not indebted to you. I don't want anything from you. To be clear—I won't accept anything from you whether it's dinner tonight or a house *ever.*"

I suck in a breath and feel tears welling. The pressure mounts. I need to get out of here before I let him see me weak.

"Thank you," I say, taking them in one by one for the final time. "Thank you for letting me see what I thankfully missed out on. Now, if you'll excuse me."

I pivot on my Target-label shoe and head to the door. Curt calls out for me, but I don't look back.

My mother knew this would happen. She said there would come a time when he would want to meet me, that he would bowl me over with gifts and promises.

"Give him a chance because you deserve that. Don't give him a second because he doesn't."

I climb into my car, the hole in my heart gaping wide open, and start the ignition.

"You were right," I say, wiping the snot off my face with the back of my hand. "That was his one chance."

I pull out of the winding, tree-lined driveway and onto the road. My heart actively breaks inside my chest as I try to stay between the white and yellow lines.

The hopes and dreams for a life with my family splinter, impaling me with open, bleeding wounds.

I smack the steering wheel with my hand.

My tears blur the road, and I wipe them with my shirt—the shirt I fretted over so that I made a good impression on the Bowerys.

So stupid.

The farther I get from the Bowery mansion, the more I know what I want.

Wade.

Being with his family today felt more like love than I've ever felt with anyone besides my mother. The Masons were so supportive, so kind, so gentle with my tender heart. Siggy seemed to know exactly what I needed from her, something that I've been missing so much in losing my mom.

An indulgent comment. A side hug. A lingering smile that said she understood my complicated emotions that I don't even know how she saw in the first place.

She made me see that I can't do life on my own ... and that there might be another option.

"I need you, Wade," I say, tears streaming down my face. "I need you so much."

I wipe my tears again but when I look back at the road, a set of bright lights blind me.

"Oh, shit!"

I pull my car as far to the right as I can.

The sound hits me first.

Screeching tires. Twisting metal. A horn that won't stop honking.

What's happening?

A pain rips through my back as I vaguely acknowledge I've stopped moving.

I try to see around the mass of metal in front of me, but I can't.

What's it doing there?

I can't do anything.

I just need to sleep.

My eyes fall closed as Wade's face drifts through my mind, and I fall into the darkness.

CHAPTER THIRTY-SEVEN

Wade

"Where the hell is she?"

I pace across the living room and try to call her again.

Voicemail.

Again.

Maybe she's just enjoying a night with her grandfather. But even though that's a logical thought, I know it's not true.

My gut tells me it's bullshit.

Worry bleeds into anger because I don't know what to do. She said she would call when she left, and she expected that to be two hours ago.

I know Dara. She would've at least texted me if things were running late because she knows I would worry.

What the fuck?

I should've made her let me go with her. It would've made me a dick, but I wouldn't be in this situation now.

Anger builds, bordering on rage, because I have no one to call. Her friend Rusti? I don't even know her last name.

She doesn't have anyone else either.

That realization hits me like a semitruck.

I pace back and forth and make a decision. If she doesn't check in with me in twenty minutes, at the top of the hour, I'm calling Curt.

Fuck it.

If she wants to be pissed, she can be pissed. I ran out of fucks an hour ago.

I should've gone with her.

I consider calling my mother and getting advice from a woman's perspective. I even go as far as considering calling Holt and listening to him babble about married life—anything to get my mind off this chill that's settled in my soul.

My feet stop walking.

A cold sweat breaks across my skin as a memory forces its way into my brain.

"Is this Wade Mason?" the woman on the other end of the phone asks.

"Yes."

"We need you to come to the hospital. It's urgent."

I know it's just a memory. It comes back a lot this time of year. That's all it is. *It's just a memory.*

I press her name on my phone again.

It rings once. Twice. Three times.

Click!

"Hello?" I ask.

"Hello."

The voice answering me is male. *Not Dara.*

I pull the phone away from my face and check her number. It's correct.

"Who is this?" I ask.

Whoever is on the other end is breathing heavily.

I close my eyes and fight a head-to-toe chill that snakes through my body. *I think I'm going to be sick.*

"First, may I ask who this is?" he asks.

"This is Wade Mason. Who the fuck is this, and why are you answering my girlfriend's phone?"

He breathes into the line. "Sir, this is Officer Wastell with the

Savannah Police Department. I regret to inform you that there's been an accident."

Oh, fuck.

No.

No. Please, no.

The bottom of my world drops out.

I fall to my knees on the hardwood.

No. This isn't happening.

This can't be fucking happening.

My hand trembles as fear dumps over me like a cold bucket of water.

I can't breathe.

"Is she all right?" I ask. "Tell me she's alright!"

God, she has to be all right. Let her be all right.

Tears prick my eyes as I climb back to my feet.

I have to get to her. I need to see her. I need to have her in my arms.

God, she has to be all right.

"Where is she?" I bark, grabbing my keys off the counter and storming into my garage. "Where is Dara?"

"She's been transported to Savannah Methodist, sir. I can't give you any more information than that."

I end the call and start my car. The tires squeal as I rip down the driveway to get to her.

To get to Dara.

To get to my lady.

I should've gone with her. I should've protected her. Why can I never protect the people in my life I lo—I …

Please, God, let her be all right.

Don't do this to me again.

I need her to be okay.

I need *her.*

I won't make it this time.

Chapter Thirty-Eight

Dara

"How are you feeling?" A redheaded woman in green scrubs looks at a screen above me. Then she clicks around a mobile computer-looking thing. "Are the lights too bright?"

My throat is so dry that I can barely speak. "They're fine."

I start to move, but everything—*every single cell in my body*—objects.

I hiss and relax as much as possible into the hard hospital bed.

My head throbs. I touch my face on the left side where it feels like I've been punched. It's swollen and warm against my hand, but my head throbs too bad to process it.

Memories of the lights coming right at me—the dazzlingly bright, blinding lights—make me squint. The smell of smoke. The voices shouting and someone tugging on my arm.

It all starts to come back to me.

"What happened?" I ask, squinting at the nurse.

"Do you remember anything at all?"

I think. "A wreck, I think?"

"Yes, sweetie. You were in an accident."

When? How long have I been here?

What's happening?

I start to sit up, but my body screams at me in protest.

"The doctor will be in now that you're awake," she says. "Can I get you anything while you wait?"

"Water," I say, the words burning my throat.

She nods and starts to leave.

"Um, hey," I say, wincing at the pain in my side.

She stops by the door.

Tears wet my eyes as I remember what I was doing. *Curt's house.*

Suddenly, the room feels really fucking big.

I'm afraid to ask the question on the tip of my tongue. I'm afraid to hear the answer. But the emptiness in my chest cries out longer and harder than the fear of being unwanted.

"Is there anyone here for me?" I ask.

Her face falls.

Tears fall down mine.

"The doctor will be right in," she whispers and shuts the door softly behind her.

My chest shakes as I cry. It's a pathetic attempt at crying because I don't even have the energy to do it right.

I lick my lips and discover that they, too, are swollen. I wonder if anything is broken besides my spirit.

Damn Curt Bowery. Damn you and your piece-of-shit son.

I look around the room for my phone. *I need to call Wade.* There's a chance no one has called him because I know he'd be here if he knew something happened.

The thought makes me smile.

He'll come for me. I know it.

The idea of seeing his face and feeling his touch slows my tears. It's the only balm to my wounds.

I just wonder how many I have.

A soft knock raps against the door. A balding man in a white coat comes into the room.

"Well, hello, sleeping beauty," he says softly. "I'm Dr. Kidmore. How are you feeling?"

"Like I got hit by a truck. Funnily enough, I'm not sure what hit me."

He sets a notebook down on a stand. "I think your instincts are probably right on that."

I try to smile.

He takes a quick glance at the machine overhead and then rolls a stool up beside the bed. "I'm going to do a few checks, okay?"

I nod, barely.

He shines his light in my eyes, which makes me squint. *Ouch.* His fingers are soft, though, as they press against what must be a patchwork of bruises given how much they hurt.

"You're doing great, Dara. Are there specific areas of discomfort for you? There is a lot of bruising and swelling."

I try to shrug but wince instead. "Well, my face hurts. My arm. It hurts to breathe too deep."

"That makes sense. You have a small fracture in your left hand that will heal on its own. And a nicely cracked rib. You're going to be pretty sore."

I wince while trying to take a deep breath. "I believe that."

He smiles.

"The other driver—are they okay?" I ask.

"He's alive. I can't say much else."

I nod, my heart sinking. "I understand."

Hearing that is a relief that I didn't know I needed. I rest my head against the pillows and sigh.

"Do you have any questions for me?" he asks.

"When can I go home?"

He grins. "We have a few more tests to run, so we'll see how that goes. Hopefully tomorrow if everything looks the way I expect it to."

"I'd like to find my phone. Do you know where it is?"

He shakes his head. "I don't. I can check with the records that came in with you, but I'm guessing if anyone has it, it's the police. But don't worry," he says upon seeing my distress. "They'll find all of your belongings and return them to you."

How can I call Wade?

"I need to call … a friend," I say, tears forming in my eyes again.

"Absolutely. There's a phone over there." He points at the table on the other side of me. "If you need help finding a number, one of the nurses will help you." He pats my hand. "Don't worry. We'll get you all fixed up and out of here as good as new."

I try to grin at his kindness. But between my tears and swollen face, who knows what it looks like.

Dr. Kidmore's face sobers. "I have one more thing that I'd like to ask you, Miss Alden."

"Okay."

"You do know that you're pregnant. Right?"

There are no bright lights this time. No smell of burnt rubber. There isn't a chunk of metal that keeps me from seeing a few feet away from my face.

But none of that means that I don't feel hit by a truck again.

"*Excuse me?*" I ask, my eyes going wide.

I gulp. *I didn't hear him right. I probably have a concussion.*

"Am I concussed?" I ask.

"No. You do not have a concussion. But you are expecting a baby."

A baby?

I squeeze my eyes shut and grab my head—only to pull my hand away because the pain from touching it is somehow even worse.

I can't be pregnant. How can I be pregnant?

Well, I know *how* but how?

Wade.

Oh, fuck.

The monitor hanging above me starts beeping. A shot of fear mixed with adrenaline fires through my veins.

A cold sweat dots my skin as I think I might vomit.

"I take it that this information is new to you," he says softly.

I laugh. The sound is hollow and breaks on a sob. "Oh, a little bit."

"We're going to run an ultrasound shortly, and we can help you schedule an appointment with your OB," he says. "I don't expect that you'll see any complications from the accident, but that's also not my specialty."

Holy shit. This is real.

"It's not mine either," I say.

He goes to the sink and washes his hands. "Do you have any more questions for me?"

"Can you hand me a puke bucket before you leave?"

"Yes. Of course." He grabs a little pale pink tub and passes it to me. "I'll have the nurse come check on you shortly. Okay?"

I nod.

I don't need a nurse. *I need Wade.*

Tears stream down my cheeks unchecked.

The tub shakes in my hand, and I wonder what part of this entire debacle is causing it. *The shock of the accident? The pain? The medicines?*

The baby?

The baby.

Oh. Shit.

I watch the doctor slowly rise and gather his notebook.

How is he so calm?

Because he's not having a baby.

I vaguely register that the door closes.

My eyes close, and I say a prayer. For strength. For peace. *And for Wade.*

If I can just see Wade, I know this will all be okay.

I know it.

Chapter Thirty-Nine

Wade

"Dara Alden." I plant my hands on the nurses' station and catch my breath. "Where is she? What room?"

"Sir, I need you to—"

"I need *you* to tell me where she is. *Now.*"

The nurse flinches at my aggressive behavior, but she doesn't look any closer to relenting.

My heart pounds so hard that I think I might pass out.

"Please. Where the hell is she?"

A man in a white coat stops at the nurses' station. He sees me and quirks a brow.

"Dara Alden," I say, nearly begging. "Do you know where she is?"

The doctor gives the nurse a small nod and then turns to me.

"You are here to see Miss Alden?" he asks.

"Yes." I move around the corner. "Please. Where is she? She doesn't have her phone. The police told me to come here, and I ... I don't know where to go. She's alone ..."

The doctor smiles. "She's in Room 304."

Three zero four.

I take off down the hall.

"Thank you," I call over my shoulder.

My shoes squeak against the linoleum. The scent of the hospital—the acrid, pungent scent that I loathe so much—attacks me full force as I try not to run down the corridor.

I count down the room numbers as I go.

Zero eight. Zero seven. Zero six.

That's not even a fucking room.

Shit.

Zero five.

I find zero four and push open the door.

My stomach heaves.

There she is.

She's in a bed that's too big for her. Her face is swollen and purple. A blanket that looks rough and itchy is pulled up to her chin.

Her wrist is curled around a pink bin.

I make my way to the side of her bed. I take her hand in mine, lacing our fingers together and avoiding her IV, and press a kiss to her forehead.

Oh, Dara. I'm so fucking sorry.

My emotions splinter as my heart breaks into two. Fear swamps me with what she's going to say when she wakes up. And what I'm going to do if she's seriously hurt.

I close my eyes and brace myself for the flurry of memories to hit me. I know they're coming. I've known since I walked through the automatic doors.

"I don't know what happened." Morgan's eyes plead with me to erase the events of the past few hours. "I couldn't find you."

My chest burns as tears well in my eyes.

"It's bad, Wade. It's so bad."

I sit on the doctor's stool as my knees go weak. I bring Dara's hand to my lips and press a kiss against it.

"I'm so sorry," I whisper to her. "I shouldn't have let you go alone."

I take in her sweet, beautiful face and wonder what happened. *Who did this to her?*

Her eyelashes flutter. I hold my breath. Slowly, as if it pains them, her eyes open. It takes a second—the longest second of my life—for her to focus on me.

Then a slow, lopsided smile graces her swollen, purple lips.

Thank fuck. She's okay.

"*Wade,*" she breathes. "You found me."

"What happened to you? I was calling and calling, and you weren't answering."

She winces as she tries to move.

"Lie still," I tell her. "Just relax. It's okay. It's all going to be okay."

I watch as her body sags in relief. The stiffness she was holding in her limbs releases. Her smile stretches a bit further. The smallest sparkle comes back to her eyes, and I'm so fucking grateful to see it.

I blow out a breath and take her in—repeating over and over that she's here. She's okay.

No thanks to me.

"I was at Curt's," she says, her forehead wrinkling. Her bottom lip trembles. "He ... It was all an act."

"What was an act?"

"All of it." She wipes a tear with her free hand. "The house is off. I never want to see him again."

What the fuck?

Fury mixes with everything else rolling inside me, and if this motherfucker did something to her—I'll kill him.

"Did he—?"

"I don't want to talk about it anymore," she says. "Not about him."

"Okay. Fine. I won't mention it again."

She gathers herself before continuing.

"I was driving and crying," she says, her body starting to shake. "And ... I don't know." She can barely get the words out. "I saw lights, and then ... I woke up here."

I gently wipe her tears off her face. Each droplet that sneaks down her cheeks is like a knife that sliced her heart.

I knew this could happen. I fucking knew it. I knew Curt Bowery was no good, and I never should've let her go there alone.

My jaw clenches as guilt hammers me from every angle.

"Wade?" she asks. "What's wrong?"

I shake my head. "Nothing. Nothing is wrong. I'm just worried about you."

She watches me closely. I have to look away. I can't let her see how pathetic I am.

"I should've been there to protect you," I tell her while watching the clock on the wall. "I should've been there to run interference between you and Bowery."

"Don't. I'm glad you weren't there."

"I was so scared," Morgan said. "I lay there thinking that I was going to die either from my injuries or the police trying to cut me out of the car. I just wanted you, and you weren't there."

Tears cloud my vision. I refuse to look at Dara.

I love Dara Alden. I've stopped myself from thinking it so many times. But seeing her like this has stripped me of the ability to stop it now.

I know that I love her because I would trade places with her without a second thought. I would die for her. I would bleed out in the most horrific way if it kept her from feeling pain.

But the truth of the matter is that I'm the one who caused her this kind of pain because ultimately, I failed her in the same way I failed Morgan.

A solitary tear slips down my face.

I know it's futile now. I know because I tried my best.

I avoided falling for Dara. I tried to keep her from falling for me. But no matter what I did, the two of us felt inevitable.

I guess this ending was inevitable too. *Failing the women I love in tragic ways. It's what I do.*

"Did you happen to talk to my doctor?" she asks with heavy caution in her voice.

I nod, smearing the tear off my face.

"Well, okay," she whispers.

A nurse pops her head in the door before walking in fully. She smiles sadly at me.

"I hate to tell you this, but visiting hours are over," she says. "Dara is in stable condition and will probably be released tomorrow. You can come back when visiting hours start at ten in the morning."

"I can't leave her alone. She was nearly killed. Look at her."

"Wade, I'll be fine," Dara says.

"Sir, I understand," the nurse says. "I honestly do. But we're getting ready to move her upstairs to a room. There's a strict no visitor policy right now due to the state of the world. I hope you can understand that."

I hang my head.

When I walk out of here, it'll give Dara time to think. And if she's smart, she'll realize that I let her walk into a lion's cage alone.

It could've killed her.

And she deserves better—so much better.

I stand and kiss her forehead, letting my lips linger against her skin. She reaches up and touches the side of my face. I can feel her body shake as she cries.

I don't say anything. I don't know what more I can say. I know I can't verbalize *goodbye*, so why speak?

She deserves better. So much better.

With a long glance, I turn on my heel and walk out.

Chapter Forty

Wade

I've never watched the sun rise from the kitchen table before.

I'm reminded that it's where Dara likes to have her coffee so she can feel the warmth of the morning rays. No amount of warmth right now can make me feel alive.

Eliza handled me not coming in today well—better than I expected. I've avoided calls from Oliver as well as from my mom. The only call I haven't gotten is the one I hoped to get: from Dara.

My clothes stink like the hospital. The odor is embedded in my hair, and a shower would do me some good. Except I know she'll call as soon as my phone isn't right in front of me.

It's how life works.

I hoped that I would have been able to justify things more by the time the morning arrived. That maybe by dawn, I would think that staying with Dara would work out. That it was the right answer. That she was the one for me.

She is the one for me. The thought of not seeing her again destroys me in a way I know I haven't fully absorbed. My life is already colder. My heart harder. My soul dim.

But this isn't about me—it's about her. It's about doing what's best for Dara. And it's obvious that doing what's best is not being with me. After all, she got hurt because of me. Because I wasn't there for her even though I knew that I should've been.

My mom is wrong. I will never make a great husband and certainly never a good father.

Why? Why am I this way? I'm so acutely detailed with every other part of my life. I'm regimented. Bold. Decisive. Yet when it comes to women ...

They nearly die.

I jump as my phone buzzes. I whip it off the table.

My heart pounds so hard that I can barely concentrate on the words written on the device.

> Dara: Rusti is taking me home. I was released. In case you might come by.

I wait for more.

Nothing comes.

Rusti is taking me home.

In case you might come by.

I run my hands over my face and feel my heart break all over again.

She's done with me. I've let her down, and she knows it. It's unforgivable.

I can't blame her.

I'll blame myself for the rest of my life.

She didn't even ask if I wanted to pick her up. She didn't assume I would be by to see her. *Because she doesn't want me around.*

Because she doesn't need me.

I get to my feet and text her back.

> Me: I'd like to see you today. Just for a little bit. Would that be okay?

> Dara: That's fine. I'll be at home.

That's fine.

My heart breaks.

As I learned from my mother, those two words together mean the exact opposite.

I'm fine means that nothing is fine at all.

My spirit falls.

My heart breaks.

My life is effectively over.

~

Dara

"Do you want to talk or sleep?" Rusti fluffs the pillow under my head. "I'll lie beside you, and we can chat or nap. Your call."

I want to sleep. I want to close my eyes and drift off to a time before yesterday when my life wasn't in shambles.

My face hurts the most from crying all night. The nurse finally gave me something to help settle me, but it didn't stop the tears from falling.

"Did you actually tell him that you're pregnant?" Rusti asks, curling up in front of me. "Because I missed that part if you did."

"He knows."

"How?"

I don't know.

"I think the doctor must've told him," I say, my voice hollow.

I still have no idea why they would have told Wade, though. He's not listed as my next of kin, and hospitals are so strict on policy.

Maybe Gramps is friends with someone high up in the hospital.

The wealthy and their connections.

"He knew. I could see it in his eyes, Rusti. He was ... he was reacting to something besides me. I'm going to be fine. Just a little banged up."

"And pregnant." She grins. "You're having a baby. There's that."

"Stop saying that."

"Well, you might as well get used to it, *Mama*."

I roll my eyes, making her laugh. But I don't laugh. I can't find humor in my life imploding.

"I wonder if my mom felt this way," I say. "My dad didn't want me either."

"Dara ..."

I close my eyes after all. "I'll raise this baby. And if Wade doesn't want to help me, then I'll do it like Mom did. It'll be fine."

"And you have Cleo and me."

I snort.

My brain starts to get fuzzy, and I yawn. The doctor said I'd be in pain, and he wasn't wrong. But I bet he didn't predict the pain in my heart or how devastated it would feel when it broke into a million pieces.

There are no painkillers for that. I probably couldn't take them now anyway.

"I just need to have a conversation with him at some point ..."

I drift off to sleep.

Chapter Forty-One

Dara

"Hey."

Wade's voice stirs me from my nap. I don't really believe it's him that I hear. I have an even harder time realizing it's him in my doorway.

He looks ... awful. Dark spots under his eyes. Unshaven. He lacks his cool demeanor, and it's been replaced with something ... else. Something detached but also affected.

What the hell?

"Can I come in?" he asks.

"Sure. Yes. Of course."

I wince as I sit up.

He lunges into action, grabbing my arm, and helps me get situated. His touch is gentle, and I wish it didn't feel like the last time I would experience it.

His face is sullen as he sits.

"How do you feel?" he asks.

"Like I got hit by a truck."

He doesn't laugh. I shrug.

"The police came by today. Told me it wasn't my fault," I tell him. "The guy fell asleep at the wheel and hit me."

"Am I supposed to say that's good?"

I consider that. "Maybe. I don't know. None of it feels good right now."

He runs his hands up and down his face.

The baby feels like an elephant in the room. At some point, I suspect it'll feel like an elephant inside me too. It's such an odd feeling to know that there's a child in there, in my stomach, when I had no idea.

It doesn't feel real. I don't feel connected to it yet, which would probably worry me if I could stay awake long enough to think about it.

I open my mouth to just sputter something into the room, to take the pressure off the situation. *Maybe if I just bring up the baby, things will get easier?*

It takes longer for words to fall past my lips than usual. That's disappointing.

And unfortunate.

"I'm sorry, Dara," Wade says before I can get a word out.

"For what?"

He tugs on his hair before raising his face to mine.

The storm brewing behind his beautiful eyes is wild and intense.

My mouth goes dry as I watch him fight an internal battle.

I place a hand on my stomach and catch myself. Slowly, I drop it to the mattress.

He shifts in his seat. His hands wring together as if he's unable to keep himself from touching me. And out of all of the things I've endured with him since the accident—this is the worst.

His refusal to touch me.

It's so many steps in the wrong direction. The Wade of late couldn't stop touching me as if he needed the connection as much as I did.

As much as I do.

He held me at night. Reached for me in the morning. Wrapped his arms around me as soon as he saw me. It wasn't always just about the kiss that would usually follow or the ass grab that was also frequent.

It was about the connection. I could feel it in the way he nestled me against his chest. I could see it in his eyes ... just like I can see now that he's not going to do it today.

Tears well inside my eyes. I'm surprised I have any more left to shed.

"Are you here alone?" he asks. "I thought Rusti was staying with you."

"She had to go to work. I'm fine, you know. Small broken bone. Cracked rib. Mostly just super sore."

He worries his hand around his jaw.

"What are you sorry for?" I ask, circling back to the topic he just began and then walked away from.

"I told you when we started this—the night of Holt's wedding—that things between us would change," he says.

I nod. "Yes. And they did."

"And you trusted me. You took me at my word and let me into your life."

"Yes. I don't see where this is going, Wade."

He stands up and paces around my room. Watching him spikes my anxiety because I know something is wrong.

Suddenly, he stops. He looks at me like he's seen a ghost. His skin is pale, and his eyes are wide and just looking at him makes me still.

"In college, freshman year," he says, his voice so low that I can barely hear him. "I dated a girl named Morgan."

Okay.

"We dated for almost a year," he says. "I don't know if I loved her or if it was just easy or if she was just the first girl I really liked." He shrugs sadly. "But she told me that she was pregnant."

What?

My brows pull together as my heart skips a beat.

He has a child?

"I didn't know what to do, Dara. Hell, I was scared shitless. I was nineteen years old, just starting my life, and—out of all of my brothers —I got a girl pregnant. It was ... It was a nightmare. For both of us."

I don't know what to say, and I'm afraid to ask questions. He may never get back to this moment of vulnerability if I do.

I suck in a breath.

"We decided to keep it," he says. "She desperately wanted to be a mother, and someone told her at some point that she might not be able to conceive. But she did. And, eventually, she was so happy."

He stares into the hallway, a smile brushing lightly against his lips.

"We decided not to tell anyone," he says. "Not until we got used to it first and could come up with a plan to tell our parents so they would know we had it handled. I knew my parents would be disappointed but would ultimately be fine about it. Hers ... not so much."

I swallow hard. My breathing picks up.

"There was a night. *A party.*" He makes a sour face. "She wanted to go. I was worried about it—about her being there with these rowdy college kids while pregnant. But she was adamant that we still have fun."

Oh, no.

My body chills as I watch a blast of fear flash across his face.

"I lost track of her somehow. Someone put something in her drink. Or at least that's what we suspected happened."

"Don't drink anything that isn't given to you by my brothers or me."

Wade ...

"She was gone." His voice is detached as he replays this moment in his mind. "I couldn't find her. I looked everywhere. Finally, someone called me from the hospital ..."

He looks at me with a single tear streaking down his face. The pain that's etched into his skin, embedded in his eyes, nearly pierces my heart with its intensity.

I want to reach for him, to hold him, to comfort him. But I know he won't let me. I can see that, too, in his face.

"She lost the baby, Dara. She lost our child *because of me.*"

My hand falls to my stomach.

I've only known that I'm pregnant for a day. I'm not even attached to the idea of it yet. But I already know that if I lost this child, I would be devastated.

Tears fill my eyes as I consider hearing the words she must've heard. My heart aches for the pain that Wade must have felt.

And also the guilt.

"We split because she went home. I thought her spirit was completely broken. She couldn't look at me, and I couldn't look at either of us. I vowed never to set myself up to feel that kind of pain again," he says. "*And then I met you.*"

My tears break the dam ... for so many reasons.

For his experience. For my experience.

For his pain. For my pain.

For his child. For our child.

And for the life I know we're never going to have.

"If that had been you last night with our child ..." He smiles sadly. "If you had been pregnant and lost our baby ..."

I open my mouth and then close it again.

Had been pregnant.

Does he not know?

"Wade, I thought you knew—"

"It's not fair to you for us to be together."

"Wade—"

"I should've gone with you. I should've been driving you. I should've been there to stand beside you to tell Curt to fuck off."

"Wade, listen to me—"

"I can't be the one. I have nothing to give you," he says, panic filling his voice. "I don't want marriage. I don't want kids. I don't want that responsibility. I can't have that responsibility, Dara. I can't. I can't risk it."

I cover my mouth with my hands and feel my world fall apart.

My body shakes as I cry. It hurts. Everything hurts. My whole existence somehow hurts.

How much simpler—how much clearer—can he be?

He stops at the side of my bed and bends down. The sweetest, gentlest kiss is placed on the top of my head. I can feel one of his tears splash against my forehead.

"I love you, Dara Alden," he whispers. "And I want you to find someone who can take care of you. Who will give you all the things in the world that you want. But that guy isn't me."

I sob as he walks out the door.

I was right all along. It was better not to trust in someone else for my joy. *Because they can take it away. They can leave. They can reject you.*

I touch my hand to my stomach.
Reject us.

CHAPTER FORTY-TWO

Wade

Fuck. All. Of. This.

I storm into the conference room of Mason Limited with a printout in my hand. I toss the stack of papers I stapled together before I came here on the table. They flutter about before landing in front of Oliver.

"Wow. Bad day?" Oliver asks, picking up the papers.

"You get this pissed off before lunch?" Boone makes a face. "Easy, brother. You're going to have a heart attack."

Holt waves at Boone to cut the shit.

"What's going on, Wade?" Holt asks, rocking back in his chair.

"That." My voice booms through the room as I point at the papers. *"That motherfucker."*

Boone whistles through his teeth. "And I thought Wade had been mad at me before. Yikes."

"This is not the day, Boone," I say, anger making my hands shake.

"Noted."

Holt peers over Oliver's shoulder as he flips the page.

in check. Will it even matter in the long run? Sure, if he really does love me, it will help. But if he still doesn't want children, then there's not a lot I can do, and no amount of love will fix that.

"I want to ..." He shrugs. "I want you in my life. I want you to be my partner. My wife. My best friend." He scoots closer. "I never want to not have you by my side. I want to be your first call. I want people to know that you are Dara Mason, and they better not mess with you or I'll come for them."

You cannot suck tears back into your tear ducts.

They splash down my cheeks.

There is something very different in his expression, especially compared to the last time he eviscerated me with his proclamation of love. The last time, he was halfway out the door—terrified, sad, immovable in his rejection.

Now? Now he's reaching into my heart, showing me it's lovable and desired and wanted—providing the balm it has needed.

His love. His desire to stay.

A future. A refuge.

A family.

This man. This fucking man.

"I can take care of myself," I say.

"I know you can. That's one of the reasons I love you. But you don't have to because you have me."

Do I?

I get to my feet and put a little space between us. It's not this easy. It can't be.

"What about your family doing business with Curt? Curt and I didn't end things well," I admit. "I'm not sure how he would feel working with you if he knew that you and I were together like that."

Wade grins. "We aren't working with him."

"No, your brothers are. The Mexico project. I heard Oliver talking about it at your mom's."

He stands too. "And when they heard about your grandfather's bullshit, they pulled the plug. Oliver and Holt sent a letter yesterday to cancel everything. It's done."

I heave a breath. I can't believe what I'm hearing.

"Why would they do that?" I ask, my hands trembling.

"Because you're family."

My face screws up into one of those ugly cry memes on the internet, and I can't stop the sob that erupts from my chest.

Wade catches me in his arms and holds me tight. He runs a hand over my head and whispers things in my ear that I can't hear over my stupid cries.

I don't know how to deal with this.

I pull back, wiping my eyes with my hands. It's a routine I'm familiar with these days.

"They would also be very pleased if you will take me back," he says.

My chest shakes as I try to calm down. I sit on the edge of the sofa and breathe.

"I have something else," he says, handing me an envelope from his back pocket.

I take it with a heavy dose of suspicion. I unfold the letter inside and gasp.

Dear Mr. Mason,

This letter serves to inform you of our agreement for purchase of the Bartholomew Gardens estate. A formal contract will be sent from our attorney to yours.

It gives me a great deal of happiness to know that my precious property will be in good hands. I hope it brings you and Dara the joy it's given me over the years.

Respectfully,
Philip Bartholomew

"Wade. What did you do?" I crack the paper against my leg and look at him in pure disbelief. "What is this?"

"I bought it."

"I ... *Why?*"

I have to laugh. I think I'm in shock.

"Because even if you don't take me back today, you will," he says. "You have to. We have this connection that will bring us together over and over until you relent. I know it. It's the only way it can be."

I hang my head and try to calm down.

"You bought the entire thing? What are you going to do with it?" I ask.

"I thought we'd figure it out. Maybe we could put a house on a piece of it."

My face snaps to his. *He's serious.*

"It would make a hell of a photography studio," he says.

"My ... I don't know what to say."

This is too much. Way too much. And way, way too much considering he doesn't know we're having a baby.

Shit.

I blow out a breath and hope that I don't puke.

I have to tell him *now*. I have to tell him even if it wipes out everything that he's said and changes the trajectory of this conversation—and our future. Because he has the right to know and the right to make decisions for himself.

How do I do this gently?

"You told me that you don't want to get married or have kids," I say carefully. "That's big stuff."

He chuckles. "I was wrong."

"Just like that? You were wrong."

He gets on one knee in front of me. "I don't have a ring. Don't panic."

I laugh, verging on panic.

"It turns out that my father isn't a complete idiot, and he taught me a few things about myself lately," Wade says. "And I guess I can't control the entire world like I thought. Crazy, right?"

I grin. "True. But you didn't answer my question."

I hold my breath while he chooses what to say. I say a silent prayer, too, that this resolves well and what that means, I don't know.

For us both to be happy. For us to be friends. For us to figure out a way to make this work for the sake of our child—regardless of anything else.

Finally, he smiles. It's a cheek-splitting, ear-to-ear smile that I've never seen on him before. It lights *me* up on the inside, and I feel like my stressors have been lifted by this one thing.

"I'll put it to you like this," he says. "If you want to get married today, I'm in. And if you told me you were having triplets today, I'd be thrilled."

"No, you wouldn't."

"Well, maybe not thrilled, but I'd be happy. Mostly. I mean, okay, maybe not triplets. But I want to have children with you, Dara. I want you to be the mother of my children. I want to ..." He closes his eyes. "I want to let go of the past and build a future." He opens his eyes. They shine like diamonds. "*With you.*"

I lean away, putting a little distance between us. "Well, I have something to tell you."

"Lay it on me."

"We are having a baby."

He laughs. "Shut up."

"No, we are."

His laughter fades as he searches my eyes.

His smile falters.

He gets up off his knees and stares down at me.

"Do you mean it?" he asks.

I nod, tasting sweet potatoes in the acid of my stomach. I grab the book with a trembling hand.

"See? Rusti bought this for me a few days ago."

"How did you ...? When did you ... find out?"

"At the hospital."

His face pales. "Oh, fuck. Are you okay? *Dara.* Why didn't you tell me?"

"You were kind of having a meltdown," I say, standing up and tossing the book on the sofa. "I didn't want to add to your mayhem."

"But I ... You let me just walk out of there."

"I wasn't going to beg you to stay with me!"

"Why not?"

"Because I have some pride. If you don't want this baby—which is what you *explicitly* said to me—then that's fine. I'll be fine. You—"

"Marry me."

I cover my face with my hands. He pries them off one at a time.

"Marry me," he says again, more emphatically this time. "I need to take care of you. God knows that I need to apologize to you and make it up to you. And I need to punish you for not telling me this and allowing me to hurt you even more." He pulls me into his chest again. "Never let anyone hurt you, Dara. Not even me."

I wrap my arms around his waist and sigh. "Don't let me hurt you either."

He grins. "I love you."

"And I love you too."

He kisses the top of my head. "And I guess we have more to love, huh?"

I can feel his body stiffen and his heart race with my hand on his chest.

"Can I tell you something?" I ask.

"Anything."

"I'm a little scared."

His body shakes as he tries to withhold his chuckle. "I'm happy to hear that ... because I'm fucking terrified."

I laugh, relieved as I've ever been to know that someone else is afraid.

"You'll be a great dad," I tell him.

"I don't know. Maybe. I'll sure as hell try." He screws up his face. "But I share DNA with *Boone. What ... What does that mean?*"

My laughter grows as he pulls me against him even more.

"Well, Boone has good points," I say.

"Name two."

"He's charming," I offer.

"Debatable."

"And he's funny."

"*Eh.* Also debatable." This time, he lets his chuckle go free. "We'll figure it out, though."

I shrug. "We don't really have a choice."

"You always have a choice, my lady."

I turn in his arms and take in his handsome face. He really is my Catnip. So beautiful. So kind. So creative and intelligent ... and *mine*.

"I choose ... this. Whatever it is," I say. "I choose the baby, and I choose ... you."

He smirks. "Damn good thing because you didn't have a choice about me. I'm yours whether you want me or not." He kisses my hand. "No big wedding, though, okay? I mean, if you really want to, but let's not."

"I haven't even agreed to marry you yet."

He laughs. "Well, hurry up and agree to it so we can move on." He looks down and smiles. "Together."

I want to tease him. I want to poke at him like I always do and make him lose his mind. But I think we've been through enough over the past few weeks to last for a while.

"Our baby is due in the summer," I whisper.

He places his hand on my stomach. "I'm going to need you to agree to be my wife *now*."

"And if I don't?"

He growls, making me laugh.

"Wade Mason, I would love nothing more than to be your wife."

"Good. Because you didn't have a choice."

He picks me up gingerly and carries me to my bedroom. He lays me on the blankets and covers my body with his.

"I thought I'd never have this again," I whisper.

He brushes a strand of hair off my face. "We needed a break to realize how much we were meant to be together."

"You think?"

"I know. I know everything, remember?"

My laughter is caught by his kisses, and I fade into his arms.

Like an old man once told me, nothing worth having ever comes easy, and this happy ending took some work.

But it was worth every second for this sweet resolution.

Epilogue

Six weeks later

Dara

"Oh! This place is cool," I say.

Wade and I walk into The Gold Room, a bar and restaurant owned by Shaye's friend Nate. Apparently, Shaye worked here for a time in her life and still comes in to help—much to Oliver's chagrin. But Shaye does what Shaye wants, and Oliver has to deal with it.

"Hey, you guys!" Jaxi waves at the tables the family has placed together to seat us all.

The family. *My family.*

I wave at her, then Blaire, and then toss Bellamy a smile. Kel is cuddled up to her, sleeping like the little love bug he is.

Wade wraps an arm around my waist and guides me to two seats near the end. Siggy and Larissa are chatting away about jewelry as Wade and I sit. He takes the chair next to Oliver to save me from listening to business chatter.

"This is fun," I say, shrugging off my jacket. "I've never been here before."

Siggy beams. "Me neither. But if all of you kids can agree on a bar for a Friday lunch the first Friday of the month—I'm in."

We all laugh.

Hollis walks in and sits across from me and next to Larissa. He nods at Wade and then smiles at me.

"How are you?" I ask him.

"Good. Had a lyric that was driving me crazy for the past two nights, but I think I've got it today. Just sent it to Coy to see if it works."

"Where's Coy?" I ask.

"Nashville. I think he's coming home tomorrow. Is that right, Bells?"

Bellamy shrugs. "I've discovered that handling two Mason men is more difficult than I expected."

Everyone chuckles.

"Imagine having six of them—five little ones and then a big pain in the butt," Siggy tells her.

"If we have another and it's a boy, I'm done." Bellamy laughs. "The testosterone is already killing me."

A server comes up to our table. "Can I get you guys anything to drink?"

I order a water and Wade a tea. Hollis orders a beer.

"We set a date," I tell the table.

This immediately gets Siggy's interest.

"You did? When, sweetheart?" she asks.

I completely love Siggy Mason. To say she was over the moon when we told her that I was pregnant is the biggest understatement in the universe. But it's also been the moments that I've had with her on my own that make me adore her the way that I do.

Nothing will ever replace the relationship that I had with my mom, and I miss her every day and hate that she won't get to meet her grandchild—the first of many, according to Wade. But Siggy has wiggled her way into my heart and welcomed me unconditionally, and I doubt she knows how much that has been a precious balm to my soul.

As for Rosie? Still working on that little monkey. I'm not sure she's ever going to approve of the woman who stole her man.

I just look at Wade and smile. He nods, encouraging me to go ahead and share our news.

"Monday," I say, laughing.

Siggy's face drops. "Monday? *This Monday?* How are you getting married *this Monday?*"

"Mother, relax," Wade says, holding a hand toward her. "We're going to go to the Justice of the—"

"At least have them come to my house," Siggy says.

Wade rubs his temples.

"If that would make you happy, then that's fine with us," I say, elbowing Wade in the side. "I don't want to get married when I'm huge and miserable. And there's really no point in throwing a huge wedding when we have everything we need, and we already live together."

"And you're building a big-ass house," Hollis says, plucking the lemon slice off the side of Larissa's tea.

At the mention of the house, I swoon and grab Wade's hand.

The house Wade designed for us is absolute perfection. It'll be situated on the back corner of the Bartholomew Gardens—a name that I can't part with—with unencumbered views of the greenery.

I lean over and kiss Wade's cheek.

"Yes, we are building a big-ass house," Wade says, resting our entwined hands on his thigh.

"Oh," Siggy says. "Why not get married at the Gardens?"

"Because Blaire did that," I say. "She should be able to keep that as her personal memory."

Blaire smiles warmly. "You know I wouldn't care. Heck, you own it now."

"I still think it's more precious if you're the only one."

"Thank you, Dara."

"Of course."

The family chatters away about different things, from business deals on one end with Holt and Oliver, to Rosie's latest antics from Jaxi and Boone. Bellamy rocks the baby while Blaire plays with Kelvin's toes.

Wade joins Oliver and Holt's conversation here and there—mostly to correct things they've said, which makes me giggle.

The server returns with everyone's drink but Hollis's. She cringes.

"I'm sorry. I need to get one out of the cooler in the back. I'll be back with it in a second," she says.

"It's fine," he says. "Thank you." Then he looks at Wade. "Do you golf?"

"Me?" Wade asks, running our hands up and down his thigh. "Not really. I mean, I can, but ..."

"He sucks!" Boone yells from the other end of the table.

Wade rolls his eyes. "I do not suck. Why do you ask?"

"Well, I'm in a golf tournament this weekend, and I thought maybe you'd like to go with me."

Wade seems surprised at the question. "Well, I can. If you need me to."

"I don't need you to," Hollis says. "I just thought it might be fun to get outside and swing some clubs."

"Go," I whisper.

Wade is still quite a private person. We both like our solitude when we're peopled out. We love the quiet, but now, our quiet doesn't equate to loneliness. For either of us.

He has made more of an effort to be with his brothers, particularly when we spend time as couples. He doesn't seek out their company, so nothing has really changed there. But he doesn't spurn their requests for his time as he did when I first met him.

Except for Boone. He still finds excuses most of the time when Boone wants to go on what Boone calls *adventures*.

Wade doesn't fill every weekend hour with work now either. That's perhaps the biggest shock. I've yet to get him to be late for anything, but I've let that go. You can't win them all.

According to Boone, Wade has loosened the stick up his ass since he met me. *His words, not mine.*

Wade nods. He stiffens and forces a tight smile. "All right. Let me know when and I'll go. Sounds ... *fun*."

Only Wade can make the word fun sound like torture. But, hey— he's going. And I think we'll all take that as progress.

Hollis laughs. He turns to the server with his beer when his hand hits the table so hard that everyone looks his way.

The woman who stands beside him holding the bottle isn't the same server as before.

This girl, a few years younger than Hollis by all accounts, has brown curly hair. She, too, looks like she's seen a ghost.

Hollis opens his mouth, but nothing comes out.

She takes a step backward, her brows pulled together.

A half-laugh escapes her throat as she points the bottle toward Hollis.

"You ..." she says, shaking the bottle so hard that some of the liquid splashes out and falls onto the floor. "Who are you?"

Hollis stands so quickly that his chair scratches against the floor and then falls over.

No one says a word.

No one moves.

We all watch this strange interaction between Hollis and the bartender girl.

He walks toward her slowly.

I glance at Larissa. She shrugs.

"What is your name?" Hollis asks her.

"Paige." She sets the bottle down on a table. "Who are you?"

"Hollis."

Paige tries to grab a chair but misses. She falls to the side, and Hollis reaches out, keeping her from falling at the last minute.

He holds her by her arms and looks at her with ... *horror? Surprise? Shock?*

My blood runs cold.

I look at Larissa again. "Hollis?" She calls to her boyfriend, but he doesn't turn around.

He stays focused on Paige.

Maybe I'm seeing things, but there's a strange resemblance between Hollis and Paige. The same color hair. The same strong jaw. The same ridiculous eyelashes and the same athletic build.

It can't be.

Can it?

Tears stream down Paige's face. Her hands shake so hard that I wonder if she's having a seizure.

"My name …" She stops to catch her breath. A sob hiccups from her. "My name is *Harlee* Paige Carmichael. My last name was Hudson. I was adopted."

Hollis lunges forward and pulls her into his chest. Their sobs rip through the restaurant as we all watch in disbelief.

His huge arms capture the girl so tightly that I wonder if she can breathe.

Their voices are muffled as they hold each other in embraces so tight that I wonder if they'll ever separate.

The Mason family looks at one another with a mixture of tears and surprise in their eyes. Wade leans into me and whispers, "Hollis has been looking for his sister for years. He thought she was dead."

Oh. My. God.

I grab Wade's hand and hold it tight. Tears flicker in my eyes too.

Hollis's back shakes until he pulls back and looks Paige in the face.

"Are you serious?" he asks her. "You're *Harlee*?" He chokes back a lump. "You're *my* Harlee? I've been looking for you forever."

Her lips tremble. "I didn't think I'd ever see you again. I have these memories of you, but …" She yelps a sob. "I didn't even know if you were actually real or if I made you up."

He grabs her for another quick hug.

"*How are you here*?" she asks, wiping the river of tears off her face. "Why? How? I'm just …" She laughs. "I'm in shock."

He runs a hand down his jaw. His hand shakes. "Dennis Egelbert told me you were dead. He said your car ran off into the river years ago. I don't understand."

"That's the story they told people around town," she says, sniffling. "Our biological mom was looking for me at one point. That's how I found out I was adopted. My parents—my adoptive parents—had to sit me down and … it was … not a good day. But it was all fine." She grins. "It's … I can't believe it's you."

Hollis hugs her yet again. "I have so much to ask you. I … Just … Can we …" He blows out a breath and wipes the tears off his face. "I can't believe it. I can't fucking believe this."

Paige takes a few napkins off a table and hands him some. They face each other as if they're afraid to look away. Afraid the other will be gone again.

"I'm working now, and we're shorthanded," she says. "I get off at ten. Maybe we could sit here and catch up? I know Nate won't mind."

"Yeah. I'll be back tonight then," Hollis says.

Paige touches his cheek and bursts out a single laugh. "You're real."

Tears come again, and they look at each other. It's an incredible scene, and there's not a dry eye at our table.

"Paige! We need you!" someone shouts from the kitchen.

"See you tonight," Paige says.

"Yes. Of course."

We all watch the two of them separate like it pains them more than anything in the world. But there's a peace on Hollis's face that warms my heart so much that I think it might burst.

I get up and get Hollis's beer off the adjacent table.

"Here. I think you need this," I say, handing him the bottle.

The table buzzes with reactions from what just happened. Hollis pulls Larissa into a deep hug.

"It's funny how things work out, isn't it?" Wade whispers in my ear. "Things always work out for the best."

I think about everything we've been through—both separately and together. And through the wins and losses, accidents and plans, mistakes and moments of inexplicable loss, we made it. It got us here. And I wouldn't want to be anywhere else.

Would you like a little more Wade and Dara? (I did too!) There's a bonus scene for you HERE.

Also ... *drumroll, please* ... Paige (Harlee!) Carmichael's family has a series! Keep reading for Chapter One of FLIRT, book one in the Carmichael Family Series.

MEET THE CARMICHAEL FAMILY

WANTED: A SITUATION-SHIP

I'm a single female who's tired of relationships ruining my life. However, there are times when a date would be helpful. If you're a single man, preferably mid-twenties to late-thirties, and are in a similar situation, we might be a match.

Candidate must be handsome, charming, and willing to pretend to have feelings for me (on a sliding scale, as the event requires). Ability to discuss a wide variety of topics is a plus. Must have your own transportation and a (legal) job.

This will be a symbiotic agreement. In exchange for your time, I will give you mine. Need someone to flirt with you at a football party? Go, team! Want a woman to make you look good in front of your boss? Let me find my heels. Would you love for someone to be obsessed with you in front of your ex? I'm applying my red lipstick now.

If interested, please email me. Time is of the essence.

My best friend, Jovie, points at my computer screen. The glitter on her pink fingernail sparkles in the light. "You can't post that."

I fold my arms across my chest. "And why not?"

Instead of answering me, she takes another bite of her chicken wrap. A dribble of mayonnaise dots the corner of her mouth.

"A lot of help you are," I mutter, rereading the post I drafted instead of pricing light fixtures for work. The words are written in a pretty font on Social, my go-to social media platform.

Country music from the nineties mixes with the laughter of locals sitting around us in Smokey's, my favorite beachside café. Along the far wall, a map of the state of Florida made of wine corks sways gently in the ocean breeze coming through the open windows.

"Would you two like anything else?" Rebecca, our usual lunchtime server, pauses by the table. "I think we have some Key lime pie left."

"I'm too irritable for pie today," I say.

"*You* don't want *pie*? That's a first," she teases me.

Jovie giggles.

"I know," I say, releasing a sigh. "That's the state of my life right now. I don't even want pie."

"Wow. Okay. This sounds serious. What's up? Maybe I can help," Rebecca says.

Jovie wipes her mouth with a napkin. "Let me cut in here real quick before she tries to snowball you into thinking her harebrained idea is a good one."

I roll my eyes. "It *is* a good one."

"I'll give you the CliffsNotes version," Jovie says, side-eyeing me.

"Brooke got an invitation to her grandma's birthday party, and instead of just not going—"

"I can't *not go.*"

"Or showing up as the badass single chick she is," Jovie continues, silencing me with a look, "she wrote a post for Social that's basically an ad for a fake boyfriend."

"Correction—it *is* an ad for a fake boyfriend."

Rebecca rests a hand on her hip. "I don't see the problem."

"*Thank you,*" I say, staring at Jovie. "I'm glad someone understands me here."

Jovie throws her hands in the air, sending a napkin flying right along with them.

Satisfaction is written all over my face as I sit back in my chair with a smug smile. The more I think about having a *situation-ship* with a guy —a word I read in a magazine at the salon while waiting two decades for my color to process—the more it makes sense.

Instead of having relations with a man, have situations. Done.

What's not to love about that?

"But, before I tell you to dive into this whole thing, why can't you just go alone, Brooke?" Rebecca asks.

"Oh, *I can* go alone. I just generally prefer to avoid torture whenever possible."

"I still don't understand why you need a date to your grandma's birthday party."

"Because this isn't *just* a birthday party," I say. "It's labeled that to cover up the fact that my mom and her sister, my aunt Kim, are having a daughter-of-the-year showdown. They're using my poor grandma Honey's eighty-fifth birthday as a dog and pony show—and my cousin Aria and I are the ponies."

"*Okay.*" Rebecca looks at me dubiously before switching her attention to Jovie. "And why are you against this whole thing?"

Jovie takes enough cash to cover our lunch plus the tip and hands it to Rebecca. *Perks of ordering the same lunch most days.* Then she gathers her things.

"I'm not against it in *theory,*" Jovie says. "I'm against it in *practice.* I understand the perks of having a guy around to be arm candy when needed. But I'm not supporting this decision ... this *mayhem* ... for two reasons." She looks at me. "For one, your family will see any post you make on Social. You don't think they'll use it as ammunition against you?"

This is probably true.

"Second," Jovie continues. "I hate, hate, *hate* your aunt Kim, and I loathe the fact that your mom makes you feel like you have to do anything more than be your amazing self to win her favor. Screw them both."

My heart swells as I take in my best friend.

Jovie Reynolds was my first friend in Kismet Beach when I moved here two and a half years ago. We reached for the same can of pineapple rings, knocking over an entire display in Publix. As we picked up the mess, we traded recipes—hers for a vodka cocktail and mine for air fryer pineapple.

We hung out that evening—with her cocktail and my air fryer creations—and have been inseparable since.

"My mom is not a bad person," I say in her defense, even though I'm not so sure that's true from time to time. "She's just ..."

"A bad person," Jovie says.

I laugh. "*No.* I just ... nothing I can do is good enough for her. She hated Geoff when I married him at twenty and said I was too young. But was she happy when that ended in a divorce? Nope. According to *her*, I didn't try hard enough."

Rebecca frowns.

"And then Geoff started banging Kim and—"

"*What?*" Rebecca yelps, her eyes going wide.

"Exactly. Bad people," Jovie says, shaking her head.

"So your ex-husband will be at your grandma's party with your aunt? Is that what you're saying?" Rebecca asks.

I nod. "Yup."

She stacks our plates on top of one another. The ceramic clinks through the air. "On that note, why can't you just not go? Avoid it altogether?"

"Because my grandma Honey is looking forward to this, and she called me to make sure I was coming. I couldn't tell her no." My heart tightens when I think of the woman I love more than any other. "And, you know, my mom has made it abundantly clear that if I miss this, I will probably break Honey's heart, and she'll die, and it'll be my fault."

"Wow. That's a freight train of guilt to throw around," Rebecca says, wincing.

I glance down at my computer. The post is still there, sitting on the screen and waiting for my final decision. Although it is a genius idea, if I do say so myself—Jovie is probably right. It'll just cause more problems than it's worth.

I close the laptop and shove it into my bag. Then I hoist it on my shoulder. "It's complicated. I want to go and celebrate with my grandma but seeing my aunt with my ex-husband ..." I wince. "Also, there will be my mother's usual diatribe and comparisons to Aria, proving that I'm a failure in everything that I do."

"But if you had a boyfriend to accompany you, you'd save face with the enemy and have a buffer against your mother. Is that what you're thinking?" Rebecca asks.

"Yeah. I don't know how else to survive it. I can't walk in there alone, or even with Jovie, and deal with all of that mess. If I just had someone hot and a little handsy—make me look irresistible—it would kill all of my birds with one hopefully *hard* stone."

I wink at my friends.

Rebecca laughs. "Okay. I'm Team Fake Boyfriend. Sorry, Jovie."

Jovie sighs. "I'm sorry for me too because I have to go back to work. And if I avoid the stoplights, I can make it to the office with thirty seconds to spare." She air-kisses Rebecca. "Thanks for the extra mayo."

I laugh. "See you tomorrow, Rebecca."

"Bye, girls."

Jovie and I walk single-file through Smokey's until we reach the exit. Immediately, we reach for the sunglasses perched on top of our heads and slide them over our eyes.

The sun is bright, nearly blinding in a cloudless sky. I readjust my bag so that the thin layer of sweat starting to coat my skin doesn't coax the leather strap down my arm.

"Call me tonight," Jovie says, heading to her car.

"I will."

"Rehearsal for the play got canceled tonight, so I might go to Charlie's. If I don't, I may swing by your house."

"How's the thing with Charlie going? I didn't realize you were still talking to him."

She laughs. "I wasn't. He pissed me off. But he came groveling back last night, and I gave in." She shrugs. "What can I say? I'm a sucker for a good grovel."

"I think it's the theater girl in you. You love the dramatics of it all."

"That I do. It's a problem."

"Well, I'll see you when I see you then," I say.

"Bye, Brooke."

I give her a little wave and make my way up Beachfront Boulevard.

The sidewalk is fairly vacant with a light dusting of sand. In another month, tourists will fill the street that leads from the ocean to the shops filled with trinkets and ice cream in the heart of Kismet Beach. For now, it's a relaxing and hot walk back to the office.

My mind shifts from the heat back to the email reminder I received during lunch. *To Honey's party.* It takes all of one second for my stomach to cramp.

"I shouldn't have eaten all of those fries," I groan.

But it's not lunch that's making me unwell.

A mixture of emotions rolls through me. I don't know which one to land on. There's a chord of excitement about the event—at seeing Honey and her wonderful life be celebrated, catching up with Aria and the rest of my family, and the general concept of *going home.* But there's so much apprehension right alongside those things that it drowns out the good.

Kim and Geoff together make me ill. It's not that I miss my ex-husband; I'm the one who filed for divorce. But they will be there, making things super awkward for me in front of everyone we know.

Not to mention what it will do to my mother.

Geoff hooking up with Kim is my ultimate failure, according to Mom. Somehow, it embarrasses *her,* and that's unforgivable.

"For just once, I'd like to see her and not be judged," I mumble as I sidestep a melting glob of blue ice cream.

Nothing I have ever done has been good enough for Catherine

Bailey. Marrying Geoff was an atrocity at only twenty years old. My dream to work in interior architecture wasn't deemed serious enough as a life path. *"You're wasting your time and our money, Brooke."* And when I told her I was hired at Laguna Homes as a lead designer for one of their three renovation teams? I could hear her eyes rolling.

The office comes into view, and my spirits lift immediately. I shove all thoughts of the party out of my brain and let my mind settle back into happier territory. *Work.* The one thing I love.

I step under the shade of an adorable crape myrtle tree and then turn up a cobblestone walkway to my office.

The small white building is tucked away from the sidewalk. It sits between a row of shops with apartments above them and an Italian restaurant only open in the evenings. The word *Laguna Homes* is printed in seafoam green above a black awning.

My shoes tap against the wooden steps as I make my way to the door. A rush of cool air, kissed by the scent of eucalyptus essential oil, greets me as I step inside.

"How was lunch?" Kix asks, standing in the doorway of his corner office. My boss's smile is kind and genuine, just like everything else about him. "Let me guess—you met Jovie for lunch at Smokey's?"

I laugh. "It's like you know me or something."

He chuckles.

Kix and Damaris Carmichael are two of my favorite people in the world. When I met Damaris at a trade show three years ago, and we struck up a conversation about tile, I knew she was special. Then I met her husband and discovered he had the same soft yet sturdy energy. All six of their children possess similar qualities—even Moss, the superintendent on my renovation team. Although I'd never admit that to him.

"I swung by Parasol Place this afternoon," Kix says. "It's looking great. You were right about taking out the wall between the living room and dining room. I love it. It makes the whole house feel bigger."

I blush under the weight of his compliment. "Thanks."

"Did Moss tell you about the property I'm looking at for your team next?" Kix asks.

"No. Moss doesn't tell me anything."

Kix grins. "I'm sure he tells you all kinds of things you don't need to know."

"You say that like you have experience with him," I say, laughing.

"Only a few years." He laughs too. "It's another home from the sixties. I got a lead on it this morning and am on my way to look at it now."

"Take pictures. You know I love that era, and if you get it, I want to be able to start envisioning things right away."

"You and your visions." He shakes his head. "Gina is in the back making copies. I told her we'd keep our eye on the door until she gets back out here, so it would be great if you could do that."

"Absolutely," I say, walking backward toward my office. "Be safe. *And take pictures.*"

"I will. Enjoy the rest of your day, Brooke."

"You, too."

I reach behind me to find my office door open. I take another step back and then turn toward my desk. Someone moves beside my filing cabinet just as I flip on the light.

"Ah!" I shriek, clutching my chest.

My heart pounds out of control until I get my bearings and focus on the man looking back at me.

I set my bag down on a chair and blow out a shaky breath. "Dammit, Moss!"

He leans against the cabinet and smiles at me cheekily.

"We're going to have to stop meeting like this," he says. "People are going to talk."

Read or listen to Flirt on Amazon and Audible.

ACKNOWLEDGEMENTS

I always thank my Creator first. This time is no exception.

My family is so patient and supportive and I am nothing without my husband, Saul, and my four sons Alexander, Aristotle, Achilles, and Ajax. I love you.

They aren't here to see me publish this book, my thirtieth. Still, I know my parents would be so proud of me. Thank you for raising me with a solid work ethic, Mom and Dad. You're incredibly missed.

I'd like to give a warm thank you to Peggy and Rob Williams. You aren't my parents but you treat me like I'm your daughter. There aren't really words to say what that means to me.

My assistant has been with me for twenty-two books now. She's more than my right hand; she's a dear friend. Thank you, Tiffany Remy, for keeping me in line and focused on all the right things. (Usually.)

Kari March is the best. She's my oldest "book world" friend and the most creative person I know. Thank you for being you.

I would like to thank Marion Making Manuscripts for working with me yet again. Your tireless energy and attention to detail are the best in the game. You helped polish this manuscript in so many ways and I'm forever grateful to work with you.

Thank you to Jenny Sims for cleaning up the edits. You do such brilliant work on my crazy deadlines. Thank you for always saying yes to me.

I've known Michele Ficht for years and am blessed to now work with her as a proofing partner. Her eyes are so sharp and her positivity and encouragement so appreciated. I adore you, Michele.

This book is what it is in large part due to Carleen Riffle. I'm floored by her mind, her creativity—her innate sense when something is just a little off. Her honesty and brilliance are two of the many things that I love so much about her. Thank you for bringing Team Mess back to life, my friend.

Anjelica Grace is a trusty critique partner that didn't quit on me, much to my surprise. This one was a challenge in a number of ways and she hung right with me. Her trademark honesty and humor really pulled me through. I appreciate you, Anjelica.

A special thank you to Susan Rayner. I rely on your positivity and energy more than you'll ever know. You are a light in my life and I can't thank you enough for your friendship.

And, I suppose, I should thank Jen Costa. You didn't quite have the endurance for this one, my friend, but I love you anyway. Ha!

Mandi Beck knows most of the reasons I love her, but I do look forward to seeing her again in person and telling her all the other reasons that probably slipped her mind. That is, if she'd let me. But she won't. It's a small part of her charm and a big part of why I love her so much.

S.L. Scott cheered me on virtually as I made my way to The End. She's the kind of friend that claps when you win, picks you up when you're down, and sends you pumpkin spice things because she saw them at Trader Joes. Thank you for making me think I could do this again. Thank you even more for your enthusiasm when I finished.

I wrote so much of this book with Jessica Prince. So many mornings, I got out of bed, made coffee, and then met Jessica on Zoom to write the words. I showed up because she showed up. Isn't that what friendship is about? Thanks for showing up for me, Jess. Thanks for everything.

I would be remiss if I didn't thank the people behind the scenes that keep things going. Kaitie Reister, Ebbie Moresco, and Stephanie Gibson —a big, huge thank you for all you do.

A couple of years ago, I was at a book signing in California and met Atlee Hayes. She was so shy and adorable. I had no way of knowing how much she'd come to mean to me in such a short time. Not only is she massively talented and overly creative, she's also filled with energy, kindness, and enthusiasm. She's the best kind of people. Thank you for stopping by to see me that day, Atlee, and for being such a bright part of my life. You inspire me and I'm grateful to know you. Also, I'm sorry for all of the torture. Kind of.

I'd also like to thank Lara Petterson for all the things. You never fail to come up with great ideas and you always know how to get things done. I respect that. I love you.

Brittni Van is a constant source of inspiration in my life. She gets stuff done in a way that amazes me. Her desire for knowledge, determination to achieve her goals, and kindness makes her a force to be reckoned with. I'm lucky to have her in my circle.

A big thank you to the top contributors per the analytics in Books by Adriana Locke at the time of publication: Lindsey Riley, Yamara Martinez, KJ Ryan, Kim Wagner Robin, Charlene Chua, Debbie Foster Berrier, Ada Undis, Sara Hubbard, and Sabrina Hayes. Thank you for always keeping the conversation going!

Oh, Books by Adriana Locke (my Facebook group). Where do I begin? The fun we've had leading up to this release will never be forgotten. You cheered me on, teased each other, created your own series endings and fed me with your energy and love while I worked on this book. You truly are the greatest group online and I'm honored to be your leader. (Am I your leader? Some days I'm not so sure! Ha!) Here's to more books and fun!

To all of my readers, bloggers, vloggers, TikTokers—THANK YOU. I know you have a million choices of books to read. Thank you for choosing mine.

Chapter Forty-Five

Dara

"That's going to hurt like a …"

The doorbell rings in the nick of time. I close the pregnancy book with a flourish and set it on the sofa.

I get to my feet, still quite sore, and pretend I just didn't see how wide my vagina is going to have to stretch for this little munchkin to come out of it.

Your body is made to do this, the book says. Maybe. But I'm definitely opting for the epidural.

Decision made.

"What did you forget … *Wade!*"

My voice raises as I set my sights on the handsome man on the porch.

Just the sight of him brings tears to my eyes. He's wearing my favorite navy cardigan that I used to tease him mercilessly about but quietly loved.

"What are you doing here?" I ask.

"May I come in?"

I want to say no, but I don't have the heart to do it. Nor the willpower.

"Sure." I step to the side and close the door behind him. "I'm surprised to see you."

"I bet you are."

Huh?

I walk around him and head to the sofa. Thinking fast, I grab the pregnancy book and shove it under the couch cushions as I sit.

"How have you been?" he asks, taking a seat on the other end of the couch.

"Fine. Just like I tell you every day in texts."

"I hate texts."

"Then stop texting me."

I really want him to stop talking to me and to grab me instead and kiss the hell out of me. But, even if he did that, I don't know that I would let him.

My heart aches from not having him around. The struggle to deal with the pregnancy news alone was my choice, one hundred percent, but it didn't have to be that way. It could've been completely different had he come to the hospital and not freaked the fuck out. And I don't want to blame him for that but ... I do.

I'm tired of making excuses for people when they fail me. And I'm tired of thinking it's okay to be failed by everyone.

I put my hand on my stomach without thinking about it. I withdraw it slowly.

"So, why are you here?" I ask. "You knew that I was fine."

"I wanted to talk to you."

"So talk."

He grins. "Why are you being so mean?"

"Because you hurt my feelings, so proceed or leave."

I mentally pat myself on the back. *Good job. Stay strong.*

He sighs. "I'm sorry."

Well, damn. I wasn't expecting that.

"For what?" I ask.

He rests his elbows on his knees. "For a lot of things."

"Like ... *words, Wade.* I know you have them."

He grins again. I try not to see it—I look away as soon as I see it start to form—but it's addictive.

"I wasn't there for you. I'm not there for you," he says. His words are crisp and clear, and he looks me in the eyes as he says them. "I should've put my fears aside and been stronger for you, but I didn't. That was my true failure in all of this. I failed you. And I'm sorry."

Wow.

His honesty and vulnerability sink some of my anger and resolve. That irritates me a bit, but I can't help it much.

"In your defense—"

"No. This isn't about defending me," he says.

"Then from my perspective," I say, "I can't imagine how that déjà vu must've felt to you. And I had no idea you'd lost a child." I frown. "That's heartbreaking."

He gazes into the distance. "It was a long time ago, but, yeah, that's a hard one."

We sit quietly, and I use the opportunity to study him.

He still has bags under his eyes, and his skin is ruddy. His hair is a bit longer than usual, but at least he's shaved.

The most striking thing about him, though, is the clarity in his eyes. I feel like I could look right through him if I wanted to.

I hold on to the armrest and try to decide if this is a good time to tell him about the baby. We've both needed a little space to heal from the accident. Maybe we can talk about it now. Maybe we can come to some sort of agreement.

Or not.

I have to be prepared for either because I won't beg him. I won't beg a man to love me or my child.

My child.

Our child.

I grin.

I imagine a little boy with Wade's dimpled chin. I wonder if he'll wear glasses like his dad or if he'll have an interest in architecture.

Or maybe it's a little girl, and she'll have his wickedly green eyes and an eye for detail. She could be an amazing photographer. Or architect. Maybe she'll want to follow in her daddy's shoes.

My eyes blur, and I blink as fast as I can to suck the tears back into my body. I don't know if that's biologically possible, but it's worth a shot.

"You know, I should've let you go with me," I say. "I'm not saying that would've stopped anything from happening. And maybe things happen for a reason." I press against my tummy. "But all I wanted while I sat in that huge house and listened to them"—I look into his eyes—"was you. I just wanted *you*."

"I knew something was wrong," he whispers. "I could feel it. I called you so many times. I was two seconds from calling your grandfather, which made me feel like a psycho, but *I just knew*."

"Thank you for caring, Wade."

He holds my gaze, and then, slowly, he reaches for me. I want to fall into his arms, but I don't. I take his hand, give it a gentle squeeze, and then let it go.

"I'm going to be super honest with you," he says.

"Okay. Please do."

I hold my breath while he turns in his seat to face me. His eyes sparkle with an excitement that I can't place. That I can't name.

"I love you, Dara."

What?

Whatever I expected him to say, it wasn't this.

I laugh in disbelief. "You're leading with *that*?"

He frowns. "That's not the reaction I was hoping for."

"I'm sorry. You threw me for a loop." *Because the last time you told me you loved me, you walked away.*

"I love you, Dara Alden. And I want you to find someone who can take care of you. Who will give you all the things in the world that you want. But that guy isn't me."

But something in his expression is different this time. He doesn't look as ... forlorn.

I raise my eyebrows at him. He needs to use more words still.

"You're lucky that I don't throw you over my knee," he says.

I give him a look. He shakes his head, unsure what to do.

"So, you love me, huh?" I ask. "In what way?"

My nails dig into the cloth of the furniture as I try to keep my hopes

how to handle asking for help when we need it because *we never fucking need it.*"

He pauses, letting that soak in.

My chest rises and falls rapidly. My mind spins. *Why the hell is he doing this now?*

"You think we're different because I turned to alcohol, and you turned to this life of loneliness. It's the same thing, Wade. Mine just killed my liver, and yours is killing your soul. We both nearly lost our families because of it."

Our families.

That's the problem. That's it in a nutshell.

Dara was my family.

I didn't realize it until now. I didn't realize that when I felt like she had worked her way into my psyche, she had really made her way into my family. Our family. That somehow, she had decided I was good enough to build a future with.

She picked me. And I chose her.

I gave Dara a reason to believe she could count on me, and I'd be there for her. *But then I wasn't.*

"You're not a dumb kid anymore," Dad says. "And at some point, you have to stop faulting yourself for the dumb kid shit you did back in the day."

I bow my head.

"You're an outstanding architect. Wildly successful. Brilliant, really. So it's time to start acting like that and stop punishing yourself for the choices that nineteen-year-old Wade made. You're not him anymore. *Let it go.*"

It sounds so easy when he says it like that. "I don't deserve a second chance, Dad. Hell, Dara was my second chance—"

"Bullshit, Wade."

"But—"

"Bull. Shit. I got lucky. Your mother is giving me another chance after I did my best to fuck our life up." He grins softly. "I think Dara will give you another chance if you haul your ass over there and explain yourself."

"What if something happens to her? What if I can't stop it?"

"You can't always stop it. Life happens. You know that." He puts a hand on my shoulder. "But when shit gets hard, you gotta ask for help. When you felt yourself spiraling like this, you should've called me. Or Holt. Or Oliver. Probably not Coy. Definitely not Boone."

We exchange a grin.

"You put too much pressure on yourself," he says. "And she's paying the price for that."

I cringe. I hate the sound of that.

I hate the truth of it more.

"It's not just about having people in your life. It's about ... being honest with them and being honest with yourself. It's the one thing you haven't learned in all your wizardry, as Oliver says." Dad smiles.

I smile too. Because there's some sense in those words that I need to ponder. There's some wisdom there that I need to consider.

But first, I need to be honest with myself, I think.

"Dad?"

"Yes?"

"Thank you."

He pulls me into a hug that I could do without and then leaves without another word.

I'm afraid that if I try to speak, my voice will share with the fury setting me on fire.

"Fill us in," Oliver says. "What is all of this?"

"Long story short," I say, gripping the back of a leather chair for dear life, "we're canceling all deals with Curt Bowery."

My three brothers' heads whip to mine.

Boone slinks back, knowing a war is about to take place. Oliver stands to fight. Holt tries to calm everyone down in his big brother bull-shit kind of way, but I'm ready.

Let's fight.

I've wanted to fight someone all day.

I've wanted to fight someone since Dara got hurt. Since I had to look in her eyes and see her pain. Since I went to her house and realized I couldn't do this again.

What happened was a warning shot by the universe. It was a taste of what could happen again.

Losing the baby with Morgan was awful. Having her leave me over it nearly broke me. That's why Dad is the only person in the world who knows what happened. He had to come and get me when I passed out from alcohol in the college library.

Like the nerd that I am.

I wouldn't make it if something like that happened to Dara.

I'm better off to leave her now and save us both the pain.

"You do realize you just said that we're canceling all deals with *Curt Bowery*, right?" Oliver raises his brows. "Because you sound very, very unwell."

"Ollie, I mean it," I say through gritted teeth.

Holt takes the papers and scans them quickly. "Does this say he's running for president?"

I nod.

"Where did you get this?" Holt looks up at me. "This says that the announcement is not for a few days."

"I have people."

"*He has people*," Boone says, snorting.

I pick up a ruler and sling it across the room. I intentionally don't hit him, but he doesn't know that.

Boone's eyes go wide. "Wow. Okay. I got it."

"I did a little digging and it turns out that Dara had a meeting with him. He told her this," I say, licking my lips. "She was in a car wreck on the way home."

"Is she okay?" Boone gets to his feet. "Is she hurt?"

"She's going to be fine."

I want to stay mad at Boone, but it's hard seeing him care about Dara like this. *Dammit.*

"But," I say, refocusing on the dirtball that is Curt Bowery, "this guy is her only family. And he basically just told her that he's buying her off with the house so she'll play her part in the happy Bowery family for the camera. At least, that's what I've stayed up all night for the last two nights and came up with. It makes sense."

Holt holds out a hand and closes his eyes briefly. "So, this is her only family? Curt Bowery?"

"Yes."

"And he's ... manipulating her?" Holt asks.

"*Yes.* The whole house thing? To put her in a spot so she has to participate in this campaign. It's so filthy."

Oliver looks at me like I'm kidding.

"Look, I'm refusing to do the house. Period. I won't work on a project attached to him in any way, shape, or form."

My brothers look at each other. It only takes a second before Oliver nods. Then he pulls out his phone.

"Shaye? Hey, it's me," he says, his eyes glued to Holt's. "Draft a letter from me that effectively cancels the Bowery Mexico project, effective immediately. Send it to Legal and copy me, Holt, Boone, and Wade. Please." He nods. "Thanks."

"*Fuck him,*" Boone says.

Oliver clears his throat. "Bring Dara over to our house tonight. I'll have Shaye cook. Dara must be really upset."

A lump settles in my throat.

"Hey," Boone says, standing up too. "I was going to tell Wade to bring Dara to our house."

My jaw sets, and I clench down so as not to cry in front of my brothers. They don't know. They don't know exactly why I'm a terrible

choice for Dara. Of course, they'd want to care for her because they know how to do that shit.

But I don't. And she's better off without such a cold bastard in her life.

Yet ...

This hurts so fucking much.

"You know what Mom's going to do," Holt says. "You know she'll demand she have us all there to rally around her."

I bite my cheek so the pain there will help detract from the fire in my heart.

"I've gotta go," I say, heading for the door.

"So, Mom's?" Holt asks.

I grab the handle and then still. I might as well get it over with.

"We aren't together anymore."

The door shuts behind me.

I make it to my car before I lose control.

Chapter Forty-Three

Dara

"You can go home now," I tell Rusti.

She sprawls out on her stomach on the living room floor, her legs kicked up behind her like a child. Cleo runs circles around her.

"Not yet," she says.

"Then when?"

"When I'm sure you're okay."

"I'm okay."

"Ha."

She goes back to watching a reality show that I can't get into.

My phone buzzes on the coffee table. I grimace as I pick it up.

Wade: Checking on you.

Why?

"Is it him again?" Rusti asks.

I nod.

I don't know what to say to him. He's checked on me every day for the past four days. He never calls, just texts, and doesn't say anything except asking how I am or how I feel and then he closes up like the Wade I knew months ago.

"Are you going to answer him?" Rusti asks.

"Probably."

She rolls over onto her back. Cleo nips at her fingers and then barks.

> Me: I'm fine. Thanks for asking.

I set my phone back on the table. I know he won't reply.

My body doesn't hurt quite as bad as it did. My doctor said I was healing nicely, to take it easy, and to see an OB as soon as I could get in.

That appointment is next week.

Rusti bought me a baby magazine at the grocery store yesterday, but I can't get myself to look at it. Not yet. Not until I get things settled inside myself and with Wade.

"When are you going to talk to him about the baby?" Rusti asks, choosing this moment in time to do leg lifts.

I roll my eyes. "I don't know yet. Maybe when you go home."

"And maybe I'll go home once you've told him and I know that you're going to be fine."

"Doesn't Zack miss you?" I ask.

"He's in Denver for the week." She rolls onto her stomach again and looks at me. "Lucky you."

Right.

I touch my face and notice the swelling has gone down by quite a bit. Easing up with the crying fits has probably helped. I'm not less sad, just more out of tears.

I'm going to be okay. Never great, probably, and never perfect. I finally believed that he and I had a future, and I wouldn't always have to do life alone. That I wouldn't have to grieve alone. Change alone. Grow alone. But whether Wade wants the baby, when I finally get the

nerve to tell him—once we've both had a bit of time and space—it'll be fine.

It has to be.

"I have nothing to give you. I don't want marriage. I don't want kids. I don't want that responsibility. I can't have that responsibility, Dara. I can't. I can't risk it."

He won't risk it. But he should at least know the truth. He deals in truths, not emotions.

Never emotions.

"I'm just going to tell him that I'm pregnant and that he can be involved or not," I say. "I won't ask him for anything, and if he wants no part of it at all, I won't force it."

I shrug as if it's easy, but it's not. It's heartbreaking.

I never thought about having kids with Wade. I'm not even sure how it happened. The doctor just said there's always a chance of failure, and it happens, even if it's rare. But this is what my life looks like now. And maybe this is a new door since the Curt one closed.

A part of me hopes that Wade will want to be a part of the baby's life, even if he doesn't want me. I know he said he didn't want kids, but he would be such a great dad.

Just when I thought I was out of tears …

Rusti makes a face as I wipe under my eyes with my shirt.

"I'm calling it now," she says, hopping up onto her feet. "You're going to tell him, and it's going to work out."

"How can you call it? You don't even know him."

She thinks about that. As do I.

She's been so wrapped up in life with Zack that the one or two times I suggested they come to dinner with Wade and me, Zack had something going on.

Maybe now I know why my best friend didn't meet my boyfriend. *My ex-boyfriend.* Zack wasn't going to stick around.

"Okay, true, but I do know him through you. From the way he made you smile. And laugh. And … the way he made you happy."

He did make me happy. So happy.

"I bet he's just scared," she says.

"Yeah, well, me too."

"But you have me."

I roll my eyes, making her laugh.

She glances at her watch. "I have a quick shift tonight. Do you mind if Cleo stays here since Zack is gone?"

I look at Cleo. She wiggles her butt at me.

"It's better than being alone, I guess," I mutter.

Rusti laughs. "I'm going to take a quick shower. Be right back."

She disappears down the hallway, leaving me with the dog.

"What do you think, Cleo?" I ask. "Will this work out with Wade?"

She barks. Then pants. Then shakes her behind again.

"No, that's what got me into this situation, you little minx," I say, laughing.

She barks again.

I feel that reaction. I really freaking do.

Chapter Forty-Four

Wade

I'm going to have to move.

I stand in the middle of my living room, and all I can think about is Dara. Not just the moments when she was bent over a piece of furniture or riding me on another but also the way she tucks her legs beneath her while watching movies. How she gets popcorn bits all over the couch every damn time. Her preference for the fireplace to be on whenever she sits down because she likes the ambiance.

It's this way in every fucking room.

The kitchen? I think of the boxes of donuts I've come to expect on the counter.

My office? The awe in her eyes at my sketch.

The bathroom? So many lewd, delicious memories that I want to punch the mirrors until they smash against the floor that no longer has strands of her hair on it.

I can't do this. I can't live in this space and be surrounded by memories of her.

But will it be easier if I do pack up and go elsewhere? Sadly, I don't think so. I think she's burrowed into my soul and will never let go.

I mosey around my house and think of her, grateful her memories aren't fading away. Dara Alden was the best part of my life. My time with her was the happiest I've ever been—happier than I ever thought I could be.

But that's over now.

Knock! Knock!

Who is here?

I make my way to the foyer and pull open the door. My father is standing on the porch. *Fuck.* I'm not sure what my face does, but he laughs.

"I know that I'm not too pretty anymore, but you could at least act like you're happy to see me," he says.

"Sorry. Come in."

He nods and steps inside.

I close the door.

"What's going on?" I ask, heaving a breath. Out of all the people I want to talk to today, he's ... not on the list at all. I'd rather talk to Boone's dumb ass than my father.

I'm not sure why I feel the way I do about him. A psychologist could have a field day with it, I'm sure. It probably has something to do with Dad seeing me at my worst—facedown in the World History section of the Georgia Tech library. I don't love that about our relationship.

Thankful that he came? Sure. Enjoy thinking that he knows that? Not so much.

"Oh, I was in the neighborhood," he says, sitting on the sofa.

I want to stop him, to ask him to use another piece of furniture because that cushion still smells faintly like coconuts. But just before I do that, I realize how fucking stupid that is.

Before long, everyone will stop smelling like her.

My stomach knots, and I reach for my phone.

"Interesting that you found a reason to be in this area," I say, typing out a text.

Me: How are you?

I hold the phone in my hand.

"Well, we both know I'm lying so let's cut the shit, huh?" he asks.

"Sounds like a plan."

He crosses one leg on the other knee. "Do you want to tell me what's going on, or should I tell you what I heard instead?"

I glare at him. "I don't give a shit what you heard, and no, I don't want to talk to you."

Dara: I'm good. Thank you for asking. Hope you are well too.

Hope I am well too? What?

I don't know why I keep texting her. I mean, I do—I need to know she's okay. But every time I get a response, it reminds me of the status of our relationship.

And I fucking hate it.

I hate the disconnect. I loathe feeling like she thinks I don't care.

But am I supposed to care since I basically broke things off with her?

I don't know. I know I can't stop caring about her.

I know I'm so fucking fucked.

"That's fine," Dad says, making me jump. I forgot he was here. "Don't talk then. Just listen."

I look at him with the blankest stare I can muster. "I'm not in a listening mood, Father."

His foot hits the floor. He leans forward and pierces me with a gaze I haven't seen in a while.

The old man still has it.

"If you're feeling froggy today, go visit another one of your offspring," I say. "Boone always has time to waste on his hands."

"Okay. We can do this the hard way."

I sigh.

"I know what happened with Dara."

"Do you now?"

He nods. "I know she had an accident and that you broke things off with her."

"Let's just *drive that pain home.*"

"I also know that your brothers canceled a massive project with Bowery Hotels because of it."

If he wants to fight, he picked a damn good day.

My jaw clenches.

"And I told them good fucking job," he says.

The tension in my face eases.

"Curt Bowery is a sonofabitch and always has been. If he can treat his granddaughter this way, we should want no part of it," he says.

Okay. Didn't see that coming.

"Glad you agree," I say.

"But that's really the least of my concerns right now. I know Holt and Ollie are going to do the right thing."

Fair enough.

"What I'm worried about is you, Wade."

"I'm fine."

"But are you, though?"

I roll my eyes and turn my back to him.

Me: I'm miserable.

Before I can send it to Dara, I delete it.

I stare at her name and feel my heart bleed. *How can it possibly feel like I've lost a part of my soul?*

I can't eat. I can't sleep. I can't even escape with work. All I can do is pace around like a deranged chicken and worry myself to death about Dara.

It wasn't this bad with Morgan. It was a whole different kind of hurt and confusion. Now, losing Dara, I can barely breathe sometimes, and there's no end in sight.

It's not getting easier. I'm not making new memories to pile on top of the ones with her, thereby making it more survivable.

She's still there. On top. Waiting to remind me of what we had.

"What's your justification?" he asks. "How do you think this is okay?"

"Simple. There is no justification. Just facts."

"Humor me."

I sit on the chaise and sigh. "You know about Morgan. I'm two for two. I've loved two women, and I've let them both get hurt."

"I've loved one, and I hurt her."

"Because ..." I shake my head and stop myself. "I'm not going there. Not today."

Dad gets to his feet. "If you're going to pull the *you're trying to protect her* card, that's fine. I get it. I respect it." He narrows his eyes. "But only if you also pull the other one."

"Which is ...?"

"You have to see that you're protecting yourself too."

I stand too in order to equal the playing field. "This isn't about me."

"The hell it isn't."

"What do you want me to do, Dad? Take her by the hand and watch her get pummeled by life and know that I didn't do something to stop it?"

"I'm sure she would appreciate someone holding her hand because life is going to pummel her anyway, Wade."

We stare at each other, our voices rising.

"You're scared," he says. "You're terrified out of your mind. I'm not judging you. But I want you to see that you're knee-jerking your reaction to the *love of your fucking life* out of fear."

I sigh. I can't argue that.

"Look," he says, exhaling. "I've told you this before. You're a lot like your old man. We excel at everything we do. We're smart. Headstrong. We can see what needs to be done, and we do it." He leans closer. "But when things don't go our way, we run. We don't know

let her books whisk you away to a world of heartwarming romance and irresistible heroes.

Join her reader group and talk all the bookish things by clicking here.

Receive a text alert for new releases, text BOOKS to 740-206-6969. US only.

www.adrianalocke.com

ABOUT THE AUTHOR

Adriana Locke is a USA Today and Amazon Charts Bestselling author with a knack for writing swoony, unforgettable contemporary romances. At nineteen, she traded her small-town roots for big-city life, only to realize her heart beats for quiet mornings and cozy chaos. These days, she's living her happily-ever-after in Ohio with Mr. Locke—her high school sweetheart—four lively sons, and two hilariously hyper Jack Russell terriers.

When she's not penning love stories that will leave you laughing and sighing, Adriana is battling the epic quest of missing silverware, "gardening" (a.k.a. chatting with her plants), or leaving her grocery list on the counter as she heads to the store. Grab a cup of coffee, settle in, and